"WILLIAM M... ARE HERE... AWARDED THE SILVER STAR."

Lieutenant Commander David Coffer adjusted his glasses as he glanced down at the paper in his hands, and began reading in a slow solemn voice. "For extraordinary heroism. Assigned the extremely dangerous task of cutting through an enemy obstruction in order that the U.S.S. *Dallas* could navigate up the Sebou River, Wallace and his shipmates, despite the treacherous surf and enemy gunfire, skillfully and courageously accomplished their hazardous mission."

He reached out to pin the award on Wallace's chest, then stepped back. Wallace gave him a snappy salute, returned with equal precision. Then he stepped back into line. The Commanding Officer gave a sign, and a burly chief bawled out a dismissal. The ceremony was over.

As the assembled sailors dispersed around him, Wallace stood still, shaking his head slowly, disbelieving.

The Silver Star had just been awarded to a coward . . .

SILVER STAR

BOOK ONE

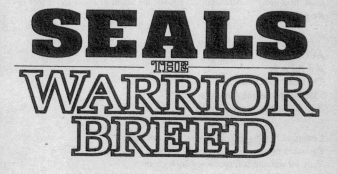

SEALS
THE
WARRIOR BREED

H. JAY RIKER

AVON BOOKS ◆ NEW YORK

AVON BOOKS
A division of
The Hearst Corporation
1350 Avenue of the Americas
New York, New York 10019

Copyright © 1993 by Bill Fawcett & Associates
Published by arrangement with the author
Visit our website at http://AvonBooks.com
Library of Congress Catalog Card Number: 93-90408
ISBN: 0-380-76967-0

First Avon Books Printing: December 1993

AVON TRADEMARK REG. U.S. PAT. OFF. AND IN OTHER COUNTRIES, MARCA REGISTRADA, HECHO EN CANADA

Printed in Canada

UNV 20 19 18 17 16 15 14 13 12 11

To the brave men of the UDT/SEALs,
present, future ...
... and past,
this book is respectfully dedicated.

Author's Note

This book is a fictionalized account of the founding of the predecessors of today's U.S. Navy SEALs—the NCDU and UDT teams of World War II. While many of the men mentioned in these pages are real, the names of some have been changed out of respect for the feelings of other brave men who swam with them. In particular, though David Coffer plays the role of the real-life Lieutenant Commander Draper L. Kauffman, no work of fiction could do justice to the founder of the UDT, one of the greatest men in the history of Navy special warfare.

The writing of any work of historical fiction requires compromises between historical fact and dramatic need; too, there is often a notable lack of agreement between different records of the same event. While I have striven for accuracy in these pages, I should mention that any changes to the actual events, whether deliberate or accidental, are the responsibility of the author and should not be construed as detracting from the deeds of the brave men described in this book.

My special thanks to a number of people without whom this book would not exist: "Andy" Andrews, president of the UDT/SEAL Museum Association (UDT 15); Dan Dillon, one of the first graduates at Fort Pierce; and Albert Stanke and Howard Dore (UDT 15) for their invaluable assistance. Thanks also to Kevin Dockery, Bill Fawcett, and especially to retired SEAL James Watson, curator of the UDT/SEAL Museum.

—H. Jay Riker
July, 1993

Chapter 1

Sunday, 8 November 1942

Combat Demolition Unit
Off Oued Sebou, French Morocco

Machinist's Mate First Class William M. Wallace groped for a handhold in the darkness as the open, spoon-nosed Higgins boat lurched and wallowed in the uneven Atlantic swell. The bobbing motion of the landing craft brought him up against the boat's coxswain, no more than a dim shape against the dark night sky that surrounded the tiny vessel. The other man rasped a curse.

"Belay that noise." Lieutenant Strickland's voice was a hoarse stage whisper. He sounded as tense as Wallace felt. "Coxswain, what's our position?"

"Comin' up on the mouth of the river, sir," Chief Boatswain's Mate Dowling, the boat's pilot, responded in the same low tones. "Won't be much longer now."

Wallace wondered how Chief Dowling could sound so confident. A thick overcast hung low over the sea, and the air was heavy with the smell of rain. Since leaving behind the tiny scout boat that had been sent in to mark the approach route to the river mouth, they'd been able to see very little of what awaited them inshore. His entire world had shrunk to this one tiny Higgins boat and the seventeen men of the Combat Demolition Unit.

The boat lurched again in the heavy seas, but this time Wallace kept his balance. He wondered what it was like for the thousands of army troops trying to board their landing craft out there in the darkness to the west, where the twenty-one ships of the Northern Attack Group waited seven miles offshore for the signal to launch the first assault wave against the beaches of Morocco. Operation Torch would mark the first major Allied offensive in the European Theater of Operations . . . and the first chance for American soldiers and sailors to come to grips with the Nazis and their allies in a full-scale combat operation.

The rough seas and heavy winds off the North African coast were a far cry from the calm waters of the Chesapeake, where the Army had done most of its amphibious training over the last two months, but at least the transports were far enough offshore to be spared the heavy ground swell of these coastal waters. Wallace had to suppress a laugh as he pictured swarms of seasick soldiers trying to climb down cargo nets into waiting landing craft that bobbed and pitched like the Higgins boat was doing now. . . .

The wind was picking up, and Wallace felt a few heavy drops of rain spatter his face. In seconds the rain had swollen from a light patter to a full-blown squall, and Wallace heard the coxswain cursing in a low-voiced monotone as he fought wind and current and the almost impenetrable darkness to keep the boat on course.

The squall might help to hide their approach, but it made Wallace nervous. Their mission was difficult enough without the added roadblocks Nature seemed determined to throw in their path. . . .

"There it is!" someone said, barely audible over the noises of the squall and the laboring engine.

Wallace peered into the darkness beyond the bow. The loom of the land was barely visible, but he could vaguely discern the low shoreline less than half a mile away. Straight ahead of the Higgins boat, the long sea walls that reached out into the Atlantic on either side of the mouth of the Sebou River gaped like the maw of a hungry predator. South of the river, low, sandy beaches stretched from the jetty to the swampy ground of a lagoon a couple of miles down the coast. Between the river and the marshes Wallace could make out a scattering of twinkling lights, the small town of Mehedia. Just north of the town, frowning down on the lower land and the curving loop of the Sebou, Wallace thought he could make out the towering bulk of the ancient Kasbah fortress dominating the landscape. The fort, according to the unit's intelligence briefings, was the principal bastion of the town's defense, garrisoned by troops loyal to Vichy France—native *tirailleurs* and tough soldiers of the French Foreign Legion. Scuttlebutt back in the fleet claimed the Vichy troops were likely to surrender rather than fight, but Wallace had his doubts. Their hearts might not be in the war, but the defenders ashore *were* protecting homes and families. . . .

In any event, the Americans had to proceed on the assumption that the opposition would be stiff. Even if the French didn't want to fight, there were German units in Morocco as well who might take over the defense if they saw their reluctant allies wavering. This was the real thing, a real clash of arms in the making.

And Bill Wallace, formerly of Norman, Oklahoma, would be squarely in the middle of it.

Six months ago he had been at Pearl Harbor, part of a team of Seabees and salvage divers working to clear up the wreckage left behind by the Japanese attack that had brought America into the war. Some of the work, dealing with unexploded ordnance left behind by the bombing, had been exacting and dangerous, but it was a far cry from his new assignment. Wallace, along with the rest of the men in the Higgins boat, had been asked to volunteer for duty with Operation Torch as a member of an ad hoc Combat Demolition Unit. Specialists in demolitions work were needed for the assault on the mouth of the Sebou River, and Wallace and the others were the closest things to specialists the Navy had today.

All of them were nervous, of course, but they were intensely excited as well. They were professionals, every one of them, and they'd been assigned a mission that only they could carry out. That excitement heightened every sense. Wallace savored the bite of the wind, the smell of salt spray as the frail, wooden boat corkscrewed through the chop.

What's it going to be like, he wondered, *under fire?*

"Goddamn!" Dowling swore suddenly. In the same instant the boat was lifted by the stern. They had been warned about the treacherous breaking ground swells that were common along this coast during heavy weather, but it was different to actually experience one. The boat hurtled forward like a runaway train, plunging headlong toward the jetty projecting from the southern bank of the river ahead. The two protective sea walls tended to channel and intensify the force of the ground swell between them, making boat handling a treacherous proposition here when the sea was running high.

The coxswain wrestled with the wheel and throttle, racing to stay ahead of a huge wave building up astern of them. Looking back, Wallace estimated the height of the breaker at thirty feet, enough to swamp the open small craft. Chief Dowling gunned the engine and the boat picked up even more speed, shooting ahead of the towering wave and angling to port as he steered away from the jetties and tried to reach the center of the river.

"Wallace, Arsenault," Strickland said. "Keep a sharp eye out. We don't want to find the damned net by getting tangled up in it."

Trying to force the image of the ground swells from his mind, Wallace moved to the bow and squinted into the darkness. Somewhere in the river ahead, probably just below the looming ramparts of the Kasbah fort, the French had strung a boom and net across the channel.

The invasion plan called for American ships to force their way up the Oued Sebou—*oued* being the Moroccan equivalent of the Arabic *wadi*, or "river"—to assault Port Lyautey with its critical military airfield, nine miles upstream. The only way to get through was to cut the barrier with charges of high explosives. That was the Combat Demolition Unit's task.

The rain was still lashing the sailors in the open boat, making it hard to see anything in the water ahead. At least, Wallace thought, the weather would keep any Vichy soldier with any common sense at all indoors tonight. That might help the team maintain the element of surprise for the critical few minutes they needed to locate and cut the boom. . . .

A bright red light streaked skyward from the jetties on the south bank. "Flare!" growled Lieutenant Dumont, Strickland's second-in-command. "Keep down!"

Chief Dowling cut back on engine power, and the boat slowed to a crawl. Here inside the river mouth the tidal swell was less of a threat, and reducing speed might lessen the chances of being spotted. That flare might have been fired off as part of a random attempt by defenders to spot activity off the coast, or it might have been a signal of some kind that had nothing to do with the Americans huddled in the bottom of the Higgins boat. By proceeding more cautiously, they might yet avoid notice.

Wallace swallowed and continued to scan the river ahead. It was hard to concentrate on the mission when stray thoughts of what might be going on ashore kept intruding. If the flare had been launched by someone who had spotted the American sailors, surely the defenders would have opened fire by now. But Wallace couldn't block out the mental image of a rifleman on the end of one of those jetties drawing a careful bead on him as he waited for the order to fire. . . .

At that moment, a shot did ring out, and Wallace ducked behind the imaginary shelter of the boat's plywood side. Suddenly the air was filled by the sharp crackling of rifle fire. Somewhere, a machine gun added its low-voiced hammering to the cacophony.

Bright light engulfed the Higgins boat. Wallace squinted up over the gunwale at the searchlights mounted on the towering walls of the Kasbah fort. He couldn't see anything against the glare, but he knew Vichy soldiers must be lining the ramparts to swell the volume of fire being directed at the landing craft.

The excitement of the mission was gone now, wiped away by the howl of bullets, the clatter of gunfire. Wallace had never felt so exposed, so naked, in his life.

The coxswain opened the throttle up all the way, and the Higgins boat gathered speed while the 115-horsepower Chrysler engine groaned and strained under that abuse. But even at full speed and steering a zigzag course they couldn't shake the searchlights spearing down from the ramparts high above the riverbank.

A deep-throated roar of artillery drowned out the rifle fire for an instant, and a shell splashed a few hundred yards away from the boat. "Seventy-fives," Gunner's Mate First

Class Bill Freemantle observed with an almost unnerving professional detachment.

"Better pray they don't decide to use their heavy stuff on us," Chief Wagner said. Wallace looked from one man to the other in sheer disbelief. How could they be so calm with death raining down all around them?

"Quiet, there," Strickland ordered. "What do you think, Jim?"

"No way we're getting near that damned boom now," Dumont replied. "I think we'd better get while the getting's good."

"Yeah . . ." Strickland hesitated an instant. "Bring her about, Chief. Let's get the hell out of here!"

Chief Dowling was quick to respond, swinging the wheel hard over to steer back for the mouth of the river and the safety of the waiting fleet far beyond. The gunfire continued to probe toward them from out of the night, kicking up tiny spouts of water all around the small craft. Occasional larger gouts marked the fall of shot from the 75-mm battery mounted in the fort.

Neither small arms nor artillery fire actually found a mark, but Wallace knew their luck couldn't hold forever. He felt totally helpless, crouched in the bottom of the boat with nothing to do but sit and wait and pray. Defusing unexploded bombs had given Wallace plenty of experience in facing danger, but at least when he was working on a bomb *he* was in control. A mistake could kill him, but as long as he stayed cool and did his job he was safe.

This was different. Any random shot could hit him, or any of those falling shells could destroy the whole boat and everyone in it. Wallace tasted sour bile, felt his guts knotting and churning.

He wasn't in control this time. . . .

U.S.S. *Dallas*
Off Oued Sebou, French Morocco

"Goddamn! Something's gone wrong!"

Lieutenant Joseph Galloway raised his binoculars to scan the distant, darkened horizon. At first all he could see was scattered lights, no different from what he'd seen the last time he's scanned Mehedia. He was about to say as much when he saw the rippling flashes from the massive bastions of the Kasbah fort. . . .

Flashes that could only be light artillery opening fire.

"They must've spotted Strickland's boat," Lieutenant Ferguson muttered. The Executive Officer of the *Dallas* was standing beside Galloway, studying the scene through his own field glasses. "That's torn it. They know we're coming now."

The destroyer's captain was frowning. "Question is, did they blow the damned boom?"

Galloway checked his watch, then shook his head. "I doubt it, sir," he said quietly. "I don't think they had time to reach the boom. They must have been spotted heading in."

"Unless it was a false alarm," someone else put in. "You know, somebody was seeing things and started firing, and that woke everybody up. . . ."

"If so, Strickland's in the thick of it," Ferguson said, his expression dour. "If he didn't get the explosives set already, he'll never get close enough to do a damn thing about it now."

Half a mile to the north of *Dallas*, the cruiser *Savannah* opened fire, the rippling flashes from the muzzles of her guns briefly lighting up the night. "If they weren't stirred up before, they will be now," Galloway muttered under his breath. He was picturing the tiny band of demolition experts in their fragile Higgins boat, suddenly caught in the middle of a major exchange of fire. The image made his stomach twist. He felt responsible for those men out there . . . and for whatever might happen to them tonight.

Of course, no one man could truly claim the responsibility for the decision to send those men ashore. But Galloway had worked with Strickland and the others from the very beginning, and it was an offhand suggestion of his that had first prompted the men planning this phase of Operation Torch to consider using naval commandos to clear the entrance to the Sebou River. Galloway had been a very junior officer on Rear Admiral Monroe Kelly's staff at the time, and his remark hadn't even been intended for the admiral's ears.

The Port Lyautey airfield was too far inland to be quickly secured by the Americans as they came ashore, but General Patton had made it a high-priority target. Though Port Lyautey was sixty-five miles north of Casablanca, the Allied strategy required it to be taken quickly as part of the northern prong of a three-front landing that would encircle the Vichy forces before they had a chance to get organized. At the very least Patton wanted to deny the airfield to the Axis so they couldn't mount an effective threat to the amphibious force . . . and ideally it could quickly be put into service to give the invaders a more reliable platform for air support through the rest of the campaign than the aircraft carrier *Ranger* and her lighter consorts could provide.

Someone had hit on the idea of sending the *Dallas*, an old four-piper destroyer of World War I vintage cut down to serve as one of the Navy's new APD assault ships, up the Sebou River with a party of Army Rangers on board to stake a claim to the airfield even as the main landings were getting started, but intelligence reports had made it clear the operation would be a dangerous one. The Kasbah fortress mounted guns heavy enough to pose a serious threat to the *Dallas*, though if she was handled boldly she could probably win through with minimal damage. It was the boom across the river that posed the real danger. If the destroyer couldn't break through that boom, the guns in the fort would smash her to pieces.

Galloway had commented on the problem to another junior aide on Kelly's staff. "What we need is a commando landing to let the commando landing go in," he'd said.

Somehow his suggestion had made its way up through the ranks, and soon Galloway had been assigned as the admiral's liaison officer, coordinating the *Dallas* operation and the deployment of the seventeen demolitions specialists hastily recruited and trained for Torch. He had followed them step by step through all the preparations.

Now they were out there in the middle of hell, and he didn't see how they could have accomplished their mission. Failure, pure and simple . . . and seventeen lives in danger because Joe Galloway had shot his mouth off.

"Well, Galloway, I guess your Navy commando scheme's going to be deep-sixed for good," Ferguson said harshly, his words an uncomfortable echo of Galloway's bitter thoughts. "Looks like your bunch of so-called experts've left us holding the bag."

"We don't know they had anything to do with this mess," Galloway snapped. "Hell, for all we know they got the cable cut . . ."

He knew it couldn't really be so, but Lieutenant Ferguson's determined pessimism was starting to grate, and automatically he rose to the defense of the CDU. The destroyer's XO had never been happy with the assignment to run the gauntlet of those shore defenses, and he'd singled out the demolition unit as the particular target of his vocal objections right from the start. Ferguson was regular Navy through and through, and he couldn't seem to accept the idea that sailors might fill any role other than as crewmen aboard conventional ships. No doubt, Galloway thought, Ferguson had been dead set against all these newfangled innovations—carriers, submarines, seaplanes. Hell, Galloway sometimes thought the man probably longed for the age of wooden ships and iron men.

He'd met all too many Navy men like Ferguson since going to work on Kelly's staff. America had never faced the need to conduct large-scale amphibious operations before, and the tried-and-true doctrines of these tradition-bound regulars just made them blind to the need to innovate.

Galloway hoped they wouldn't learn their lessons too late. Planning for Torch, he'd studied plenty of accounts of the British landing at Gallipoli in the last war, and the horror stories from that deadly campaign haunted his dreams sometimes. The Brits had paid a heavy price in lives to learn how not to run an amphibious operation. Now it seemed that the Americans would end up repeating all the same old mistakes.

Nearby, Captain Brodie was studying the coast through his binoculars. "Looks like *Savannah*'s teaching them some respect," he commented grimly. "Maybe if she can silence those guns we can take a chance on running the river anyway. What do you think, Monsieur Malavergne?"

René Malavergne, the dapper Frenchman who'd been assigned to pilot the destroyer up the Sebou, shrugged expressively. "I cannot speak for the guns or the nets, *mon capitaine*," he said. "The river I know well enough . . . and I know we will have trouble enough navigating the shallows even without the . . . complications. I would not advise making the attempt without being sure we can get past the Kasbah fort."

"Yeah," Brodie said, nodding solemnly. "That's what I was thinking." He was silent for a long moment, obviously weighing his options. If he went in, he risked his ship and everyone on her . . . but holding back would jeopardize Patton's entire invasion plan. He looked painfully young to be responsible for such a major decision . . . though Captain of the ship, he was still just a junior lieutenant commander, and in far over his head. But when he spoke again, he sounded confident. "All right. Pass the word to Communications. Message for Admiral Kelly. We cannot proceed unless that fort is neutralized or we get some kind of proof the commandos did their job. Until then, all we can do is wait and see how much luck *Savannah* has."

"It'd take some pretty damned lucky shots to knock out all the guns in that fort," Galloway said darkly. Inwardly he was torn between guilt and anger. These Navy regulars seemed to think there was nothing that couldn't be solved by a sustained offshore bombardment. He *knew* a crack team of demolitions experts could do more in a situation like this than all the ships in the Atlantic Fleet . . . but his team had obviously failed. It would be twice as hard to convince anyone to try this kind of op next time around. . . .

"Unless you people can give me a miracle, Mr. Galloway, luck is about all we've got left," Brodie told him coldly. "Meanwhile, I want you to pass the word to our passengers that they might be in for a long wait."

"Aye, aye, sir," he responded stiffly.

The problem was, Brodie and Ferguson were right. The mission had failed . . . so perhaps the whole idea had been wrong from the very beginning. Perhaps this was one job the Navy simply wasn't ready or able to undertake.

It was a sobering thought.

Combat Demolition Unit
Off Oued Sebou, French Morocco

The bright flash of an explosion on shore turned night into day for one brief moment. Wallace looked up in time to see the fortress open fire with its main battery of coastal defense artillery, not at the Higgins boat this time, but at the distant American ship that had started shelling the shoreline.

But that didn't mean the defenders had forgotten about the American boat in the mouth of the river. The smaller seventy-fives were still firing, though their gun crews were evidently having trouble tracking the moving target. There were still periodic bursts of small arms fire, too, most of it the random shots of confused soldiers whose only instinct was to shoot even when they weren't sure of their exact target.

"Hang on, boys!" the coxswain shouted over the noise of gunfire and the laboring engine. "This is gonna get rough!"

For a moment Wallace didn't catch the man's meaning. Then he realized what Dowling meant . . . just as the first heavy swell lifted the bow with a sickening, twisting motion.

They were leaving the relative calm of the river mouth now, fighting against the rolling waves that continued to pound the coast. This time there was no escaping them. The boat plunged straight into the ground swell. . . .

The first wave lifted the boat high, then suddenly slammed her back down. It was as if some giant child had grown tired of his bath toy and thrown it aside in a tantrum. Wallace, still crouched low in the bow, was able to brace himself against the impact, but not everyone in the boat was quite so lucky.

"Lieutenant! You okay, Lieutenant?" someone asked, voice ragged.

Wallace turned in time to see Strickland struggling upright, both hands clutched over his face. Blood streamed freely through his fingers. The lieutenant had fallen against the coaming, and from the looks of it he'd taken the full force of the fall straight across his nose. Chief Wagner was beside him, tearing a strip of cloth from his shirt to stanch the flow of blood.

Close by another sailor had tripped over a coil of line in the bottom of the boat. The man tried to move and cried out in sudden agony. "My legs! Christ! I think I broke my legs!"

Freemantle dropped to one knee beside the man. "Wallace!" he barked. "Give me a hand with Johnson here!"

Wallace hesitated, realized his hands were shaking. With a tremendous effort of will he forced himself to half walk, half crawl back to the injured man. Freemantle already had a first aid kit open, and somehow Wallace managed to focus his attention on the task at hand. He held the stricken man down as Freemantle examined the injuries.

"This is gonna hurt," Freemantle said gruffly. Shipfitter Third Class Johnson thrashed and bit back another cry as Freemantle's fingers probed his legs and ankles.

Wallace could see the way the sailor's feet were twisted, knew what Freemantle was going to say. "I think you managed to get both ankles broken, Johnson," he said. "Looks like you won't be going dancing for a while. . . ."

The injured man tried to muster a smile at that, but it was more of a grimace. Wallace shuddered himself as Freemantle started to cut away the man's pants legs and went to work immobilizing the shattered ankles. He couldn't bear to watch the man's pain and found himself looking back toward the hostile shore instead.

They had failed their mission. And Wallace wasn't sure he could ever face another night like this again. . . .

Chapter 2

Sunday, 8 November 1942

Combat Demolition Unit
U.S.S. *George Clymer*, off Mehedia, French Morocco

"Ahoy the *Clymer!*"

Wallace looked up as the coxswain's voice resounded from his speaker horn, hailing the transport that loomed out of the darkness dead ahead of the Higgins boat. It was hard to believe that the hell of the past two hours was finally coming to an end. Somehow they'd made it through the surf and free of the falling shells from the Kasbah fort at Mehedia. Despite everything they'd been through, only Johnson had been seriously injured. Lieutenant Strickland's nose was swollen where he'd caught it on the coaming, and some of the others, Wallace included, had a collection of bumps, scrapes, and bruises from the rough ride, but they'd made it.

He still wasn't sure how they could have escaped. The memory of bullets and shells probing for the fleeing boat made Wallace cringe, and it still took an effort of will to keep from giving in to a bad case of the shakes.

"Ahoy the boat!" The voice of the Officer of the Deck aboard the *Clymer* was tense, nervous. Everyone in the fleet would be on edge now, as the hours and minutes ticked down to the moment when the admiral would give the signal to launch the landing craft massing around the assembly point in toward the beaches around Mehedia.

Chief Dowling raised his bullhorn again. "Ahoy the deck! I have a casualty! Where do you want him?"

13

There was a short pause, presumably while the OOD double-checked to be sure there was space for the Higgins boat to come alongside. It looked as if the *Clymer* had launched all of her boats in readiness for the assault, but it was hard to be sure, from Wallace's vantage point, at least. "Tie up below the portside boom!"

The coxswain increased power to the engine and steered to port. Wallace looked up as they passed down the side of the towering transport, marveling again at her graceful lines. The Combat Demolition Unit had made the crossing of the Atlantic in two separate groups. Wallace had traveled with the larger party, Strickland's, aboard the U.S.S. *Cherokee*, while a few of the others sailed aboard the *Brant*. They had only transferred to the *Clymer* for the attack on Oued Sebou just before the fleet had broken up into the three Attack Groups required to carry out the separate landings of General Patton's invasion plan. So Wallace had been on the *Clymer* only a few days and still couldn't get used to the difference between this large, well-appointed transport and the cramped quarters of the *Cherokee*, an oceangoing tug that hadn't been designed with either speed or comfort in mind.

By contrast, the *George Clymer* had been planned to enjoy both those benefits. She had begun life as the *African Planet*, a luxury liner plying the sea routes between the United States and Africa. But with the coming of the war the *Clymer*, like so many other passenger ships, had been pressed into duty under the bald Navy designation of APA 27. Nonetheless she kept many of her luxury features right through the transformation from liner to troop transport, such as the graceful double staircase that led down from the main deck.

As the coxswain guided them in close alongside the hull, Wallace and Gunner's Mate Freemantle grabbed boat hooks to fend off in case a wild wave tried to batter the frail wooden Higgins boat against that massive barrier. He heard the loudspeaker blaring orders on the deck far above. "Now hear this! Now hear this! Casualty coming aboard! Stretcher-bearers to main deck, port side! On the double!"

He craned his neck to look up as deck crewmen finished securing a line on a cleat on the main deck, then threw the free end down to the Higgins boat. Seaman First Class Wieniewski caught it, secured it forward, and drew them closer in as the coxswain cut the engine. In a few seconds the boat was tied up fore and aft.

A boom on the main deck swung out over the Higgins boat. An empty litter basket, an openwork wire-mesh stretcher with sides about eight inches high and a ridge running down the middle of the lower half to separate a patient's legs, dangled from a line at the end of the boom. Wallace watched as the deck crew slowly lowered it into the boat. At a barked order from Chief Wagner, he grabbed one end of the litter as it came within reach and eased it down to the deck next to Johnson. They quickly unhooked the line to make it easier to transfer the patient from his resting place in the bottom of the boat.

"This is going to hurt, kid," Wagner told the injured man as he spread out a blanket in the bottom of the basket. "Perry . . . Joyce . . . get him secured."

The two sailors lifted Johnson and eased him into the litter, not without eliciting another cry from the man. They gingerly made sure his legs rested comfortably in the shallow depressions that were intended to keep them separate and secure, then folded the blanket around him and strapped him in tightly. Then Wallace and Wagner hooked up the harness to the four corners of the litter, attached the line, and signaled their readiness. Someone up above started the winch to haul the stretcher up, and Wallace grasped a line dangling from the front end of the stretcher and pulled on it, manipulating his end to keep stretcher and patient from banging into the hull. Dowling did the same with a line from the aft end of the litter.

Finally it was done. The stretcher was swung inboard and eased to the deck, out of sight of the men in the boat. Meanwhile, deck crewmen had tossed the free end of a rope ladder down so that the other members of the team could disembark. Wallace, the fifth man up, reached the deck in time to see a pair of burly stretcher-bearers lift Johnson's stretcher. With the duty pharmacist's mate in close attendance, they walked quickly toward the nearest hatch, maybe fifteen feet from the boom. He saw Strickland with them, no longer bleeding but with his face puffy and bruised from his fall.

Something drew Wallace after them. He hadn't known Johnson that well, though they'd trained together after being dragooned for the CDU assignment. But the man's injury had affected Wallace more deeply than it should have. It was so sudden, so senseless that he should come through the hail of rifle fire unscathed and then fall victim to an accident, and Wallace couldn't help but be reminded of the old phrase: *There, but for the grace of God, go I. . . .*

He followed the little procession forward to the kneeknocker hatch that led into the superstructure. Inside, the passageway was spacious, though Wallace ducked a bit as his head brushed some emergency equipment secured along the top of the corridor walls. They turned left at the first cross-corridor and headed forward, past a pair of doors on the outboard side of the passageway. At the third door the pharmacist's mate opened it up and let the stretcher-bearers through, then he stopped Strickland and motioned him toward another door farther down the corridor. He turned to follow the others into the examination room, and Wallace, unnoticed, trailed after him.

Someone switched on brilliant lights over the table in the middle of the examination room as the stretcher carriers transferred their patient, blanket and all, from the litter to the table. The light glittered off gleaming surfaces and highlighted the red ceramic floor tiles, a legacy of the *Clymer's* luxury liner lineage never seen in the sick bays of more mundane Navy ships. As Wallace watched from just inside the door, the men went to work, cutting away Johnson's outer clothes and boots while someone wheeled in a portable X-ray machine and the pharmacist's mate explored the shattered ankles with a delicate, sure touch.

The X-ray technician pressed a button, repositioned his machine, then took a second picture. He removed the bulky film cassette from the machine and turned away from the table. As he brushed past Wallace he muttered, " 'Scuse me, buddy." Then he was gone.

A few seconds later the door behind Wallace opened again. A commander with a medical corps caduceus on his shirt hurried past him. "How's it look, Marshall?" he asked briskly.

The pharmacist's mate turned from the table. "The fractures are bad, Doc, but it looks pretty straightforward . . ." The petty officer trailed off, noticing Wallace for the first time, and the commander turned to face him as well. "You need a doctor, son?" the officer asked, frowning.

"N-no, sir," Wallace stammered. "I . . . just wanted to make sure Johnson was all right. . . ."

"We'll let you know after we've finished examining him," the doctor told him. "Meantime, you'd best be back to your outfit." He gave a brief smile. "Don't worry, son. He's in good hands. I'm letting Marshall here do all the hard work. . . ."

Marshall and a couple of the others chuckled, and Wallace stammered an apology as he backed out.

Outside the examination room, he gave way to the shakes at last. His head was pounding, and for a moment he was dizzy and having trouble seeing. After a few minutes the pressure behind his temples eased, and he was able to make his way to the compartment assigned as the CDU's shipboard berth.

Wallace didn't know why he'd been hit so hard by everything that happened, but he had his suspicions.

He was beginning to think that Bill Wallace was nothing more or less than a coward.

Scout Boat
Off Safi, French Morocco

Boatswain's Mate Second Class Frank Rand peered through the early morning gloom, studying the dark outlines of the shoreline ahead. Dawn was still a long way off, but there were a few lights showing from the town of Safi, and they helped Rand gauge the distance between the tiny, bobbing scout boat and the waterfront town that had been selected as the target for the southernmost prong of the assault on North Africa, over a hundred miles south of Casablanca.

The mission the scout boat had drawn this morning would be long, difficult, and tedious, with a little danger thrown in for good measure. The landings planned for Safi were complicated by the need not just to capture the long, broad mole that protected the harbor but to capture it intact so that the port could be put to immediate use unloading tanks and other heavy equipment and supplies that wouldn't be able to handle the heavy North African surf of the open beaches. So a picked landing force had to grab the waterfront first, and that required careful guidance by someone willing to take a small boat in close to shore and direct the incoming traffic from the invasion fleet.

Rand glanced back at Ensign John J. Bell, the commander of the scout boat. The young ensign looked cool and composed as he swiveled his head back and forth from the looming land ahead to the dumpy silhouette of the APD *Bernadou* a few hundred yards astern. The mission had been touted as a risky one, but it seemed all too dull as far as Rand was concerned. He'd entertained hopes that the scout boat would actually hit the beach itself, her crew serving as amphibious commandos to scout out the beachhead before signaling the rest of the armada to land. But that wasn't the way things had turned out. The scout boat would remain offshore, exposed to fire once things started to heat up, but too far away to take any real part in the action. And action was what Rand had been looking for.

It seemed as if the Navy was determined to block his every attempt to win the same kind of glory his father had earned in Belleau Wood in the last war. Frank Rand had gone into the Naval Academy at Annapolis in the summer of 1941, determined to follow in his father's footsteps and become an officer in the Marine Corps. But then the Japanese had struck at Pearl Harbor, and that changed everything. Rand had left Annapolis at once to enlist, figuring he'd see action a lot faster if he didn't have to sit through long years as a midshipman. Along the way he'd also decided on the Navy instead of the Marines, since after Pearl Harbor it looked like the Navy would be in the forefront of the fighting, at least for a while. Frank Rand wanted a chance at glory above all other things, a chance to finally prove to his hero father that the weak and sickly child he had long scorned was worthy to carry on the family name and tradition after all.

But instead of action, he'd wound up posted to the Philadelphia Naval Yard after boot camp, a dead-end job that offered nothing of the action he craved. For months Rand had applied for every active assignment he could think of, from destroyers to bomb disposal school to the Seabees. Something, *anything* to get him into the war. He'd even requested Scouts and Raiders, amphibious commandos who warned that the odds against just surviving in their ranks ranged somewhere between slim and none. But the wheels of the Navy bureaucracy followed their own tortuous pace, and for a long time none of his applications had elicited a response.

Then, abruptly, he'd been assigned to the transport *Harris* in Chesapeake Bay. It wasn't exactly the posting Rand had been looking for, but at least the ship had been assigned to Operation Torch. He'd been given the chance to get into the war zone, at least, even if it was only as a junior petty officer on a poorly armed transport. And when the Captain had asked for volunteers to man the scout boat that would guide the invasion in, he'd jumped at the chance. Perhaps the experience would even count in his favor when the paper pushers finally got around to considering him for Scouts-and-Raiders school.

All in all his long-anticipated chance at adventure and glory had been something of an anticlimax. He had ended up bobbing around in an open scout boat, just one of the small party under Ensign Bell's orders. Any glory tonight would be shared . . . and there'd be precious little to go around.

He returned his gaze to the shore. He could just perceive the long sea wall that marked the mole off the starboard bow. "Coming up on our mark now, sir," he said quietly. "Steer three degrees starboard."

"Coxswain, dead slow," Ensign Bell growled softly. "Get ready . . ."

Their job was a simple one. In order to seize the mole and put the port into operation, the *Bernadou* was to land two companies of specially trained assault troops from the 47th Light Infantry on Green Beach, located at the landward end of the mole. To reach the position, the *Bernadou* had to steer north of the mole and through the shallow harbor. A mistake of even a few yards could put the APD on the wrong side of the sea wall or, worse yet, fetch her up against the end of the barrier in a collision that would wreck the ancient ship.

Astern of her, another APD followed, the *Cole*. The second ship carried naval specialists who were supposed to get the heavy cranes and other port facilities up and operating as quickly as possible. And somewhere behind the two destroyers, a narrow, elongated wedge of small landing craft was following along, ready to hit the beaches after the initial assault on the port had been successful.

Everything depended on getting the two assault personnel destroyers into the port, and that was where the scout boat came in.

"This is our mark, sir," Rand said after a few long moments of silence.

"You're sure?" Bell asked sharply.

"Yes, sir." His reply was equally sharp. "We're exactly where we're supposed to be." He was wishing, though, that he was somewhere else. Perhaps on the end of the mole itself, marking the end of the obstacle instead of a point a few hundred yards away from it.

"Very good. Do you want to do the honors, Rand?" Bell's voice was even, but Rand thought he could hear a hint of mockery in the words. His views on using commando parties ashore to mark the landing zones, well known to his companions, were generally regarded with anything from skepticism to scorn.

"Aye, aye, sir," he said, keeping his reply neutral. He produced a lantern from the bottom of the boat and turned to face aft. Checking to make sure that he had the light set up so that it could only be seen by friendly eyes, Rand switched it on and off rapidly, giving the prearranged signal.

U.S.S. *Bernadou*
Off Safi, French Morocco

Lieutenant Commander Robert E. Braddy, Jr., lowered his night glasses. "There's the signal!" he said. "Make the reply. Bring her five degrees to port, Helm."

"Aye, aye, sir," came the prompt replies. A signalman flashed a light toward the scout boat, and as he finished making the signal the light ahead went dark. The APD settled into her new course, avoiding the end of the mole and steering parallel to the long sea wall as she started the final run to shore. All according to plan . . .

Minutes passed like hours, and Braddy had to struggle to keep his face impassive. It wouldn't do for his bridge crew to see their captain betray any sign of strain, though they all knew that this mission was considered by all the experts Stateside to be a "suicide lash-up." But maybe there wouldn't be any resistance. . . .

The hope vanished together with the darkness, both driven away by the bright flashes of artillery batteries opening fire from shore. There were two batteries, one north of Safi, the other located to the south, and both had opened fire almost as one.

Braddy reached for the TBS microphone. "Play ball! Play ball!" he said sharply—the code signal giving the order to begin the attack on the African coast. He glanced at the ship's clock. It was not yet 0430 hours.

Bernadou's Gunnery Officer was already passing orders to the APD's gun turrets to open fire, and in seconds the six three-inch main guns and the five 20-mm mounts were all in action.

A moment later, a streak of light rising in the sky caught Braddy's attention. It burst suddenly in a bright polychromatic glare that lit up the whole harbor, and someone on the bridge let out a groan. "Oh, great," one of the crewmen muttered. "Hurrah for the red, white, and blue!"

Braddy was too angry to reprimand the sailor. He knew exactly how the young man felt. Someone back in the States with more power than sense had conceived the brilliant idea of having the Americans launch their attack with a sky-rocket set to burst into an aerial representation of the American flag. Obviously something had gone wrong—perhaps the powder in the rocket had gotten damp, or maybe it had just been an impossible idea from the beginning. At any rate, the only result of the patriotic display was this bright multihued flare, like some demented Fourth of July display gone horribly wrong, that illuminated the incoming American ships and made them easy marks for the batteries ashore.

Braddy had a brief image, quickly suppressed, of the confusion the display must be creating among those, friend and foe alike, who hadn't known about the fireworks plan in advance. Then he forced himself to consider the pressing realities of their situation.

From farther out to sea, the destroyer *Mervine* was starting to pour artillery fire toward the northern French battery, designated on Braddy's charts as the "Batterie des Passes." As he watched, the two French 75-mm guns there spoke, the muzzle flashes renewing the light that was fading as the failed skyrocket fell back to the sea.

"Number-two gun!" the Gunnery Officer snapped suddenly. "Target, range one-five-zero-zero, elevation two degrees. Fire!"

It hadn't registered on Braddy until that moment that one of the converted destroyer's main guns happened to be trained almost dead-on to the French battery, but the Gunnery Officer had seen it and acted promptly. In seconds the naval gun opened up, and after one near miss and a slight adjustment in trajectory they scored a direct hit on the position. The whole bridge crew let out a cheer, but the voice of the Gunnery Officer overrode the noise as he shouted orders. "Hit! Hit! Maintain fire! Pour it on, boys!" And the gunfire continued, pounding the battery as quickly as fresh rounds could be slammed into the breach of the three-incher and flung at the target.

More shells were falling around *Bernadou* and *Cole* now, plunging fire from the 155-mm guns of the Batterie Railleuse, perched on a 460-foot cliff south of Safi. Those guns were out of the APD's reach, but the covering ships offshore quickly answered the fire. After only two quick salvos it fell silent, apparently out of action. The Batterie des Passes was silenced now, too.

Then they were passing the head of the mole and coming under fire from small arms and machine guns. Bullets clanged and whined as they struck the ship's armored sides. Braddy saw a pair of soldiers in position on the destroyer's fire-control platform rise up almost in unison and throw grenades at the nearest muzzle flashes. They continued their dangerous work as *Bernadou* bore steadily down on her target, the jetty closest to the landing site designated Green Beach.

"Get ready!" the helmsman called. "Bottom's coming up fast!"

The keel scraped the sandy bottom, and *Bernadou* jolted to a halt. As she did, the men of K and L Companies began pouring over the side into the shallow water, swimming or wading toward shore.

The Americans had taken a big step toward the defeat of the Axis powers in these predawn hours. The first amphibious assault against the forces of Adolf Hitler had hit the beaches of North Africa. . . .

Scout Boat
Off Safi, French Morocco

Rand watched as *Bernadou* slid past the scout boat and into the inner harbor of Safi, the uneven, rippling illumination of muzzle flashes from her guns and the thunder of each deep-throated report lending a nightmare quality to the whole scene. The last flickering glare of the weird multicolored signal rocket had already died away, but explosions, muzzle flashes, and bright, stabbing searchlight beams continued to turn night into day.

Something whined past his ear, and Rand swiveled his gaze toward the sea wall. A small knot of soldiers was visible there, shouting, gesticulating. One of them was pointing toward the scout boat, and another raised a rifle and squeezed off a round. Rand flung himself to the deck and felt the bullet pass within inches of his head.

"Coxswain!" Bell shouted. "Take us out of range! And steer for the second control point!"

"Aye, aye, sir!" the sailor responded, his voice ragged.

Inwardly, Rand was seething. No one in the boat had any weapon heavier than a pistol, so there was no chance to return fire effectively. If this operation had been planned right, he thought angrily, they would have been sent into the harbor loaded for bear. A well-trained amphibious commando force could have done plenty to secure the mole in advance. . . .

There was another shot. Then, suddenly, a grenade exploded among the party on the end of the mole. Someone screamed, a chilling, inhuman sound. But Rand felt nothing but elation. Action at last! This was a real battle, even if he was still on the edges of it all.

The scout boat shot forward, steering to port and into the inner harbor in the wake of the *Bernadou*. Now that the lead ship was headed into the harbor, Bell's crew had a second task—to be sure the *Cole* arrived at the Mercantile Dock where most of the unloading equipment in the port was located. Once again, the job was a simple one, calling for no more than showing a light to guide the second APD in. They exchanged flashing recognition symbols with the *Cole*, then watched as she steered for the Mercantile Dock, crashing alongside and disgorging a Navy landing party. The resistance there was scattered and ill-organized, and it took only minutes for the sailors to secure the pier, the cranes, and a trio of small boats moored close by.

In the meantime, Bell had ordered the scout boat into motion again, steering to the outside of the harbor this time to guide in the waves of landing craft that had followed the two destroyers from the assembly point eight miles away. Their principal beach was south of the mole, beyond the sea wall and the cliff where the Batterie Railleuse had by now been silenced.

This final phase took over an hour to complete, as wave after wave of landing craft had to be steered to their designated beaches. The sky beyond Safi was beginning to grow lighter with the approaching dawn, and everyone in the cramped scout boat was growing stiff and sore from the prolonged ordeal. But Rand was still feeling frustrated at the essentially passive role they had played. All of the work they had done through the early morning hours could have been handled by any competent boat crew. Surely amphibious commandos could have accomplished more?

"Looks like we're finished here," Bell said at last. "Guess we should head back to the *Bernadou*—"

"There's more we could do, sir," Rand interrupted. He jabbed a thumb in the direction of the Batterie Railleuse. "Take those guns up there. If we got in close we could find out if they're really out of action or just playing possum. They stopped firing awfully damned quick, you know. If they're just waiting for a chance to nail some of our boys on the way in to the beach . . ."

The ensign shook his head. "That's not our mission, Rand," he said. "Leave that for the spotters ... or the fly-boys off the *Santee*. Our job was to mark the beaches and guide the boys in, and we did that. Now it's time we headed on in."

Rand started to open his mouth to argue, then caught the look in Bell's eye and fell silent again. Time and again he'd let his enthusiasm and a mouth that was too big for his own good get him into trouble, but Rand was finally starting to learn that it was never a good idea to talk back to officers, even wet-behind-the-ears ensigns. "Aye, aye, sir," he said at last, but he didn't bother to hide his disgust.

It was the same old problem all over again. The Navy was just too set in its ways, too dull and plodding and slow, to make the best use of its resources ... including a sailor named Frank Rand. Maybe the decision to leave Annapolis had been the wrong one, after all. It looked like he'd never get the recognition he craved on his present path. As an officer he might have missed out on some of the action, but at least he would have entered the war with enough authority to take the initiative and do the things he knew had to be done.

You'll never amount to anything. He could hear the echo of his father's harsh words in his mind even yet, and it seemed now as if they had been prophetic after all. Howard Rand had won the Distinguished Service Medal and a field commission as second lieutenant for his part in the Marines' fighting at Belleau Wood; and even without the eye and leg he'd left there, he remained an imposing, forceful figure of a man, a hero who carried his scars as badges of honor. But he'd never been proud of his only son. Frank had been small as a child and the target of every childhood disease that came along. Weak and sickly, he'd been nothing but a disappointment to the man who looked to him to carry on his name.

That disappointment, those barbed comments, had hurt. And the younger Rand had resolved to do something about it. His father wanted a hero; therefore Frank Rand would be a hero, no matter what it took. He had worked out, running, lifting weights, learning to box, and going out for sports in school. And his efforts had paid off. Though he was still small, he was now tough and wiry instead of frail. He'd played quarterback on his high school football team and had been deluged with offers from colleges interested in signing him up. But he'd set his aim higher, on Annapolis and the officer's career his father had never been able to pursue because of his wounds. And there, too, he had overcome the odds. His father had grudgingly approved his efforts, used his name and fame to get his son the coveted appointment.

And then Rand had thrown it all away in his impatience to get into the war....

He ignored the frown Bell directed his way and looked back at the shoreline. That was where the action was. And that was where he wanted to be, with all his heart and soul.

Chapter 3

Monday, 9 November 1942

Mercantile Dock
Safi, French Morocco

Frank Rand looked up sharply when the air raid siren started wailing. There was nothing to see, really, not with the fog that had settled over Safi in the early morning. The activity on the dock was almost surreal, distorted by mist and punctuated by the siren's piercing, ululating scream. All around him men were looking, shouting, running.

"Take cover! Take cover!" someone yelled.

He caught a brief glimpse of men on the deck of the transport *Lakehurst* uncovering machine guns and snapping back their bolts, ready to open fire at the first target that came near. But the heavy, fog-laden sky revealed nothing,

and the sirens were too loud to allow anyone to hear if there
were engines passing overhead.

Rand stood still, squinting into the mist. He was more excited than frightened or concerned. At least this was action
of a sort. He'd volunteered to join a work party ashore
rather than remain cooped up aboard the *Harris,* but all the
resistance in and around Safi had been put down by nightfall on the first day. By D+1, all that had remained for Rand
in Safi was tedium and hard work ... until now. The air
raid siren changed everything. Maybe he'd have a chance to
prove himself after all ...

Close by, the crew of a light antiaircraft gun were hurry-
ing to ready their weapon. The barrel lifted slowly skyward,
like a giant finger pointing to danger. "Take cover, you idiot!" one of the gunners shouted. It took Rand a moment to
realize the yell was directed at him.

Suddenly a shape took form against the overcast
above—a plane, dropping low and skimming over the harbor straight toward the *Lakehurst.*

The machine guns aboard the transport opened fire, and a
moment later the antiaircraft gun joined in. Nothing seemed
to affect the plane, though. The pilot simply held his course
as if he were a barnstormer putting on a display for an appreciative crowd.

Rand heard the whistling sound of the bombs falling, and
the whole world seemed to slow down. The plane passed
right overhead, and the antiaircraft gun swung to follow it,
still firing without noticeable effect.

Then there was a flash and a roar from the far side of the
gun, and a moment later Rand was flattened as if by a
giant's fist.

Consciousness returned an unknown period of time later.
Rand was lying on the pier, listening to shouts and the
sounds of booted feet running nearby. Flames crackled
somewhere out of his line of sight, and over it all he heard
the sound of someone moaning. He started to struggle into
a sitting position and realized that his left leg felt like it was
on fire. He looked down and saw blood. . . .

"Whoa, there. Take it easy, kid." A pharmacist's mate
dropped to one knee beside him, started to examine him
with a cool, professional detachment. "It's nothing serious.

You took some shrapnel, that's all. Might've broken a bone.
If that bomb had been a few feet closer you'd've been
headed for Arlington, like those poor devils who were manning that gun over there." He jerked his thumb toward the
antiaircraft position, and when Rand turned his head he
could see the twisted wreckage . . . and a body stretched out
nearby, already covered by a blanket. "You were lucky. But
some flyboys off the *Santee* are heading for Marrakech to
hit the airfield they came from. Those bastards won't be
coming back soon, I bet."

"Yeah," Rand muttered, groggy. "Yeah. Lucky."

The last thing he remembered as he slipped back into unconsciousness was a mixture of regret and embarrassment.
Regret that he'd be sidelined yet again . . . and embarrassment at the way he'd been sidelined. *Too stupid to come in
out of an air raid*, he thought bitterly.

He knew what his father would say about it all. . . .

U.S.S. *Texas*
Off Mehedia, French Morocco

Lieutenant Joseph Galloway climbed the rope ladder from
the launch up the steep-sided hull of the battleship *Texas,*
pausing at the top to salute the colors and the OOD at the
rail. He fell in behind the others who had made the crossing
from the *Dallas*. Captain Brodie and the Army captain who
commanded the Ranger detachment were crisp and correct
in their carefully pressed and well-starched uniforms, like
Galloway. The French pilot, René Malavergne, made a startling contrast in his civilian clothes.

"If you'll follow Ensign Harlow, gentlemen," the OOD
said with an apologetic smile. "He'll show you to the briefing room. You'll have to forgive us if we seem at sixes and
sevens right now. You don't generally get VIPs dropping in
out of nowhere in the middle of a war zone. But the
admiral'll be down in a few minutes . . . if he lives that
long!" The officer turned away suddenly in response to another hail. Another small boat was coming alongside, presumably from the *George Clymer.* Galloway was tempted to
linger to greet Strickland and Dumont in person, but de-

cided against it. He followed the others, instead, as the fresh-faced ensign conducted them below.

At this juncture, it was enough to know that the men of the CDU had lived through their disastrous raid after all.

The briefing room was already filled up with officers, mostly Navy but with a sprinkling of men from Brigadier General Truscott's battle staff looking distinctly uncomfortably and out of place. The party from *Dallas* found a spot near the foot of the narrow table, and Galloway cocked an ear to listen as half a dozen somber conversations unfolded around him.

It was plain that things weren't going well around Mehedia.

Despite the initial debacle with the demolition unit's failure on the Sebou River, landing operations had proceeded smoothly enough, mostly according to the original plan ... all except the attempt to force the passage of the river with *Dallas* and her Ranger contingent. Wave after wave of landing craft had hit the beaches around Mehedia soon after dawn, striking at points north of the Sebou, south of the flanking lagoon, and in the center just below the jetties along the riverbank. The northern and southern beaches had fallen easily, taken totally by surprise, but the defenders around Mehedia itself had still been edgy enough after the initial disturbance to be on their guard. Although offshore bombardments had suppressed the defensive batteries long enough to allow the Americans to gain a foothold on the central beach, the fighting had been unexpectedly heavy all day.

The principal objective of the troops on the center beachhead had been to capture the Kasbah fort, which would have essentially eliminated all serious resistance by the Vichy troops. Around noon, the Army had, with minimal casualties, secured a lighthouse south of the fortress, but from that point on the fighting had bogged down. After a long and bitter struggle a small force had finally reached the base of the fort and settled in for the night. The fighting had died down after darkness fell, but it was clear that the resistance on shore was still unbroken.

Soon after dawn on D+1, the depth and determination of that resistance had been proven all too plainly. A counterattack from the Kasbah fort had rounded up the sixty-odd soldiers who had reached the position the night before, and much of the rest of the morning had been spent fighting off a series of attacks by French tanks that had threatened for a time to roll the American attackers back into the sea. Only the guns of the fleet, directed by spotter planes and naval gunfire liaison personnel ashore, had been able to turn back the armored thrust.

And that was where matters stood. Noon had come and gone on D+1, and they were no closer to resolving the situation around Mehedia. Port Lyautey's airfield was still safe behind the double bastion of the boom and the Kasbah fortress, and Mehedia itself still stood firm against the inexperienced American troops ranged against the town.

It didn't help that the other landings had gone ahead with barely a hitch. The invasion forces at Safi and Fedhala were both poised for the final thrust to take Casablanca, while all along the Mediterranean coast similar landings threatened Oran, Algiers, and other key cities of Vichy North Africa.

No wonder, then, that the Northern Attack Group had drawn the Task Force commander's ire. . . .

Galloway looked up as new arrivals were ushered into the briefing room. As he'd suspected, they were the CDU leaders from the *Clymer,* Strickland and Dumont. The former had a bandage across the bridge of his nose, and his face had been cut up and bruised. Galloway nodded a greeting to the two of them, but they had to find chairs in the corner of the room, away from the table.

It was a minor miracle that the team had come away from that disastrous raid with only one major injury and no deaths. The news had been a big relief to Galloway.

"Attention on deck!"

Galloway and the other officers came to their feet quickly in response to the barked command from the petty officer beside the door.

"As you were," Admiral Monroe Kelly growled, stalking into the compartment with a dark scowl creasing his bluff features. He wasn't alone. Two men in Army uniforms were with him, and Captain Baker, CO of the flagship, brought up the rear with the harassed look of any naval officer whose life has been made miserable by visiting brass.

Ordinarily Brigadier General Lucian K. Truscott cut an imposing figure, but today he was eclipsed by the larger-than-life figure who strode ahead of him. Major General George S. Patton, Jr., tall, stocky, his hair going gray but the fire in his eyes making him seem younger than the greenest ensign in the room, stalked through the door like some frowning, implacable juggernaut ready to crush anyone and anything that dared stand in his path. From his position Galloway could just catch a glimpse of one of the general's famed ivory-handled pistols.

Unlike the Navy men in the room, Patton looked distinctly rumpled. His uniform was creased and wrinkled, spattered with dust and dirt in places. That was only to be expected. Less than two hours before, he had been in his headquarters on shore near Fedhala, when a sudden impulse had made him commandeer a seaplane for a lightning trip north to visit the stalled scene of the operations off Mehedia.

The assembled officers, Galloway among them, settled back into their seats as the admiral took his place at the head of the narrow table. But Patton remained standing, leaning forward over the tabletop, a grim expression on his face.

He started speaking in a low but penetrating voice. "So far, Northern Attack Group is the only force under my command with the dubious distinction of letting the goddamned French kick it in the ass! So I'm here to administer an even harder kick, one that'll make you people forget all about the French and start worrying about me instead! When I get through with you, you're going to be so damned eager to lead your boys into battle that you'll probably march all the way across Africa and link up with Montgomery and the British just because you'll be afraid to stop moving while I'm still behind you." Patton took a seat, heavily, and leaned forward. His voice was lower, but no less intense. "So . . . tell me why the hell the American flag isn't flying over Mehedia yet."

"General, the resistance ashore has been heavier than we expected," one of Truscott's staff officers ventured. "The men aren't at fault—"

"I agree," Patton cut him off. "Those boys out there are

damned fine fighting men, and man for man they can take anything the French *or* the Germans can dish out. That leads me to look a little higher in the TO. . . ."

"It's that damned fortress!" someone swore. "We had a couple of ships pounding it with everything we had, and they never even slowed down. Until we can break them there, we're not going to make much headway."

"The fort . . ." Patton looked thoughtful. "And I take it the fort's the reason why you didn't get the Rangers up the Sebou to the airfield, too."

"The fort," the Ranger captain next to Galloway said quietly. "And the boom in the river. The Navy claimed they could get us to the airfield, but they fell down on the job."

Some of the other Army men chuckled. Everyone in the invasion force knew Patton's feelings about the Navy. Early on in the planning he'd expressed doubts that they could deliver the invasion on time and on target, but at the same time he'd gruffly promised, "If you land us anywhere within fifty miles of Fedhala and within one week of D-day, I'll go ahead and win. . . ."

Patton directed his glare on Brodie. "You couldn't break past the fort and get my boys ashore, Captain?"

"No, General, we couldn't," Brodie told him, standing his ground. "As I have said all along, sir, *Dallas* can't maneuver up that river as long as that boom is intact. When the attempt to blow the boom failed, I made the decision to abort our part of the mission. If *Savannah* had been able to knock out the battery inside the fortress we would have made an attempt, but the combination of obstacles and those guns makes any attempt to run up the Sebou a suicide mission. As we agreed before." He nodded toward the French pilot, Malavergne.

"*Oui,*" the Frenchman agreed quietly. "The boom is too great an obstacle. I would not wish to make the attempt as long as it remains."

Other officers around the table were nodding thoughtfully. Plainly Malavergne's words carried weight. He had picked up the nickname, in the American fleet, of "the Mark Twain of Morocco" for his vast experience as a pilot on the Sebou before the war, but the humor went together with a lot of respect for the man. He'd turned Free French after Morocco declared for the Vichy government and had been spirited out of North Africa early in the fall by agents of the fledgling O.S.S. It was Malavergen's report that had first revealed the presence of the boom that had prompted the formation of Strickland's Combat Demolition Unit.

Patton's abrupt nod cut off a babble of comments from around the table. "Understood. But it leaves us with a problem. You know the goddamned Germans hit Southern Attack Group with an air raid this morning. As long as Port Lyautey airfield remains in enemy hands, there's the threat they'll hit some of your ships too. I still say we have to neutralize that field, and the only way to do that is to land the Rangers!"

"Well, unless the Navy can come up with something that works this time, it looks like the only option is to take out the fort with an all-out push," Truscott said. "That'll be a damned expensive operation."

"My people did everything they could," Rear Admiral Kelly said sharply. "Everything humanly possible. And I resent any suggestion that we did less than our best."

Kelly's Chief of Staff looked straight at Galloway as he spoke. "The real problem, I'd say, is expecting the Navy to do something it isn't equipped to do. The Navy isn't designed to support a commando unit. The demolition team did their best, but they're just ordnance-disposal people . . . and they were in over their heads, that's all. We should never have taken on the job in the first place. It isn't what the Navy's all about."

Galloway darted a glance at Strickland and Dumont. Both looked angry, but neither one had the rank to break in on so many senior officers, no matter what the provocation.

Well, neither did Joe Galloway, but he was damned if he was going to let that condemnation of the CDU stand. "With all due respect, sir, that's a load of bullshit!" he said.

There was a murmur of disapproval, a few nervous laughs. The captain smiled, but his eyes were cold. "Is that your expert opinion, Mr. Galloway?"

"The demolitions unit didn't fail because the men weren't trained for it. Or because they were doing something God didn't intend the Navy to do! That's like saying that we shouldn't have started using submarines or carriers just because they were new. The Navy's now responsible for delivering large numbers of troops ashore in amphibious operations. Army troops here in Europe, and the Army and the Marines both against the Japs. Part of that responsibility is going to be clearing the beaches of obstacles. And I can't think of too many ways to do it aside from sending in men to take them out with explosives. The CDU can still do the job, sir. All we need is the chance."

"You're the liaison with the demolitions unit, aren't you?" Patton asked. "Galloway, isn't it?"

"Yes, General. Yes to both." He swallowed. He'd managed to do it again, shooting off his mouth in front of the brass. But he wasn't about to retract one word of his outburst, not even if it meant he'd end up as a coastwatcher in the Aleutians for his insubordination.

"And what is it that makes you think your people can do any better this time than they did the last time?"

"General—"

"May I answer that, sir?" Strickland broke in, coming to his feet. His voice was blurred by his swollen nose.

"And you are?"

"Lieutenant Mark Strickland, General. I'm the senior officer in the demolition unit. And I was in command when we went in the other night." He paused, then plunged on. "General, we damn near made it the first time. It was sheer bad luck that we were spotted before we could get in and cut the cable. I'm convinced we can do the job if we just manage to get in close enough. And now that our troops are on shore and hold the mouth of the river the chances of our being detected before we get up to the fort and the boom are a lot lower."

Patton frowned, looking back at Galloway. "You agree with that assessment, Lieutenant?"

"Yes," General," he said, glad that Strickland had taken the lead. He was convinced that the CDU could do the job, but he had been reluctant to commit the team members to another raid without knowing if they were willing to try. This had to be a job for volunteers. "The basic idea, I think, is still sound. A small unit, infiltrating to the boom, will have a good chance of cutting it before they're discovered." He looked at Truscott. "And it won't put as many lives at risk as an all-out attack would. Isn't that an important consideration?"

"And if it fails again?" Truscott said harshly. "It sounds good, Lieutenant Galloway, but so far your people haven't exactly done much to inspire confidence."

Patton held up a hand. "Now, Lucian, let's not get personal with all this. We're supposed to be on the same side." He paused, looking thoughtful. "I want your honest assessment, Lucian. Can you mount your attack this afternoon, if you start now? Guarantee taking the fortress today?"

The other general didn't answer right away. Then he shook his head slowly. "I doubt it, General. Not with all the pressure this morning. Switching from defense to offense is never easy. . . ."

"The Army ought never to be *on* the defensive," Patton flared. Then, more quietly, he went on. "But I'd agree there isn't much chance of getting a fresh attack organized before we lose the light, and I don't want to risk any more screwups by trying to make it a night assault. That's just inviting extra casualties to no good purpose." The general looked at Galloway. "Well, if you can do it tonight, take out that boom and get the *Dallas* up that goddamned river by morning, we won't have lost any more time. The question is, can you do it, Lieutenant?"

Galloway looked at Strickland. "What about it? Is the CDU up to another try?"

Strickland nodded. "We'll be ready tonight, sir. Guaranteed."

"General, I can't speak for the Rangers or for the *Dallas,* but *my* people will be ready." Galloway smiled. "And this time we'll take out that boom."

"And *Dallas* will be waiting," Brodie put in. "Unless they drop a shell into the engine room as we go by, we'll get your men to the airfield. And if they do knock out our engines, I'll have my men get out and haul her there, like a barge on the Erie Canal!"

"Now that's what I want to hear!" Patton said, slapping the tabletop. "You listening, Lucian? As long as we have the American spirit behind us, we're invincible. Invincible! And the sooner those goddamned Nazis realize it and surrender, the fewer of the bastards we'll have to kill." He smiled coldly. "I don't think Adolf Hitler or any of his god-damned thugs are smart enough to give up. We'll have to dig them out of Germany one foot at a time. And that's just the way it's supposed to be, eh, boys?" There were appreciative chuckles, especially from the Army men.

The meeting turned to other matters and broke up within an hour with Patton's announcement that he had to get back to his own sector of the front. "And have no doubt about one thing, gentlemen," he said as he stood up. "I don't expect to have to come back here. If I do, God help you all!"

As the party from the *Dallas* started to leave the room, Patton stopped Galloway by holding his riding crop up at chest level in front of him. "You made good sense in there, son," he said. "We need more of your kind of original thinking in this war. Down through the whole history of mankind every War Department starts off a new conflict by trying to refight the last war, and it never works. It's the original thinkers, the people who can see how to use the new technologies and the new ideas that are always out there, they're the ones who make the real difference. So keep on plugging for your notions, Lieutenant. And don't let the bastards get you down."

"Thank you, General," Galloway said, uncomfortably aware of too many eyes on him. "I'll do my best."

His mind was a whirl of confused thoughts and emotions as he boarded the launch and headed back across to the *Dallas*.

U.S.S. *George Clymer*
Off Mehedia, French Morocco

"Now hear this! Now hear this!" Bill Wallace looked up as the tannoy blared. "Casualties coming aboard! Duty pharmacist's mate and stretcher-bearers to main deck, port side! Casualties, main deck, port side!"

"Another batch," Boatswain's Mate Second Class House commented glumly. "Poor devils."

Though the *Clymer* had debarked her full contingent of troops, activity to and from the beach continued almost constantly as the fighting ashore dragged on. With her superb sick bay facilities, the transport served as one of the primary platforms for handling casualties brought off the beaches by relays of small boats. One of the *Clymer*'s doctors had even taken charge of a medical team ashore to handle initial treatment and to sort and route casualties as they came off the firing line.

The regular arrivals of boatloads of wounded was a bitter reminder of the dangers ashore, and Wallace couldn't get his mind off the demolition team's narrow escape less than two days ago.

And now the word had come down that they were going in again tonight, to make a second attempt on the boom.

Strickland and Dumont had returned from their meeting with the brass aboard the *Texas* with the news of General Patton's decision. Now, with the afternoon wearing on toward sunset, the remaining sixteen members of the unit—Johnson, of course, was still confined to the casualty ward with his shattered legs—had gathered on the deck of the *Clymer* to check and stow their equipment aboard another Higgins boat and finalize preparations for the new raid. Most of them seemed cheerful enough, ready, even eager, to tackle for a second time the daunting task of blowing the boom.

Wallace, though, was far from happy at the prospect of another raid. The demolition team's failure had left him shaken and unsure of himself, and it wasn't a feeling he relished.

But even though Lieutenant Strickland had made it clear that any of them could bow out of the second raid if they wanted to, Wallace couldn't bring himself to quit. To do so would be to admit to the fear that was gnawing at him, and that would brand him a coward for all to see. And whether or not anyone else saw it that way, Wallace knew that he himself would never be able to live down an admission that he couldn't face the raid.

He glanced around the deck, wondering how many of the others secretly harbored the same doubts. Was he the only one? Or were they hiding their real feelings behind false bravado and gallows humor?

"Hey, Billy, you think that thing's big enough yet?"

He started at the sound of his name, then realized the comment was directed at Bill Freemantle. The gunner's mate was just coming out on deck with Boatswain's Mate House, the two of them wrestling a huge metal canister like a misshapen garbage can that must have weighed a hundred pounds or more. It was an underwater incendiary device Freemantle and Lieutenant Dumont had started assembling soon after Strickland's announcement of the new raid, designed to cut the submerged net that made up part of the Sebou boom.

"Never" was Freemantle's phlegmatic reply.

"Billy won't be satisfied unless he can use that sucker to set fire to everything from here to Berlin," Ed Sperry said, spitting eloquently. He patted the .303 Lewis gun he'd been stripping and checking, a twin to the one Wallace was working on. Tonight, at least, they would be going in loaded for bear, with machine guns, extra explosives, and other equipment. It might just make the difference between success and failure.

"I just like to know I've got things covered," Freemantle said with a grin. "No sense leaving things to chance this time around. I plan to cut that cable tonight if I have to use my teeth."

"Yeah, I'm with you," Chief Dowling said. "Better to get my teeth broken chewing on the boom than get my ass broken when General Patton comes looking for explanations."

"That's just about what he was threatening to do, Chief," Strickland said. "I gotta tell you, that's one scary guy. Makes going up against the Krauts look pretty easy by comparison."

"Hey, Strickland, you planning to go in with that bandage on your nose?" Dumont asked, his tone bantering. He mimed aiming a rifle at the senior lieutenant. "That big white thing in the middle of your face is better'n a bull's-eye, especially in the dark."

"Don't you worry about me," Strickland replied with a grin. "Takes more than getting my nose bashed to put me out of action."

"Yeah," Dumont said. "Lucky you fell on your head. Nothing vital there, huh?"

"Look, I volunteered for this little vacation, didn't I? Of *course* I'm a little short in the brains department." He paused. "Out there, you guys are taking orders from me, so what does that say about *your* smarts?"

"It says we're *all* in trouble," Sperry said without looking up from his machine gun. After a moment he added, "Sir."

Wallace listened to the banter with a sinking feeling in the pit of his stomach. These men weren't afraid of what was out there. They could face another foray under the guns of the enemy ashore and still crack jokes about it all. None of them, it seemed, shared his fear. His cowardice.

I won't give in, he told himself firmly. *I won't quit now.*

But all the determination in the world couldn't completely overcome the fear he felt inside. . . .

Chapter 4

Tuesday, 10 November 1942

Combat Demolition Unit
Off Oued Sebou, French Morocco

Bill Wallace watched while the crew for the Higgins boat scrambled aboard the LCP(R) as it swayed from davits alongside the *Clymer*'s leeward rail. While Chief Dowling took his position at the coxswain's station on the port side near the bow, Machinist's Mate First Class Zymroz made his way back to the engine housing amidships. The third member of the crew, Wieniewski, was right up in the spoon-shaped bow with a boat hook, fending off as the roll of the transport threatened to batter the boat against the *Clymer*'s hull.

Members of the transport's deck crew started lowering the boat slowly, carefully. From his vantage point along the rail, Wallace could look down into the Higgins boat and see Dowling running through his checks of the engine. Zymroz was poised to go to work in case the starter didn't work or the engine needed to be primed. This was the trickiest part of deploying a boat, particularly when the seas were running high, as they were tonight. If the engine didn't catch right away, the boat would bob alongside the *Clymer*, out of control, and slam into the larger vessel with each passing wave.

They could barely feel the motion on *Clymer*'s main deck, but Wallace thought the action of the waves was even worse tonight than it had been during the first raid. That didn't make much difference here at the assembly point, but it meant they'd be in for another rough ride when they got in close to the mouth of the Sebou. There were squall lines in the area, too, which didn't help the situation much.

The engine caught as the Higgins boat touched the water, and Dowling flashed a quick thumbs-up to the rest of the demolitions men up on the *Clymer*.

Crewmen quickly started draping cargo nets along the side, and a few moments later Strickland gave a quick, approving nod. "All right, boys, let's mount up," he said, his voice still slightly distorted by his swollen nose. He'd taken off the bandage Dumont had joked about earlier, and with his face blackened by camouflage paint his facial injuries weren't obvious.

Wallace wanted to hate the man. Banged up as he'd been, he could have opted out of leading the team in tonight. Dumont could have taken command. But even with a perfectly acceptable excuse, Strickland had insisted on going in. With that example in front of him, Wallace certainly couldn't back out now, no matter how tempting the idea might be.

He swarmed down the net, painfully aware of the towering sides of the *Clymer* and the pitching motion of the LCP(R) below him. Wieniewski steadied him as he stepped across into the bow of the Higgins boat, and he in turn helped Freemantle and Lieutenant Dumont get aboard.

Strickland, as the senior officer, was the last to descend. Wallace saw him pause at the top of the cargo net, turn to deliver a snappy salute toward the stern of the ship where the flag would have been flying had it been daytime. Then the lieutenant saluted again, to the OOD this time. "Request permission to leave the ship," he said formally.

"Granted, Lieutenant." Wallace was surprised to hear that voice. It wasn't the Officer of the Deck at all, but Captain Arthur T. Moen, the transport's skipper. "Good luck . . . and Godspeed."

Strickland descended quickly, and Freemantle helped him aboard. "Wallace, Sperry, take the gun tubs," the lieutenant ordered. "Don't fire unless I give a direct order. We've got the firepower to defend ourselves, but everything still depends on stealth and surprise tonight. I don't want any screwups."

"Aye, aye, sir," Wallace acknowledged. Sperry echoed his words.

He took the portside gunner's post, a cylindrical tub just forward of the wheel, and quickly found the Lewis light machine gun stowed inside. It had been modified by having its wooden buttstock replaced by a D-shaped spade handle so that it could be maneuvered around within the confined space of the gunner's cockpit. Wallace slipped a loaded forty-seven-round pan magazine into the feed tray on top of the machine gun, then pulled the cocking knob back and forced a safety strip up into place. The weapon could now be fired at a moment's notice.

"Everybody set?" Strickland asked. "Right, then. Cast off!"

Dowling pushed his throttle forward and the Higgins boat crept away from the *Clymer*, gathering speed slowly. He steered toward the transport's stern, moving parallel to the leeward side until they were well clear of the ship before turning toward the land. As they crossed the *Clymer*'s stern, darkness closed in around the boat. The transport kept the side facing the land entirely blacked out at night, carrying out all boat operations under the lights on the opposite side, which couldn't be seen from shore. Now that the boat had moved out of those lights, the darkness was almost complete.

Just like the first night.

The trip went smoothly enough, but the closer they got to shore the worse the ground swell grew. Once again they were plowing through towering waves and pounding surf, and Wallace couldn't help but dwell on what had happened the last time. But they managed to avoid the worst, and eventually they were back in the quieter, more sluggish waters of the Sebou River.

It started to rain, another eerie parallel to the first mission. Visibility had dropped to near zero, but at least that made them harder to see from shore.

With the weather closing in, they couldn't see much from the boat, but Wallace knew from the afternoon planning that the area right at the mouth of the river, including the jetties where they'd seen the flare that first night, was now in the hands of American infantrymen. That meant the risks of detection were a lot lower this time out. Still, Dowling cut back on the engine, proceeding up the very center of the channel with just enough headway on to counter the sluggish current of the shallow waterway.

"Eyes open, people," Chief Wagner growled, sounding nervous. Maybe Wallace wasn't the only one who was remembering the first raid, after all.

Long minutes passed as the boat slipped farther and farther up the river. They had to be past the front lines now, and that meant they could be spotted and challenged at any moment. The LCP(R) had already pushed farther than on the first night, but that just meant they'd have that much farther to run if things went sour again. And they were closer to the guns of the Kasbah fort, too. . . .

The rain eased, and Wallace caught a glimpse of the frowning walls of the fortress perched high on a rounded knoll just above the riverbank. A few lights were shining high on the ramparts, but there was no sign that anyone had spotted the Higgins boat. Barely making headway, the landing craft eased slowly up the waterway, hugging the north bank. Wallace realized he was holding his breath, as if that could make a difference in their chances of being discovered. Sheepishly he let it out again, a ragged sigh. They were almost to their goal.

Their intelligence, based on Malavergne's report, said that the boom was just beyond the curve where the river bent around the high ground that held the citadel. Through the rain, Wallace could just make out the gradual sweep of the riverbank, the beginning of the elbow-shaped bend. He turned to touch Dowling on the arm and point, and the chief gave him an approving nod. Dowling, in turn, leaned close to whisper something to Strickland.

More time passed. Wallace tried to guess how long it had been since leaving the *Clymer*, but estimates were hard. They'd set off shortly after midnight. Had it been an hour? Two? He wasn't sure.

The boat cut through the mist, painfully slow, edging closer to its goal. Seaman Wieniewski spotted the line of the boom first, and Dowling reduced the boat's speed to a crawl as he steered toward the middle of the barrier. Wallace glanced up, painfully aware of the possibility of patrols on either bank, of hostile eyes looking right down into the American landing craft from the top of those sheer stone walls.

All Wallace could see of the boom from his vantage point was a thick cable strung across the half-mile width of the river, held up in several places by small boats. It didn't look particularly formidable from here, but he knew that a heavy net was suspended underwater, making the barrier that much harder to break as well as raising the specter of tangled propeller shafts should a ship like the *Dallas* try to force her way past.

Wieniewski used his boat hook to snag the low hull of one of the boats, and Dowling adjusted the throttle so that the engine was barely turning over, putting out just enough power to maintain position against the current. The chief dropped the boat's small bow ramp so that it was just level with the water, and Strickland and Freemantle moved out on the makeshift platform and crouched down to study the boom. Wallace could see it better now, and followed their low-voiced conversation carefully.

The main cable was one and a half inches in diameter, sagging slightly between the boats. The net wasn't noticeable from the Higgins boat, but there was a second wire strung above the main cable that caught the lieutenant's attention immediately. Unlike the boom itself, the wire was taut, running straight from shore to shore about a foot above the cable. It didn't come into contact with any of the supporting boats.

Strickland pointed to it and spoke in a whisper that barely carried to Wallace's position. "Alarm wire, I'll bet," he said.

Freemantle nodded. "Or a booby trap."

"Be careful not to break it," Strickland ordered. "Or even to touch it. Whatever else it is, it's trouble. At the very least it'll probably bring down the whole damned garrison on top of us if we break it." The words made Wallace glance up again involuntarily. The Kasbah loomed in the darkness, its size magnified by the shadows that gathered around it, a gigantic, menacing presence that might almost have been some horrible medieval monster waiting to pounce on its prey.

He shook off the feeling as Strickland and Freemantle straightened up and turned back to the rest of the team. The lieutenant moved back to consult in quiet tones with Dumont and the two CPOs. Seconds passed, slow, painful seconds that weighed heavy on Wallace's imagination.

Off in the distance he could hear the crackle and pop of small arms fire, punctuated by the occasional crump of a grenade or larger explosion. That would be American soldiers along the beaches mounting a diversionary attack, stirring up trouble to distract the Vichy troops from the sector along the river. It was a potentially dangerous operation, for the demolition team as well as for the soldiers involved. The attack might well distract the French, but it might also be enough to stir up troops who would otherwise not have been alert. One of them could notice the men in the river. . . .

Finally the team members started to work, moving quickly and efficiently despite the cramped quarters, knowing that time was against them. In the stern of the Higgins boat, Dumont directed the deployment of the two rubber boats into the water.

Wallace started as Strickland put a hand on his shoulder. "Dowling and the boat crew are staying here with me. Everyone else goes to work on the boom." His voice was a hoarse whisper, barely audible over the sound of rain lashing the river.

Wallace nodded slowly and climbed out of the gun cockpit. Making his way carefully to the stern of the boat, he was one of the last to scramble over the port side and into the water.

Though they had two seven-man rafts, most of the raiders were swimming. One team, the men from the *Cherokee* under Chief Wagner, with Wallace among them, went to work placing charges along the cable and in the supporting boats. They had one of the rubber boats for the job, carrying their explosives and other demolition gear. The second team, Dumont's men, paddled the other raft carefully along the length of the obstacle. They were playing out two lengths of primacord line as they went, stopping to secure them to the bottom from time to time as well as taping the two strands together every few feet.

Strickland remained in the Higgins boat, having decided that his swollen nose might hinder his breathing if he was trying to stay afloat. He knelt again on the lowered bow ramp and picked up a U-shaped Mark I explosive cable and chain cutter and fitted it over the boom. Within the cutter's metal case was a shaped charge liner and a packed one-and-a-quarter-pound charge of the new Composition C explosive. He fitted the securing hook, an inverted metal question mark spring-loaded in the bottom of the case, carefully around the cable to hold the cutter in place. It was supposed to be able to cut through a two-inch steel chain or cable, though it had frequently failed to work properly when the team practiced with it back in Norfolk.

It was because of the cutter's unreliability that Strickland had ordered the rest of the team to string additional charges along the length of the boom. The men in the water placed charge after charge, working swiftly and professionally, just as they had trained back in the Chesapeake. The backup charges were placed at regular intervals along the boom, with two half-pound blocks of TNT lashed to the front of the cable and two more positioned on the opposite side, slightly offset from the front two. In theory, the conflicting forces of their blasts were supposed to tear the boom apart. Wallace followed along after Bill Freemantle, who was setting the charges in place. His job was to tie dangling lengths of primacord hanging from each TNT block into the main lines of primacord using simple girth hitches. Primacord was a new development, introduced to the members of the team for the first time during their training period at Norfolk. A fabric-covered line of PETN high explosives that detonated at over 24,000 feet per second, primacord was an

ideal way to set off large numbers of charges almost simul-
taneously.

Over, around, over, over, and through, then move down
and repeat the girth hitch for another set of charges. It was
tedious, exacting work, and for Wallace, at least, there was
the constant gnawing awareness that sentries ashore might
spot them at any time. With the men spread out along the
entire length of the obstacle, there wouldn't be time to reach
the Higgins boat and escape once their presence became
known. Searchlights from the walls of the Kasbah fort could
illuminate the boom if someone raised the alarm, and the artillery mounted there would start raining down among the
Americans in short order. Those not killed outright by the
concussion of explosions in the water around them would be
easy prey for soldiers on shore, and even if a few men on
the Higgins boat made a run for it they'd have to pass right
under the guns of the fortress. So Wallace worked with one
ear cocked for the sound of a challenge or the crack of a rifle shot from the bank above them, knowing there was nothing he could do if one came.

But they were not seen. Eventually, the job was done, and
the swimmers and the two rafts were gathered together
again alongside the Higgins boat. "Looks good," Strickland
said softly, almost the first words any of them had said since
going to work. "Let's pack it in."

Freemantle was frowning. "You want me to set the incen-
diaries, Lieutenant?" he asked in a whisper.

The officer hesitated a moment, then shook his head. "If
the stuff we put on the boom isn't enough, nothing is," he
replied at last. "We don't want to delay any longer."

Someone had secured the Higgins boat to the cable with
a single line, though Dowling was still at the controls, holding her position against the current so that they wouldn't put
a strain on the cable or accidentally drift into the alarm
wire. The other two crewmen left aboard were keeping a
sharp lookout. Seaman Wieniewski had a Tommy gun cradled in his arms, while Zymroz held a 1903A Springfield at
the ready. The engineer set his weapon down in the bottom
of the boat and went to the side to help the men in the water
climb aboard. Quickly the team members hauled themselves
out.

While Chief Wagner took charge of getting the rafts and equipment back into the rear section of the boat, Strickland produced a package tightly wrapped in oilcloth and opened it up. Inside were a pair of fuse assemblies, kept carefully protected from the water. The lieutenant had made up two separate fuses, one timed to allow them to pass down the river and back to sea, the other much shorter. Wallace saw him weighing the two flat wooden boards in his hand, frowning, before he picked one. Even in the dark Wallace noticed the colored band they'd used to tell the two apart. Strickland was setting the short fuse.

He knew the officer's decision made the most sense for the success for the mission, but that thought wasn't comforting. The shorter fuse would go off within minutes of being ignited, giving the boat just enough time to back away to a safe distance. Given the high failure rate of the M1 friction fuse igniter in use around water—it was prone to fail if just a little bit of damp crept into its inner workings—Strickland had probably decided to use the shorter delay first so they could go back and try again if it failed. And a faster fuse meant less chance the explosives might be discovered by some random patrol and rendered harmless before they could go off.

But the choice of that fuse also meant they'd be giving themselves away at once. The Higgins boat would have to run the gauntlet with the entire Kasbah garrison alert and ready for them. Wallace felt the blood pounding in his temples and almost dropped Freemantle's incendiary device as he tried to stow it under a bench. He fought for control and forced himself to get back to work.

In the bow, Strickland taped the blasting caps of the firing assembly to the two lines of the primacord main, keeping the fuse up high to hold it clear of the water. Then he straightened up and looked back at Chief Wagner.

"Equipment's aboard, sir. All men accounted for," the CPO said quietly.

"Very good, Chief. Stations, everyone, and look sharp." As Wallace and Sperry took their places in the twin gun cockpits, Strickland turned back to the fuse igniter and yanked on the T-shaped handle at the end of the firing wire.

"Fire in the hole," he said crisply. "Coxswain, raise the ramp and back us out of range."

Long seconds passed as the boat pulled farther downstream. Then, suddenly, an explosion lit up the night as the primacord main went up and detonated the charges all along the line. In the eerie glow of the blast, Wallace turned to see Strickland's satisfied smile. Looking back up the river, he watched the cable come apart. The heavy explosive cable cutter had done its job after all, parting the boom almost dead center. The secondary charges blasted the rest of the cable into fragments, though the heavy net underwater continued to hold the small boats together. Slowly at first, but then with gathering speed, the boats drifted with the current. The weight of the waterlogged net, unsupported now by the cable, slowly dragged them underwater. The channel was clear.

"Get us out of here, Chief," Strickland ordered.

"Qui va la?" The shout was thick, hoarse. It came from the darkness. After a moment, it was repeated. Then a gunshot rang out, and a bullet whined past the Higgins boat.

Seaman First Class Wieniewski opened fire with his Thompson, firing blind. More shots, more shouts, rent the night. Now the enemy knew they were there. If the blast itself hadn't been noticed—and after all, there was enough intermittent artillery fire from both sides around the beachheads to make most people ignore one more random explosion—the severing of the alarm wire above the cable would certainly have alerted the garrison to the raiders' presence . . . and now this exchange of fire so close to the fort made it plain that this was no mere spillover from some clash near the front lines.

Somewhere an alarm bell rang out, and then sirens were starting up again, as they had the first night. Searchlights blazed to life on the walls of the Kasbah fort, sweeping back and forth along the river, hunting for their prey.

This close to the fort, the boat and its passengers would be sitting ducks if the lights were as effective in illuminating them as they'd been the first time out.

"Knock out those lights!" Dumont ordered. "Fire! Fire!"

Sperry's machine gun chattered as Dumont barked out his command. But Wallace didn't seem to be able to force his body to obey. He was frozen, thoroughly in the grip of a horrible paralysis as all his fears came to the fore at once.

"Fire!" Dumont shouted again, but Wallace barely heard him. "Fire! Fire!"

The shouted order finally penetrated the fog that clung to Wallace's mind. He had no idea how long Dumont had been yelling the command, seconds or minutes or hours. His finger tightened on the trigger of the machine gun at last, and he pivoted to aim in the direction of the parapets of the Kasbah fort.

He was vaguely aware, as he turned, of one of the searchlights going out. "Good shot, Sperry!" Dumont said. "That'll teach the bastards!" The junior lieutenant had drawn his Colt M1911 A1, and he snapped off a pair of quick shots even though the range was far too long for the fire to be effective.

The other searchlight went out as well, probably cut off rather than hit. The men on those walls would know their lights were the surest target for the gunners in the boat, and that would make them cautious. Maybe too cautious to try very hard to nail the Americans. . . .

The night sky turned day-bright in an instant. "Flare!" Chief Dowling called needlessly.

Up above, one of the 75-mm guns spoke, and a splash a few dozen yards off the Higgins boat's bow marked the fall of the shell. Wallace continued to fire, his finger clamped down tight on the trigger, until his ammo ran out. He changed magazines automatically, going through the motions without thinking about anything. His mind still had trouble accepting the reality around him, and he was operating more on reflex and training than on any conscious level.

Another shot, another miss . . . but nearer this time. A second flare lit up the night sky as the first one faded out.

"Gun it, Chief," Strickland ordered, and Dowling rammed the throttle forward and threw the helm hard over, steering downriver. More rounds arced toward them, some of them coming entirely too close for comfort. Through his private fog Wallace heard a machine gun rattling, heard round after round come smashing through the wooden hull somewhere behind him. He opened fire again, not really aiming at anything in particular now but just maintaining a steady stream of bullets in the general direction of the fort behind and to port of the racing LCP(R). Several of the other team members had carbines out now, and Wieniewski had again grabbed his Thompson to add an insistent, chattering voice to the argument.

"Freemantle! House! Start jettisoning everything that isn't nailed down!" Strickland's shout was loud enough to be plain even over the roar of the engine. "If we hit those waves at the river mouth with all this extra gear and a leaky hull, we'll sink like a rock!"

As he turned to fire aft, he saw the two sailors dumping the rafts and their deadly cargoes over the side. Freemantle picked up his incendiary device, now a dangerous liability in the fragile wooden boat, and pitched it out as well.

The light faded again as another flare died out, but for all of the zigzagging Dowling tried, the artillery fire continued to fall all too close to the Higgins boat. From shore, a machine gun rattled, and Wallace heard the bullets passing close overhead. Bullets struck the hull, punching clear through the thin wooden sides in tiny bursts of whirling splinters. Turning in the cockpit, he directed his fire toward shore, but instead of making the enemy keep their heads down, it only seemed to provoke more shooting.

"Cease fire!" Strickland called, hoarse-voiced. "Cease fire! They're tracking us by muzzle flashes now! Stop firing!"

Sperry released the trigger of his LMG and Wallace paused to glance over at the other gun tub. A few more shells probed after them, along with random fire from shore, but both grew less accurate and more sporadic as the seconds ticked slowly by. Soon the only noise left was the roar of the engine, and after the chaos of combat it was almost eerily quiet.

"Mouth of the river coming up fast," Dowling warned. "Everybody brace yourselves. We don't need anybody else ending up like Johnson. . . ."

With a clank the Lewis gun jammed as the machinist's mate fired a last burst at the distant fortress. Cursing under his breath Wallace dismounted the weapon to stow it before they hit the rough seas, but he mistimed it. They hit the first of the high swells just as he lifted it free of its mount, and the sudden lurching of the Higgins boat knocked it loose from his grasp. The machine gun tumbled into the sea alongside, and Wallace barely grasped the sides of the gunner's cockpit in time to avoid following it into the water.

"That's coming out of your pay, buddy," Freemantle shouted as he threw the remaining cases of Lewis gun ammunition in after the weapon, sounding almost exhilarated. He had every right to sound that way. They'd made it out of the jaws of death alive a second time, and this time the unit had accomplished its mission. The boom was gone, and the assault on Port Lyautey could proceed according to plan at long last.

The CDU had proven itself ... but Bill Wallace knew that he'd failed miserably tonight. He'd allowed his fears to get the better of him, and when the crucial moment had finally come, he'd frozen up, unable to function. That could have cost the lives of every member of the team.

Strickland gripped the sides of the two gun cockpits and leaned close to Wallace. "Good job back there," he said. "Damned good job."

Before Wallace could frame a reply, someone called from farther aft. "We're making a lot of water back here, Lieutenant!"

Strickland turned away, leaving Wallace more confused and uncertain than ever. The lieutenant's praise had sounded genuine enough. Had he really not noticed how Wallace had frozen? Or were the words supposed to be some kind of gentle encouragement to make him feel better?

He wasn't sure, but whatever the others thought of him, Wallace knew that his own worst fears had been confirmed tonight. He was a coward, pure and simple, and he had no right to be a part of this team of brave men who had dared to strike at the very heart of the enemy's resistance.

U.S.S. *Dallas*
Oued Sebou, French Morocco

"Dead slow, Helm. Easy ... easy."

Galloway could hear the tension in Captain Brodie's voice. *Dallas* was just entering the Sebou, fighting the surf and steering carefully to stay well clear of the jetties on either side of the river mouth. It was just a few minutes past 0530 hours, according to the bridge clock. The upriver attack was finally getting under way.

They'd spent long hours cruising off the river mouth in company with one of the Task Force destroyers and the *George Clymer*, waiting for word from Strickland's raiding party. At about 0230 all hell had broken loose around the Kasbah fort, beginning with an explosion followed by a flurry of searchlights, alarms, and gunfire. But there was no way to know with any degree of certainty what was going on, and the waiting had been nothing short of sheer agony.

But then, at last, word had come from the *Clymer*. Strickland's Higgins boat had come limping out of the mouth of the Sebou to meet one of the transport's scout boats, and together they'd made their way out to where the APA waited. According to the *Clymer*'s signal, the CDU's Higgins boat had been holed in thirteen places, and every man aboard had gotten banged up when they hit the ground swell beyond the river mouth, but no one had been killed or seriously wounded this time, and the mission had been accomplished.

So now it was time for *Dallas* to take over.

She was really not the ideal vessel to tackle the shallows of Oued Sebou, but she was the best the Americans had for the job. There was actually only one ship in the fleet with a shallow enough draft to run safely up the Sebou, the clunky old merchantman *Contessa*. But she was no combat craft; her job would come later, ferrying supplies to Port Lyautey to get the airfield into operation once the Army had secured the area. *Contessa* just wasn't a suitable assault craft, though. She was old and slow, leaky and prone to breakdowns. In fact, she'd been sidelined by engine trouble just as the rest of the invasion fleet was setting out from Chesapeake Bay, and her original polyglot merchant crew had scattered during the long wait for the repairs to be completed. The old freighter had caught up with the fleet just in time for the invasion, manned by a crew of Norfolk jailbirds offered parole in exchange for volunteering, but by the time she'd reached the assembly point, the *Dallas* had already been locked in to the role of assault ship for this mission.

Though her draft would make it hard to navigate the seventeen-foot main channel, the destroyer was the best compromise they had between shallow water capability, speed, and protection.

Galloway prayed the compromise would turn out to be a sound one.

"Watch the 'elm," the French pilot warned the helmsman. "You are drifting from the channel."

"But this is the center. . . ." the sailor protested.

"The channel runs very near the south jetty," Malavergne said harshly. "You are too far north!"

"Take the wheel, Monsieur Malavergne," the captain ordered. "You know the channel. We're in your hands."

"And God's," someone else muttered.

Galloway glanced to starboard and was horrified to see the stone sea wall close up alongside them, near enough to touch. The side of the converted destroyer scraped along the jetty once, a frightening sound.

Then the ship lurched suddenly, yawing as Malavergne tried to fight the wheel. "Goddamn it!" Lieutenant Ferguson shouted. "Meet her! Meet the helm!"

"It is the surf," Malavergne told them, still struggling to control the helm. "Between the jetties it is always like this."

Machine gun fire raked the hull from the bank. "Increase our speed," Brodie ordered quietly. He seemed totally imperturbable despite the nightmare quality of the scene around him.

A seaman sent the signal on the engine telegraph, but there was no apparent change either in the sound of the engines or the speed of the plodding destroyer. Brodie ordered the signal repeated, still with no effect. "Damn it, Smith, what are you doing to me?" the Captain muttered.

"Sir!" Another sailor had appeared in the doorway, his face and uniform caked with grease and dirt. "Sir, Mr. Smith's compliments and we've got the engines opened full up already."

"Full!" Ferguson snorted. He pointed through the bridge windscreen. "Look out there, sailor. If we're making more than five knots, then I'm Eleanor Roosevelt!"

The sailor stammered his reply. "B-but, sir . . . sir, we're showing the engines revved to twenty-five knots! She can't take much more."

Ferguson looked angry, but as he opened his mouth to chew the helpless snipe out, Malavergne spoke up from the wheel. "'E is not lying, Lieutenant," the Frenchman said quietly. "It is the mud. We are probably sailing as much through the bottom mud as we are through water. I was afraid this might 'appen with a deep-draft ship like this one."

"Sailor, my compliments to Mr. Smith," Brodie said, waving off Ferguson with a curt gesture. "Squeeze every bit of power out of those engines. We can't afford to get bogged down in this damned muck."

"Aye, aye, sir!" The sailor seemed relieved as he hurried outside.

Ferguson pointed. "Look there, Skipper. Goddamned demolitions men screwed us again!" He shot a withering look toward Galloway.

There was just enough light to see the river up ahead. The boom no longer blocked the entire river, but one segment of it had apparently not been completely destroyed. A pair of small boats were hanging in the river, apparently still held together by a fragment of the cargo net.

And they were squarely across the channel along the southern side of the river, the only place deep enough for *Dallas* to even attempt the passage.

"We'll have to abort," Ferguson went on, voice tense.

Brodie shook his head. "No way, Mr. Ferguson. They gave us the call sign 'Sticker' for this mission, and by God that's just what we're going to do. We'll stick to it if it takes everything we've got." He turned to the man on the engine telegraph. "Signal for full speed."

But as the sailor complied, the destroyer gave a sudden lurch. She had run aground. . . .

The engines whined and strained and she slowly started to make headway through the soft bottom mud, but Galloway knew there was no way she could build up the speed to break through the remains of the boom. After all this, to have come so close, and still fail, was more than he could stand.

At that moment guns of the Kasbah fort opened fire,

dropping a 75-mm shell just off the ship's bow. A few moments later a second shell whistled overhead and struck astern.

The explosion lifted her stern free of the mud, and the laboring engines suddenly raced. *Dallas* surged forward, her gauges suddenly registering her speed at eighteen knots. Her bow struck what was left of the boom dead center, and she barely shuddered as the net came apart and the APD drove on up the river.

The guns continued to fire from shore, but Brodie brought *Dallas*'s own three-inchers into play to reply to the shelling, and after a short and ineffectual exchange the French batteries stopped firing. By now additional gunfire from the supporting ships offshore was diverting their attention, and despite the mud and the narrow channel and the poor light the destroyer pushed on, rounding a bend that took her out of the immediate line of fire.

It took close to two hours, all told, to thread the needle upstream and come within sight of the Port Lyautey airfield.

But one final obstacle remained in their path, at the last bend of the river between the ship and her goal. A pair of river steamers, the same type of vessels René Malavergne was used to piloting, had been scuttled, one on either side of the Sebou. They all but blocked the narrow river. . . .

Malavergne steered for the opening between the two hulks. With her keel grating over the riverbed, *Dallas* drove forward. She passed right between the hulks with a screeching sound of metal scraping against metal. Galloway could picture the reaction among the crewmen who'd soon be turned to to replace the paint they were scouring off, but a scraped-up paint job was a small price to pay for success. The destroyer almost hung up at the last minute, but then she was through the gap, rounding the last bend, and the airfield spread out ahead of her, the end of her quest.

Some American soldiers were visible ashore along the north bank of the river, men of the Third Battalion, who had been trying to win across against resistance around the airfield for most of the day. Some of them dropped a rubber boat they were carrying and raised a cheer as *Dallas* passed.

The pilot ran the ship up alongside the airfield dock, and as *Dallas* slowed to a stop the Rangers were already spilling

over the side. But before the last man had swarmed down
the cargo nets a field battery farther up the river opened fire,
dropping 75-mm shells within thirty feet of the destroyer,
and Brodie barked quick orders at his gunnery officer to return fire with the three-inch battery. Just as the turret swung
around, though, the drone of aircraft engines filled the air
overhead, and the spotter plane off the cruiser *Savannah*
roared past the embattled destroyer. Somehow the pilot
managed to plant both his bombs squarely on the twin guns
of the French battery, silencing them.

In short order, all resistance had ceased and the objective
was in American hands at last.

When the Rangers reported their success, Galloway finally let out a sigh of relief. The mission, despite everything, had been completed. It could only be a matter of time
before Patton broke the spirit of the Vichy defenders and
forced a surrender, and that would make Operation Torch
the first real victory of the Allied counterattack against Hitler's Europe.

They'd made plenty of mistakes along the way, mistakes
that Hitler's generals might have exploited far more effectively than these French garrison troops. Future invasions
would be far more bitterly contested, and Galloway knew
the Americans would have to hone their skills at amphibious
operations before they could hope to crack the tougher
beaches that lay ahead.

The first Combat Demolition Unit had shown one way
they might cope with the defenses they were likely to face,
but they'd need plenty of training and practice before they'd
be ready to play their part.

Galloway hoped they'd get that time . . . and that chance.

Chapter 5

Sunday, 24 January 1943

Port Huron, Michigan

"What's the matter, Frank? You haven't said more than ten words all afternoon."

Frank Rand looked up, feeling suddenly guilty, and tried to muster a feeble smile. "Nothing . . . nothing, honey. Just wishing my leave wasn't up next week. It'll be hell . . . er, I don't want to have to leave you again."

He knew he was being bad company, but he couldn't shake himself out of his glum mood. Coming home for his convalescence leave, he decided, had been a big mistake. The chunk of shrapnel they'd dug out of his leg after the air raid at Safi had given him a nasty fracture, and Rand had sailed home on a hospital ship to spend Christmas and New Year's in the naval hospital at Portsmouth. He'd been given thirty days to see his family and finish his recovery before reporting back for duty.

So he'd gone home, back to Marine City, near the banks of the Saint Clair River near the border between Michigan and Canada. Returning to his boyhood home had been a strange experience for Rand. Navy life had changed him more than he'd realized, and he didn't feel a part of his hometown anymore. The war was still comfortably distant, only intruding when the radio or the papers carried some suitably edited account of events in North Africa or New Guinea or on Guadalcanal . . . or when rationing or shortages happened to inconvenience the routine of civilian life.

Nancy Brown made a face. "It's your own fault, you

know," she said, pouting. "You know Daddy was ready to offer you a tester's job at the yard. You'd have been 2A for sure, and we could be getting ready to get married this summer. But you had to go off to the Navy . . . to your stupid war."

"We've been over all that before, honey," he said, trying to keep his tone light. He didn't want to dredge up the old argument again. Nancy Brown was a year younger than Rand, the same age as his sister. They had been an item for two years, and she'd mapped out a plan for them to marry just as soon as she graduated from Saint Stephen's High School in June. Nancy had never really accepted his announced intention to go through Annapolis and become a Marine officer. For her, their whole future together had been perfectly mapped out. Her father, who owned one of the largest boat yards on this stretch of the Great Lakes, had been hinting that Frank Rand could go places at Brown's Marine, especially as the owner's son-in-law. College at Ann Arbor, a degree in business, an assured future . . . those were the things that mattered to Nancy. So when he'd gone ahead and applied to Annapolis, they'd broken up.

Now he was back. He'd looked her up despite the quarrel, hoping his new role as a wounded warrior fresh from danger and excitement in North Africa would be suitably impressive. Perhaps, he had told himself while lying in his hospital bed trying not to think about the itch under his bulky cast, perhaps she'd had a change of heart. He remembered Nancy Brown as everything a young man could want, beautiful, blond, bright and cheerful, with a family with some money and some clout in the community. A man could do a lot worse. . . .

But she hadn't changed, after all. She'd been eager enough to see him, acting as if the quarrel had never split them up and even inviting him to come out to her family's Port Huron vacation cottage for the weekend. They'd gone ice skating in the morning, until a snow squall and dropping temperatures drove them indoors. Now they were sitting in front of a roaring fire. It should have been the picture of domestic bliss, but Rand knew it was all wrong. She would never understand what drove him, never accept him for who and what he was

Like his father, he thought bitterly.

He was saved the need to try to steer the conversation away from the future he'd passed up by the sound of a car pulling up in front of the cottage. After church Nancy's parents had driven back to Marine City, just under twenty miles south of the Port Huron cottage, in response to a panicky phone call from the boat yard. Rand had entertained ideas of using their absence to reopen a two-year-old campaign to seduce Nancy, but now he was just as glad they'd come back. If he'd managed to get her in bed, he probably would have felt bound to make an honest woman out of her, and right now he doubted she was really the wife he wanted after all.

The Browns were an ill-matched couple. Christopher Brown was large, hearty, with iron-gray hair and a firm jaw, more like one of the boat builders he employed than one of the richest men in Saint Clair County. His wife, Louise, was small, with an air of elegance and patrician haughtiness about her. The money behind Brown's Marine came from her family, and everything about her, from her tailored clothing to her impeccable manners to her fastidious disdain for anyone and anything that didn't measure up to her standards of culture or breeding, was calculated to elevate her above the common folk.

For a time Louise Brown had been heartily in favor of Frank Rand. Unlike her daughter, she'd seen plenty of advantages in a son-in-law with an Annapolis background and a Marine Corps commission. But after Rand had left the Academy and signed up as an ordinary enlisted man, her favor had vanished overnight. She tolerated him for Nancy's sake, but that was all.

Fortunately Nancy's father still looked on Rand favorably. Frank had worked for him summers since he'd been sixteen, and Christopher Brown had accepted him at every turn. He'd offered Rand a job but seemed pleased when the Annapolis appointment had come through—pleased for Frank Rand, not for the status the Academy conferred. But when Rand had come home after Pearl Harbor and announced his intention to enlist, Brown had taken him aside privately to express his approval. Brown had been in the Navy himself, in the Great War, and seemed genuinely happy at Rand's decision. At Nancy's prompting he'd offered the tester's job with its draft-deferred 2A status, but he'd been even happier when Rand turned it down.

Sometimes Frank Rand wondered if his real attraction to Nancy had been the prospect of Christopher Brown as a father-in-law. Certainly he was the kind of father Rand wished he'd grown up with.

"Nancy," Brown boomed as he came in, shedding his winter coat. Rand got up quickly from the floor in front of the fire, though Nancy stayed where she'd been. "Frank. Too cold for skating, huh?"

"Yes, sir," Rand said. "We thought it would be best to get in and get warm."

Brown nodded. "Snow tonight, I'd say. We'll be wanting to allow a little extra time heading back tonight."

Nancy looked up at her father. "Was everything okay at the yard, Daddy?" she asked.

He shrugged. "I've had better days. Some damned fool was careless with his cigarettes and started a fire. Nothing major, but I had to make sure all the government's precious papers were still in the safe...." He trailed off, frowning. Brown's Marine was one of several yards in the area that had won government contracts to develop, test, and produce variants on the Higgins boat design for the War Department, and Brown fought a never-ending battle with the bureaucracy to keep up with its conflicting demands for secrecy, security, and mountains of paperwork on every subject under the sun.

His wife came up beside him. "We saw your parents in Marine City, Frank," she said, somehow managing to imply with her tone that she wished they hadn't. "Christopher, give Frank his letter, won't you?"

"Letter?" Frank asked, raising an eyebrow.

"Your father thought it might be important, Frank," Brown said. "It came in the mail yesterday. Looks official." He fished a large buff envelope out of one pocket of his coat and passed it to Rand. He stared at the return address thoughtfully for long seconds, his mind prey to a swirl of emotions.

"Well, aren't you going to open it, Frank?" Nancy asked.

He nodded absently and finally turned the envelope

over in his hand and ripped it open. He pulled out the small bundle of papers inside and studied the covering letter. Orders ... travel documents ... his future decided upon at last.

Rand's eyes fixed on one line of the document. *Report to Commanding Officer, Fort Pierce, Florida, for assignment to top-secret school.* Fort Pierce was where they trained the Scouts and Raiders. He was in!

"You look like a rich uncle just died, Frank," Brown said with a gentle smile. "Good news?"

"I got my assignment," he said in an excited rush. "Scouts and Raiders, the school I've been asking for since last summer!"

"Scouts and Raiders," Louise Brown said, mouth pursed disapprovingly. "It sounds so ... so underhanded. Couldn't you get some kind of more *honorable* job? It's such a comedown, after Annapolis, isn't it?"

He stammered, not wanting to contradict her but eager to defend his choice. Her husband saved him.

"Now, dear, all jobs in the Navy are honorable. And this is the posting Frank's been wanting. Navy commandos, no less ..." He trailed off, his eyes meeting Rand's. "I've heard of this outfit, son. They say they expect to take seventy-five percent casualties when they see action. It takes a brave man to sign up with odds like that."

"Seventy-five per*cent*?" Nancy said, suddenly wide-eyed. "Frank ... !"

But Rand ignored her. "Thank you, Mr. Brown. I ... well, I figured it was the closest I'd get to the Marines, and that was where I was heading before Pearl Harbor. I found out the Navy wasn't getting into the action as much as I thought they would. At least not the part of the Navy I've been in."

"Frank Rand, look at me," Nancy demanded, finally standing up. "Why would you go off and sign up for a suicide mission? Why?"

He sighed. "It's not, Nancy. Really. They do dangerous work, yes, but the Scouts and Raiders are going to be an important part of the war soon. Scouting the beaches before our troops go ashore in an invasion. It's the kind of job I wanted since the day I joined up, contributing ... doing something worthwhile. Something that'll make my dad proud."

"He will be, Frank," Brown told him firmly. "He will be."

Frank Rand wished he could feel as certain of it as Nancy's father sounded.

Monday, 25 January 1943

Marine City, Michigan

The Browns dropped Frank off at home late on Sunday night, and his parents and his sister were already asleep when he let himself into the house. It wasn't until the next morning, with everyone gathered around the breakfast table in the corner of the kitchen, that he was able to tell his family about his new orders.

But their reaction wasn't what he'd hoped for.

"It sounds so *dangerous*, Frankie," his mother was saying for what seemed like the twentieth time. Looking at her across the table, Frank noticed how thin and drawn her face had become just since he'd enlisted. Elizabeth Rand had aged ten years in as many months. She'd been against his decision to enlist, and his announcement today had brought her to the verge of tears.

But she was proud of him, he knew, unlike his father. He'd heard that she made the most of every chance to let everyone in Saint Clair County who would listen hear about how her son had been wounded in the invasion of North Africa.

"The war is dangerous, Mom," he said. "I'm being sent for training right now. It's not like I'm shipping out for Guadalcanal or to go fight U-boats or something."

"But when you're done training . . . ?"

He shrugged. "Who knows? I hope I get a chance to do something worthwhile, whatever that turns out to be. But there's no telling what they'll do with me."

His father looked up from his newspaper with its headlines about the British occupation of Tripoli. "Don't worry about the boy, Elizabeth," he said gruffly, taking a pull on his pipe and fixing Frank with a steely look from his one good eye. "From the sound of it, the training will be pretty tough. There's no guarantee he'll even pass the course."

Rand felt a surge of anger. "Come on, Dad! I'm not going to wash out! I'm going to pass the course, and I'm going to take everything they throw at me. The Navy . . . or the Nips . . . or the Krauts . . . whoever!"

His mother ran out of the room at that, and the elder Rand slapped his paper down and stood up slowly, painfully. "Fine work, boy," he growled. "You *had* to go and upset your mother with all this nonsense about Navy commandos, didn't you?" He took his cane from its place leaning beside his seat and hobbled toward the door, but paused there and looked back at Frank. "It's all very well for you to go chasing after your damn-fool dreams. Action. Glory. Danger. But do you have to make your mother suffer because you want to play soldier?" He was gone before Rand could answer.

"Wow," his sister commented. "You don't need to go to school to learn how to start a war."

Rand looked at her. Sue was the same age as Nancy, a high school senior who had her pick of the boys at Saint Stephen's. Her dark eyes were mocking.

"You don't seem to care much one way or the other," he said, trying to get control of his seething anger with his father.

"Hey, I'm happy for you. You got your chance to pull even with Dad, and I know that's all that really matters to you. And I'm making out pretty well. I mean, Mom mothers me a little more when she's worried about you, and Dad thinks of me as the one who isn't crazy, even if I'm not a boy. And you wouldn't believe what it can do to a girl's popularity to have a war hero for a brother."

"War hero," he said. "Yeah, right."

"Well, okay, so that's just the way I tell it." She grinned at him, and despite his turmoil he smiled back. "Not many people here in Marine City can say their brother was wounded in an air raid in North Africa, you know. Your little Nancy can't even say that . . . she has to be content with claiming you for her one true love."

"She what?"

"Didn't she say anything over the weekend? You must be

losing your touch, big brother. 'Cause when you were in the hospital, she was sure staking a claim."

He opened his mouth, then closed it again. He'd already decided that Nancy wasn't for him, but he wasn't going to get drawn into talking about it with his little sister.

The silence in the kitchen went on for a long time before Sue Rand spoke up again. "You know, Frank, you don't really have to push so hard with Mom and Dad." This time her voice was quiet, serious, with no trace of mockery or banter. "Mom thinks you're the greatest thing ever, when she's not worried sick about you. And Dad—"

"Dad!" The anger came flooding back. "He'll never accept me unless I show him I've got what it takes. Never."

"You're exaggerating," she said. "He's proud of you for volunteering. For what you did in Africa."

"Yeah. Some pride." Maybe the hospital in Portsmouth had been too far from Marine City to allow for a visit, but his father not only hadn't made any effort to see him, he hadn't even written. Rand's only contact with home during the whole Christmas season had been through his mother and Sue.

And when he'd come home, it had been to find his father as gruff as ever. He'd tried to entertain his family with stories of the landings, tried to describe what it had been like to be in the scout boat guiding *Bernadou* and *Cole* into Safi's harbor. Rand had spun out a long story one night about the air raid where he'd been wounded, doing his best to put a light face on it all to keep from worrying his mother or his sister unnecessarily, but when it was all said and done his father's only comment had been: "Sounds like they didn't teach you much about taking cover when you're under attack. Anyone in my outfit in Belleau Wood who pulled a stunt like that didn't just end up with a pretty little scar. He was dead."

"If he's so proud," Rand said bitterly, avoiding his sister's eyes. "If he's so damned proud of me, why can't he say so just one time? I'm not the kid who couldn't climb up into the treehouse he built me. Maybe I didn't do that much in Africa, really, but I tried. And I'll try even harder next time I get a chance. All I ask of him is a little bit of support. . . ."

He pushed his chair back suddenly and stood. "I guess

even that's too much to ask from *him.* He wanted a junior edition of himself, and I'll never be that. But at least in Scouts and Raiders I'll show him what *I* can do."

Rand left the kitchen in an angry mood and stomped up the stairs to his bedroom. Inside, he pulled his seabag out of the closet and started to pack.

He didn't have to report for another week, but there wasn't anything to keep him in Saint Clair County anymore. Not Nancy, not his father . . . not even his mother. Sue was the only one who understood him at all, and even she didn't realize the needs that drove him.

No, there was nothing for him here now. He'd catch a train from Port Huron to Detroit this afternoon and be on his way to Florida by morning.

And he wouldn't come back again, not until he had proven himself once and for all.

Wednesday, 27 January 1943

Navy Yard, Washington, D.C.

"Wallace, William M., Chief Machinist's Mate, United States Naval Reserve!"

Wallace stepped forward from the ranks of sailors, his back ramrod straight, his face impassive. The ceremony on the Navy Yard's parade ground, on the shore of the Anacostia River and just a few miles from the Capitol Building, was being staged with a maximum of pomp and circumstance, but he found it hard to take it very seriously. He still felt quite out of place in his brand-new chief's uniform and visored hat.

Lieutenant Commander David Coffer adjusted his glasses as he glanced down at the paper in his hands, then started reading in a slow, solemn voice. " 'For extraordinary heroism as a member of a demolition party attached to the U.S.S. *Cherokee* during the assault on and occupation of French Morocco from November 8 to 11, 1942. Assigned the extremely dangerous task of cutting through an enemy obstruction in order that the U.S.S. *Dallas* could navigate up the Sebou River, Wallace and his shipmates, on the night of November 9, proceeded with grim determination toward their objective. Despite the treacherous surf, he and his comrades skillfully and courageously accomplished their hazardous mission of cutting the cables at the mouth of the river, as guns from the French fort opened fire. Countering the enemy's attack until out of range, Wallace and the other members of his party, in spite of enormous breakers which battered their boat, brought her back to safety.' " Coffer paused. "William M. Wallace, you are hereby awarded the Navy Cross."

He reached out to pin the award on Wallace's chest, then stepped back. Wallace gave him a snappy salute, returned with equal precision. Then he stepped back into line. The commanding officer of the Navy Bomb Disposal School gave a sign, and a burly chief bawled out a dismissal. The ceremony was over.

As the assembled sailors dispersed around him, Wallace stood still, shaking his head slowly, disbelieving. The Navy Cross had just been awarded to a coward. . . .

The decoration might have meant more if they hadn't been passed out wholesale. Several members of Strickland's demolition team had ended up in the Bomb Disposal School at the Navy Yard after the Torch landings. A few had gone on to other duties; Lieutenant Dumont, for instance, had earned a promotion to lieutenant commander and an assignment as the senior salvage officer in North Africa. But the bulk of the outfit, including Freemantle and Wallace, had ended up here, assigned as instructors in bomb disposal techniques. And every man from the CDU had been given the Navy Cross, whether they were here or at another duty station. Each award had been couched in virtually identical language, with no regard at all for individual exploits or accomplishments. To have his efforts put on the same level as those of men like Freemantle, Dumont, Strickland, or Chief Dowling struck Wallace as little short of ridiculous. It cheapened the Navy Cross to hand it out to everyone in the unit together, whether they'd done well or not. There was even a rumor circulating at the Yard that Johnson, the man who'd broken his ankles on the first raid and missed out on the second in consequence, had received exactly the same award with the very same description of his part in the operation.

And what had they really accomplished, after all? They'd failed their first attempt. And while the second raid had been a success, the achievement had been virtually nullified a short time after the *Dallas* had steamed up the Sebou to the airfield. They'd secured Port Lyautey as planned and flown in twenty-seven U.S. Army P-40Fs from the escort carrier *Chenango*, but to little effect. The tramp steamer *Contessa* with her jailbird crew had broken down on the way up the river with her load of parts, fuel, and supplies, further delaying the opening of the airfield. The whole of the tenth of November had been taken up by these misadventures, and at ten o'clock that evening all their efforts had become moot when Admiral Michelier, the French commander for the area around Casablanca, had agreed at last to cease hostilities.

So in the end nothing the demolition team had done had really contributed much to the outcome of Operation Torch. But clearly someone in the War Department had decided that a few flashy medals would be just the thing to motivate the men in ranks—and the civilian population at large—to believe that North Africa had been a major step forward in the war effort. The wording of the citations was carefully phrased to leave out any hint of the initial defeat or the total irrelevance of the whole CDU exploit.

Wallace looked down at the medal with a frown. A shiny bit of ribbon and metal didn't turn a coward into a hero. That was one thing he knew for sure. He had allowed fear to overwhelm him that night under the walls of the Kasbah fort, and the memory of it still made the blood pound in his temples. He had to overcome the fear, to put it behind him.

A phony medal for a phony exploit couldn't do any of that. Only Bill Wallace could turn his life around. Only Bill Wallace could force himself to face down his fears and put the coward inside him down once and for all.

But he wasn't sure how he was going to do it.

Thursday, 4 February 1943

Navy Amphibious Training Base
Fort Pierce, Florida

"Reporting for duty, sir," Rand said, holding himself rigidly at attention.

The big man with the ensign's insignia on his collar gave a casual nod. "At ease, all of you. My name is Bucklew, and I've been assigned to process in our new trainees here."

The four sailors standing in a row in front of his desk relaxed a little, but not much. Rand studied the ensign as the man leafed through the personnel files on his desk. Bucklew was no typical fresh-faced young officer just out of school, that much was for sure. Rand estimated his age at close to thirty, tall, stocky, thickly muscled. Nothing at all like the typical recruiting-poster image of a Navy officer, he thought, though perhaps he was just what the Scouts and Raiders wanted.

If so, would they really want Frank Rand?

"Hmm." Ensign Bucklew put down a file and looked up at Rand. "Interesting record, Rand. You were in North Africa?"

"Yes, sir," Rand replied. "With the *Harris*." The words were no sooner out than he was cursing himself inwardly. Bucklew knew that already.

"File says you volunteered for the crew of one of the scout boats."

"Yes, sir." This time he resisted the impulse to elaborate.

"What did you think of the performance overall? Were the scout boats useful in getting the troops ashore?"

Rand hesitated. "Er . . . permission to speak freely, sir?"

The ensign smiled. "You'll find we all speak pretty freely in this gang, Rand. Say what you think."

"Sir, my boat guided two APDs into the inner harbor at Safi. It was absolutely essential work, and the attack couldn't have proceeded without it, but I feel it could have been handled better."

"How so, Rand?"

"Sir, one scout boat bobbing around in the middle of the harbor wasn't very efficient. I felt then . . . I still think . . .

we should have put men on shore. They could have marked the jetty much more effectively. And scouts on shore could have done a better job at showing the exact dimensions of the beaches. That didn't matter much with the APDs, but for the smaller landing craft going in blind ... I just think lights showing from the beach itself would have been useful. I urged my CO to let us try that, but he turned the suggestion down."

"I see." Bucklew looked thoughtful. "Interesting observations, Rand. I wish I'd been able to see things from the same vantage point."

"Sir?"

He smiled. "I was in Africa too, in the Algiers part of the operation. Had to pull every string I could find to get there, too. The powers that be thought me and my buddies in the first S&R class would be more useful as instructors Stateside, but I told them we had to see an invasion up close if we were going to be effective later." He spread his hands. "So of course we got all the way to Algiers and then got our transport torpedoed out from under us before we had a chance to do much observing. Looks like you got to see all the things I was there to look for."

Rand thought of his own embarrassment at being wounded in the air raid and fought back a grin. "I don't know if I saw anything useful, sir. But I know what I was thinking at the time."

"Impressions can be as important as anything else, Rand. I'll be wanting to pick your brain later." He looked down at the file again. "Says here you were wounded. Broken leg."

"Yes, sir. Air raid, the day after the landing."

"The physical training here is pretty tough. Sure you're up to it?"

"Yes, sir," he said, more emphatic than he'd intended.

The ensign's calculating eyes lingered on him for a long moment, then he nodded. "Very well. We'll find out, I guess. Now ... Havlicek, Peter Thomas."

"Sir." The first class boatswain's mate next to Rand stiffened again. He was almost as tall and broad as the ensign, but younger, only a year or two older than Rand.

"From Columbus ... that's my hometown." Bucklew smiled.

"Yes, sir." There was a moment's silence. Then Havlicek's eyes widened. "Sir . . . are you Phil Bucklew? The football star?"

The ensign shrugged. "Don't know if star's the right word for it, but I played a little. And coached a little, too, until Pearl Harbor."

"You only took the Bulls to three consecutive league championships! I . . . sir, it's a real honor to get to meet you. I played high school ball . . . and wanted to go to Xavier College, just like you. But then the war . . ."

"Yeah, the war," Bucklew said, shrugging. "Well, Havlicek, it might not be football, but Scouts and Raiders takes a lot of hard work and discipline. And teamwork, too. Most of our original gang are all football players. Big John Tripson, Buck Halperin, Jerry Donnell from the Bulls . . . you'll be in good company, I guarantee it. But just like in pro ball, if you don't make the cut you're out. So give us everything you've got, Havlicek."

"Yes, *sir*!"

Bucklew turned his attention to the other two sailors in turn. When he'd finished, he leaned back in his chair and studied all of them through narrowed eyes. "All right, you men'll do. For the moment, at least. Now, listen up. We're still pretty damned new here. My class was the first S&R gang, put together last summer out of Gene Tunney's phys ed program. We made things up as we went along. Your group's going to be the first organized class to go through training, so there'll be some rough spots while we work things out. Hell, we've only been here at Pierce since last month. I expect you to roll with the punches. Scouts and Raiders are going to have to know how to handle surprises. You got me?"

"Yes, sir," they responded in chorus.

"Good. We've got ourselves the only real live building here on the island as our HQ, so you won't have to be out there in that tent city they call a base. Two men to a room. Havlicek, Rand . . . you two're bunkmates. Same for you two, uh . . . Shelby and O'Hara. See the yeoman outside for your assignments. Get settled in over the weekend, gentlemen, because come Monday we're gonna work you until your asses fall off. Dismissed."

They left the office, stopping outside to ask for their room assignments and collect their seabags. The building that housed the Scouts and Raiders had been a casino before the Navy had taken over. Somehow Bucklew and the other Scouts and Raiders had finagled their way into possession of the facility at a time when the rest of the Amphibious Training Center was little more than tents, swamps, and bugs. As Rand followed his new roommate to their quarters, he was already starting to feel like one of the Navy's elite.

Chapter 6

Monday, 15 March 1943

Washington, D.C.

The taxi turned left off of the Francis Scott Key Bridge and began traveling south along the west bank of the Potomac. Lieutenant Galloway, in his blue uniform and with his briefcase on the seat beside him, sat in the backseat and watched the early morning light touching white marble and winterdead trees. Behind him, high on the hill on the other side of the river, Georgetown University brooded over the valley below like some medieval castle. Left and ahead, the whitemarbled panorama of Washington, D.C., was spread out for his inspection, gleaming, pristine, less national capital, it seemed, than monument to the Republic.

Even yet, fifteen months after Pearl Harbor, Washington in many ways seemed only distantly touched by the war, though ramshackle government buildings, barracks, and warehouses continued to crop up everywhere, from the Tidal Basin and the shores of the Potomac up the Mall to the very gates of the Capitol Building itself. The city was bustling, growing, thriving as it had never thrived before, and yet the people remained strangely insular, somehow isolated from the greater events of the world outside their narrow lives.

Elsewhere in the country, people were holding rubber drives, buying war bonds, and planting Victory gardens. Women were coming out of their homes and going to work in the nation's shipyards and factories. In cities along the coasts, blackouts were the rule now, after a series of appalling incidents the year before, when German U-boats had actually torpedoed merchant ships backlit by the glow of American cities. In Washington, however, life, *all* life, it seemed, revolved around the government. Since the late 1930s, people had been descending on what once had been a provincial, almost a backwater town that rarely, if ever, intruded upon the thoughts and perceptions of the country's citizens. The Depression and the New Deal had changed all that, of course. And now the war was changing it far more than mere politicians could ever hope to manage. But sometimes it seemed as though the town's citizens were so wrapped up in themselves and in their work that they had no attention left to spare for events transpiring beyond the Potomac's muddy banks.

Past the Jefferson Memorial Bridge, the cab slipped beneath the proud, green rise of Arlington National Cemetery. Looking up, to his right, Galloway could see the long lines of tombstones stretching beneath the hill's crown of winter-barren trees and the red-and-white presence of the old Custis-Lee mansion.

Tombstones. There would, Galloway thought glumly, be a lot more of those grim white markers planted on that sacred hillside before this war was over. Between the first landings in August of 1942 and last month, when the Japanese had finally evacuated the last twelve thousand of their troops from battle-savaged Guadalcanal, seventeen hundred American boys had died.

And there were going to be so very many more.

He didn't want to think about those neatly arrayed tombstones. Shifting in the cab's backseat, he turned again to watch the Washington panorama.

A boom town. That, he thought, described the marble city

perfectly. The government was growing so quickly now that anyone who could type and file was hired on the spot for ninety-five dollars a month. Apartments and rooms for rent were pricelessly rare, and a kind of black market in spare bedrooms was making neophyte landlords rich. After coming back from North Africa, Galloway had lived in bachelor officer's quarters clear out at Fort Meade for two months before he'd finally managed to find a shabby little two-rooms-and-a-bath apartment in a run-down part of Georgetown. The apartment, a sectioned-off upstairs part of a larger townhouse owned by a widow named Mrs. Dilmore, had its own access to the outside and enough room for him if he didn't collect too many more books or personal items during his stay. To win the place, though, he'd had to endure a two-hour interview with Mrs. Dilmore, answering shockingly intimate questions about his private life, his personal habits, and even his sexual activities, then endured a lecture about smoking, cooking, loud talking, swearing, or entertaining women in his apartment. He'd answered all the questions, and smiled and nodded pleasantly throughout the lecture; he would have done *anything* by that time to get a room that close to downtown Washington, even if the hot running water was rusty and lukewarm, the wallpaper was peeling, and his landlady was a pinch-faced, snoopy old battle-ax.

He still hadn't been able to buy a car, which left him depending on taxis and rides from co-workers at the Pentagon.

God, how I hate this town, he thought.

Duty in Washington, Galloway thought, was penance for his sins off the coast of North Africa last November. Or had he actually been killed, and this . . . experience was Purgatory? No, no, this couldn't be Purgatory, or even Hell. He would have expected something more in the way of sulfur and brimstone. The sisters back at Our Lady of Mercy in Boston had never hinted that punishment for his mortal sins might consist of mind-numbing boredom . . . or being forced to endure the shortsighted stupidity of others.

There could be no question that his assignment to Washington was punishment of a sort, even though he'd arrived with a glowing citation from General Patton entered in his service record. The service record also contained a fitness report written by Admiral Kelly's chief of staff.

"Although he shows great promise as a naval officer," that damning-with-faint-praise narrative ran, "Lieutenant Galloway must learn to work within the set guidelines and boundaries of the Navy chain of command. Though bright and innovative, he has on numerous occasions circumvented the established chain of command in order to gain support for his ideas which, though highly inventive, are frequently impractical. . . ."

Impractical, yeah. Like sending a handful of men out in a tiny, open boat in thirty-foot waves, braving enemy machine guns and shellfire to blow a boom across the Sebou River and open the way for a commando assault. The plan *had* worked, and not a man had been lost . . . but Galloway was still well aware of how close Lieutenant Strickland's tiny command had come to total disaster.

More damning in official eyes was the fact that the operation really hadn't been necessary. Yes, the *Dallas* had slipped past the wrecked boom and offloaded the Rangers at the Port Lyautey airfield. But in less than twenty-four hours, Vichy resistance had ceased and the Americans had entered Casablanca. It was unlikely that capturing that airfield had contributed much to the campaign.

As for the citation from Patton, well, George S. Patton, Jr., was not exactly a prominent or well-known officer, and among those who knew him, he was not well liked. He certainly was not one of those movers and shakers of the high military command, the men who got things done, whose word could actually change a system that clung to the old ways of doing things with all the tenacity of a bulldog. Like Galloway, Patton was perceived as a maverick, a visionary who pursued his own impractical schemes, bypassing the established order of things to fulfill them and to hell with any toes that might be stomped on along the way. Praise from General Patton was about as valuable for Galloway's military career as written praise from the Devil himself.

As a result, Galloway had run into some trouble in finding his niche after his rather precipitous transfer to Washington. He'd spent most of December in a junior officers' replacement pool, waiting for assignment. Then he'd been dropped behind a desk in the personnel office at the Washington Naval Yard on the north bank of the Anacostia River. There, mingled with the tedium of filling out forms and writing evaluations, he'd typed up report after report on the tactical potential of Navy special operations, concentrating on the value of teams consisting of six to eight highly trained and highly motivated men, drawing on Strickland's mission for proof of what such teams might accomplish. The reports had gone out to the staff officers of a dozen separate commands, to Ordnance, to Weapons Testing, to the Bomb Disposal School at the Navy Yard, even to CINCPAC out in Hawaii.

Predictably, perhaps, nothing had happened . . . except that someone in the exalted, gold-plated ranks far above a mere lieutenant's mean existence had sent a complaint down the chain of command. He'd spent another couple of weeks in an officer's pool before being reassigned across the river to the Pentagon. There, he'd been working for the past month in Supply, processing requests for mimeograph paper, for carbon paper, for typewriter paper, for filing cabinets and desks and lamps and typewriters. The job was less interesting than his work in Personnel at Anacostia, if that were possible, and it left him with far less free time. In four weeks, he'd been able to write only a single report on Navy special operations, plus two requests for transfer to combat duty.

Sometimes he thought that if he had to spend one more minute in this insane, intensely political city, he would go stark, raving mad.

The cab swung through a gentle curve along the Potomac, and the enormous, five-sided edifice that was the brand-new headquarters for the War Department appeared ahead, rising from a vast and ugly red scar in the earth. It was an imposing and, for Galloway, a detested sight. So big there'd been no room for it anywhere in Washington proper, with over seventeen miles of corridors and three times the floor space of the Empire State Building, the structure known even during its design phase as the Pentagon had been completed in an astonishingly short period of time. In the early spring of 1943, it still showed signs of haste employed in its construction. Huge, blunt, and ugly, it was no less a monument than smaller structures honoring men like Washington and Jefferson. It was a monument, Galloway thought, to the runaway bureaucracy that was rapidly threatening to bury the military in an avalanche of paperwork.

"So what's it like, Lieutenant?" the cabby asked him, suddenly breaking the spell of depressed silence. "Workin' in that big building, I mean."

"What, the Pentagon?"

"Yeah. They say people get lost in that thing."

"Oh, it's not so bad," Galloway said, smiling despite his mood. "We do occasionally get requisitions for balls of string from small parties of workmen who've been wandering around in there since they put the walls up. I guess they're still looking for the front door."

"What I wanna know," the driver said, "is what's gonna happen after this here war's over. I mean, when the Army goes back to peacetime size, there ain't no way in Hell they're ever gonna use all that space, right?"

"You got me," Galloway said. "I've heard they might use it to store records."

"Aw, hell, Lieutenant. Now pull the other one, okay? How many records could one government want to keep, huh?"

"You'd be surprised," Galloway said. "You'd be real surprised."

Before the Pentagon had been built, the Department of the Army alone had maintained its offices in twenty-three separate buildings scattered throughout the city of Washington. Since 1917, the Navy Department had kept its offices in a dilapidated and supposedly temporary structure erected on the Washington Mall by no one less than then–Assistant Secretary of the Navy Franklin D. Roosevelt, a structure that it had long since outgrown. In September of 1941, while Congress, the President, and the public continued an ongoing debate over just where the Pentagon was to be built—and on whether or not it was even needed—the Army's General Somervell, the West Point graduate engineer already credited with building New York's Idlewild Airport, ignored the debate over whether such a structure would desecrate the hallowed ground of Arlington and ordered the construction begun in a field known as Hell's Bottom, south of the National Cemetery. Work proceeded at a furious pace, with as many as thirteen thousand men working around the clock, under banks of arc lights at night, in a sea of mud during bad weather. So rushed was the work that architects could not keep ahead of the building contractors. Blueprints were frequently taken from the abandoned aircraft hangar where the architects were working before they were completed, and in one notorious case, one designer had asked about the shape of a particular load-bearing beam in his plans, only to be informed that the beam had already been installed the day before.

By May of 1942, half a million square feet of the building were ready for occupancy—assuming the words *ready* and *occupancy* were not too closely examined, and the first convoys of troop-guarded armored cars laden with secret files began wending their way through the fields of mud surrounding the five-sided monster. For almost all of another year, the Pentagon's inhabitants dodged hordes of construction workers, wet paint, wet cement, falling debris, a steady din of noise, and choking clouds of plaster dust as they attempted—mostly in vain—to coordinate the work of dozens of separate departments in a complex enterprise that was rapidly becoming a logistical and bureaucratic nightmare. Completed in January of 1943, it now housed forty thousand people, the largest office building on Earth, and there were those who claimed it already was too small.

Would order ever be established in this steel-and-concrete altar to the pagan gods of universal chaos? Galloway sincerely doubted it.

"That's sixty cents, Lieutenant," the cabby said, dropping the meter flag.

"Right. Thanks." Impulsively generous, Galloway handed the man three quarters, then climbed out of the cab. The building loomed above him, monolithic and oppressive. He felt very small.

Squaring his shoulders, Galloway clutched his briefcase and began picking his way across a path of scrap lumber that workmen had used to bridge a muddy swamp close by the building's river entrance.

Officially, construction work on the Pentagon had been completed a month ago, though bulldozers continued to rumble on the grounds outside and gangs of tool-wielding men still banged away in some unfinished corridors and rooms. Most of the facilities inside were still primitive, and every steel desk top in the building was coated daily with a layer of plaster dust thick enough for its occupant to write his name legibly with a fingertip.

Most disconcerting, though, was the sheer size of the place, that and the sheer anonymity of the faceless hordes of officers, secretaries, and harried office workers who swarmed through the place like ants in some colossal, five-sided hill. In ten thousand years, Galloway would never be able to learn the names of more than a few of them. Most he would never even meet, save as part of the milling throng that seemed more like part of the background than individuals, his co-workers.

Betty Finster, the secretary who worked the front office for Supply, looked up as he walked in. "What did you do now?" she asked. She was a heavyset, plain-faced woman of about fifty, and she was worth her weight in gold. Galloway was fairly certain that she was the only person in the whole building who knew where everything was and where everyone worked. Certainly, it was she who ran the Supply Department, rather than Captain Long, her purported boss.

"What do you mean, my beautiful Betty?" He grinned easily, but his stomach twisted inside. God, what *had* he done now?

"Can the blarney, Lieutenant. And you might want to clean up that uniform a bit." She handed him a memo. "Report to my office as soon as possible," it said in a hastily scrawled handwriting that required some effort to decipher. It was signed, simply, "Metzel," and included a room number on the Pentagon's C-ring, third floor.

Galloway raised his eyebrows. "Metzel? Who is Metzel?"

Betty sniffed. "*Captain* Metzel is on the Commander-in-Chief-Atlantic's planning staff. Just who did you insult this time, Irish?"

"I'm not sure," he said, handing the memo back. "But I guess I'd better get up there."

"I guess you're right."

Technically, this could be about that last report he'd submitted. It had been addressed to the Office of Amphibious

Operations and had detailed how small teams of men trained in demolitions work could slip unobserved onto a hostile beach, blowing paths through mine fields and obstacles before an invasion began. In particular, he'd stressed how important this might be in the expected future landings in the Mediterranean, in Sardinia or Sicily, or Greece, possibly, or even in Italy itself. Maybe the report had found its way all the way up the pyramid to CINCLANT, but that scarcely seemed credible.

Was somebody very high up the official totem pole about to come down on him for meddling in things beyond his ken? That seemed a lot more likely.

Ten minutes later, the mud wiped off his shoes and the lint patted off his blue jacket with a strip of paper tape wrapped around his fingers, Galloway knocked on a wooden door, unadorned save for its number, then walked in. An attractive civilian secretary with neatly bunned, brown hair eyed him suspiciously from her desk, as though she weren't used to dealing with mere lieutenants. "Yes?"

"Lieutenant Galloway," he said. "To see Captain Metzel."

She consulted with an intercom box on her desk, the exchange too low for him to hear. Elsewhere in the large room, ranks of office workers, military and civilian, clattered away at their typewriters like so many human typing machines.

When the secretary looked up again, she wore an expression of mild disapproval. "You're to go right in, Lieutenant. He says, 'Hurry.' "

Inside the inner office, Captain Metzel was just putting on his coat. "You're Galloway," he said, his manner brusque.

"Yes, sir."

"Afraid something's come up. Got to go. I'm late as it is." The man spoke in harshly punctuated bursts, almost as though his speech couldn't keep up with his thoughts. "I need to talk to you, though. Free tonight?"

The unexpected question confused Galloway, who'd been expecting a chewing out. "Er . . . that is, yes, sir. I am."

"Good." Metzel tore a sheet from a notebook on his desk, plucked a fountain pen from his jacket, and rapidly scrawled an address. Handing the paper to Galloway, he nodded satisfaction. "There's a party at that address, starting at eight. Just tell them that you're with me. They'll let you in. It's a formal dinner. Full dress, whites, gloves, and sword."

"Aye, aye, sir. Uh . . . may I ask, Captain, what this is all about?"

"Eh? Don't you know? Never mind. I'll talk to you tonight."

And then Metzel was gone, leaving Galloway alone in his office. Bemused, he pocketed the address and left the office, pulling the door shut behind him.

"You're lucky," the secretary told him as he came out. "He gave you a whole thirty seconds. Most officers don't get half of that."

Galloway studied her speculatively. If she was as efficient as Betty down in Supply, she'd have a handle on what the hell was going on. "Listen, I'm afraid I'm lost. Can you tell me what this is all about, Miss . . . Miss . . ."

"Miss Lewis. You're the lieutenant who wrote that report that has everyone so shaken up, aren't you?"

"I don't know. Am I?"

"The word, Lieutenant, is that you've rattled some bars in some very high cages. All I know is that Captain Metzel wanted to see you. I take it he wasn't very informative."

"I'm afraid not. He wants me to meet him at a party. Tonight."

Her eyes opened wider. Galloway could not help noticing that they were very, very blue.

"At the Gilmans'?"

He reached into his pocket, fished out the address, and studied it, trying to read the crabbed handwriting. Failing, he handed it to her.

"That's it. Franklin and Rita Gilman. It's in Georgetown, near the university. Here." She wrote down a more legible version of the address, then handed it back to him.

"Thank you, Miss Lewis." She really might be somewhat pretty, he thought, though having her hair in a bun gave her a rather severe, no-nonsense look. Her suit, a gray, extremely conservative jacket over a plain white blouse and gray skirt, did little to flatter her.

"Anytime, Lieutenant," she said. Surprisingly, she winked. "Good luck."

He wondered exactly what she meant by that.

A few minutes past eight that evening, Galloway rang the bell at a brick townhouse at a fashionable Georgetown address. It was actually less than five blocks from the room he'd been renting for the past month, but in the Washington area, five blocks could spell the difference between whole, separate universes of social orders. A pretty maid in traditional black and frilly white answered the door and accepted his hat.

Some thirty guests were gathered in a drawing room larger than he'd imagined possible in the townhouse. The sexes seemed evenly divided; the men were, for the most part, senior military officers, admirals and generals, colonels and captains. A few civilians were present as well, in formal evening dress, while the women in the room provided a glittering background of color and expensive jewelry.

One of them saw him standing in the foyer and walked toward him, a glass in one slim hand.

"Good evening, Lieutenant," she said, smiling. "Still lost?"

Galloway didn't answer at once. He couldn't. At first he didn't even recognize the young woman standing before him, and when it finally dawned on him that this was the secretary from Metzel's office, he found himself completely tongue-tied.

Her hair was down, stylishly swirling about her bare shoulders, and in this light it looked more dark blond than brunette. Her evening gown was dark blue and strapless; his eyes followed the plunge of her décolletage and he found it all but impossible to tear them away.

"Or have you lost something?" When he looked up, her smile was dazzling.

"Uh, sorry," Galloway said. "Miss Lewis! What are you doing here?"

She took a sip from her glass. "Working supper, I'm afraid. With old Idea-a-Minute."

"I beg your pardon?" He was beginning to feel like he was entirely out of his league.

She dimpled. "Haven't you heard that? We call him 'Idea-a-Minute Metzel.' The man's amazing, really. Brilliant. If they put him in charge of this war, we'd have Hitler,

Mussolini, and Tojo all on their knees inside a year, begging for mercy. Come on. I'll take you to him."

"Lead the way."

The view, he noted, was nice from the back as well. He was sorry when she ushered him into a small study leading off the back of the drawing room. A fire crackled in a stone fireplace, and the walls were hidden by shelf upon shelf of books. Galloway still didn't know who this Gilman person was, but he certainly had a well-furnished library.

Captain Metzel was there, in uniform. With him was another man, this one in civilian clothes, and without a uniform it took Galloway a moment to recognize him.

"Ah! Galloway," Metzel said. "Glad you could make it!" He turned to the other man. "Admiral King, this is the report writer I told you about."

Galloway found himself shaking hands with a spare, hawk-faced man. "Admiral King, sir. This is certainly an unexpected honor."

Earnest J. King was Chief of Naval Operations, and the highest-ranking naval officer in the American armed forces. His handshake was firm and dry, and his eyes missed nothing. "Captain Metzel has been telling me about your demolition team idea," King said. "You say you were there when it was tried at Torch?"

"I was aboard the *Dallas*," Galloway said, "not with the CDU. But I was involved in the planning, yes, sir."

"And you think that a small team could go ashore on an enemy-held beach at night, fasten explosives to the obstacles and landing craft traps there, and make their escape?"

"They could go in by boat, or they could swim ashore, sir. Yes, they could do it. I'm convinced of that."

"You've made more than a few enemies along the way, son. Are you award of that?"

"Yes, Admiral. I gather that some people feel . . . threatened by the idea of elite forces."

"Damn right, they do," Metzel put in. "Just try going up to some station CO and tell him you want the best five percent of his people."

"It's money, too, Captain," King said. "Money and politics always go together. And a unit like this is going to be expensive."

"It needn't be, Admiral," Galloway said. "They won't be able to carry weapons, for instance. Maybe a knife for cutting line and fuses, but that's all. They'll have their explosives, and that's it."

King smiled, but his eyes were still hard. "There's more to it than that," he said, "as I'm sure you realize. Boats, maybe special boats, tailored to special missions. Special explosives, waterproof detonators, things of that nature. And above all, training. We'll need to get the best people, skilled in demolitions work, available. Build a whole new school. That will take money. And time."

"You sound as though you've already worked this out, Admiral."

"Not me. But others have. Captain Metzel here, for one. And I've seen reports from other people. There's a young lieutenant commander running the Bomb Disposal School over at the Navy Yard who's been thinking along these lines for some time. No, Lieutenant, yours is not the only voice for naval combat demolition teams by a long shot. I'd have to say that it is simply an idea whose time has come."

"That may be true, Admiral," Metzel said. "But we've still got a hell of a long way to go."

"And that, Captain, is why I want you to take this project. Put together a research team and tell me if the idea is feasible. What will we need? Where can we set up the school?" King turned and faced Galloway, his eyes suddenly fierce. "You."

"Sir?"

"Captain Metzel tells me you're in Supply down in the five-sided squirrel cage basement."

"Uh, yes, sir."

"Damned waste. Okay. As of tomorrow morning, you're working for Captain Metzel. Report to him. I'll see that the paperwork gets put in the pipeline to clear your transfer."

Galloway was stunned. He would be leaving Supply? At last? "I'm not real sure what his new assignment entails, Admiral, but sight unseen I've got to thank you with all of my heart!"

King grinned. "Don't mention it. Believe me, after you've worked your tail off trying to keep up with this guy, you'll rue the day you ever met me. You certainly won't thank me for the favor!"

Dinner and the endless round of small talk with naval officers, minor politicians, and their wives went by in a blur. Galloway kept trying to arrange an apparently casual and accidental meeting with Miss Lewis, but Metzel's secretary attracted young and unattached officers like a flame attracting moths. Fortunately, most of the officers present were more senior and had their wives in tow, or Galloway never would have had a chance. Still, he saw more than one admiring or openly lustful glance directed at her from captains or admirals from the opposite side of the room.

"... and I was telling my husband just the other day that one sees so many *strangers* in this town these days, and they're not at all an attractive class of people. These New Dealers and agronomists and economists and university professors all strike one as so, well, *common. . . .*"

"Ah, please excuse me, ma'am," Galloway said, disentangling himself from the elegantly attired dowager as gently as he could. Across the drawing room, the cloud of moths had momentarily opened up, and he wanted to take his chance now, while he could.

"But I wasn't *finished*!"

But Galloway had already crossed the room, plucking a glass of champagne from a servant's tray along the way. "Miss Lewis?"

"Hello, Lieutenant. The boss through wringing you out?"

"I suppose he is. For now, anyway. Champagne?"

"I don't drink. But thank you."

He blinked. He'd seen her with a glass earlier. "But I thought—"

She dimpled. "Actually, I put soda water in a glass so that people aren't always trying to give me a drink," she said. "But, you see, you caught me with my defenses down."

"Ah. Right." Deftly, he turned and dropped the champagne on a passing servant's tray. "Lieutenant Galloway, in the best Irish tradition, boldly puts his foot in it once again."

She laughed. "Not at all. So. How are you enjoying the party?"

He took a look around the room, scanning the glitter and

finery and self-importance. The dowager was giving him a fish-cold glare at a range of seven yards. Turning to face Miss Lewis again, he pulled an elaborate grimace. "Is *that* what you do at these things? Enjoy them? Darn! Nobody ever told me!"

"You looked a bit out of your depth there with Mrs. Morely. The Dragon Lady of Georgetown."

"You saved me, you know. From a fate worse than death."

She curtsied slightly, and the movement did wonderful things to the engineering of her dress. "Happy to be of service, sir."

"I'll tell you the truth, lass. Every time I go to one of these full-dress-with-sword affairs, I learn again why the ancient Romans threw themselves on their swords."

"You'll do nothing so drastic, I hope!"

"Well . . ." He paused, as though thinking about it.

"Please," she said, taking his left arm. "It's such a lovely sword, and I wouldn't want it to get bent. Besides, I happen to know that Mrs. Gilman just had her floors done specially for this party, and if you bleed on them, the captain and I would become persona non grata. Outcasts, forever barred from Washington society."

He reached across to his left hip and touched the hilt of his sword. "Sure you don't want me to do you a favor?"

She laughed. "I'm sure."

"Look, ah, Miss Lewis—"

"Please, call me Virginia."

A warm, lovely name. "Virginia, then. I'm Joe."

"I know. I had your personnel record on my desk yesterday."

"I'm not very good at this sort of thing, but . . . can I see you again?" He felt clumsy and foolish. He didn't know if she was spoken for, knew nothing about her. . . .

"That might be possible," she said.

"Great! It looks like I'm going to be working in your office, for Captain Metzel, so—"

"Oh." She looked disappointed. Her hands slipped from his arm.

"What's the matter? I say something wrong?"

"Oh, it's not you, Joe. But I do have a rule, an absolutely inflexible rule. I don't date guys in the office. Never."

"Why? What difference does that make?"

"Let's just say 'Once burned, twice shy' and leave it at that, okay?"

"What if I get myself fired?"

"Joe!"

"I could throw myself on my sword. Just for you. That would get me fired. You see, we're not allowed to damage government property."

"You nut!"

"Or . . ."

"Or what?"

"Or you could see me tonight."

"I *am* seeing you tonight. Right now!"

"Not what I mean. Look, I won't be working for your boss until zero-eight-hundred tomorrow, right? I could date you until then, couldn't I?"

She gave him a long, appraising stare. "You're sweet, Joe. I like you. But I don't think so. I've got a lot of work to go over tonight." She glanced at her watch. "In fact, I'd better be going pretty soon or it won't get done."

"Walk you home?"

"No, thank you."

"You want to walk me home?"

"*No!*"

"Just thought I'd ask."

Chapter 7

Thursday, 6 May 1943

Georgetown

Galloway was awakened by a knock at the door. Blearily, he reached across and looked at the alarm. Zero-five-twenty ... forty minutes before it was due to ring. Now who in the hell could be calling at this hour?

He'd been on Metzel's staff for seven weeks now and was beginning to think the entire world consisted of his office and this apartment. Idea-a-Minute was a human dynamo who tended to run his people as hard as he ran himself. Galloway had been working late the night before—again—and felt now as though he'd just closed his eyes.

The knock came again, a little louder this time, and he groaned. Rising from the creaky spring mattress, pulling a threadbare robe from a coat hanger and slipping it on over his boxer shorts and T-shirt, he shuffled to the door, opened it a crack, then threw it wide open.

"Virginia! What are you doing here?"

She was standing on the wooden landing outside his apartment door, a briefcase in one hand. She was wearing a white pullover sweater and the long khaki pants she often wore to work. Women wearing slacks was a shift in fashions that Galloway hadn't gotten used to yet. Not that he minded. On Virginia they looked great, hugging her hips and accentuating her long legs, but it was only during the past year or so that women had started wearing pants in factories, offices, and on the streets.

The war had changed a lot more than national boundaries.

"Morning, Joe," Virginia said. "Sorry to barge in on you so early."

"No problem. No problem at all." He stepped aside, ushering her into the apartment. "Please, won't you come in?"

"Well . . ."

"Can I get you some coffee?"

That decided her. "Oh, that would be wonderful. Okay." She entered his living room, and he closed the door behind her.

"Grab a seat," he said. "And let me get presentable. I won't be a moment."

He set up his hot plate and plugged it in. He wasn't supposed to cook in this apartment, but without his morning coffee he was useless . . . and what his landlady didn't know wouldn't hurt her.

And what applied to the coffee went for Virginia as well. His relationship with Metzel's secretary over the past weeks had progressed from mild flirting to a deep respect. His several offers of dinner had been turned down, but in a lighthearted way that left no bitterness or even regrets. She was smart, cheerful, professional . . .

. . . and *damn* she looked good in slacks!

As the water hissed in the percolator, he went into his bathroom, shaved, and brushed his teeth, then dressed in his whites. When he emerged, the coffee was merrily perking and he poured Virginia a cup.

"Milk? Sugar?"

"Black. And strong. What you Navy boys call 'battery acid.' "

"Not that bad, I hope. We serve 'jamoke'-grade coffee at this establishment. Some mornings it's even up to 'java' grade."

"What? Not 'joe'?"

"Only if you ask very nicely." He handed her the cup and saucer.

"Thanks," she said, gratefully accepting it as she perched on the edge of Galloway's sofa. "I was up late working on this stuff at home and then up again early."

He took the ladder-backed chair opposite. "Don't you ever sleep?"

"Not enough, sometimes. Anyway, I'm on my way to

work, but Captain Metzel called me half an hour ago, since you don't have a phone, and asked if I'd drop that off with you." She gestured toward the briefcase, sitting now by the door.

"Oh? What's in it?"

"Some papers he wants you to look over before your big zero-eight-hundred meeting."

"Ah . . . I know I'm going to regret this. *What* zero-eight-hundred meeting?"

She grinned at him across the rim of her cup.

"The meeting you and Captain Metzel are having with the CNO."

"My God. Why do I have to see Admiral King?"

Setting her cup back on its saucer, she leaned forward far enough to place one hand on his knee. "Because you've done it, Joe! Admiral King is going to issue the order today."

He blinked. He was not a morning person at the best of times, but he was feeling unusually slow this particular morning. "Order? What order?"

Rising gracefully, she crossed over to the briefcase and returned with it to the sofa. Opening it, she removed a file folder and handed it to him.

"Read," she said.

He did, excitement quickening inside him. The directive, already typed up for Admiral King's signature, was in two parts. The first section directed that men be assembled and trained for a "present urgent requirement" for the Atlantic Fleet amphibious forces. The second ordered procurement, experimental work, and training begun for "permanent Naval Demolition units," which would be attached to other amphib forces throughout the fleet.

The order was to be effective on May 6—today!

Galloway leaned back in the chair, the folder open on his lap. It was happening! It was really happening!

"Captain Metzel suggested that you might want to go over all of these papers on your way to the Pentagon this morning," Virginia said. "Seeing as how you're delivering the briefing to Admiral King and his planning staff. Congratulations, Joe. This is what you've been working for all this time!"

It was still a little hard to take it all in. Things were happening so fast. Since he'd been working with the planning staff, Galloway had known that King was inclined to accept Metzel's recommendations about forming a Combat Demolition Unit, but he'd not expected any action from the bureaucracy-tangled upper echelons of Pentagon management for another month at least.

But he was holding the orders in his hands now, today.

"I guess I'd better get moving, then," he said.

"I'll drive you," Virginia said.

"Is this trip really necessary?" Galloway quipped. He had his own car now, a '37 DeSoto he'd bought for a hundred dollars from a lieutenant commander being transferred to the U.S.S. *Boise*.

"It is if you want to have a chance to go over this briefing material before you see the CNO. Or would you rather call a cab?"

"Oh, no! No! If I'm going to be driven, by all means let it be by you! I'll get my hat."

"And I'll go start the car."

A few moments later, Galloway had reached the bottom of the stairs below his apartment and was about to go out the front door. On the street, Virginia was just climbing into her car, a black, '41 Ford. *Damn*, but she looked good in pants!

"*Mister* Galloway! A word with you, *if* you please!"

He started, immediately guilty even though he wasn't sure what he was guilty of. "Oh, ah, good morning, Mrs. Dilmore."

"I am shocked, Mr. Galloway, positively *shocked*! You know the rules. I will not stand for my tenants entertaining women in my apartment, and here I find you have had one up there all night! All *night*! I let that room to you because I was confident of your straight moral character, but this is just too much! I simply do not know what to say! I . . . well, words fail me, that's all. I am shocked!"

"Whoa, there, Mrs. Dilmore. It's not what you're thinking at all."

"I catch a girl leaving your apartment at six in the morning! What am I supposed to think?"

"Mrs. Dilmore, Miss Lewis works with me at the Pentagon." He hefted the briefcase for her to see. "She simply delivered some paperwork for me—"

"I know all about you Navy men!"

". . . to go over on the way to work! I invited her in—"

"But I thought you were different! Ha!"

". . . for a couple of minutes, no more! She's a very nice girl. You'd like her."

"A nice girl?" She sniffed, a toss of her head indicating the woman in the car. "Dressed like *that*?"

"What's wrong with the way she's dressed?"

"*Mister* Galloway! Merciful heavens, do you think I'm *blind*? Why, why, she's dressed as a *man*! It's not decent!"

"Please, Mrs. Dilmore. This—"

"I'd heard some girls had started wearing men's clothing, but I'd certainly never expected to see it myself, and in *my* house!"

". . . is all perfectly innocent! She wasn't—"

"Oh, I saw that cover article in *Life* last year about women in pants and I stopped buying it. I wrote them a letter, too. Imagine, such filth!"

". . . wasn't here last night! She simply—"

"Hmpf! Let me tell you, young man." She leaned forward, shaking her finger furiously. "I *will* not tolerate moral turpitude on these premises. I will expect you to have that apartment vacated and you gone by Monday next! Do you hear me? Monday! There are plenty of nice, decent young men looking for a room in this town. I do not have to tolerate such shocking, *shocking* indecency! And in my house!"

There was no winning her over. Once Mrs. Dilmore had set her mind a certain way, Galloway knew, there was no changing it.

"Trouble?" Virginia asked as he settled into the passenger's seat.

"Um," he said, a bit distractedly. "I seem to have just been thrown out on my ear."

"What! Oh, no! Because of me?"

He smiled. "Well, I have to admit it did look a bit suspicious, having you leave my place at zero-six-hundred. I guess she didn't see you arrive."

"Oh, Joe!" She placed one hand on his knee. "I'm so sorry!"

"Ah, well. The water wasn't hot anyway. I'll scare something up." Perhaps there was room now at the BOQ over at the Navy Yard. They'd been full up in December, but with so many officers coming and going in wartime Washington, perhaps something had opened up. But God, the waiting lists . . .

"Nonsense!" she snapped as she put the car in gear and pulled out onto the street. "You can stay at my place!"

"I . . . beg your pardon?"

She twinkled. "No, Lieutenant, I'm not making indecent proposals. I live with my parents, up in Dumbarton. My brother is away, with the Marines. I'm sure you could use his room. At least until you can find a place of your own."

"I wouldn't want to be an imposition."

"No imposition. I'll call Mums and square it with her." She glanced at him, one eyebrow arched. "Remember, though, Mr. Galloway. I don't date co-workers, even when they're living in my home."

He winced. It was the second time in five minutes someone had called him "Mr. Galloway." It made him feel like his own father. "Yes, ma'am. I remember. I'll be good."

The briefing session with King and his staff went better than Galloway had been expecting, given that he'd not even started preparing for it until that morning. King, of course, had already made up his mind about the combat demolition teams; he was the one who'd ordered the directive written. His senior staff officers, however, had been only marginally involved in the planning, and it was up to Galloway to fill them in on the concept.

"We are issuing two directives," Galloway said, "because we have two specific needs, one long-term, one short-term. In the long term, of course, we will begin work immediately on establishing a training program for combat demolitions teams, which will be attached to our amphibious forces all over the world. We will need a truly elite force, men of superior health and conditioning, thoroughly trained in sophisticated demolition techniques. The bad news is that, as yet, we don't even know what those techniques are. We're going to have to learn them, or invent them, as we go. We also do not yet have the men. We will need volunteers, of course, and we will need men physically fit enough to meet the challenges of this service and smart enough to learn the intricacies of modern demolitions work. Perhaps most important, we will need men willing to volunteer for a unit where, we estimate at this time, there is a distinct possibility that combat casualties will run on the order of seventy-five percent."

There was a low-voiced murmur at that from the crowd of admirals, captains, and commanders sitting in the CNO's briefing room. Some were taking notes or leaning over to whisper to their neighbors. Seventy-five percent casualties was an outrageous figure—ten percent was considered high—but the combat demolition teams would be expected to take on extraordinary challenges.

The admiral in charge of the Amphibious Operations Staff was watching Galloway attentively. Galloway wondered if the man remembered the report he'd routed to his office a few months earlier.

"It will take time to set that program up, procure men, get funding, and begin work. We don't even know yet where training will take place. All of which means that, in the short term, we're in real trouble with 'that present, urgent requirement.' Planning has already begun for Operation Husky, and Admiral King wants the men and equipment ready to handle beach demolitions for that invasion."

Operation Husky: the invasion of Sicily, and the first Allied step back into Europe. Expectations were that the beaches would be heavily defended, that the Axis forces would have obstacles and boat traps in all of the likely landing zones, and that casualties would be heavy.

"We plan to look for volunteers from two sources," Galloway continued, "from among men who have already acquired some of the requisite skills: the Navy Seabees and the Navy bomb and mine disposal people over at the Navy Yard."

The bomb disposal people, of course, had plenty of experience working with high explosives, and there was no question at all about their bravery. The Seabees, the Navy's Construction Battalion, was a new outfit, just over a year old. It had been organized in January 1942, less than a month after Pearl Harbor, but its men had distinguished themselves several times already, at Guadalcanal and elsewhere. They knew how to handle explosives, which they used for excavations and to blast through coral reefs, and at the Canal, some of them had fought off Japanese attacks while working to clear Henderson Field.

But how many of them would be willing to reconnoiter a Japanese beach armed with nothing but a knife? Or plant explosives on a mined obstacle with enemy mortar fire bursting all around?

"That concludes our presentation today, gentlemen," Galloway said. "If you have any questions, I'll be delighted to try to answer them."

There was the usual string of questions making him repeat things he'd already covered in his briefing. *Where are you planning to set up this new training center?* That had yet to be decided, but they were looking into the possibility of using the Naval Amphibious Training Center at Solomons Island, Maryland. *Do you actually believe that a handful of men, armed with nothing but a knife and some explosives, can make any difference at all in a heavily defended beach?* Obviously, sir . . . or we would not be here wasting your time and ours. *Where do you expect to find volunteers for so dangerous and demanding a specialty?* And on and on and on.

When he left the Pentagon late that afternoon, he felt certain that the thing could be done—*if* it was given the proper support from the higher levels of the Navy command hierarchy. But convincing them that it could be done, that it *should* be done, was going to be well-nigh impossible.

The encounter left Galloway feeling bitter and angry, resurrecting emotions he'd not allowed to surface for a year and a half. It was a little scary to realize that he was partly responsible for instigating a chain of events and decisions that might one day create a whole new Navy command.

He tried hard not to think about the seventy-five percent casualties part. Could he pick four men for training, then pack them off, knowing that three of the four would not be coming back?

More than ever, Joseph Galloway hated Washington; he hated the blind, idiot stupidity that lurked just behind the mask of official bureaucracy, and he hated being stuck there, behind a desk, when his proper place was aboard ship, doing what he'd originally signed up to do. What he was doing now was important, no mistake . . . but how important would it be in the long run if no one took notice, if nothing got done?

He took a cab back to his Georgetown apartment—his former apartment—then spent an hour packing before climbing into his DeSoto and driving up to Dumbarton. The area was definitely one of the ritzier parts of the town, with shaded, cobblestone streets, elegant and gracious homes, and even a little bit of lawn outside each house.

Following Virginia's directions, he found the Lewis home. To his relief, she was already there to introduce him to her parents. Her mother was a slim, elegant woman with an aristocratic bearing, much like Mrs. Gilman, who'd given that party a couple of months before. Her father, Howard M. Lewis, was a small, dapper Harvard man. "Glad to meet you, Lieutenant," Lewis said, shaking his hand. "If my daughter here vouches for you, you're certainly welcome to stay here until you can make arrangements, of course." His eyes narrowed. "Galloway. You're not Catholic, are you?"

Something about the man's tone set warning bells going in Galloway's mind. "Not really, sir. I guess I'm not much of anything. Is that a problem?"

"Ah!" Lewis clapped him on the shoulder. "Don't sweat it, son. It's a free country, right? We're Episcopalians, here, but this country was founded on the principle of freedom of religion." He kept glancing past Galloway at Virginia as he spoke.

The conversation turned to other matters, the war, and Washington politics. Lewis called himself a simple lawyer, but Galloway learned later in the evening, to his considerable surprise, that Lewis worked at the White House. Once a congressional assistant, he was now a senior aide to no less than Secretary of War Henry L. Stimson. A Democrat who wholeheartedly endorsed Roosevelt's New Deal, he referred to himself lightly as one of the President's spies on Stimson's personal staff. The Secretary of War, as was well-known, was a prominent Republican, chosen both for his very real talents as a cabinet officer and to disarm the Republicans at the next election.

Later, after dinner, Galloway and Virginia sat together in the ornate swing on the front porch. The sun had long since set, and the lights of Georgetown and, beyond, Washington glittered like a sea of stars. Sometimes, Galloway thought that the town never slept.

"By the way," Virginia said after a long and comfortable silence. "That was a good response you gave Dad when he asked you about being Catholic. I, um, know it's none of my business, but you *are* Catholic, aren't you?"

"You've been reading my personnel records again."

"Yes. . . ."

"Well, I was raised Catholic, yes. Went to a Catholic school. I wasn't lying to your father, though. I haven't been to Mass in years."

"For God's sake, don't ever admit to Dad that you were raised Catholic! He's a Freemason. He still thinks the Catholics are behind some kind of Popish plot to take over the country."

"What?"

She pointed off to the right. "See Georgetown U, over there?"

The university's spires, rising above trees and houses, were lit by the streetlights below them. "Uh-huh."

"A Catholic school, right?"

"Well, I guess it started out that way. I don't really know the history."

"On the school grounds, there's a stone wall on the heights overlooking Washington. They have these cannons mounted there—"

"Sure, I've been there. I've seen them."

"Right. Old, black, cast-iron cannons left over from, what? The American Revolution, maybe. They look like the guns off an old pirate sailing ship. I don't think you could actually fire them."

"It'd be kind of hard. Their bores are plugged up with cement."

"Anyway, a few years ago, a distinguished representative stood up in Congress and gave a blistering speech against the Catholics, claiming they were plotting to take over the country." She dropped her pitch of her voice, beetling her brows, raising her arm, imitating a politician in full sound and fury. " 'Even now,' this idiot congressman said, 'even now, the Catholic enemies of this great nation of ours have occupied the heights above this city and have their cannon trained on the dome of this Capitol Building!' And my Dad was up there in the visitor's gallery, applauding as wildly as the rest."

"Jesus," Galloway said, slumping back in the swing. "Sometimes I wonder how we ever managed to get anything done!"

"People are so *stupid* sometimes," she said, her fists clenched tightly in her lap. "Vicious and prejudiced and narrow-minded."

He had the distinct impression that at least some of her anger was directed at her father, but that she couldn't bring herself to admit it. There were tears glistening on her cheek.

"I don't really know what I believe anymore," Galloway said softly. He felt like he ought to change the subject, but he didn't know how.

She changed it for him. "Tell me about yourself," she said at last.

"You're the one who's been reading my personnel files," he said, lightly bantering. "You probably know more about me than I do."

"I know that you're sharp and bright and you're the first officer I've seen who can hold his own with Idea-a-Minute Metzel. I know you're unorthodox. You have ideas that tend to upset the proponents of the conservative tried-and-true, for which I heartily congratulate you. You're not career Navy, though, are you?"

"Nope. I'm in for the duration, and that's it."

"Why'd you join?"

He hesitated for a moment, staring out across the lights of the city. "Actually, I started out in the Merchant Marine."

"A feather merchant? You?"

"Yes, me. Then the Germans sank my first ship out from under me. That was a month before Pearl Harbor. There was a program going at the time, with the Navy handing out reserve commissions to merchant officers. I applied, and they took me up on it."

"You were torpedoed?"

"Yeah. The *Orleans Merchant*. There's not much to tell, really. We were in a convoy six hundred miles west of England when it happened. Hell, it was our fault, really. We still didn't know what we were doing. The convoy wasn't zigzagging, and the tin cans weren't patrolling properly. They hit us just about at dawn."

She shivered. "What was it like?"

"To tell the truth, I don't really remember a lot about it. I'd had the midwatch, so I was in my bunk, fast asleep. It was night, and I was off watch. Next thing I knew, I was out on the deck, stark naked, with men screaming around me and oil on the sea and the sky on fire. We'd taken a fish forward. God, the whole ship forward of the stack was just . . . gone. There was a lot of smoke, there was a pillar of fire that looked like it was going up forever, and the deck was heeling so far forward I could hardly stand up." He smiled, a humorless twitch of his mouth. "I wasn't thinking real straight. Guess I'm just not a morning person. I kept trying to go back to my compartment to get a pair of pants.

"Fortunately, my best friend, Jeff O'Brien, grabbed me and put me over the rail." He sobered. "They called us the Terrible Irish Twins. Jeff didn't make it, though. He never got off."

"I'm so sorry."

He shrugged. "War's hell, right? That's what General Sherman said. I lost a bunch of friends on the *Merchant*. She just went down so fast. I was in the ocean, looking up at her, and suddenly her stern was sticking straight up out of the water, the propellers still turning, and then she started sliding straight down. I was floundering around on the surface with a bunch of other guys. They were covered with so much oil they looked like shiny black seals, and I was laughing at them. Didn't even stop to think that I must've looked the same way. I remember thinking how cold the water was, and that I wasn't going to get out of this.

"I guess I must've lost consciousness, because the next thing I knew, I was lying across a piece of deck planking, there was a life raft alongside, and they were trying to get me to climb aboard. They had to come in and get me. After a while, one of the destroyers came up."

He still remembered the cold, the stink of oil and death.

"After all, well, the idea of neutrality just didn't have any meaning for me anymore. The *Orleans Merchant* had a crew of sixty men. They rescued fifteen of us, one quarter. Jeff O'Brien, he saved my life. I know that, know it as well as I know my own name, and he was gone. Left a twenty-two-year-old widow in New York."

"Sometimes in the last few weeks, Joe, you've seemed, well, angry. At the Navy? Because the Germans got your ship?"

"No." He sighed. "No, not at the Navy. At stupidity. At incompetence. At people who shut their eyes tight and refuse to see things that a blind man could see. At *willful* stupidity, I suppose.

"Anyway, when I got back to New York, it seemed astonishing that nobody knew what happened. There it was, a month before Pearl Harbor and they didn't even care. The Hearst papers were pushing isolationism. Pro-neutrality letters were piling up in the Senate mailroom. What was it, two hundred thousand a day? I heard that when the *Reuben James* was sunk, the public was more interested in the score in the Army-Navy football game." The *Reuben James* had been a Navy destroyer, torpedoed late in October of 1941.

"But Pearl Harbor changed all that."

"Yeah, it took a sneak attack to open our eyes. For some of us, anyway. Well, I knew we were headed for war with Germany, sooner or later. I wanted it to be sooner, and I hated like hell the thought that Jeff and the others had died for nothing, you know? I wanted to do something. I don't know, pay him back for saving my life, maybe."

"I don't understand. How does what you're doing now help him?"

Galloway shrugged. "We were hauling supplies to England, trying to help them hold out against the Nazis, so I guess you could say that's what Jeff died for. Maybe I was thinking, even back then, that when America got into the war, we'd be doing more than just carrying supplies to England. We'd be storming ashore on some beach, wresting a foothold away from the enemy and using it to pour in more troops and tanks and equipment. Hell, we have all of Europe to take back, and half the Pacific.

"Anyway, I had my chance during Operation Torch, when Patton wanted an airfield captured and there was a boom blocking the river he needed to go up. I was part of the staff that worked out a plan to send a few picked men in to blow the obstacle out of the water. One man, a few men, can make a difference, even in a war as big and crappy and dirty as this one.

"Fortunately, someone in the War Department was thinking the same way, because someone read my report on combat demolition teams and, well, here I am."

She leaned closer, taking his arm in hers. "I'm glad."

There was a long silence after that. Somehow, Galloway was not sure how, his arm was around her and he was looking down into those impossibly blue eyes.

They kissed.

After a while, he pulled back a little. "I thought you never dated guys from the office?"

"We're not dating," she said. "We're necking on the front porch."

"Ah," he said, pulling her close again. "That's different."

Chapter 8

Friday, 7 May 1943

Norfolk, Virginia

Ensign Henry Elliot Richardson drew closer to the girl, putting his right arm around her bare shoulders and holding her tight. "Aw, come on, pretty baby!" he murmured in her ear. Her hair was like pure, spun gold. "You just have no idea at all what you're missing!"

"Gee, Hank, I don't know. I always thought nice girls

didn't do things like that! I wouldn't want people to get the wrong idea about me. . . ."

"You are a nice girl, Peggy! Listen, you can believe me! Everybody does it, and it's no big deal! They just talk about it like it's dirty, but everybody does it! And I promise, I'll never tell a soul." Well, except maybe for some of the guys back at the base. Man, oh man, were they going to be green-faced, blue-balled jealous when he told them about *this* one! "I promise, Peggy! I love you!"

Richardson and the girl were sitting in her living room, curled up on the sofa with the lights turned down low. Richardson wished it was winter. Then there'd be a big fire going in that stone fireplace across the room next to the patio doors. Girls ate up romantic junk like that. Still, he was doing pretty good with her so far. They'd spent half an hour kissing on the sofa, and she'd let him slide his hand up under her skirt and stroke her thigh, and put his hand on her breast. Victory in sight . . . full speed ahead!

He let his right hand slide gently down her shoulder, the fingertips trailing down behind the low-cut top of her blue silk dress, exploring beneath the elastic pinch of her bra. She shivered at the touch.

Richardson had met Peggy Cartwright at a party thrown by some Norfolk civic group for junior Navy officers that evening down at the Y. He'd been captivated by her from the start, and, obviously, she'd been taken by him. Hank Richardson had the easy self-assured manner, self-confidence, and quick wit that gave him a way with girls. He was also well aware of his debonair appearance; he was twenty-four, had blond hair, an affected Clark Gable mustache, and the boyish good looks that girls, he knew, found irresistible.

He'd never failed yet.

After dancing with Peggy a time or two, he'd suggested that they go somewhere to get better acquainted, away from the press of the crowd. She'd readily agreed and brought him back here, to a swank home in Norfolk's Bayview district, explaining that her parents were out at a party for the evening and would not be back until very late, midnight or even one in the morning. That suited Richardson fine. It was only nine-thirty, which gave him plenty of time to make his move.

"Are you sure, Hank?" she said, looking up at him from beneath lowered lashes.

Yeah, she was ready. He could feel her quivering with anticipation. She just needed to feel that *he* had made the move. She was asking, she was *begging* him to make the decision for her.

"Sure I'm sure," he told her. "I wouldn't lie to you, baby."

"Gee, I wouldn't want anything to . . . happen. . . ."

"Not to worry, sweetheart. I came prepared. I brought protection." He always carried a good supply of condoms when he went ashore, though the pharmacist's mates at the dispensary tended to look at him a bit strangely when he showed up weekend after weekend, asking for more. He rather enjoyed the notoriety it gave him.

"Well," she whispered. "I *guess* it's okay. . . ."

"Hey, trust me, baby."

Deftly, he slipped first one strap of her dress off her shoulder, then the other. With a practiced touch, he slid his hand down her back, found the zipper, and gave a long, smooth, downward tug. The top of her dress fell away. Another deft move, and her bra followed the dress, loosing firm, delectable breasts capped with pert nipples, stiffly erect. Leaning over, he lightly kissed her left breast, drawing the nipple into his mouth, suckling her, circling it with his tongue. Her head shot back, her arms clasped tight about his head as she held him to her, and she moaned with shivering pleasure.

His left hand dropped to her leg, slipping up once more beneath the hem of her blue silk dress. "Wait," she whispered in his ear, then slid out from beneath him and stood up. For a moment, he thought she was backing off, and he started to muster his arguments anew. She surprised him, though, by reaching behind her back . . . and suddenly her dress pooled around her ankles in a loose shimmer of silk. He stared, astonished at her daring, as she unhooked her stockings and rolled them off, then wiggled out of garter belt and panties. Kicking the garments aside, she took a step forward and stood directly in front of him, bold, gloriously naked except for her jewelry, hands defiantly on hips. His eyes locked on the sweet delta of gleaming, golden curls lining the crease between her belly and her thighs, and he could not tear them away.

She laughed, a musical sound. "Well, sailor," she said. "Are you going to keep a lady waiting, or are you going to get naked too?"

Richardson stood and fumbled with his buttons, his shoes and socks, the fastenings of his trousers. He couldn't get undressed quickly enough, though all the time he was wondering about this girl. He'd thought Peggy was a virgin; hell, she'd *told* him she was a virgin! But, good God, she certainly wasn't acting like one now! He wondered if she was telling the truth about being twenty-one.

Naked at last, he reached for her, but she stopped him with an upraised hand. "Wait, Hank. You said you brought protection?"

He found one of the prophylactics he always carried in his billfold, and she helped him roll it on. He was certain then that Peggy knew exactly what she was doing, that she'd done this before.

They sank again into one another's embrace on the sofa, their arms entwined about one another, restlessly caressing and exploring. The smell of her, of perfume and of woman, filled his nostrils, driving him wild. He'd never known a girl like this. When she opened her legs to receive him, it was like sinking into a hot, wet, clinging ecstasy.

She *wasn't* a virgin! And now she was revealing a practiced expertise that he'd never dreamed the shy, demure blonde he'd met at the party possessed. He'd known so-called Victory girls before—young women who deliberately sought liaisons with men at nearby military bases—but he'd never seen anything like this. Peggy was transformed, writhing wildly, grinding beneath him and against him, clawing at his back with her long nails, locking her legs around his hips. She let out a keening, animal wail, and Richardson wondered if the neighbors were close enough to hear.

A key rattled in the lock to the front door.

"Oh, *shit*!"

Peggy shrieked again, with passion rather than the fear suddenly possessing Richardson. Desperately, he clamped his hand over her mouth. "Shh, *Shh!* Peggy! Someone's coming!"

He heard the door open, the sound of footsteps on the stone floor of the foyer. "Peggy?" It was a man's voice. "Peggy, we're home. . . ."

Peggy's blue eyes flew wide open above the trembling cup of her hand. When he uncovered her mouth, she gasped. "It's Daddy!"

He pulled out from between her legs and she gave another involuntary yelp as he rolled off her and onto the floor. Their clothes were all mixed up together. He scrambled about, reaching for his boxer shorts, his shoes, his billfold . . .

A man walked into the living room, a big, heavyset man, and Richardson felt the ice-cold grip of impending doom. Peggy's father was wearing a white uniform, the left side of his tunic plated with colorful ribbons, his shoulder boards solid masses of gold. Peggy's father . . . an *admiral*?

The girl rose to her knees on the sofa, arms crossed protectively and uselessly across her breasts, her golden hair in wild disarray. "Daddy! What are *you* doing here?"

"What the fuck is going on?" The admiral advanced, face darkening with rage. At his back, a slim, birdlike woman yelped and clutched white-gloved hands to her mouth.

Richardson made a last, desperate scoop for his trousers and bolted across the floor. The Cartwright living room had a set of tall double doors, wood and glass, opening to the right of the fireplace onto a backyard patio. He lunged for this slender chance for escape, his clothing in a tight bundle clutched against his bare chest, praying that the doors were unlocked, that they opened *out* instead of *in*. . . .

They were unlocked, but they were hung to open inward. He struck them with his shoulder and felt them give; glass shattered, wood splintered . . . and then he was rolling head over heels across the flagstones of the patio outside as glass shards tinkled around him.

"Come back here you fucking little bastard!" Admiral Cartwright's bulk filled the now-wide-open patio door, a fireplace poker in one upraised hand.

Somehow, Richardson got his bare feet beneath him, took three running steps, and cleared the ornamental shrubs bor-

dering the patio with an Olympic hurdler's leap. He'd lost
his trousers and one shoe in the fall but he didn't even consider going back for them. God, did he still have his wallet?
Ah! There it was! This was no place to leave his ID! The
grass was wet beneath his feet as he sprinted for the picket
fence; there was blood on his face but he hadn't even felt
the cut. His shoulder hurt, though, and it hurt more when he
scrambled over the fence.

The Shore Patrol walking Norfolk's streets picked him up
an hour later, wearing only his shirt with his ensign's shoulder boards and his boxer shorts. He pretended to be drunk,
explaining with a dramatically slurred voice that he'd fallen
through a window when they asked about the cut over his
eye. They wrote up a report, dressed his wound, and called
his base watch officer for someone to come pick him up. He
was an officer and so wouldn't spend the night in the S.P.
drunk tank. It would be up to his CO to render whatever
discipline was necessary in his case.

And that didn't worry Hank Richardson in the least. Not
with *his* connections. . . .

Monday, 10 May 1943

HQ, 12th Naval Construction Battalion
Norfolk, Virginia

"What the hell am I supposed to do with you,
Richardson?"

"I assume that's a rhetorical question, sir."

"Rhetorical question my ass. I've got a rear admiral on
my tail, a rear admiral who's mad as hell. He's sent down
a directive that he wants the man responsible for this . . .
this outrage found. I believe he said something about a
court-martial or maybe reviving keelhauling. Or was it a firing squad? Actually, the way he was carrying on, I suspect
it was both."

"I, ah, really don't know what could have upset the admiral so, Commander."

Commander George Aimes, commanding officer of the
12th Naval Construction Battalion stationed at Norfolk, Virginia, glared across his desk at the sun-bleached youngster

standing at attention before him. His eyes went to the gauze
pad taped over the kid's right eye.

"You don't, huh?"

"No, sir."

"No idea at all?"

"Not in the least, sir."

"Was she a good lay?"

"Uh ... I beg your pardon, Commander?"

"Was the admiral's daughter a good lay? Never mind,
never mind!" Aimes studied the ensign for a drawn-out moment. There were beads of perspiration on the side of Richardson's face, and his white shirt was damp. True, it was a
typically muggy summer's morning in Norfolk, but Aimes
suspected that more than the temperature was making the
kid sweat.

"Admiral Cartwright saw you the other night. Are you
aware of that? He got a real good look, described you well
enough for me to know damned well who he was talking
about. Blond hair. Neat little movie star's mustache. Baby
face. You're not fooling anyone, you know."

"I really think, sir, that this must be a terrible case of
mistaken identity. Someone else who looks a little like me,
seen in the dark ..."

"Hmm. And how did you know it was in the dark?"

"Well, I guess ... I guess I assumed from what you
said—"

"The way I hear it, little Peggy Cartwright told her father
who it was. That's how he knew who to call."

"Really, sir. I don't know the lady."

"You were with her at a party earlier in the evening."

"Oh, *that* Peggy? Well, I took her home. And that was
all, sir. I swear!"

"Shut up, Richardson. Stop moving your mouth for a
minute and listen for a change. Son, ever since you came to
this outfit, you have been a royal pain in the ass. Mouthing
off about how things would be different if you were in
charge, about how you'll shake things up some day when
you're an admiral. But you know what, sonny? I don't think
you're going to make admiral. You are a cocky, arrogant,
shave-tailed, pussy-happy little bastard who thinks with his
balls if he thinks at all. Someday, *some*day, either you're go-

ing to end up in Portsmouth Naval Prison for insubordination, or your CO is going to shoot you just to get you out of his hair, or some irate father or husband is going to cut off your pecker and feed it to you. And your rich daddy ain't going to be able to save your ass."

Aimes considered Richardson for a long moment, wondering just how far he could go. His own ass was in a sling this time, and the insolent young puppy knew it. He was keeping his face straight, but Aimes had the distinct feeling that behind that bland expression, Richardson was laughing at him. Again.

What the kid needed to straighten out was discipline, but damn it all, he wasn't going to get much of that when his father was R. Vaughn Richardson of New York. Aimes had lost track of the number of times Senator Morton had telephoned the base "at the behest of my good friend"—not to mention important campaign contributor—Vaughn Richardson.

The Seabees had been organized by Admiral Moreel just over a year ago with the idea of creating a Navy construction unit that could both build and fight, replacing the civilian engineering contractors the service had relied on until then. Men with construction experience had signed on as enlisted men; men with training as engineers or contractors had been given commissions with the Navy's Civil Engineering Corps.

God alone knew why Henry Richardson had decided to join the Navy. His father was one of the wealthiest building contractors in New York State; the son had followed in his footsteps, taking an engineering degree at MIT and going to work in one of his father's companies. Hell, they must have known the right people to bribe to keep him out of the draft . . . so why the hell had he joined the Navy? And why, *why,* dear God, had he ended up in Norfolk, under Aimes's command?

Every time the younger Richardson got into trouble, it seemed, the old man came down on Aimes's superiors like a shitload of bricks. Boys will be boys, and besides, everyone knew the Seabees didn't adhere to the rules and regs like regular Navy. All charges dropped. Don't let it happen again. And generally it was Aimes who ended up looking bad.

But, good Lord! This time it was Admiral Cartwright's daughter! Shit, Cartwright was out for blood, Senator Morton wanted all charges dropped, and Aimes was caught in the no-man's-land in between.

"Richardson," he said slowly, "I'll tell you what I'm going to do for you."

"Yes, sir?"

"I pride myself on being a fair man. Strict, but fair. In my sixteen years as a naval officer, I've never once skinned a man alive unless I was damned sure he deserved it."

"All of the men in my division say that you're the best there is, sir."

"Can the grease, Richardson. You've got a smart-ass mouth and it's not helping your case any. Now, I'm sure you'll be very relieved to know that I don't have one scrap of solid evidence that you're the man Admiral Cartwright chased out of his house Friday night."

"Sir, I—"

"You're at attention, mister!"

Richardson stiffened to full attention, hands at his sides, eyes held rigidly focused on a spot on the wall behind Aimes's head.

"As I was saying, I have no proof. However, of all the junior officers on this base, you, Ensign Richardson, have been the most trouble ... and every goddamned incident has involved girls. There was that whore you smuggled into the junior BOQ two months ago."

"That wasn't me, Com—"

"Then why was the story circulating that you were the one going around saying, 'She followed me home, can I keep her?' Then there was the incident with that nurse over at Portsmouth Navy Hospital, skinny-dipping up at Willoughby Spit. There were the, um, items of intimate apparel found in your bunk space. What was that, your collection? Or are you moonlighting as a lingerie salesman?"

"Just mementos, sir. From friends. And Lieutenant Carruthers and I were just—"

"Richardson, I just don't understand you. You're from a good family. Your daddy's got enough money to buy you a yacht all your own, so why did you feel you had to come play with the Navy's ships?"

"Sir, I wanted to serve my country, sir. I thought I could be a force for good and contribute to my nation's war effort. Sir."

"Oh, don't make me puke. I'm going to give you a choice, son. And the choice will be entirely up to you." Aimes picked up the BUPERS directive that had come across his desk that morning. "The Navy is experimenting with a new outfit, something called a Naval Demolition Unit, and they've put out a call for volunteers. The NDU is looking for men, Richardson, either Seabees or men with bomb disposal or explosives handling experience, twenty to thirty-five years of age, reasonably fit, able to swim two hundred yards, and with no fear of explosives. You're not afraid of explosives, are you?"

"I've worked with dynamite, sir. In my father's company." He looked interested.

"Good. Good. The directive indicates that you must volunteer for, ah, let's see ... 'hazardous, prolonged, and distant duty.' " Aimes looked up from the order, smiling pleasantly. "It's that 'distant' part I like most, Richardson. The farther away from Norfolk and my battalion you are, the happier I will be. I gather they're talking about duty overseas. Maybe in the Med."

"What's this team supposed to do, Commander?"

"I haven't the faintest idea, Richardson. And I don't really care. All I know about is that you are going to volunteer for this NDU stuff, and you're going to get shipped the hell out of Norfolk, and I will never, ever see your insolent, snot-nosed, pussy-stinking face again."

"You said something about a choice. Sir."

"Ah. So I did. Your alternative, Richardson, if you don't want to volunteer for this NDU outfit, is to take a little walk with me over to Mainside and Admiral Cartwright's office. I will walk in there and introduce you to each other and then turn around and leave. It will then be out of my hands completely, and your father's powerful friends can go breathe down somebody else's neck for a change. And, hey. Who knows? Maybe you can convince the admiral that it was your twin brother he saw running around his house bare-ass naked last night, screwing his daughter on his couch and busting up his patio door. Christ, Richardson, were you aware that that girl is just *seventeen*? Jail bait, son! I don't think even your daddy and all the senators in Washington could squelch something like that!"

Ha! That got to him, Aimes thought with satisfaction, watching Richardson's eyes widen, his nostrils flare. The Cartwright bitch must have told him she was older. He'd heard some wild stories about the admiral's daughter, and this incident tended to confirm them. He almost felt sorry for the poor son of a bitch standing before him.

Almost. "Maybe, though," Aimes continued reflectively, "just maybe, Admiral Cartwright will let you telephone your father, and the two of them can cut some kind of deal. The admiral seems like a reasonable, levelheaded guy, man of the world and all that. You think maybe he'd be willing to do that? Nah, I didn't think so either. Well? What do you say? Is it the NDU, or should I give Admiral Cartwright's office a ring and let them know we're coming over?"

"Uh, if the admiral knows I'm over here, sir . . ."

"If you volunteer, I will act surprised and say you had already volunteered. I can show him your orders and I doubt that even he will follow you. Especially if he pictures you hitting the beaches in a war zone lugging around a pack full of dynamite! If I were you, I would worry about what might happen if I introduce you to the admiral formally. I suspect that even Senator Morton wouldn't be able to find all of the pieces, and I doubt that Admiral Cartwright cares a fig for Morton. He's a Republican, I understand."

"I think, sir, that I would like to volunteer for that special duty."

"Smart choice. Very smart choice. Maybe you have a brain in your skull after all. Or maybe that's just your instinct for survival speaking. That's good, because you're going to need a survival instinct where you're going. And you know what? I'll tell you something else. I'm going to cut your orders today, and I'm going to mail off the usual copies to your new duty station. And I'm going to include in there a note to your new commanding officer, something to the effect that if you wash out, you get assigned right back here to Admiral Cartwright's command, because he has taken a personal interest in your naval career. You hear what I'm saying, Richardson? You're going to go to this new unit, and you're going to stick with them and not try to pull any strings to get reassigned, because if you don't, you're going to find yourself face-to-face with the man whose underage daughter you deflowered last night. You read me, boy?"

"Y-yes, sir."

For once the kid didn't have a smart answer. Good. Maybe he'd gotten through to him for a change. God, if this didn't straighten him out, nothing would.

"Dismissed. Get out of my sight."

"Aye, aye, sir."

Richardson spun in a smart about-face and banged out through the door.

That fat-assed, bureaucratic, bean-counting bastard, Richardson thought later, as he stowed his uniforms and other belongings in the brand-new matched set of luggage his mother had given him when he'd gotten his commission. Seabags were for enlisted pukes and the hired help.

Yeah, Aimes probably thought he was teaching him a lesson, threatening him with a combat outfit heading for a war zone. Ha! Hank Richardson had seen variations on that maneuver before, but he was too smart for them. Chances were, he'd be able to drop out of the program as soon as it got tough—hey, it was a volunteer unit, wasn't it?—and he'd find a way to finesse himself an assignment somewhere else. Maybe on the West Coast. Or Hawaii. Yeah. He'd always wanted to see Hawaii. Soft duty, warm sun, pretty girls. That was the ticket, brother. *Ow!* He winced as he slung the first packed suitcase off his rack. His shoulder was still mighty sore where he'd smashed open that door.

Failing duty in Hawaii or California, he'd be able to hang on. Old Admiral Cartwheel wouldn't be at Norfolk forever. Hell, he might even be able to pay another call someday on the delightful and delectable Peggy.

Deflowered? Peggy? Yeah, that slut had been deflowered, all right, but a long time ago and not by him. He sure wouldn't mind having the chance to continue the process, though, picking up where he'd left off. Sometime when the bitch's bull-necked father wasn't likely to come barging back in early from a party, swinging a fireplace poker. It might be a good idea to wait until her next birthday, though, just to be on the safe side. *No* lay was worth going to jail for!

In the meantime, what he'd heard so far about NDU sounded interesting. Talking to some of the other Seabees on the base, he'd not been able to pick up anything he could pinpoint as the straight dope, but it sounded like hush-hush commando stuff. Why not? The girls loved war heroes. He might just be able to become one with a chest full of medals. Girls just *loved* guys with lots of medals.

Besides, he had a feeling that this NDU outfit wasn't so tough. They were looking for Seabees, right? That meant bulldozers and airfields and construction work out in the jungle. A piece of cake.

Richardson was whistling as he finished packing.

Chapter 9

Monday, 10 May 1943

The Pentagon

Galloway walked into Metzel's outer office, winked at Virginia, and nodded toward the inner sanctum. "I think I'm expected."

Virginia smiled. "Indeed you are. Go on in, Joe."

He rapped three times at the office door and, at Metzel's gruff "Enter," walked in.

"You wanted to see me, sir?"

"Ah, Galloway." Metzel stood and walked around from behind his desk. Another naval officer in the room rose from a chair by the wall. "Good. Want you to meet some-one."

That someone was a tall, angular man with thick glasses, long-nosed, big-eared, and wearing the two-and-a-half stripes of a lieutenant commander on the shoulder boards on his full-dress whites. When Galloway glanced down to read the medals on his left breast, he had to suppress a small start of recognition. One of those medals, opposite the Navy Cross, was a Maltese cross centered by a heroic, laurel-wreathed profile and two crossed swords, handing from a red ribbon with four vertical gold stripes.

What the hell was an American naval officer doing with the French Croix de Guerre?

"Commander," Metzel told the officer, "this is Lieutenant Galloway, the young man I was telling you about. Lieuten-ant, this is Lieutenant Commander David L. Coffer."

"A pleasure, Commander." Galloway extended his hand and the other man took it.

"Same here, Lieutenant." His grip was firm, his toothy and generous smile quite genuine. "I gather we're going to be doing some traveling together."

Galloway's eyebrows raised, and he glanced across at Metzel. "Oh, really?"

"Commander Coffer here is our head of the Navy Bomb Disposal School, over at the Navy Yard. In fact, he founded the school back ... what's it been, David? A year now?"

"Almost a year and a half, Captain. We started it the month after Pearl Harbor."

"That's right. God, time flies when you're having fun. Lieutenant, do you remember Rear Admiral Blandy?"

"Chief of the Bureau of Ordnance back in late '41, wasn't he, Captain?"

"Affirmative. And one of the damned few flag officers at the time who could glance at the newspaper headlines and determine that the Navy was going to need some people trained in bomb disposal, and damned soon. Coffer was working with the British UXB people at the time. Blandy snagged him, wangled him a Navy Reserve commission, and told him to set up the unit."

Galloway looked at Coffer with interest. Working for the

British . . . and wearing one of France's highest military decorations? He was intrigued.

"Anyway, I should say that Commander Coffer *was* CO of our Bomb Disposal School, since he's just been transferred here for new duties. He got here late, but he got here, and now it's time to go to work. Right, Commander?"

"Yes, sir."

Metzel glanced at Coffer, then looked back at Galloway and grinned. "You'll have to watch out for this character, Lieutenant. He's had some damned interesting adventures, let me tell you. You'll have to get him to tell them to you sometime."

"I'll look forward to that, sir."

"Good. Okay, I don't have much time, gentlemen," Metzel told them. "I'm due at a briefing upstairs in ten minutes. But I wanted to get you two together and fill you in a bit on what I have in mind. Grab a chair, Commander, Lieutenant." The captain uncovered a map of the world tacked to an otherwise bare wall behind his desk. "I don't need to fill you in on the situation out there, do I?"

Both men shook their heads. Red lines had been drawn across the map, marking the limits of the Axis powers, the ground held, the peoples conquered. In the east, Imperial Japanese troops controlled half the western Pacific, from little Attu and Kiska at the trailing end of Alaska's Aleutian Islands to the Solomon Islands and New Guinea in the south, from the borders of India in the west to the Marshall and Gilbert Islands in the east.

In Europe, the entire continent save isolated Britain and neutral Spain, Sweden, and Switzerland was ringed in by jagged red lines. Eastward, the Nazi high tide had made it to Leningrad, the outskirts of Moscow, and the charnel house at Stalingrad, then ebbed. The Russians had recovered a lot of ground since their triumph on the Volga four months earlier, but the Nazis were still deep inside the Russian heartland, and no one knew how much longer the Soviets could keep up the long and extraordinarily bitter fight.

South, the situation was better. The Germans and the Italians still held most of the Mediterranean, except for British Malta, of course, but only a sliver of German resistance remained in Tunisia. Rommel's surprise strike in February at

the green American troops at Kasserine had only delayed
the inevitable, and the Americans were squeezing the enemy
from the west as Montgomery's Eighth Army closed from
the east. Very soon now, all of North Africa would be in Allied hands, the first real territorial advance won against the
Axis now in three and a half years.

But, by the gods of war, there was still such a long way
to go.

"We're on our way back," Metzel said simply, pointing at
the liberated sweep of North Africa. "And Operation Torch
showed us the way. The landings in Algeria and Morocco
did a lot more than let us liberate French North Africa.
They proved that amphibious landings can work, that they
will work, that if we have to, we can fight our way back to
the enemies' capitals beach by beach and island by island.
The future of this war will be determined by amphibious
operations, by landings on a scale never before attempted.
The Western Task Force at Torch employed one hundred six
major ships and thirty-five thousand men. The landings
we're planning now will make that look like sandlot baseball. But none of it is going to be easy."

Metzel pointed with an outstretched finger, indicating
France, Greece, and a scattering of islands in the Pacific.
"During the next few years, we are going to be making amphibious landings all over the world. In Europe, we'll be
opening up the second front the Russians want so badly. In
the Pacific, Guadalcanal and New Guinea are tiny first
steps. We're going to island-hop all the way up to Japan.
We learned some of the techniques we're going to have to
perfect during Operation Torch.

"The problem is, the enemy knows we're coming. He
knows as well as we do where we're going to have to land
and what we have to do to get our troops ashore. If he has
any sense at all, he is going to protect his beaches. He's going to put obstacles far enough off those beaches that they'll
stop our landing craft well offshore and make our soldiers
disembark in water five or six feet deep, out where they'll
either drown or lose their equipment.

"Commander Coffer, your job is going to be to find a
way to cheat the enemy, to stop him from blocking our
landings. You are to gather some good men and train them

in methods for clearing those obstacles. Your orders will allow you a lot of leeway. Go anywhere you think best to set up a base for training. You've got a blank check. You can have any man you ask for, in or out of the Navy. Frankly, gentlemen, this is an emergency, and we're damned short on time. Are you with me?'

"Yes, sir," both Coffer and Galloway answered, almost in unison.

"Lieutenant Galloway, I've been pleased with your performance for the past couple of months. You are an inventive and intelligent officer, if not always precisely the soul of tact. Now I want you to go to work with Commander Coffer. Give him the same enthusiasm and cooperation you've given me. Help him set up this new demolition unit."

"Aye, aye, sir," Galloway said. He felt lightheaded with excitement. They were going to use his ideas! Combat demolition teams, demo experts able to slip onto an enemy beach and take out the enemy obstacles!

Metzel glanced at his watch. "Gentlemen, you must excuse me. I'm late for my staff meeting. As usual." He gathered up his leather briefcase and stuffed in some manila folders scooped from the pile on the top of his desk. "I suggest that you two knock off, go get a drink some place, and get to know one another. Tomorrow, I want to hear some ideas from both of you about this new team. Okay?"

"Yes, sir," Coffer said. He glanced at Galloway and winked. "We'll both be here."

"Whew!" Galloway said, moments after Metzel had strode from the office. "He didn't give you much time to get acclimated, did he? Just drag you in and pile it on."

Coffer grinned easily. "My fault, actually. They delivered the telegram to me yesterday, transferring me over here from the Navy Yard, but I bribed the delivery boy into taking it back until this morning. I, ah, didn't care to be interrupted."

Even Galloway's nonconformist soul was shocked at this admission of . . . not wrongdoing, precisely, but certainly a bending of the rules. He kept his face impassive, though. "Must have been something pretty important for you to do that, sir."

"It was. I got married last week and I was still on my honeymoon."

Galloway brightened. "Gotcha. Congratulations, sir."

"Thank you, thank you. But I guess now the honeymoon is over. Shall we go someplace to get acquainted?"

"Aye, aye, sir. Where do you want to go?"

Outside, workmen dropped something with all the acoustical suddenness of an exploding bomb. "Anywhere," Coffer said, "away from here. I *hate* loud noises."

"Right. Grab your hat, sir, and follow me."

They paused in the empty and echoing passageway outside Metzel's office. "My God," Coffer said, surveying the seemingly endless corridors. "How do you ever find anything in this place?"

Galloway laughed. "It ain't easy, Commander. They say people get lost in this place and wander around for months at a time. Sort of like the Flying Dutchman."

"I can believe it. You could die of old age just trying to find the exit."

"Well, it's not *that* bad, actually," Galloway said. He frowned to convey the properly thoughtful consideration of the problem. "There is the story, though, of a young woman working here who was going into labor."

"Oh?"

"Yeah. She walked up to a guard and told him it was time. She was already in labor, she said, the contractions were coming every few minutes, and she needed to get to a maternity hospital, fast."

"Christ. What happened?"

"Well, the guard looks at her, ah, ripeness, let's say, and he says, 'Madam, you never should have come here in that condition!' She looks him square in the eye and says, 'Sergeant, when I came in here, I wasn't.' "

Coffer guffawed, doubled over, and slapped his thigh. "Ha! Oh, great! I believe that one, too. So tell me, Lieutenant. How do we get out of here? I'm not in labor, but I sure as hell could use a drink."

"Yes, sir." Galloway held up his watch and studied the dial with assumed gravity. "If we start right now, we should be able to make it to O'Keefe's before the dinner crowd arrives . . . early next Thursday evening."

Their escape was not as difficult as Galloway had pretended. Some forty minutes later, they were sitting in a booth in O'Keefe's Bar. The darkened room was not yet crowded this early in the afternoon, and the two men had found a measure of privacy in a place that was a bit more conducive to conversation than the new-wrought chaos of the Pentagon. Styled as an Irish pub just a short drive south in the neighboring town of Arlington, Virginia, O'Keefe's had already acquired a reputation as a popular watering hole for Pentagon officers.

"So you were at Annapolis," Galloway said. He sipped his drink—a whiskey and soda on the rocks—and felt the warmth and flavor of the place seeping into his bones. After a day in the War Department's five-sided pressure cooker, this was his favorite place to unwind.

"Yes, I went through the Academy. Class of '33." Coffer rapped his open hand twice on the tabletop, eliciting a double click from the gold ring he wore on his right ring finger. "I'm a ring-knocker from way back. My father was an admiral, you see. I was following the glorious family tradition."

"Who— Wait, not Vice Admiral Coffer. *James* Coffer?"

"The very same. But when I graduated, they wouldn't give me a commission. Weak eyes."

"Damn!"

"Yeah, I said the same thing. And then some. So did Dad." He took a sip from his own drink. "I re-tested a couple of years later, but I still couldn't get in."

"So what'd you do?"

"Well," Coffer said, "it was late '39, right? The Germans had gone into Poland, first of September, and now the British and the French were squared off with them along the Maginot Line. All quiet on the Western Front, and all of that."

"The Sitzkrieg."

"Uh-huh. Anyway, I decided I'd be damned if I was going to let a little thing like being half blind keep me out of the war, right? So I packed away my Navy togs, put on a French army uniform, and joined the American Volunteers Ambulance Corps."

"You're kidding."

"Nope. *Allez!* Lafayette, we are here!"

Galloway gestured with his raised whiskey toward the Croix de Guerre on Coffer's chest. "That where you picked up that itty-bitty red-and-gold trinket, there?"

Coffer glanced down, then dismissed it with a shrug. "Yeah. Things got pretty hot over there a time or two."

Pretty hot indeed. After months of Sitzkrieg—the "Phony War," as the newspapers had called it—the German divisions had come storming into France in June of 1940, not through the iron-and-concrete bastions of the invincible Maginot line as expected, but around the French left flank, through neutral Holland and Belgium.

Just as the bastards had done in the *last* great war in Europe.

"I was captured," Coffer went on. "Ended up in a prisoner of war camp at Luneville. But I guess the Germans thought me and some of the other American ambulance drivers they'd caught were too small, so they threw us back."

"What, for public relations? Propaganda?"

"I guess. In any case, they let us go, and I got across the Channel to England just in time to go through the first big Blitz. That was, let's see. September. September 1940."

"Hell, talk about out of the frying pan."

"You said it, brother. Well, I had some connections over there. I was able to wangle myself a slot as a sublieutenant with the Royal Navy Volunteer Reserve."

"And this was all before Pearl Harbor."

"Hey, I didn't want to miss anything."

"What about your eyes?"

He chuckled. "Well, by that time the Brits were desperate. Any warm body suicidal enough to volunteer for duty with Mine Disposal. You don't need eyesight to disarm bombs, you know." He held up his hand, rubbing his fingertips lightly across his thumb. "You need touch. Like a safecracker. And nerves, of course."

"Of course."

Coffer tugged at the lobe of one large ear. "You've heard about the UXB work over there, haven't you?"

"Unexploded bomb disposal squads? Yeah, I've heard." Men brave—or crazy—enough to walk up to a one-ton mountain of steel casing and high explosive which, for one reason or another, had failed to explode on impact. Maybe the thing was defective. Maybe some tiny internal wire or battery contact had jarred itself loose in the fall and was waiting just the lightest of touches to make electrical contact and detonate.

Or maybe the thing had been *designed* not to explode until some UXB disposal expert arrived on the scene in order to try to take it apart. Galloway had heard of young men being blown to bits while trying to disarm a German bomb. He'd heard of plenty of others who'd cracked under the terrific strain. Crouching in some dark, rubble-filled basement—or in a fifty-foot-wide crater half full of ice water—face-to-fuse with a bomb deliberately engineered to baffle the best demolitions experts the British could muster, knowing full well that the next quarter turn of a wrench could complete some unknown Third Reich bomb designer's parameters and set the whole thing off in an instant of pyrotechnic fury . . . Galloway could imagine no task more stressful, more hellish than that.

"Well," Coffer continued, "the Jerries were starting to get real cagey. Special fuses. Booby traps. False detonators. Duplicate wiring. Double blinds. Magnetic exploders. Contact exploders. One wrong guess and—" He threw open his hands, fingers up, pantomiming an explosion. "Wham! Tinkle-tinkle-tinkle. Dear Mrs. Coffer. We regret to inform you that your son died last week because he was exceptionally stupid. His last mortal remains will be forwarded to you just as soon as we can find enough of them to fill a cigar box for burial."

Galloway chuckled at the gallows humor. He was fascinated by Coffer's story. The man must have acquired tremendous firsthand knowledge of Nazi bombs. "So, were you ever stupid? Have a bomb blow up on you while you were taking it apart?" He meant it as a joke.

"As a matter of fact, yes."

Galloway blinked. "I beg your pardon?"

"Yes, I had a bomb explode while I was working on it."

"You seem to be in remarkably good health for someone who's been fitted for a cigar box casket."

"Appearances can be deceiving, you know." He grinned.

"Actually, there's not a lot to tell. It was right around Christmas 1940. A one-ton naval mine—the Germans had been dropping mines by parachute into the Thames and the port harbors, you know. Anyway, this one came down just a bit off course. It smashed through the roof of a whore-house in Liverpool."

"Oh, no!"

"Oh, yes. Down through the attic. Down through an up-stairs bedroom, somewhat to the consternation of the girl working there and her client. It finally came to rest in the, ah, gentleman's sitting room downstairs, squat in the middle of a sofa, wreathed in Christmas decorations gathered on the way down and with its parachute tangled up in a chande-lier."

"Cleared out the place pretty quick, I bet."

"So I gather. I guess the all-clear had already sounded, and everybody was back in the bordello, hard at work, when it happened. Naked girls and naked johns pouring out onto the street. Anyway, the thing didn't go off. They called the Mine Disposal Squad, and I got the baby.

"I'm still not sure what happened. The fuse might have been a new type, one I hadn't been briefed on. I was using my nonmagnetic wrench on the fuse guard when suddenly the damned thing started buzzing. I could *feel* those little wheels spinning inside."

"What did you do?"

"I ran, of course. Vaulted a couch and a portrait of the King, raced down some steps and straight out the front door. I don't really remember the explosion. I remember running over wet cobblestones outside, and I remember seeing the police crowd-warning line a long, long way off. The next thing I know, I was flying through the air. Landed plop on the street a lot closer to the police line than I'd been a sec-ond before. I walked away from it, though."

"I'll be damned." Galloway wasn't sure whether to be-lieve Coffer's tale or not, but the correct response to any war story told by a superior officer was polite incredulity mingled with admiration, so that was what he gave. "Some guys have all the luck."

"Well, I didn't think so at the time. I ended up in the hospital for a while. Kidney injury. That's where they told me that I couldn't go back."

"Why not?"

"One of the rules. No one goes back to Mine Disposal after one's blown up on him. Just after I got out of the hospital, another unexploded mine came down on an airfield a mile away. The nearest disposal officer was eight hours away, so I called up London and got permission to disarm it."

"Did you?"

"I squatted there on the runway fifty yards away for five whole minutes—one cigarette's worth—and stared at that infernal thing. It stared back. It was the same damned type that had touched off on me at the whorehouse, and I still didn't know what the hell I'd done wrong. Then I screwed up my courage, went in, yanked out the fuse, and that, as they say, was that."

"Something of an anticlimax, wasn't it?"

"Hell, I didn't mind. Like I said, I don't like loud noises. After that, in November of '41, I went back to Stateside on leave. I happened to be here in Washington, and that's when Admiral Blandy tagged me for organizing a Navy bomb disposal school. He was the one who wangled a commission for me in the Naval Reserve. I guess my vision didn't seem like such a big deal to the brass by that time."

"You disarm any more bombs after that?"

"As a matter of fact, yes. I flew out to Pearl right after the Jap attack. There was a shitload of unexploded Jap bombs—on the base, in the water, jammed into the hulls and superstructures of our ships—and they had me go out there and help dispose of 'em. No story there, though. Those things were simple after the German devices. No booby traps. Hell, it was no challenge taking them apart at all. Hardly even worked up a sweat."

Later, they talked about Morocco and about attaching explosive charges to river defense booms while riding a pitching, open boat in monstrous seas, with unpleasant people armed with machine guns and artillery trying to get your range. They talked about demolitions and what a combat demo team would need to learn about if it was to take on the mission outlined by Captain Metzel.

After driving Coffer back to his quarters, and with the hour too early yet for dinner, Galloway made his way to the Library of Congress, that ponderous, gray edifice squatting just across First Street from the Capitol Building. He'd decided that he liked Coffer and he was fascinated by the stories his new boss had been telling at O'Keefe's ... but could they possibly be true? Coffer's easy manner and disarming smile inspired confidence; he certainly didn't seem to be the typical spinner of sea yarns that Galloway had met more than once so far during his naval career. Hell, he'd loaded on the blarney a time or three himself.

There was, in his opinion, nothing wrong at all with a little embellishment around the edges, just to add to a sea story's texture. That, after all, was the nature of the art form. What was that comic opera line from Gilbert and Sullivan? Something like "adding corroborative detail to lend verisimilitude to an otherwise bald and unconvincing narrative." Yeah, that was it. Poobah in *The Mikado*. Galloway had met plenty of Poobahs in the Navy and had played the part himself more than once. Embellishment was virtually a Navy tradition, as well as a harmless and entertaining pastime ... except when the listeners were expected to trust the yarn spinner with their lives. Then you'd damn well better be able to separate fact from fiction.

After getting help from a pretty, brown-eyed librarian, Galloway made his way deep into the library's stacks. His goal was a back-issue collection of the *Royal Military Review,* a quarterly publication that included official after-action reports and citations. If Coffer's wild story about that bomb in the London whorehouse was true, there ought to be some mention of it ... probably in the January 1941 issue.

There it was. He pulled the thick volume off the shelf and paged through to the index. Sure enough, there was Coffer's name. He turned to the page and read the citation, written by Captain C. N. E. Curry of the Royal Navy's mine disposal organization.

Son.

Of.

A.

Bitch.

Brit action reports generally carried all of the excitement

and hot-blooded pacing of a naval shipboard stores inventory list, but this one, written with the characteristic dry humor and studied understatement of the British, suggested that Coffer hadn't told the half of it.

When the mine's anti-tamper fuze was triggered, Galloway read, *Lieutenant Coffer quite correctly evacuated the area. The resultant explosion obliterated the structure and hurled Lieutenant Coffer through the air. He sustained injuries in the blast requiring subsequent treatment in hospital.*

The explosive mechanism had a three-second timing fuze, but Lieutenant Coffer managed to cover forty yards before the device went off. This would indicate that Lieutenant Coffer did the equivalent of 100 yards in 8 seconds; it is possible that his extreme sense of urgency enabled him to do so.

Extreme sense of urgency? Yeah, right. Galloway tried to imagine the sour rasp of that activated fusing device, and an Olympic sprint through a Christmas-decorated sitting room turned into a hellish obstacle course by overturned furniture and pieces of collapsed ceiling. Coffer's long legs must have really been shifting.

And Lieutenant Commander David L. Coffer had been telling nothing less than the truth. Galloway was impressed.

Chapter 10

Tuesday, 11 May 1943

Navy Bomb Disposal School
Navy Yard, Washington, D.C.

"I'm sorry, Wallace, but I'm afraid I can't approve this."

"But, sir. . . ." Bill Wallace didn't go on. If the Navy had taught him one thing, it was never to argue with an officer once he'd made his mind up about something.

"Look, Wallace, if it was up to me you'd be on your way in no time flat." Ensign Jack Fagerstal spread his hands helplessly. He was the duty officer today, the only officer available in the HQ building, in fact. For the past few days everything at the Bomb Disposal School had been chaos, with wild rumors of shake-ups and personnel changes. And, of course, there was the request that had drawn Wallace here, the notice that the Navy was seeking volunteers for a mysterious new assignment. But it seemed they weren't seeking *some* volunteers, after all. "Hell, I'd be glad to trade places with you myself. Some paper pusher out of D.C. tapped *me* for the job, and I didn't even volunteer. So I'd be glad to let you go in my place, but that's not my decision to make."

"You're going, Mr. Fagerstal?"

"Yep. Soon as they finish cutting my orders. Then it's off to beautiful Solomons Island and points unknown. Like I said, I'd rather stay here. But it just ain't up to me."

Wallace didn't bother to hide his disappointment. The request for volunteers had called for men with blasting experience, Seabees, civil engineers, and bomb disposal men, unmarried, willing to face a high-risk mission of an unspecified nature. Most of the people at the gun factory or anywhere in the Yard didn't know anything about it, though there were plenty talking about volunteering to get away from the dull routine of the school. But Wallace recognized what that order was about. It was almost a twin of the one that had called Strickland's men from Pearl before Operation Torch. Wallace was certain they were putting together another Combat Demolition Unit for some upcoming amphibious assault. With German resistance in Tunisia on the verge of collapsing, odds were there were plans afoot for another invasion somewhere in what Churchill was fond of calling "the soft underbelly of Europe."

A new CDU was exactly where Bill Wallace wanted to be.

Wallace wasn't sure just how he'd come to that conviction. He'd had plenty of time to think these last several weeks, time for all the soul-searching and agonizing one man could take. His failure at Oued Sebou still haunted him, and it probably always would. Wallace knew, even if no one else seemed to, that he'd frozen up at a crucial moment and could easily have put the entire operation, the whole *unit,* in deadly danger. He'd called it cowardice, but he was beginning to think it was something more complex than that.

After all, he'd handled unexploded bombs without a qualm, and most men couldn't have faced that kind of danger. And he'd been eager enough to go in on the Sebou raid at the beginning. Could a coward have faced anything like that without throwing in the towel?

Wallace still didn't know the answer to that one, but he thought he knew what was at the heart of his problems. Any sane man would be afraid of being killed or wounded in combat; that wasn't cowardice, that was good, healthy, survival instinct fear. The thing that had made him freeze so badly wasn't the fear of death so much as it was the realization that death was so *random.* At Oued Sebou, Strickland's men had never even *seen* an enemy soldier, never had a more definite target than the walls of the Kasbah fort to fire at. And the enemy, for the most part, had been firing just as blind, filling the air with shot and shell and hoping something would hit. Any stray round might have killed Wallace, any wild accident might have left him injured like that shipfitter who'd broken his legs.

Wallace thought he could probably face death eye-to-eye, but he couldn't stand the thought of his fate being so completely outside his own control. *That* was what made his pulse pound and his head hurt every time he thought back to Oued Sebou.

And the one way he could think of to beat that helpless feeling was to force himself to go back into combat again, to face his fears and make himself the master of his destiny once more. Another CDU mission would be perfect. But it seemed he wasn't going to have that chance....

A thought struck him. "Couldn't Commander Coffer help me out, Mr. Fagerstal?" he asked. "Maybe he'd let us switch assignments."

Fagerstal laughed. "Boy, you really are behind the times, aren't you, Wallace. Old Four-eyes has already shipped out.

Didn't even get to finish up his honeymoon. Things are so snafued around here now they haven't even named a permanent replacement for him. Anyway, it wouldn't help if he *was* still here, Wallace, 'cause he's the one who *doesn't* want you going anywhere."

"Sir?"

"Look, Coffer's just drawn some new hush-hush assignment. The way I hear it, he's started co-opting a whole bunch of guys from the school here, but he doesn't have a permanent setup of his own yet. So he just issued a blanket order to hold up all transfer requests for anybody on his list until he can get around to getting his new outfit organized. And you're one of the ones on the list." Fagerstal laughed, a harsh, unpleasant sound. "Better enjoy it while you can, Wallace. I may be heading for dangerous, distant parts, but I bet old Four-eyes has something *really* big planned for you."

Wallace didn't know if he should feel excited or depressed at that comment. He needed a combat slot if he were ever to face down his fears. But was that what David Coffer had in mind for him?

Perhaps it would turn out to be something worse than mere combat.

Monday, 17 May 1943

Naval Amphibious Training Base
Solomons Island, Maryland

The Nissen hut looked as if it had been placed in one corner of the compound as an afterthought, and that was probably the exact truth. Bases everywhere were hard-pressed to keep pace with the rapid expansion of America's war machine, and that was especially true the closer they were to the nation's capital.

The jeep that had deposited him in front of this dubious-looking, ramshackle structure was already out of sight, but Ensign Richardson continued to regard the rounded, corrugated metal walls with a critical frown. He had grown up watching his father's construction business at first hand, and these makeshift ersatz buildings favored by the military never failed to strike him as the inferior products of a mass-production mentality.

"Well, Ensign, are you going to stand there gawking all day? Or are you coming inside?" The voice at his elbow came close to making Richardson jump.

He whirled, mouth open to make an angry reply, but caught sight of the speaker's rank insignia in time to stop himself. Instead he managed a hasty salute. "Sorry, Lieutenant. I just . . . wasn't sure if this is where I'm supposed to be."

The other officer returned his salute crisply, but his reply was laconic. "If your name is Richardson, Henry E., Ensign, USNR, then this is exactly where you should be," the lieutenant drawled. "That's the last name left on my list. If you're anyone else, you're in the wrong place at the wrong time, 'cause this area's for authorized personnel only."

"I'm Richardson, Lieutenant, ah . . ."

"Then you're in the right place at the wrong time, Mr. Richardson." The man continued as if he hadn't spoken. "You were supposed to report here an hour and a half ago. So get your ass inside, Ensign. We've been waiting for you."

"Yessir," Richardson replied. The lieutenant's manner had thrown him off balance, and he had to force himself to calm down and get back in control as he turned to pick up his bags. It looked like he was being put through a classic "hurry up and wait" scenario. Commander Aimes, true to his word, had pushed through the orders transferring Richardson to the new NDU command in record time, but on arriving at Solomons Island he'd found that nobody knew anything about it. He'd spent most of the past week spinning his wheels and wondering if he was far enough out of Admiral Cartwright's reach here on the outskirts of Washington.

Finally someone had deigned to admit that the Naval Demolitions Unit had indeed been assigned a building at the base, and he'd been ordered to report for duty this morning to a Lieutenant Fred West. Richardson was running late today, having been held up getting a haircut, but the way the bureaucracy had been jerking him around so far, he'd doubted that he was keeping anyone waiting.

He'd just have to see what he could do to let his new lords and masters know who they were screwing around with, starting with this pushy lieutenant. . . .

But when he turned around to speak his mind, the man had gone, as quickly and as quietly as he'd appeared. Richardson shrugged and headed for the door.

Inside, the Nissen hut was set up as a small barracks area, with tiered bunks and an open space at one end where about twenty men were gathered around a couple of folding tables, talking, laughing, playing cards, and generally goofing off. They all fell silent and looked up, interested, as Richardson came in, but after sizing him up they returned to their own pursuits once more. The buzz of a dozen different conversations filled the cramped quarters, and the newcomer was all but ignored.

One man, though, didn't turn away, an ensign in undress whites at the fringe of the group. He half rose from his chair and stuck out his hand in greeting. "I'm Culver. Pull up a chair and join the party."

"Party?" Richardson echoed.

"Well, so far none of us has the slightest idea why the hell we're here, but me, I'm an optimist. I figure I'll pretend we're here to have a good time until someone decides to be a wet blanket and tell me different, y'know?" Ensign Culver studied Richardson through narrowed eyes. "How about you, buddy? Do *you* know what's going on here?"

"Not a clue. My CO told me I wasn't supposed to like it much, so I think maybe your party idea needs a little work, but other than that I'm in the dark." He set down his bags and pulled out a folding chair. "Oh, yeah. I'm Richardson. Hank Richardson."

Culver jerked his thumb at the rest of the crowd. "I came up here from Virginia middle of last week with Lieutenant West and a dozen Seabees. The others have been trickling in ever since. Civil Engineer Corps, Seabees . . . all engineering people with blasting experience. We've got miners, roustabouts, powder monkeys, oil field roughnecks, just about anybody you can think of who knows how to make things go ka-boom."

"Yeah," Richardson said. "Yeah, I got this gig 'cause I had some blasting experience too. Must be some god-awful big construction job coming up. You know, now that the Krauts've surrendered in Tunisia, there's probably going to be a big push on to build airfields and ports and that kind of thing. Turn that whole stretch of coast into one big advanced base so we can use it to stage attacks in Greece or Italy or wherever the brass decides to send the Army next. My CO said something about the Med, but I don't know if he knew anything for sure or if it was just wishful thinking."

Culver raised an eyebrow. "Wishful thinking, huh? Sounds like you and your CO didn't exactly see eye to eye."

"Let's just say we had a little difference of opinion about how I should spend my free time."

The other ensign looked at him blankly for a moment, then shrugged. "Well, that's more'n I've heard, anyway," he said. "But you know, I don't really buy the idea of doing construction work. They could've sent in a regular Seabee outfit for that. I think this is something bigger, some kind of a—"

"Attention on deck!" someone barked, and everyone surged to their feet.

"As you were." They all looked toward the door, where a newcomer wearing a commander's strips and a haggard, harassed look on his face had just come through the door, trailed by three other officers. Two of them were lieutenants—Richardson recognized one of them as the pushy guy from his encounter outside—while the third was another ensign. The little knot of new arrivals pushed through to the center of the common area. Though most of the men in the Nissen hut had resumed their chairs, the silence now lay as thick and heavy as centuries-old dust in some ancient tomb as they watched the four officers.

The commander glanced around the room. "You men are all volunteers," he said coldly. "And you will be shipping out to Africa in ten days."

A confused hubbub broke out, and Richardson grinned at Culver. "See, I told you. Tunisia, like I said."

"Silence!" the commander rasped, and the room fell quiet again. When he went on, his tone was softer, but still forceful. "My name is Commander Daniels, from the Amphibious Operations staff in Washington. I've been assigned to

bring you people up to speed and get you started training
for a special mission as quickly as possible."

" 'Scuse me, Commander," a sailor drawled, sticking his
hand up. "But I reckon there's been some kind of mistake.
I didn't volunteer for nothing. They just ordered me to report here. My old pappy always told me that the first rule
of military service is never to volunteer, and I ain't never
gone against that yet."

Some of the other men laughed, but Daniels turned an angry scowl on the man. "Get this, and get it now, sailor," he
said in a low, deadly voice. "We need men with blasting experience for some potentially risky service in the Mediterranean. The powers that be say it's a mission for volunteers,
but they also say we only have ten days left to get this outfit
together, train it, and ship it off, and that's not enough time
for me to go through all the usual folderol of asking for volunteers. Ergo, you all just volunteered, and I don't want to
hear anything more about it. I strongly advise you all not to
rock the boat, because we don't have time for a lot of shit."
Was he looking straight at Richardson when he said that, or
was it just a guilty conscience that made it seem that way?
The officer turned his glare back on the sailor who'd interrupted. "You get my drift, mister?"

"Er, ah . . . yessir."

"Good." He gestured to the three men flanking him.
"Lieutenants West and Smith are the two senior officers in
your unit. And Ensign Fagerstal, here, is a specialist sent
over from the Navy Bomb Disposal School over at the
Navy Yard. He'll be part of your outfit, but he's also responsible for checking you people out on the latest explosives and demolitions techniques we've been working on.

"Now . . . your assignment. Our British allies have
learned that the Krauts are working on ways to plant obstacles along damn near every decent beach in Europe. They'll
be dumping all sorts of steel and concrete between the high-
and low-tide lines that'll tear the bottoms out of our boats
if we try to go in across them. They haven't got very far
yet, and we still don't know exactly what we're going to be
up against, but we've got to be ready to clear the beaches
any time our boys go in."

Commander Daniels paused. "We're going to deal with

these obstacles by forming a new outfit, Naval Combat Demolitions Units, that can go ashore in front of an invasion and clear away those obstacles. They're getting ready to set up a new school to train these NCDUs, but the formal program won't be off the ground for a while yet. Meantime, we've got a more immediate problem. Within the next couple of months FDR and Churchill want to launch another strike. Somewhere in Europe, this time. In the Med, that's all I can say right now. We can't hold up the timetable just to train the first NDU gang from scratch, and we're worried that the Krauts might've started building up their beach defenses getting ready for us to come. So we need some experienced demolitioneers who can serve as a stopgap until we get our regular teams into place. That's where you come in. Your unit will be designated a Naval Demolition Unit—we'll hope we don't have to include the word 'Combat' in your job descriptions."

"We're gonna invade *Europe*?" someone said, sounding incredulous. Then, belatedly, he added, "Sir?"

"That's about the size of it," Daniels said with a weary smile. "You'll be given a week here at Solomons Island to practice with landing craft—LCP(L)s—and all the latest military explosives. We'll put you through your paces out on the Chesapeake and along some of the beaches near here. And in another ten days you'll be on your way. Any other questions?"

"Ah, sir," Richardson ventured hesitantly. "Commander Daniels, this sounds like quite an opportunity and all, but a *week* to train? That isn't much. Shouldn't we get some of the training these new NCDU thingies are getting?"

The commander shook his head. "Even if we had the extra time for a real training course, it wouldn't do any good right now. Hell, they don't even have a base set up yet for the NCDU project. They sure as hell don't have any standard training program worked out. No, you men'll be showing the way. Later, if you want, you'll be given the chance to fold right into the new teams. Maybe even get a shot as combat demolition instructors, if you have the right background. But that'll have to come later. The work you've got in front of you right now is what's important. It'll be dangerous, I won't try to kid you about that. But it could also save a hell of a lot of lives on some hot beachhead some-where." Daniels paused and glanced over at the officer who had chewed Richardson out before. "You have anything to add, Lieutenant West?"

"Just this," the man said, and his eyes *were* fixed on Hank Richardson. "This is a team effort. Every man in this room is depending on every other man, maybe for his life. We're going into an unknown situation with damn little time to get ready for it, and that means that we need everybody pulling together. You start fucking off, you shirk a job or try to play a bunch of dumb-ass games 'cause you think you rate special treatment or something, and I guarantee you'll wish you'd just gone and sat on a live grenade. So pull your weight, do your job, and help your buddies. That way we'll all have a better chance at seeing the end of this damned war." West paused. "All right, ladies, you've got fifteen minutes to stow your gear and muster out on the grinder out back for a little bit of good old-fashioned drill! Show a leg! Move it!"

The inside of the Nissen hut dissolved in chaos as the men scrambled to comply. Richardson could feel the lieu-tenant's cold eyes on him as he manhandled his bags to an unused bunk and started to change into shorts and a T-shirt. Plainly Commander Aimes had followed through on his other threat to inform Richardson's new CO of his spotty record, and West was setting out right from the start to make it clear that he wouldn't be getting away with any-thing here.

Well, that was fine. Risky mission or not, he would man-age just fine. He'd go along with this Lieutenant West as long as he had to, but in the end Richardson knew he could always find a way to turn things around. Meanwhile, he'd make the best of it. And maybe, just maybe, he'd find a way to make this new gig pay off.

Friday, 21 May 1943

The waters of the Mediterranean Sea were choppy this morning, and the two-man kayak carrying Frank Rand and Peter Havlicek made poor progress. Around them was nothing but dark seas and dark skies, though Rand could sense the far-off loom of land along the distant northern horizon, the southern coast of Sicily, hostile, menacing. Rand and Havlicek had spent most of the night paddling their tiny boat right up along that coastline, taking depth soundings, studying the lay of the land, learning the details of villages and beaches and landmarks against the day they'd come back in the vanguard of an Allied invasion armada.

That was the job of the Scouts and Raiders, after all.

Rand and his classmates at the S&R school at Fort Pierce had been through an eight-week daily grind of running, swimming, canoeing, and training with weapons of all kinds from knives to mortars and rockets. The object of the training was to prepare them to perform advanced beach recon, both early scouting of a prospective landing area—the work Rand and Havlicek had been doing all the past night—and the actual preinvasion task of marking out a beach and guiding the first invasion wave ashore. And every step of the program had been designed to toughen them up, turn them into competent, hardened commandos.

The first class to graduate, Rand's class, had been assigned to the Mediterranean early in April. Ensign Bucklew had been replaced in his training duties at the same time so that he could take command of the unit. More training had followed after their arrival, this time at a British submarine base on the island of Malta. Here the Americans had been matched up with their opposite numbers from the British Combined Operations Pilotage Parties to learn additional skills, including such specialties as assault tactics, climbing, demolitions, and the use of .50-caliber machine guns.

But Malta hadn't been all training by any means. Several times in the course of their stay on the tiny island, the Scouts and Raiders teams had been dispatched to perform real reconnaissance missions along the coast of Sicily. Rand had been on his share of the missions, usually teamed with Havlicek. They'd been under strict orders, though, not to go ashore or let the Germans or Italians discover them, so all in all Rand hadn't seen any more action here than he had with Ensign Bell off Safi.

The Americans had performed these raids time after time without incident, though some of their British colleagues had run into trouble on occasion. One British team, deployed from its submarine in a two-man kayak, had missed its pickup rendezvous and ended up paddling the whole eighty miles between Sicily and Malta. Rand hoped nothing like that would happen tonight.

Something was moving in the black water ahead, a low, ill-defined shape knifing through the darkness. At a signal from Havlicek they stopped paddling, letting the kayak drift and praying that whatever it was didn't turn out to be a German patrol ship making its rounds.

"Ahoy the boat! Waterloo!" The hail dispelled Rand's fears instantly. He doubted any German could have packed quite that much sheer Britishness into four simple words. And "Waterloo" was the challenge the sub's skipper, Commander Richard Randolph Kent, RN, had selected for the night's business.

"Trafalgar!" Rand shouted the countersign through cupped hands, then grasped his paddle once more and started toward the submarine.

"Damn, those things are spooky," Havlicek grumbled from the rear of the kayak. "I don't think I'll ever get used to the way they just come up out of nowhere like that."

"Me, neither," Rand answered him absently. He was focusing most of his attention on maintaining the tricky little kayak's trim.

The sub's deck was almost flush with the water, and a trio of British sailors was there to lend the Americans a helping hand as the boat bumped alongside. Rand found himself looking up into the grinning face of the sub's navigator, a cheery young Scots lieutenant named MacLeod. "Good to have you back, chaps," he said as he helped pull Rand aboard. "Successful run tonight?"

"About like always, sir," Rand responded. "I've seen just about all of that bloody beach that I care to see!"

"Frank, my boy, it's about time you had yourself some leave," Havlicek said, scrambling onto the metal deck behind Rand. "You've been hanging around these Brits so long you're starting to sound just like them."

"And what's wrong with that, mate?" MacLeod said, exaggerating his accent into a loose parody of Cockney.

"Corblimey, you toffs 'ad best not go round talking down the King's English, if you know wot's good for you!"

There was scattered laughter. Rand turned to his partner. "You got the camera, Havlicek?"

"Right here. *And* the notebook. Let's hope we got all the stuff Mr. Bucklew wanted this time. Otherwise he'll skin us alive and then make us swim around Malta in the salt water."

"You'd think by now we'd have enough info to go on," Rand griped as he bent over to help the Brits hoist the kayak aboard and start breaking down the collapsible boat. "Damn it all, I thought this S&R work was going to be more than just taking pictures and sampling bottom mud!"

"Be patient, Frank," Havlicek told him. "You know as well as I do these scouting missions are important."

"Yeah ... yeah, I know. But I'm just about ready for some *real* action. . . ."

"You're always ready," his partner countered. "But maybe you won't have to wait much longer."

Rand looked up at him sharply. "What do you mean? You heard something?"

"Just scuttlebutt. But word has it the final invasion plans were okayed by the brass the other day. We really are going in."

"Any idea when?"

"Think they're gonna tell us that? Sometime in the next couple of months, I'd guess. Maybe the middle of July. And you know what that means."

"You bet I do! Some real action, for once. And about damned time, too!"

Rand returned to his work eagerly, excitement coursing through every vein. When the Allies launched their invasion of Sicily, it would be the Scouts and Raiders who'd lead the way.

Wednesday, 26 May 1943

USNATB
Fort Pierce, Florida

"Gentlemen," the stocky Navy captain said, rising from behind his desk. "I'm Clarence Andersen. Welcome to Fort Pierce."

Galloway stood by as Coffer shook the man's hand, ignoring the trickle of perspiration running down his spine. It was early afternoon, and the mid-June heat and humidity of Florida's Atlantic coast had already taken its toll of his Navy whites.

The two of them, Galloway and Coffer, were on the final leg of a whirlwind inspection tour that had stretched from the amphibious training center at Solomons Island in the Chesapeake all the way to Camp Murphy, in nearby Martin County, Florida.

"Good afternoon, Captain Andersen," Coffer said. "This is my aide, Lieutenant Galloway. I hear you might have some rooms for rent."

Andersen laughed as he waved his visitors to a couple of chairs next to the wall of his office. "Well, not much in the way of rooms," he said, resuming his seat behind the desk. "More like prime swamp real estate. *If* you can convince the 'gators and the mosquitoes to let you have some."

Captain Andersen's office was little short of luxurious—unsurprising since it was a large and well-furnished room in what once had been a resort hotel. A ceiling fan stirred the air, and a pot of coffee was warming on a hot plate in the corner. The sounds of hammering and sawing floated through an open window from the raw, partly finished naval amphibious training center outside.

"I understand you've only been here a few months, sir," Coffer said. "You've accomplished quite a bit in a short time."

"Amazing how fast the buildings go up in wartime, eh? Yes, I read myself in as CO down here in January. Of course, all of the available buildings were snatched up right away. That doesn't leave much for the Johnny-come-latelies, I'm afraid."

Galloway had been surprised to learn that there were
buildings in what, on the maps he'd seen, was little more
than a strip of barrier island a couple of miles off the Florida coast. It turned out that Fort Pierce, a town with a population of about eight thousand, located on the mainland,
had been a small but popular tourist resort before the war.
Causeway Island, separated from the town by a narrow
strait, boasted two hotels, the Burston and the New Fort
Pierce, both now taken over by the Coast Guard and the
Navy as headquarters and barracks spaces. A slender spit of
sand, submerged at high tide, connected Causeway Island
with the northern tip of Hutchinson Island, a long, slender
barrier island, part sand dunes, part swamp, separated from
the mainland by a sluggish one-to-two-mile-wide saltwater
barrier.

The site offered everything Galloway and Coffer had
been looking for: uninhabited real estate where the nascent
NCDU could play with noisy substances without
bothering—or killing—the locals; a rugged surf and long,
empty beaches where they could practice coming ashore in
landing craft and small boats; plenty of secluded rough terrain for the training program; and the close-by convenience
of the Fort Pierce Naval Amphibious Training Base for supplies, matériel, medical facilities, and communications.

Coffer smiled. "We're not really interested in the tourist
accommodations, Captain. We'd like a place where our new
outfit can rough it."

"Then you've come to the right place. The Scouts and
Raiders are already down here, had you heard?"

"Yes, sir."

"Back last January, just a week before I came aboard,
some of them were passing through on their way to Camp
Murphy. They liked what they saw here so much they had
their orders changed. Now they're set up in what used to be
a casino across the way."

"Frankly, sir," Coffer said, "that's one of the things that
attracted us to this base. We're hoping to get some help
from the Scouts and Raiders in getting this thing organized,
right, Joe?"

Galloway grinned. "If you can call it that, sir. We've

heard they have a pretty tough training course going down here."

"Tough? Hell, eight weeks of calisthenics, running through beach sand, an obstacle course as tough as any in the Marines, paddling rubber boats through Atlantic surf . . . a damned picnic!"

"Well, maybe we can talk some of the S&R people into letting us in on some of the goodies," Coffer said. "We're particularly interested in picking up on some crossover with them. Sharing instructors, training, and maybe equipment."

"Training with the S&R? Good God, why?"

"From what we've heard, sir," Galloway pointed out, "their training program emphasizes the teamwork and the toughness that we're going to need to make the NCDU work."

"I still haven't been told anything about this new project of yours," Andersen said. "Combat Demolitions . . . is that Seabee work or ordnance disposal?"

"Actually, it'll be a bit of both," Coffer said. "And we hope to draw experienced personnel from both groups." Briefly then, he sketched in the outlines of the program, as he and Galloway had worked it out during the past month. Afterward, Galloway took over, describing the CDU action at Oued Sebou.

"The whole idea more or less grew out of the Port Lyautey raid," he concluded. "Amphibious warfare is going to come into its own in this war, and we're going to need people trained to deal with obstacles like the boom at Oued Sebou, mines, maybe anti-boat beach defenses we haven't even seen yet."

"You know," Andersen said, "I was an acting commodore in Africa. I heard about that business at the Sebou River. Incredible! And now, you two are setting up a training center for that type of operation here?"

"That's the idea, Captain," Coffer said. "We'll be creating a new elite unit. One that can go onto a beachhead with the first wave and take out the obstacles. Possibly chart approaches to the landing areas ahead of the invasion. You can see, we'll be dovetailing nicely with the Scouts and Raiders, who are supposed to investigate beaches ahead of the landings."

"Splendid! Splendid!" Andersen said, enthusiasm animating his voice and face. "Captain Coffer, I'll arrange for you to meet the skipper of the Scouts and Raiders down here. Maybe you two can work out some sort of arrangement with the training."

As Coffer and Andersen continued to discuss the creation of the NCDU training facilities at Fort Pierce, Galloway leaned back in his chair and listened to the rasp and bang of construction work continuing outside. *Damn!* he thought. *What I wouldn't give to be a part of it!* He'd discussed the matter at length with Coffer during the past few days, all but begging to be assigned here as a member of the first class. Coffer had turned him down cold.

"I'm afraid not, Joe," Coffer had said during their inspection of the Solomons Island facility the week before. "At least to start with, I'm going to need people with bomb disposal experience. I've already gotten in touch with some people I know in D.C. at the Navy Yard, and they've agreed to come on board. I need you up in Washington, guiding this monster through the red tape! Maybe later, after we've gotten this thing under way."

Maybe later . . .

Galloway doubted that there would be a later. Once things got rolling, there would be a carefully defined set of requirements specifying who could apply for the new program, and combat experience would almost certainly be one of them. The time to get in on the ground floor was now, while the unit and the program were still being put together.

And he would be sitting it out back in Washington.

At least he had a place of his own now, another small Georgetown apartment created by the partitioning of a larger townhouse, and this one with a far more reasonable landlady than Mrs. Dilmore.

He'd been delighted to get out from under the Lewises' roof. The day-to-day dread that he would say or do something to excite the man's anti-Catholic prejudices had made living there almost intolerable, even for those few, short weeks. He'd continued seeing Virginia, though. In her unbiased attitude and open-mindedness she was as unlike her father as could be imagined. Just before he'd left with Coffer on this tour, she'd told him that, last year, she'd been en-

gaged to a young naval officer in Metzel's department, a
Lieutenant Bernard Goldman.

A *Jewish* officer. When Howard Lewis had found out,
he'd actually pulled strings to send Goldman to the Pacific.
Virginia's fiancé had died aboard the cruiser *Vincennes,*
sunk at the Battle of Savo Island off Guadalcanal.

Which explained her reluctance, Galloway thought, to
form further liaisons among her co-workers at the Pentagon.
Despite that, the two of them had been growing closer
lately, especially since he'd moved back to a place of his
own. Staying in Washington, he reflected, would have *some*
fringe benefits.

Assuming he survived the Battle of the Red Tape in
Hell's Bottom.

Chapter 11

Saturday, 10 July 1943

Assembly Area
Off Scoglitti, Sicily

Ensign Richardson was almost beginning to look forward to
the prospect of battle.

Since the Naval Demolitions Unit had left Norfolk aboard
the APD *Alcyon* over a month ago, life had settled into a
dull monotony that made Richardson edgy. No women, no
privacy, not even the promise of better things to come . . .
it had been so dreadfully boring that Richardson had started
dreaming fondly of the danger Commander Aimes had
wished on him. He was even beginning to think life in the
shadow of Admiral Cartwright would have been preferable.

At first the NDU had been an enjoyable enough experience. Oh, they'd had to sweat through some calisthenics and some running, but because time was so short they'd spent most of their efforts on getting familiar with some of their gear. Richardson had taken the instruction in handling the LCP(L) in stride. It had taken him back to lazy weekends on his father's small yacht on the Hudson. And the new military explosives had really piqued his interest. The War Department was coming up with new ways to make a bang all the time, things like the primacord Richardson had heard about but never encountered before. Since the NDU had been denied liberty during training and Richardson had thus been cut off from access to the outside world, about the only recreation he could indulge in was planning ways to use these new explosives to make Richardson Enterprises tons of money after the war.

But after ten days they were loaded aboard the *Alcyon* in Norfolk Harbor. They still did calisthenics out on deck every morning, and Lieutenant West, Ensign Fagerstal, and some of the other officers endeavored to keep their days filled with everything from lectures on explosives to taking inventory of the mountain of equipment that had been issued to the unit, but none of that was as interesting as going out in a Higgins boat to make a mock landing on some Chesapeake beach and test out some new way to blow up obstacles and obstructions. *Alcyon*'s captain made it clear that he wasn't about to let anyone from the NDU start playing with explosives on *his* ship.

The passage to Oran had taken just over three weeks. There they joined the Sixth Fleet at anchor, and they waited. They had found a harbor almost bursting with shipping, and new vessels had crowded in day by day, but still the order to sail hadn't come. Richardson had started to wonder if the rumors about invading Sicily were true or just a lot of wishful thinking.

On the eighth day of July, the Sixth Fleet had finally steamed out of Oran, heading eastward along the northern coast of Tunisia. The course had been devised to keep Axis spies guessing as to the destination of the Allied armada: Sicily, Italy, Greece, the Greek Isles, perhaps, all possibilities planted in the minds of the Nazi leadership over the past few months by means of a thorough campaign of disinformation.

Of course, it might have gone better if Allied officers hadn't started distributing maps of Sicily and guidebooks for Italy before the invasion fleet sailed. But even that typical snafu couldn't do much to throw the attackers off their stride, or so it seemed to Ensign Richardson. Nothing the Axis could throw into the fray could defeat the massive armaments arrayed against them in Operation Husky.

The ships turned north on the ninth, sailing into a fast-rising storm front along the west coast of Malta. The storm was breaking as they reached their designated assembly area in the Gulf of Gela, making visibility poor. *Alcyon*'s radar broke down soon after 0300 hours, and she narrowly avoided a collision with another ship of the task force as she plowed through the heavy weather. But she made it to her assigned position, and the PA speakers began blaring the orders to prepare landing craft and start loading up in anticipation of the assault to come.

The Naval Demolition Unit had been assigned three LCP(L)s, and the men were broken up into teams accordingly. Boat Number One was commanded by Lieutenant West in person, while Lieutenant Robert C. Smith had Boat Two, and the ranking ensign, Harold Culver, commanded the last of the landing craft. The NDU men labored in the rain to load their explosives and other demolitions gear into the LCPs. Included with their gear were rubber rafts fitted with outboard motors, and each boat carried enough explosives to wreck anything the Nazis might have set up in their path.

With crews aboard but passengers waiting on deck, the landing craft were swayed out on their booms and lowered into the water. Then the call went out for the NDU teams to go down the cargo nets and take their places in their respective boats.

Richardson had been assigned to Boat One, where Lieutenant West had expressed a desire to keep a personal eye on him. As he scrambled down the netting and dropped into the open LCP(L), Richardson heard GM2 Simms chuckling behind him. "Hey, Mr. Richardson, do you have permission to leave the ship, sir?"

That evoked a chorus of laughs. Back in Oran, Richardson and the others had gone to work drilling with the rubber boats in their store of specialty supplies. As it happened, Richardson had been the only one in the team who had any knowledge of outboard motors, so he'd ended up with the job of teaching the others. They had inflated one of the boats, lowered it into the water, then carefully lowered the motor aboard on the end of a line. Then Richardson had gone hand over hand down the same line to get aboard the raft and secure the outboard to its mount. Other NDU men had followed, and they'd spent a good part of the afternoon circling the ship and putting the big raft through its paces. Later they'd gone through the whole process in reverse.

It had only been after they were back aboard and had everything secured that Richardson had been summoned to the Captain's presence. There he was questioned, kindly but firmly, about details of his past Navy experience. Finally the Captain had come to the point. "You say you've been in nearly six months, Mr. Richardson," he had said quietly. "Tell me, in all that time didn't anyone ever tell you to ask permission before you leave the ship?"

Thinking back to the incident now, Richardson suppressed a grin. He wondered what the Captain would do if he climbed back aboard and ostentatiously sought him out on the bridge in the midst of a tense unloading process just to ask for his formal permission to leave the *Alcyon*.

Somehow he didn't think the gesture would be appreciated.

The rain let up after a time, but everyone in the open landing craft was soaked to the skin by then. The swells were high, the darkness well-nigh impenetrable, as the LCP(L) slowly circled near the very edge of the assembly area. Unlike most of the landing craft, each with an assigned place in the grand scheme of the invasion, the NDU boats were designated as being on call. If there was any sign of an obstacle, natural or artificial, anywhere that threatened the smooth deployment of the troops, one of the NDU boats would be sent to deal with the situation.

It promised to be a long and tedious night. But as he sat in the cramped boat, with few passengers but mounds of supplies and explosives around him, Richardson was just as happy they weren't going to hit those beaches until they'd been softened up for a while.

Off Beach Yellow
Licata, Sicily

The Higgins boat was idling, barely making headway as it ran parallel to the coastline. Under the faint illumination of the quarter moon, with no lights showing, the landing craft was shrouded in darkness. Frank Rand could make out a few scattered points of light from buildings or bonfires on shore, but nothing more.

Ensign Bucklew, though, seemed to know exactly what he was looking at as he scanned the coast through field glasses. "Okay," he said quietly. "If Licata is off there to the left and that mountain over on the other side is Monte Gallodoro, then this is just about right. The boundary of the beach should be straight inshore of here, Rand, so you'll have an easy shot. Get yourself ready."

"Aye, aye, sir," Rand responded quietly.

They had rehearsed the operation hundreds of times, or so it seemed, yet Rand knew this time out would be different. This time was for real. By dawn, the Allied invasion of Sicily—Operation Husky—would be under way, and it was his job tonight to get in to the beach and guide the attack in.

As he clambered awkwardly over the side of the LCP(L) into the small rubber boat alongside, Rand couldn't help but feel a rising tide of excitement, elation. This was what all the training, all the preparation, had been leading up to. Tonight Frank Rand was finally going ashore onto a hostile beach, and that meant a chance to come to grips with the enemy.

A chance for glory.

He checked the equipment lashed down in the bottom of the raft. It didn't seem like much for a man about to go up against the first line of the Axis defense of southern Europe. His only weapon was a Colt M1911A1 pistol with two spare clips. Far more important, at least as far as Bucklew and the high command were concerned, was the small chart of the landing area in its waterproof pouch and, of course, his flashlight. Rand checked the latter, flicking it on and off with the beam pointing into the bottom of the raft, then nodded approval. "I'm ready," he said quietly.

Aboard the Higgins boat, Pete Havlicek gave him a quick thumbs-up and then cast off the raft. Almost immediately the landing craft picked up speed, moving toward the opposite end of Beach Yellow to deploy another man to complete the task of marking out the beachhead.

On his own at last, Frank Rand smiled coldly and picked up his paddle. This was the moment!

As he paddled, he couldn't help but think back to his bitter thoughts during the Safi operation. This time it was being done right. During training Bucklew had picked Rand's brains as promised, putting his suggestions together with ideas brought up by other trainees, instructors, and the occasional visitor to the S&R base. The doctrine of the Scouts and Raiders was built on personal reconnaissance and individual initiative, and Frank Rand liked to think that was due in no small part to his own contributions to the evolving process.

Rand steered as straight as possible, keeping Bucklew's instructions in mind. Most of the beaches assigned to General Patton's force were hard to distinguish because of the dull sameness that characterized much of the southern Sicilian coast, but Beach Yellow was one of the best beaches for a night landing on the whole island. In the darkness it was hard to pick out any details, though the starlit sky did help him pick out the bulk of Monte Sole off to his left, rising above the scattered lights of the Sicilian town of Licata. The other most noticeable landmark for Beach Yellow, Monte Gallodoro, was harder to see even with night-adapted eyesight.

He heard a distant drone of engines overhead, the sound of warning sirens on the shore. That would be a wave of bombers coming in, timing their attack to coincide with the airdrops set to go in down the coast around Gela, and with the naval bombardment that was supposed to soften up the beach defenses. He paddled faster, knowing that the serenity of the quiet little coastal town ahead would soon be transformed into a scene from Hell.

A pair of powerful searchlight beams suddenly stabbed

skyward, bright enough to make the stars grow dim. The lights threw Monte Sole into sharp relief and lit up the sky like the lights in front of a Broadway theater on opening night. Rand guessed they were the lights around the Licata airstrip, located well inland. The Germans and Italians were on alert now, though so far they seemed to be reacting entirely to the air assault.

He was glad the searchlights that overlooked the sea hadn't been turned on as yet. Training and practice had taught him that a small boat was awfully hard to spot even with a really powerful light, but that was cold comfort for the man in that boat. There was nothing to make a raider feel quite so naked as a searchlight beam passing right over his boat as he approached a well-defended beach.

Suddenly German searchlights didn't seem to matter much, as the guns of the Allied naval squadron opened fire, transforming night into day. The flashes and reports from the fire support ships rippled along the surface of the sea to the south, and when Rand glanced over his shoulder he could see the tracks of shells arcing up into the sky, bright white balls that drifted overhead almost lazily, interspersed by streaks of red.

More sirens sounded ashore, and in minutes answering shots were coming from dozens of points ashore, mostly machine guns, but interspersed with antiaircraft and artillery fire. Farther back, new lights were appearing, including the flickering, wavering glows of fires started by the hails of shells and bombs falling on the Axis positions.

Rand could hear the surf now, and knew he was getting close. Slowly, carefully, he brought the rubber boat into the beach, trying to watch for any sign of activity on shore. Finally he rolled out of the raft and into the waist-deep water. A wave helped him steer the raft up onto land. He dragged it up from the waterline toward a wheat field in stubble that the earlier S&R excursions had identified as a likely place to hide the boat. It didn't take long to round up his gear and conceal the raft. Then Rand crouched down and studied his surroundings once more.

He had come ashore a little farther west than he'd planned, near the low-lying bog and the oblong pond that separated Beach Yellow from the mouth of the Salso River.

He would have to make his way to the east a few hundred yards in order to mark his side of the landing area.

Before he stirred, he watched and listened carefully. The bombardment and bombings went on undiminished, drawing sporadic replies from the defensive positions, but he couldn't detect any sign of organized troop movements. Satisfied that his only real danger was from random fire, not active resistance, Rand set out at a trot. He took his bearings on Monte Gallodoro and the lower slopes of Saffarello in front of it, clearly visible now in the intermittent light of the bombardment.

He estimated he'd gone about two hundred yards when he saw the cluster of low concrete buildings that lay very close to his goal. They were perhaps a thousand yards inland from the beach, on the lower slope of Saffarello Hill, but they directly overlooked the spot he was supposed to set up on. They hadn't been there the last time they'd scouted these beaches. That was the problem with beach reconnaissance. The longer the time between the initial survey and the actual invasion, the more chance there was that the enemy would add new defenses.

He dropped down in the midst of a tomato garden and studied the enemy strongpoint. He couldn't see much from his present location, but he was sure there was more than one building there. As he watched, explosions nearby briefly illuminated the position. Rand was fairly sure of two bunkers, and on rising ground behind them he thought he could make out the skeletal shapes of four field guns, probably a 75-mm battery, barrels pointed at the sea but not yet firing. About halfway between the strongpoint and the beach, there was at least one additional bunker.

That made his job a lot more complicated. How was he supposed to mark the edge of Beach Yellow without being noticed by the soldiers in those bunkers?

Rand lay very still, his mind racing. The landing craft were supposed to start their run at 0300 hours, and he didn't have much time to come up with an answer. Without a good fix on the western flank, some of the Allied boats might come in too far to the left, just as he'd done in the raft. The terrain around the mouth of the Salso, marshy and soft, wasn't suitable for a landing, especially by tanks. A mistake could spell disaster for the whole Beach Yellow landing. . . .

He came to a decision. There was really only one answer that would work here.

Rand scrambled to his feet and started to work his way forward, moving more slowly than before, staying in a low crouch and moving from cover to cover. It was like one of the exercises back at Fort Pierce, creeping up on an objective using stealth and caution. The only difference was that failure here would result in consequences far more dire than a noisy chewing-out by an angry instructor. Here the first he'd know of an alerted enemy would likely be a rifle shot whistling past him or the nearby rattle of machine gun fire.

He angled toward the bunker closest to the beach, dropping to his belly to crawl the last hundred yards. Now he could see a light showing from within, and as he reached the side of the structure he heard voices inside. Rand froze and listened. He spoke a little French, and the words he heard sounded enough like that language for him to guess it was Italian. A part of him felt a little let down. Everyone knew the Eye-ties weren't in the same category as the Germans, so there was a lot less glory in going up against Italian soldiers. On the other hand, if all the scuttlebutt about the poor morale of Mussolini's army these days was true, perhaps he'd stand a chance of carrying out his plan.

He crawled around to the front of the structure and settled down just under the firing slit that looked out over the beaches. The blunt nose of an outmoded Fiat-Revelli machine gun protruded above his head, but there was no sign that the men inside were about to use it. From where he was, he doubted anyone in the bunker would be able to see him, and if someone did they wouldn't be able to get a good angle to fire at him.

On the other hand, if the Allies picked out this bunker as a target, nothing in the world would save him from the effects of friendly fire. . . .

Frank Rand, commando hero, does it again, he thought wryly. In Safi he hadn't shown enough sense to come in out of an air raid. This time out, he'd like as not end up getting hit by his own side because he chose to take cover in front of an enemy strongpoint.

He grinned, though, as he pulled out his light. Even his father wouldn't be able to deny his son's courage this time.

Rand aimed the shielded light toward the sea and flicked it on and off in the prearranged signal that would tell Ensign Bucklew he was in position. Now things would really get interesting. . . .

Scout Boat
Off Beach Yellow
Licata, Sicily

"There!" Peter Havlicek lowered his field glasses and pointed toward shore. "That's the signal. Rand's in position."

"Good," Bucklew said. "I was starting to get worried. Now we've got both flankers spotted. Coxswain, center us between those two points. Havlicek, get ready to show our light. It's getting late."

Havlicek moved to the stern of the boat and set up the lantern they'd use to guide the first attack wave into Beach Yellow. He was glad Rand had finally shown his light. Although they had little in common, he and Rand had hit it off during S&R training. Everyone in the unit had volunteered for the job of marking the beach, but Havlicek knew it meant more to Rand than just a mission. Despite the friendship that had grown up between them these past six months, he still didn't know exactly what it was that drove the little second-class, but his dedication and intensity were undeniable.

Ensign Bucklew, Havlicek knew, had come close to rejecting Rand for the mission for that very reason, claiming that the last thing they needed on the beaches today was a hero. The best man for a dangerous Scouts and Raiders operation was someone who was competent but cool and cautious, someone who'd keep his mind on the primary objective. The officer had gone so far as to ask Havlicek's opinion of his bunkmate when considering his list of volunteers, and Havlicek had been forced to admit he didn't know how reliable Rand would be in action. There was something of the daredevil about Frank Rand, something wild, impulsive.

But he was also one of the best in his class, a man who could certainly handle the physical demands of the job. Bucklew had finally decided to let him go in, but Havlicek had been worried for his friend ever since he'd shoved off in the raft. Now it seemed he was in position and secure enough to signal the fleet. So perhaps the doubts and concerns had all been groundless after all.

"In position, sir," the coxswain reported.

"Very good. Havlicek, show the light. Let's get this show on the road."

He switched the lantern on and steadied it on the stern, peering aft into the gloom. Almost immediately he heard the low mutter of distant motors as the landing craft of the Salso Attack Group started toward shore. Operation Husky was under way for real.

At first nothing changed. The bombardment from the fire support ships assigned to Beach Yellow and Beach Blue continued unabated, and there was some answering fire from shore, but it seemed that the defenders hadn't yet identified the boats of the Attack Group that were steering for the beaches. And the signal lights continued to glow, bright and steady, evidently unnoticed by the Axis troops preparing for the attack. The scout boat led the first wave of landing craft right up to the beach, only turning aside at the last minute to back out and pick up the second wave. As they swung away, Havlicek watched a line of LCTs and LCPs running up on the sandy beach, their bow ramps dropping almost in unison. And at that moment someone raised the alarm on shore.

More sirens rose and fell, eerie in the predawn darkness. The crack of rifle fire rang out, scattered at first. The volume of fire quickly swelled as the Americans returned fire. Here and there the deeper chatter of a machine gun spoke in counterpoint, and once a field gun opened up to lob shells toward the beach. The defenders were finally beginning to react to the landings, shifting their attention from the cruisers and destroyers to the beaches themselves. From Havlicek's vantage point in the stern of the scout boat, it appeared the invaders had managed nearly total surprise despite the intense opening bombardment. The defenders simply weren't ready for the attack.

He was just starting to voice the observation out loud when bullets raked the side of the scout boat. Everyone dropped low behind the dubious shelter of the hull. Havlicek peered over the side, saw the muzzle flash of an MG firing off on the left side of the beach. Suddenly he realized what else he could see there.

"God damn! What the hell's going on with Rand?" he said out loud.

Bucklew joined him at the rail. "That MG fire's coming right from Rand's position, for Christ's sake," he said. "What the hell's going on over there?"

A cold chill ran up Havlicek's spine. "You don't suppose they caught him, sir? Set up his light in a phony position to screw up our boats coming in?"

The ensign frowned for a moment, then shook his head. "It's in the right spot," he said. "I'm sure of it. Why would the Krauts set the thing up where it belonged, when they could move it a couple hundred yards over and maybe lure half our boys into the marsh?"

Havlicek shook his head. "Doesn't make any sense. 'Cause I sure don't see why Rand would set up his beacon inside a machine gun nest."

The MG fired again, but the boat was quickly moving out of range and most of the bullets never reached her. Havlicek continued to stare at the beacon and the muzzle flash just above it. Just what was Rand doing out there?

Beach Yellow
Licata, Sicily

The hammering noise of the machine gun over his head made Rand flinch involuntarily. The Italians in the bunker had held their fire until an LCP(L) had run up on the beach a few hundred yards away. The boat's arrival on shore had elicited shouts and harsh orders within the pillbox. Then the Fiat-Revelli had started up, swinging back and forth as the defenders sprayed fire at any American soldier they could spot.

Kneeling below the firing slit, he considered half a dozen plans for suppressing the bunker, but none of them stood much chance of success. Perhaps if he'd been given some grenades or explosives, he'd have been able to do something worthwhile. But one man with a pistol couldn't be sure of taking out the pillbox alone ... and if he was killed or wounded trying, the defenders might discover his beacon and spoil the attack.

But he was all too conscious of the firing right over his head. If he came up with a way to take out those men inside, no one could doubt his heroism. Not even his father.

Dawn was starting to light up the eastern sky. Rand glanced at his watch. It was 0345, and the sun would be fully up in less than an hour. The almost constant light of explosions and fires and muzzle flashes showed him some detail of the activity on the beaches. Soldiers of the Third Battalion, Fifteenth Infantry poured ashore, dispersing as quickly as they could leave their landing craft. Despite the pockets of resistance like Rand's own pillbox, they moved forward quickly without becoming bogged down. Fortunately the beaches hadn't been mined or blocked by obstacles, so there was little to slow the attackers down except for the flurries of bullets, grenades, and shells.

The determination of the defenders was by no means a constant across the beach. Rand spotted some strongpoints that weren't responding at all to the assault, and he could see knots of Italian soldiers streaming back from forward positions, confused, panicky.

Rand spotted a clump of fleeing soldiers rushing up the slope straight toward his position. He drew his pistol, ready to defend himself. One of the Italians noticed him before any of the others and raised his rifle, and Rand rolled sideways to duck behind the corner of the pillbox. The rifle shot pinged and whined as it ricocheted off the concrete. From farther down the beach an automatic weapon barked and three of the Italians fell. The rest dispersed quickly.

Rand crawled toward the bodies sprawled on the hillside, intent on their weaponry. The move took him away from the protection of the bunker, but whoever was inside firing the machine gun apparently didn't notice him as he reached the closest of the casualties. The man had a rifle but no ammunition for it. What he did have, though, was a grenade of the German potato-masher type tucked into his belt. That was what Rand had been wishing for. He grabbed the device and started back toward the bunker, still on his belly and praying he wouldn't be spotted.

He was almost up to the firing slit when a loud engine drowned out the noise of the Italian machine gun. Rolling over, Rand saw the bulk of an American Sherman tank climbing the slope below him, headed right for the bunker. There were American GIs advancing in a loose skirmish line on either side of the vehicle, zigzagging from cover to cover but advancing remorselessly.

The tank rumbled and groaned as it came up the last bit of the slope, and its turret swung toward the pillbox. Rand muttered a curse and dropped into a nearby shell hole, expecting the tank to open fire. But it didn't.

The Italian machine gun fell silent, and in seconds the door at the rear of the bunker was flung open. Holding out a white flag, with hands up, half a dozen men burst out into the open. "Surrender! Surrender! We your prisoners!" one of them was shouting in broken English.

Something jabbed into Rand's back. "What about you, Luigi?" a gruff voice demanded.

He twisted his head around, saw an infantry man holding a BAR. "I'm an American!" Rand said. "Scouts and Raiders!"

"Yeah, and I'm the Pope," the GI said, grinning. "Drop that grenade and the pistol and stand up real slow."

Rand had no desire to demonstrate his bravery by provoking a nervous American soldier. He did as he was told. Another American, a corporal, stooped to pick up his M1911A1. "Well, he's got him an American pistol," the noncom said. "His uniform ain't Italian, or German either. And he sounds American enough. Maybe he's telling the truth."

"Yeah," the man with the BAR grunted. "And maybe he clobbered the real Navy guy to get it."

"My dog tags—" Rand began.

"Send the prisoners down to the CP we captured," a fresh-faced young officer with a second lieutenant's bars said. "They'll sort it out down there. Reynolds, you and Nicholls take him in."

Rand was seething as he allowed himself to be herded down toward the beach among the Italian prisoners. He'd been so close to taking out the bunker on his own, but instead of tossing the grenade through the firing slit and singlehandedly silencing the enemy MG, he'd managed to blunder into a comedy of errors. He'd never live this one down, he thought bitterly.

The little party's destination was another concrete strongpoint closer to the beach, evidently a command post. A few American soldiers were there, together with a harassed-looking Army captain who didn't have time to deal with prisoners of any kind, much less one who claimed to be an American. Corporal Reynolds and the BAR man, Nicholls, were told to keep an eye on their charges until the officer could spare a few minutes.

Through the open door of the CP, Rand could see a few GIs inside poking around the building. An older man wearing fatigues but no rank insignia was with them, sitting behind a desk at the very edge of Rand's line of sight. He carried no weapons and looked distinctly out of place. Unlike the others, he was scribbling notes in a pocket notebook and paying no attention at all to the contents of the command post.

Suddenly a phone rang inside the building, a loud, incongruous sound that made every head nearby swivel. The ringing went on, and the men started exchanging uncertain looks.

The unarmed man broke the spell when he suddenly reached across the desk and picked up the telephone. *"Che è?"* he said calmly, smiling. Then he cocked his head for a moment, listening to a voice at the other end of the line. After a few moments he spoke again in voluble Italian, too fast for Rand to make anything out. Finally he hung up and leaned back in his chair, laughing.

The captain fixed the man with an angry glare. "What the hell was that about?" he asked.

The other man laughed again. "That was the general in command of this sector. He said somebody woke him up claiming the Americans were landing at Licata, but I told him it was all a false alarm and everything was quiet. I think he decided to go back to bed."

That made the other Americans start laughing. "Mr. Chinigo," the captain finally got out. "Mr. Chinigo, I was against having any war correspondents along when we hit the beach, but by God I'm going to ask for one every time we go in! Wait'll they hear back at headquarters that a reporter single-handedly threw the whole damned Eye-tie HQ into a tailspin just because he knew enough Italian to answer the phone!"

Rand slumped against the outer wall of the bunker, more dejected than ever. Not only had he almost managed to take out the enemy pillbox, but there had been a reporter right in the area all along. If he'd been successful, Rand's name would have been in every paper Stateside, a genuine war hero. Surely that would have impressed his father. But instead he'd missed his one chance. The story everyone would remember from Licata would be the tale of how Chinigo had used a captured telephone to throw the Axis defenders off stride. No one would remember Frank Rand, except for the ones who laughed at the commando taken prisoner by his own side!

Chapter 12

Saturday, 10 July 1943

American Sector, Sicily

The original plan for Operation Husky had conceived of American and British forces landing across a wide arc sweeping from the ancient city of Syracuse in the southeast corner of the island all the way to Palermo at the northwestern tip of the triangular island. The British Eighth Army, under Montgomery, was to have gone ashore between Syracuse and the southern town of Gela, with Americans of Patton's Seventh Army guarding their flank as well as concentrating on Palermo itself. Lieutenant General Patton himself had endorsed the plan thus presented, claiming the Germans and Italians could never protect the vital city of Messina—and with it the way across the straits into the toe of Italy—from an advance on two fronts.

But it quickly became clear that in this case no battle plan would survive contact with the General Staff. Two British officers had their doubts about the plan. Sir Bernard Law Montgomery, the hero of El Alamein, was a cautious man but also an egotist. No one was ever entirely sure if his objections to the original version of Operation Husky stemmed from a concern about flank security or a fear that his flamboyant rival Patton might make good his vow to be the first one into Messina. As for General Sir Harold Alexander, commander of the Fifteenth Army Group and direct superior to both Patton and Montgomery, his objections went back to the poor performance of the American army at Kasserine in February. Alexander simply didn't believe the American Seventh Army could protect the British and still take Palermo.

Alexander's superior, Eisenhower, wasn't inclined to press the American army's case. He wanted to preserve the alliance above all else, no matter how loud and often George S. Patton, Jr., might have protested.

Rumor had it that Husky took its final form in a map drawn on a steamed-up mirror in a hotel lavatory, with Montgomery suggesting a narrower version of the landings and General Bedel Smith, Eisenhower's Chief of Staff, agreeing that the man who had conquered Rommel had the best grasp of the situation.

So the British force was going in through the southeast corner of the island, while Patton's men were to land along the south coast to safeguard their flank. The Seventh Army was assigned beachheads in three separate places fairly close together along the coast. CENT force, built around Major General Troy Middleton's Forty-fifth Division, was given the task of securing Scoglitti, the town in the American sector closest to the British. Close by, at Gela, DIME force went in under Major General Terry de la M. Allen and his deputy, Brigadier General Theodore Roosevelt, Jr. The First Infantry Division, known as the "Fighting First" or

"Pershing's Own," was the core of DIME, and General Patton accompanied this centrally placed unit in person. Finally, up the coast a short way from Gela at the town of Licata, JOSS force had the assignment of securing the American left. General Lucian K. Truscott, who had brought the American army ashore along the banks of the Sebou in Operation Torch, commanded the Third Infantry Division that formed the core of JOSS.

Each portion of the American sector offered its own unique problems. Truscott's men, for instance, found Licata ill-defended at best. A few pillboxes and machine guns had put up a brisk resistance for a while, but many of the Italian defenders simply melted away. Even the Germans at Licata didn't have much fight in them. Officers in the landing craft plying back and forth from fleet to beaches reported that the German 88 batteries commanding the approaches fired with amazing accuracy and precision for quite some time but were very careful not to actually hit the boats themselves. Within a matter of hours Licata was completely secured, and reinforcements were pouring ashore across the beaches and through the town itself as fast as they could be off-loaded.

At Gela, the initial resistance was sporadic, but large numbers of German and Italian troops were posted in reserve not far inland. As the landing developed, the Italians mounted an early afternoon counterattack with tanks and infantry, but it failed to dislodge the American beachhead. Strangely, the Germans, part of the dreaded Hermann Göring Division, remained inactive throughout D-Day.

Scoglitti was an altogether different proposition. Here the defenders proved poorly organized, their reactions slow and their defense halfhearted, much as at Licata. But the beaches at Scoglitti were treacherous. Owing to some last-minute confusion, not all of the Scouts and Raiders got in to mark the CENT landing areas, and those that were marked proved treacherous in another way. Scoglitti's coast was protected by several undulating sandbars that lay in shallow water, parallel to many of the beaches. Some landing craft ended up stranded on these unless they were lucky enough to catch a surging wave to carry them across. Others lost control in the ground swell, going off course or even colliding with one another. And the sandbars made the surf particularly treacherous, so that dozens of boats became stranded in the soft sand of the Scoglitti beaches and were unable to return for additional loads.

What might have happened if the German resistance at Scoglitti had matched that around Gela—or if the Americans going ashore at Gela had been as badly disorganized by conditions outside their control as the men of CENT force—was a question no one in the Allied High Command cared to think about.

But it did prove, once and for all, the need for intensive scouting both before and during a landing operation. And a few high-placed naval officers would also argue that those sandbars might have been opened up by naval demolitions if there had been time enough prior to the invasion. While there were few similar beaches anywhere in the European Theater of Operations which might one day be assaulted, the sandbars of Scoglitti did bear a resemblance to the coral reefs of the Pacific Islands, and thoughtful officers began to turn their minds to ways to prevent the same kind of misstep in future campaigns.

Naval Demolition Unit #1
Scoglitti, Sicily

The LCP(L) chugged into the cramped harbor of Scoglitti and headed for the only free pier available. The harbor was long and narrow, and the boat's coxswain had his hands full threading the needle past the little white church on the headland in the middle of the town and along the shore lined by sad-looking, dilapidated old houses. A few of them showed definite signs of damage, whether from the naval bombardment or from street fights after the landings Richardson didn't know and didn't particularly care.

He tried to stretch cramped legs, but it wasn't easy in the loaded boat. All three of the landing craft assigned to the NDU had been hanging around at the fringe of the assembly area for half the night and all morning, waiting for orders, waiting for some kind of purpose. But the call had never come. After all the buildup, all the waiting, the NDU had never been called upon to do its job.

Richardson was relieved they hadn't seen any fighting, but he couldn't help but feel a little let down at the same time. Was this all there was?

As the boat pulled up alongside the pier and a linehandler forward looped a length of line around a convenient bollard, a j.g. charged down the long wooden structure with fire in his eyes and a BEACHMASTER band worn prominently on one arm. "You can't tie up here! For Christ's sake, get this heap outa here so I can get my next scheduled LCM alongside!"

Lieutenant West stepped to the rail, looking up at the beachmaster. "Look, buddy," West said. "I just want to know where the hell *we're* supposed to be? And when? We've been circling out there in the assembly area all night. Damn boat's gonna run out of fuel pretty soon if we don't find a home."

The j.g. frowned. "What's your unit?" he asked.

"Naval Demolitions. Boat Number One. We're off *Alcyon.*"

The other officer scanned a list in a clipboard clutched in one hand. "Naval Demolitions, huh?" he said. "Hell, it's pretty damn late for you guys to show up now. Ain't nothing left naval to demolit, know what I mean?" He laughed as if trying to prove he'd said something riotously funny.

"All I know is, they said we'd be called when needed, but nobody the hell called," West said, a ragged edge in his voice.

"Well, you're not on my list. And I figure if nobody's needed you yet, they ain't ever going to. We got all the beaches secured, and anybody what couldn't get over the sandbars found themselves an alternate beach. All we're doing now is bringing up reinforcements and resupply, Lieutenant. Beats the hell out of me where you're supposed to go."

At that moment another man hurried up, an Army first lieutenant who managed to look at least as harassed as the beachmaster and a lot dirtier and more tired. He was tall, skinny, and young, with prominent teeth. "You in charge of this circus?" he demanded of the j.g.

"I'm the beachmaster. If it's already on shore I can't help you with it. And if it ain't here yet it ain't my fucking fault!"

The Army man plowed ahead as if the beachmaster hadn't spoken. "Well, I'm from General Middleton's staff. The general wants to know where the bloody blue blazes the division engineering supplies are. Our engineers don't have any goddamned explosives to blow up any of the goddamned barricades the Krauts and the Eye-ties put up across the goddamned roads in that goddamned town!"

"They haven't come ashore here, Lieutenant," the beachmaster said. "Why don't you try down on the beach?"

"I've been to the goddamned beach!" the Army lieutenant exploded. "They're the ones who said to check with you!"

West broke in before the beachmaster could make an angry retort. "Ah, Lieutenant, we're Naval Demolitions men, and we've got some explosives on board. What say we lend you a hand?"

For a moment the Army officer looked ready to shout again. Then relief flooded his face. "God bless you!" he said, smiling for the first time. "I knew the whole Navy couldn't be snafued!"

"Looks to me more like a janfu," West said.

"Janfu? I ain't heard that one before."

"Joint Army-Navy Fuck-Up," Richardson put in blandly.

The Army man laughed. "You can say that again." He shook his head. "You know, I was in the Sixtieth Regiment for Torch, and we got screwed coming ashore at some little shithole called Mehedia. Boats going the wrong way, obstacles that didn't get taken out in time to send a ship up the river, a fortress that wouldn't give up ... it was a mess. They said we'd learned how to do an amphib op in Torch." His gesture took in the whole of the Sicilian coast around the dirty little town. "Now I ask you, did we learn how to do it? 'Cause it sure don't look like it."

"Well, Lieutenant, ah ..." West trailed off.

"Rogers. Doug Rogers. My friends call me Doug. My enemies call me Buck ... once."

"Well, Lieutenant Rogers, if you'll show us the way we'll bring our toys—"

"Now wait a minute," the j.g. protested. "I told you you can't dock here."

Rogers swung on him. "Look, buddy, there's two ways we can do this. You can let these helpful gents unload their gear, thus earning the undying respect and gratitude of every soldier in this godforsaken little town and maybe, just maybe, seeing to it that future Army-Navy relations aren't left stuck on the same level of cooperation and goodwill currently enjoyed by Hitler and old Uncle Joe Stalin. Or, you can be an officious little bastard and make this boat move, whereupon we'll lose another hour or two clearing those barricades. That'll make General Middleton mad. And when General Middleton gets mad, the division gets mad. Now it just so happens that the division didn't just pick up its Thunderbirds nickname because of our unit patch. Seems like we have a whole bunch of Red Injuns in the outfit, and if they get riled there ain't no telling what's likely to happen. So if you don't want your scalp adorning the wall over our O club, you'll keep General Middleton happy. Now how about it?"

The beachmaster looked from Rogers to West and back again. "All right," he said at last. "All right, you win. But if I catch hell from this from *my* CO, I'll let him have it out with your Middleton and his redskin buddies."

He hurried off again, heading for the far end of the pier, where a commotion had broken out between the crews of two LCP(L)s. West ordered Richardson to take charge of the first party to go with Rogers, while he and two of the men stayed back and continued to sort through demolitions gear they could use if the first party ran short.

Rogers led them into the middle of the town. The first barricade was a crude wall of rubble and shattered concrete that had been raised across the widest of Scoglitti's narrow streets, evidently as a defensive position that hadn't actually seen any use. But now it was blocking vehicular traffic. The only major artery linking the harbor, poor as it was, with the interior of the country ran right up this street, and without it trucks, tanks, jeeps, and half-tracks would soon snarl into the worst traffic jam ever seen.

Richardson and the petty officer named Simms studied the wall carefully. It was only waist-high, but thick, and it would have made things worse to try to batter it down.

"Hey, Mr. Richardson," Simms said suddenly. "How 'bout we try out some of those shaped charges?"

He frowned. Along with their other explosives, they'd

been issued a number of the new M2A3 fifteen-pound shaped charges, described in their manuals as being intended to penetrate almost three feet of reinforced concrete or twelve inches of steel. This wall wasn't nearly that strong, but he knew it would take a lot of conventional charges to do much with it. Unfortunately, the NDU had never had a chance to practice with the shaped charges back at Solomons Island, so none of them knew anything about what to expect if they tried.

Still, it was the government's money, not Richardson's, and he didn't have any better ideas about how to get the job done. "Okay," he said finally. "Let's give it a try."

They had two crates of two charges each with them, and since he didn't know how effective they'd be, Richardson decided to place all four at regular intervals along the barricade. The theory of shaped charges, or so said the hastily assembled manual they'd been studying, was to use a conical charge to direct an intense explosive jet against a relatively small area. Looking at one of the charges, Richardson wondered just what kind of area effect it was likely to have. Sixteen inches long and six inches in diameter at the narrow end, the cone-shaped explosive with its scalloped, open-ended face didn't look very formidable.

They placed the four charges low on the wall, two on each side in staggered positions. A string of yellow primacord served to connect them all, and Richardson found a fuse igniter still snug in its waterproof wrapping that he crimped onto a length of fuse. Crimping a blasting cap to the end of the fuse and then taping the cap to the primacord line completed the charge assembly. When it was done, he signaled everyone to move well back. "Fire in the hole!" he called, tugging at the T-wire. He backed off hurriedly and took cover around the corner of a nearby building.

When the charge went off, it literally tore the wall apart. As the demo men came out into the street, they saw they'd blasted it so thoroughly that vehicles wouldn't have any trouble making it through.

"Okay," Richardson drawled, surveying his handiwork. "Make a note, Simms. Four charges is a little bit of overkill for one rubble wall. Got it?"

"Got it, sir," Simms replied, straight-faced.

They were all laughing as they moved up the street to survey their next obstacle. It was as if they'd gone back to training at Solomons Island again. The war, at that moment, seemed a long, long way off.

Command Post, Beach Yellow
Licata, Sicily

The scout boat ran up on the beach alongside an LCT and dropped its ramp, and BM1 Peter Havlicek followed Ensign Bucklew onto the beach, trying to match the officer's long, impatient stride.

The fighting around Licata had died out by noon of D-Day, and S&R guidance into the beaches was no longer needed. The scout boat had made a few runs between the LSTs offshore and the shores of Beach Yellow through the morning hours, ferrying extra troops and supplies in. Eventually even that role was no longer necessary, and they'd been freed up to recover the Scouts and Raiders they'd put ashore the night before. All but two of those had now been accounted for, but one of the missing was Frank Rand, and Havlicek was beginning to believe he really had been taken prisoner, as they'd feared.

It had been a long and harrowing night. The boat had taken hits from machine guns and even a few light field pieces, though no one aboard had been hurt. And except for the two missing flankers, the same was true of the men who'd been in the most danger ashore. All in all, the landings at Licata had been smoothly carried out, and the Scouts and Raiders had good reason to be proud of the role they'd played in it all. Reports from some of the other beaches indicated that a few of the S&R teams hadn't been able to mark their landing areas in time, but in each case it had turned out that they'd been delayed because the transport carrying them had been late making the rendezvous before the attack. Where the Scouts and Raiders had gone in, they'd done their work well.

But the prospect of even two men lost was enough to make Bucklew anxious. Havlicek had known the ensign felt strongly for all the men in his command, but until this morning he hadn't realized the full extent of Bucklew's devotion to them.

They'd been asked to come ashore in response to a query from an Army unit on the left flank of Beach Yellow. Apparently they had a lead on one of the missing men and wanted Bucklew to make an identification. This had been Rand's stretch of beach, and Havlicek couldn't help but be worried that they were about to be confronted with his bunkmate's dead body.

"You the S&R boys?" a tall GI asked casually as they approached a concrete building near the edge of the beach.

"I'm Ensign Bucklew, soldier," Bucklew snapped irritably.

"Er . . . sorry, sir. Didn't know you were an officer." The soldier gave him a quick salute. He had good reason for confusion. None of the Scouts and Raiders team had worn insignia with their uniforms when they went in, and Bucklew's fatigues didn't give much of a clue even as to what branch of service he belonged to, much less his rank. "Come this way, sir."

Havlicek followed them around to the back of the building, where a group of Italian prisoners lounged on the sand, trying to stay cool in the midday sun. They didn't look much like defeated men, for the most part. Smiling, laughing, joking among themselves, they looked more relieved than anything else. There were a few American GIs there too, standing guard over the POWs.

The glummest face in the whole crowd belonged to none other than Frank Rand. He looked up sharply as Bucklew and Havlicek came around the corner, coming quickly to attention.

"Rand?" Bucklew demanded. "What the hell are you doing with this bunch?"

An army corporal spoke up. "Then this one really does belong to you swabbies? Hey, Nicholls, you owe me a buck!"

A couple of the other Americans in the neighborhood laughed. Rand's face flushed.

"I'm waiting, Rand," the ensign said.

The red-faced sailor spread his hands helplessly. "The

dogfaces wouldn't believe me," he said, sounding bitter. "I tried to tell them . . ."

"We found him next to a bunker full of Eye-ties who were firing a machine gun at us the whole way up from the beach," the soldier named Nicholls said defensively. "What were we supposed to think? And he had a Kraut grenade, too."

"I was trying to blow the damned bunker and save your asses," Rand shot back. "Would've done it, too, if your bunch hadn't come along."

"That's enough, Rand," Bucklew said wearily. Havlicek thought he was looking relieved as well, though. "We'll sort everything out when we debrief you. Right now let's head back out to the ship, okay?"

Rand didn't look happy. Heading back toward the scout boat, no one spoke, and Havlicek found himself wondering just what it was that had upset his friend so much.

Blue Beach
Near Scoglitti, Sicily

They had spent a good chunk of the afternoon blowing up obstacles for the Army, but eventually the men of the NDU ran out of work to do again. The division engineers had finally caught up with their errant boatload of explosives and were quick to assure the Navy men that they'd be taking over once more.

That left Richardson and the others largely at loose ends. After checking all the beaches they could reach on foot for additional obstacles or obstructions, West had decided they should head back to the ship to see if they could be of use anywhere else. Lieutenant Smith and Ensign Culver had already been in contact by radio to report they'd done the same. Some of the others had also been helping the Army, working to blow up strongpoints farther from the shore.

All in all, it was one hell of a way to run a Naval Demolitions Unit, Richardson decided.

Their boat had finally been moved out of the harbor and beached at the close strip of sand designated Blue Beach on West's charts. Invasion planners, it seemed, had a rather limited repertoire of code names for their landing sites. All three of the main American zones included at least one, and sometimes two or three, different Blue Beaches. It was no wonder the engineers had misplaced their gear.

So now the little party was walking along the beach, headed for their LCP(L). Richardson thought they were more like picnickers on a stroll down the seashore somewhere back home than military men on an enemy coast, but he kept his thought to himself. No doubt if he started mouthing off again Lieutenant West would find some unpleasant little chore for him to do.

Up ahead, a bulldozer was laboring over the soft sand, trying to reach a landing craft that had broached as it came ashore. Stranded, the boat looked like some prehistoric sea creature that had beached itself by accident. The Seabee driving the bulldozer was having trouble getting in close enough to do anything. The sand made traction difficult here. Richardson had heard Rogers remark earlier that only six of sixteen bulldozers had made it ashore and off the beaches, making the job of getting things around Scoglitti into some reasonable order all the harder.

West flagged down the driver, who stopped the 'dozer long enough to answer the lieutenant's hail. "Any idea if there's anything blocking the beach around here?" he asked. "You need any demo work?"

The driver shrugged. "Hell if I know, sir," he said, and spat eloquently. "I wasn't even supposed to come ashore here. Rest of my unit went in up there at Wood's Hole, but the idiot driving my taxi took a wrong turn and let me off here."

"So who told you to go to work on these boats?"

"Nobody, sir. I just saw 'em all stranded and thought it might be neighborly to give 'em a little push back into the water. You have any different orders for me, Lieutenant?"

West shook his head. "Not me. My boys and I are just about as much out of place around these parts as you are. Keep it up, sailor!"

The Seabee started up the bulldozer again and went back to work trying to push the stubborn landing craft back to its natural element.

Farther down the beach, with their landing craft finally in sight, they were accosted by a gaggle of people wearing all manner of clothes. It took Richardson a moment to register them as civilians, townsfolk. A number of the local men were swarming over an LCM, unloading its cargo under the watchful eyes of the boat's coxswain. Some of them broke off at the sight of West and the others and intercepted them.

"Eh, you got the boat to unload?" one of them asked in thickly accented English. "We unload the boats, you give us carton of smokes, *si?* We like the American smokes . . . like all you American boys." He thumped his chest. "Me, I have many relatives in New York. Many relatives. Maybe I go to New York myself, some day, now that you come and you throw out that Mussolini! So what you say, eh? You need the work done? We do it."

West shrugged. "Sorry, we don't need any workers. And anyway, I doubt anybody has a decent cigarette left on them. Not after a night tossing around in an open boat the way we did. Sorry."

"Hey, that's all right. We catch you tomorrow, maybe you have work for us then, eh?"

On impulse, Richardson reached into his waistband. "Hang on, Luigi," he said cheerfully. "Tell you what. I've got half a pack left. You and your buddies can have them. Free of charge. Think of it as a bonus from Uncle Sam."

"Aw, come on, Richardson," West said. "You can't think any of your cigarettes are any good, can you? Or are you just playing one of your damned jokes on the locals?"

"Not me, Lieutenant," he protested. He pulled out his cigarettes, neatly wrapped in a spare prophylactic since the storm the night before. "See? Take a look. The Hank Richardson patented waterproof cigarette case. Guaranteed for life or until your first lay."

That got a laugh from the sailors, but West just fixed him with a sour frown. Richardson extracted the cigarettes and pocketed the rubber. The Sicilian leader took the Camels, grinning broadly. "Thank you, thank you, you Americans always welcome here!"

Richardson wasn't paying much attention to the man, though. There were a handful of Sicilian women standing at the fringe of the group, and a couple of them weren't half bad in a dark, Italian sort of way. He wondered how much action a pack of cigarettes would buy from one of them.

Too bad he didn't have any good connections in the fleet. A really good scrounge could've scared him up enough smokes to corner the market on pussy in the whole god-damned American sector.

Ah, well. No doubt West wouldn't be letting him off his leash. Otherwise he just might be tempted to sample some of the local delicacies.

Sunday, 11 July 1943

American Sector, Sicily

The Hermann Göring Division finally launched its long-anticipated counterattack on D+1, but this time it was the exhausted and discouraged Italians who failed to coordinate with their allies. The attack nearly cut the Allied beachheads around the Gulf of Gela in half, until General Patton himself arrived at a forward HQ and ordered a Navy ensign to get on his walkie-talkie and call in naval gunfire on the advancing tanks. At one point the situation looked so grim that a Navy lieutenant, John T. Koehler, was ordered forward with the men of his Advanced Base unit to hold the lines at all costs, but the situation stabilized before Koehler and his men reached the front. With devastating accuracy the guns of battleships, cruisers, and destroyers rained shell after shell down on the advancing tanks, until finally the German commander ordered his men to withdraw. Never again would the issue in Sicily truly be in doubt, though a tenacious German resistance in superb defensive terrain would extend a campaign once confidently predicted to last no more than two weeks into an ordeal that took thirty-eight days and many Allied lives to resolve.

In the end, sheer frustration caused Patton to make an end run around the coast of the island by way of Palermo, the port he'd once planned to make his base of operations. His flanking maneuver brought him into Messina only hours ahead of his rival of El Alamein, though the Americans had been forced to go the long way around to get where they were going. The whole exercise proved that the original plans for Husky had been sound after all, and never again would the fighting quality of the American servicemen be doubted by the British or anyone else.

No one could have called Operation Husky a textbook success, but it had proven once and for all that a large and varied invasion force could be put ashore even in the face of an active enemy defense without suffering more than minimal disruptions. But Husky was always a sideshow, and everyone knew it. They also knew it was only a prelude to new landings in Italy . . . and no more than the opening bars of a grand symphony that would reach its triumphant crescendo when the Allies launched the real Second Front with a cross-Channel invasion into France.

Every group that had a part in Husky took away its own lessons from the campaign. The landings in the Gulf of Gela proved conclusively that the Scouts and Raiders could perform a vital service. Beachhead reconnaissance long before the assault had been invaluable. More important, they had proven that skilled commandos going ashore just ahead of the attack could further increase the odds in favor of victory at a comparatively low risk. Bucklew's entire S&R force lost only one flanker; he was captured by the enemy and later liberated as the Italian resistance collapsed. Nothing was said about flankers taken prisoner by their own side. That was the sort of thing that was just chalked up to the infernal confusion of war.

As for the Naval Demolition Unit, their experience suggested quite a different lesson. The NDU hadn't been necessary to Husky after all. The threatened Axis Army beach defenses hadn't turned up, and for the most part Army engineers—when their explosives were delivered on time— easily dealt with the pillboxes and obstacles encountered inland. It seemed as if the highly touted pressing need for Combat Demolitioneers had been greatly overstated, even by Admiral King. There was a tendency, in Navy circles, to regard the idea as a novel luxury but no burning necessity. Combat Demolitioneers might someday come into their own, but in the aftermath of Operation Husky very few in the upper echelons of the Allied High Command felt there was any reason to press the issue.

Chapter 13

Fort Pierce, Florida

He handed his orders across the makeshift desk, then stood to attention. "Chief Machinist's Mate Wallace, reporting for duty, sir."

"Stand easy."

As the officer behind the desk leafed through the top couple of pages of his orders, Wallace studied both the man and the room. He knew Lieutenant Commander Coffer, of course, from the Navy Yard, though he no longer had the same spit-and-polish look he'd had as CO of the Bomb Disposal School. Coffer was wearing green fatigues splattered with mud and showing dark streaks of sweat beneath the arms and down the front, and his wet hair was matted across his forehead. There were white salt stains on the black frames of his glasses, on each side at the temple and again at the curves above his ears. A steel helmet was perched on the upright of a straight-backed chair in the corner. His sleeves were rolled up to the elbows, and the nails of his hands were black with grime.

The headquarters for the NCDU training camp was better than the canvas tents that appeared to be the predominant architectural style of the Fort Pierce base, but only just, an obvious rush job of lumber, canvas, and scraps. A battered, black, wire-frame fan was perched on a rusty fifty-five-gallon drum in one corner, but it did not appear to be working. The air inside the building was sweltering, the humidity standing a hair under one hundred percent.

171

As he stood there, Wallace could feel his own uniform quickly becoming saturated with sweat. A small, green lizard clung to one wall of the room. A cloud of gnats buzzed and danced in the steaming air by the door. From close by, outside the ramshackle building, he could hear the shouted "One! Two! Three! Four!" of trainees going through physical calisthenics.

Finally, Coffer looked up from the orders. "So! More fresh meat. We're glad to have you here, Chief."

"Thank you, sir." He looked around the room again. "I think."

Coffer slapped a mosquito that had landed on his bare arm, leaving a bright, tiny streak of red. "It may look like Purgatory, son, but believe it or not it takes a special kind of man to get the kind of slot we're offering you. The Navy Cross—field experience in combat demolitions in North Africa. That's just the sort of material we need here."

Wallace's eyes widened. So that was it. He knew Coffer had requested him for this assignment, even blocked his own attempts for a transfer to Operation Husky. But he hadn't known why his old CO had wanted him so badly.

"I'm not so sure my Navy Cross counts, Commander. They gave 'em out to everybody who was there, you know. Party favors."

"I wouldn't exactly call the Navy Cross a 'party favor,' Chief." He closed the record folder. "Well, all I can say is welcome to Fort Pierce." He plucked at the front of his fatigue shirt and tugged at it as though airing himself out. "Or maybe I should say 'Welcome to Hell.' What have you been told about our operation down here?"

"Not a whole lot, Commander. Some scuttlebutt, of course. Wild stories about commandos and suicide squad stuff, but nothing solid. Security has been amazingly tight."

"Good. We want it that way."

" 'Loose lips sink ships,' sir?"

"If you like. They also get boys ground up into hamburger if the enemy knows they're coming ashore.

"Chief, you've been asked to volunteer for what could be the most important single contribution you, personally, could make to this war. By directive of the Chief of Naval Operations, we are down here in this God-forsaken swamp to create the Naval Combat Demolition Units. I want you to be one of my team instructors."

Somehow, Wallace managed to mask his disappointment. An *instructor!* "Yes, sir."

"You've got a damned impressive background, Chief. I knew I wanted you with us right from the start, when they first told me I'd be in charge of putting the teams together." Coffer looked up into Wallace's face and seemed to read the reluctance there. "Question? Out with it."

"Uh, sir, I was just wondering how long this assignment might last."

"I can't say yet. Why?"

"Well, sir, I'm not really instructor material." He could feel the pounding starting again behind his eyes. He clenched his hands at his sides, steadying himself, slowing his breathing. Gradually, the pounding receded. "I mean, I would really much rather have a combat assignment."

Coffer appeared to consider his request. "Mmm. Chief, you've been in the Navy long enough to know that our personal preferences don't pull much weight." He paused, leaning back in his chair and raking Wallace up and down with his eyes. Wallace had the uncomfortable feeling that Coffer was reading everything he was still holding inside.

If he was disappointed by what he read there, however, he didn't show it.

"Well, I'm not going to play games with you. I don't have the time." He tapped the orders on his desk. "You've been ordered to Fort Pierce, but the assignment I have in mind for you is strictly volunteer. You don't have to accept it. In fact, there are people right outside that door who would tell you that you're crazy to accept it. The fact of the matter is, I need you. Bad. Men of your caliber, with your experience and expertise, are rare, worth your weight in solid gold, because men like you can take a hundred raw, fumble-fingered kids and turn them into a hundred more men like you. I need someone who will take these kids in hand and make them into combat demolitioneers. You follow?"

"Yes, sir."

He rapped the top of his steel desk, which was showing pockmarks of rust peeking from beneath its flaking outer layer of battleship-gray paint. "I can promise you that this duty will be every bit as unpleasant, dirty, wet, stinking, exhausting, and out-and-out nasty as combat. The only difference is that nobody will be shooting at you.

"If you don't want to volunteer for this duty," Coffer went on, "no one will think the worse of you. I'll pass you on to the amphib base across the way. Captain Andersen—he's the CO of the Fort Pierce amphibious base—Captain Andersen might be able to use you. You could work for him until the paperwork goes through to send you back to the Navy Yard."

The pounding was still there behind his eyes, a faint throb. He remembered bullets slamming through the hull of the Higgins boat off the Oued Sebou. The heat was making him feel light-headed.

The prospect of working in some base personnel office, or of going back to disassembling bombs in D.C., was not pleasant. Wallace stood there, sweat dripping from the end of his nose and pooling up and down his spine as he considered the alternatives. "Might there be a chance of combat in the future, sir? If I stick it out here, I mean."

"Hell, yes. You don't think I want to stay in this swamp forever, do you? I don't expect you to either. My guess at this time is, we'll have our instructors rotate through here for nine months or a year, then assign them to a combat team."

"That sounds satisfactory, sir."

"You want to volunteer?"

"Yes, sir."

"Glad to hear it. But maybe you'd like to hear the bad news first, before you commit yourself."

"The bad news, sir?"

"What we're trying to build here is not just a demolition team. We're drawing our expertise from the Bomb Disposal School and the Seabees, but when we're finished here, we're going to have something brand new. Combat demolitioneers. Men we can ask the impossible of, and have them do it. The men's morale, their motivation, their esprit de corps is going to be the single most important element of the team. Understand?"

"Yes, sir."

"An elite fighting unit. To create it, we're going to have to instill the men with a sense of unit integrity. Chief, you've been in combat. You've been under fire. What's the most important thing to a man in a situation like that? What keeps him going?"

Wallace thought carefully about that one. Not bravery, certainly. He'd frozen in that boat off the North African coast but still managed to come through somehow. And every other man in the boat had been scared too. Leadership? Not really, though a bad leader could screw up a unit's fighting spirit faster than almost anything else. The other men . . .

"I'd have to say that it's the other guys, sir. The men on either side of you. You fight because you know they're there, that they're depending on you."

"Bull's-eye," Coffer said. "Each man in the unit has to trust every other man, to know that he's carrying his own weight, to know that all of them are in the same leaking boat together."

Coffer stood up from behind the desk. He was rail thin, and Wallace had the impression that he'd worked a fair number of pounds off an already lean frame in the past few months. When he grinned, it was like looking into the face of a skull, except that the eyes were fiercely, keenly alive.

"In this organization we're not going to pay as much attention to rank as they do in the rest of the Navy. More important than rank will be the knowledge that the guy telling you to do something impossible, something that's likely to get you killed, has been there too." The death-head's smile widened. "For that reason, all the instructors here, officers and men, are expected to go through the exact same training course."

"I . . . see, sir."

"When we started out down here, back, the first week of June, there were just four of us. Me. My Exec, Lieutenant j.g. Warnock. Ensign Francis. You remember Warnock and Francis from Bomb Disposal, of course."

"Yes, sir."

"There was also Lieutenant j.g. Wetzel. He started off as a civilian. Worked with one of the big powder companies, but he got a special commission to be our technical man.

"That was it. We started from scratch. One tent in the jungle, and the sand fleas were so bad you wouldn't believe it.

"As the new recruits started trickling in and we began to try putting the unit together, we decided that we needed some sort of organized training. Not just instruction in how to blow things up. Most of us knew something about that already. We needed a good, hard physical training program that would toughen us up and, more important, make us a team.

"As it happened, there's a Navy Scouts-and-Raiders group stationed at the amphibious base. That was part of the reason I chose Fort Pierce as the site for our training center. We went over there, sat down with some of their physical training instructors, and asked if there wasn't some way they could compress their eight-week training program into a single week. They were more than happy to comply."

"One *week?*"

"We call it 'Indoctrination Week.' The class starts off as a bunch of individuals. By the end of the week, if they make it through, they're a team. After that, they get to the fun stuff, playing with TNT, C-2, and primacord. If you want to be an instructor at this school, we'll expect you to go through the same training as the men. I did. All the other officers did. Believe me, it makes a difference to the men, knowing that whatever we tell them to do, we've been through it ourselves, just like them. Still want to volunteer?"

Another lizard had just dropped with a tiny, scrabbling plop from the ceiling onto some papers on the corner of Coffer's desk. Wallace stared at the beady-eyed creature for a moment, wondering just what the hell he'd managed to get himself into. The lizard stared back, somewhat unhelpfully.

The choice seemed plain. Accept Coffer's offer of mud, sweat, and "Indoctrination Week," with the promise of a combat assignment later on . . . or an uncertain future of desk jobs and Stateside assignments.

Unconsciously, he raised his hand and rubbed his eyes.

"Sir, I would like to volunteer for this assignment."

Coffer extended a dirty hand. "Outstanding. Welcome aboard!"

Thursday, 22 July 1943

Fort Pierce, Florida

They put Wallace into NCDU Class One-C, beginning the Monday after he arrived. The numbers of trainees still weren't large—there were only fourteen men in his group—but that was just as well since equipment was still in woefully short supply. There weren't enough rubber boats or paddles, not enough helmets, not enough shovels, and not enough explosives. Most of what they needed they borrowed from the Scouts and Raiders.

There was a hell of a lot of work yet to be done.

It was strange, Wallace thought, that he was already thinking of the NCDU as something more than a brief stop on his way to back into combat. For the past four days, he'd been studying every aspect of the intensified Scouts and Raiders course, thinking about what he might be able to add.

Marine sergeants and Navy chiefs with the Scouts and Raiders school paced up and down the beach, encouraging the trainees. "Crawl! Crawl, you turtles! You sand lice! Flatten down there, Collins, before I take a two-by-four to your tailbone. You wanna get your fuckin' ass shot off? Flat! On your bellies! Crawl! Now *freeze!*"

On the order to freeze, Wallace hugged the sand, not moving, scarcely breathing. A sharp pain nipped at his arm, followed by an intolerable itching, but he managed to hold his position. America, Wallace decided, did not need to worry about a German invasion of the Florida coast. The sand fleas and the mosquitoes on this beach were more effective than an interlocking network of coastal forts, steel-and-concrete obstacles, and sixteen-inch guns.

Once, two days before, a trainee had yelped and slapped his arm when a sand flea bit him. He'd spent the next several hours digging a grave for the hapless flea with his helmet. Since it had to be three feet deep, according to the gunnery sergeant running the class, it filled up with water before it was done ... forcing him to move to another site and dig another grave. When the hole finally met the instructor's grudging approval, the entire class had stood at attention in the hot sun, listening to the trainee's eulogy for the flea. After that, they'd all pitched in to fill the holes.

A thunderous explosion erupted in the sand twenty yards to Wallace's left, showering him with grit and giving him further incentive to worm his way even deeper into the sand.

The use of explosives was a new twist; there was still very little in the way of an organized curriculum for the NCDU classes, and the instructors were obviously making up a lot of it as they went along. Wallace had already thought of some ideas of his own, some new approaches that he might be able to apply once he got through his introductory week.

Another explosion thundered nearby. What was needed, he thought, was an intensive period of blast after blast that would simulate a heavy bombardment. If anything short of real war could separate the men from the boys, that would be it. He'd have to see if he could talk to Coffer when—

WHAM!

"Awright, you mud-sucking gooney birds, let's see you hit those dunes! Up that beach! Move it move it move it!"

So tired he could scarcely move, hammered by the incessant noise and storm of the explosives, Wallace staggered the next fifty yards.

At least no one was *shooting* at him.

Friday, 23 July 1943

USS *Alcyon*
Oran, Algeria

"All right, all right, move along, you goddamned wops!"

The line of Italian prisoners started moving up the gangway again, urged on by growling, irritable American sailors who made clear their resentment at being turned out to deal with these captive foreigners under the harsh noonday sun. Some of their charges grumbled, a few in heavily accented English, but most speaking incomprehensibly in their own singsong native tongue. It was yet another job the men of the NDU had drawn that bore no resemblance at all to their original assignment, but Henry Richardson, lounging in the

shade of a warehouse across the pier from the work party
and their prisoners, was perfectly happy with the whole arrangement. He had to fight back a grin as he remembered
how Commander Aimes had hoped he'd end up in a war
zone. Hell, this Naval Demolition shit was better than the
regular Seabee routine!

"Hank," Ensign Harold Culver said as he came up beside
Richardson, looking sweaty and irritable. As the unit's senior ensign, he'd been put in overall charge of the detail, but
he was having to divide his time between supervising on the
pier and trying to keep both the POW handlers ashore and
the Exec aboard the *Alcyon* happy. Richardson didn't envy
him his job. "I want you to pass the word to the men to
knock off harassing the prisoners."

"Harassing?" Richardson asked, raising an eyebrow.
"What are you talking about? Nobody's touched any of
'em."

Culver frowned. "The language, man! The epithets!
There's no need to insult the poor devils, for crying out
loud!"

Richardson didn't see what he was driving at at first.
Suddenly it dawned on him. "What, you mean calling them
wops? Come on, Harold, what's the big deal about that? It
ain't like they spikka da Inglish well enough to know what
anyone's saying to them anyhow."

"Some of them do," Culver said. He shook his head wearily. "You just don't get it, do you, Hank? Those men de-
serve a little dignity. How'd you like it if *they'd* captured
you and started treating you like dirt, huh?"

"It wouldn't be the same thing," Richardson protested. "I
mean, what are they going to call me? A damned Yankee?
That's something to be proud of!"

"You're hopeless, Richardson," Culver said. "However,
fortunately, you're also under my orders. So *pass the word*
that the name-calling and the insults are out of bounds. Let's
just get the job done so the rest of us can get in out of the
sun like you, okay?"

"Aye aye, sir, Ensign Culver, sir," Richardson said. He
moved out into the glare of the sun and down the line of
sailors posted between the Army trucks unloading the Italians and the gangway up to the *Alcyon*'s main deck, quietly

passing on Culver's instructions. It was clear most of the men felt the same way he did. And why shouldn't they? Everybody knew the Eye-ties were lazy, vain, and stupid, and their army was the laughingstock of Europe. They'd damn near got themselves beaten by a bunch of spearchuckers down in Ethiopia, and the Greeks had whipped them so bad in 1940 that Hitler'd been forced to bail out his pal Mussolini by sending in the Wehrmacht to save the day.

The Americans had taken more than three thousand Italians prisoner in the first two days of Operation Husky. As the transports of the invasion armada had finished unloading their troops and supplies, the prisoners had been ferried out to them for shipment back to Africa. Now, in Oran, they were being herded aboard the vessels that were due to head back for the States.

Richardson came up behind the last sailor in the detail, one of the demolition team, just as the man spoke up. "Hey, Guido," he called out cheerfully. "Hey, you're gonna be right at home when you get to the States. Half your family's probably already over there, and you'll find most of them right in prison with you doing ten-to-twenty on racketeering and tax evasion!"

One of the prisoners stopped suddenly, holding up the line as he turned to look at the jeering sailor. "Do not laugh at us," he said, his accent thick but understandable. "We are going to New York and you are going to Rome. Who has the better deal, eh? Think about it, my friend."

"All right, move along," Richardson growled, and the line started forward again. "And you, Simms . . . Mr. Culver wants you to quit baiting the prisoners. The faster we get 'em aboard, the sooner we can knock off and catch up on some rack time."

"Uh, yes, sir, Mr. Richardson," Simms said, looking confused. Perhaps he was remembering the night on the trip out from Norfolk when Richardson had entertained some of the NDU men with a whole string of Italian jokes.

Richardson didn't stay to help him sort it out. He was thinking of the POW's words. *We are going to New York and you are going to Rome.* Unfortunately, that wasn't true. The NDU would be sailing home in the *Alcyon* along with the prisoners, with orders to return to Camp Bradford in Virginia.

Once he would have been elated at the chance to get back Stateside, but Camp Bradford was part of Admiral Cartwright's bailiwick, and Richardson didn't relish the prospect of putting his head back into the lion's jaws quite so soon. But there didn't seem to be many options open right now.

Evidently Sicily had shown the Allied High Command that there wasn't as much to fear from Axis beach obstacles as they'd first believed. There were plans to follow up the resolution to the campaign in Sicily with another landing somewhere—the scuttlebutt said Italy—but it seemed the makeshift NDU was no longer considered necessary. So it was back to the States . . . and back to square one for Hank Richardson.

And that, he thought, was just too bad. He'd decided he really liked this NDU business. After that one day's work in Scoglitti there'd been no further call for demolitions experts, so Richardson and some of the others had been put to work unloading cargo from the *Alcyon* and doing other odd jobs. They'd spent a sleepless night aboard ship when Stuka dive-bombers launched a raid on the fleet, but even that had turned out more funny than dangerous. The bombers had come in high and released parachute flares, then dropped their bombs from above the level of the slowly falling lights to make it hard for the defenders to spot them. Between the bombs, the roar of aircraft engines, and the clatter of the ship's antiaircraft batteries, the noise had been fearful, but finally British flyboys in Spitfires had come north from Malta to fly high cover for the fleet. *Very* high cover, as it turned out. The American gunners, still on edge, had kept on firing, forcing the Spitfires to dodge friendly fire. At one point a clipped, ever-so-proper British voice had been heard to exclaim over the ship's radio, "If you sons of bitches don't stop shooting at us, we're going home!" After that the captain had passed the word for gunners to be a little more discerning when they picked their targets.

But aside from that one brush with the war, things had stayed quiet. And if that was the worst Richardson was going to encounter in Naval Demolitions, he was all for sticking with it. He'd have all the advantages of claiming the mantle of dashing war hero, but with none of the dangers. An ideal combination . . . except that it was coming to an end.

He rejoined Culver. "Hey, Harold," he said casually. "Do you think we'll be seeing any more action?"

The other ensign shrugged. "Who knows? It'd be pretty silly to ship everybody back to the States and then turn around next month and send everybody back out again for another op, but the War Department does crazier things than that just to work up an appetite before breakfast. Whatever you guys do, though, you'll be doing it without me."

"What do mean? You leaving us?"

"Lieutenant West got special orders covering me and Fagerstal along with the word to head back to Bradford. He showed them to us yesterday. Jack and I are being assigned to the regular NCDU gang down in Florida once we hit port. They've got me lined up as an instructor. So I guess I'll be busy shaping your replacements, whatever it is they decide to have you guys do."

Culver caught sight of *Alcyon*'s Exec and went across to talk to him, leaving Richardson in charge of the detail with plenty on his mind. Culver and Ensign Fagerstal had it made, he thought bitterly. They'd be going full-time into the demolitions program. If that assignment was anything like this easy duty, they'd just coast through the rest of the war.

And Florida was a long, long way from Norfolk. And from Admiral Cartwright.

Richardson frowned. He wanted a shot at a permanent NCDU slot. Well, according to the scuttlebutt he'd heard lately, the demolition teams were looking for Seabee volunteers. If he could swing it, he could set himself up on Easy Street for the duration. . . .

There would just be time after he got off duty today to send a cable or two back home before *Alcyon* was due to sail. He'd put in for a transfer to the NCDUs, all right . . . and he'd have his father and Senator Morton pull a few strings to make sure he got it, too. When *Alcyon* docked in Norfolk next month, his orders would be waiting for him.

Good-bye, war zone! Hello, sunny Florida!

Chapter 14

Monday, 26 July 1943

Bizerte, Tunisia

"Reporting as ordered, sir." Rand tried to hide his apprehension as he waited for Ensign Bucklew to acknowledge his arrival.

"Take a load off, son," Bucklew told him, gesturing to the chair in front of his desk. As Rand sat down, he wondered if the ensign's easygoing manner boded good or ill. It wasn't anything like their last face-to-face meeting, that much was certain.

Once the Allies had secured their beachheads in Sicily, the S&R team had been deemed unnecessary and shipped back to Bizerte on an LST carrying Italian prisoners. Rand had seen very little of Bucklew during the quick passage across the Mediterranean, but soon after they had started settling in to their new quarters, Bucklew had summoned him for a scathing interview.

That time, Bucklew had kept Rand standing rigidly at attention the entire time. He'd had plenty of opportunity to study Rand's detailed report of his role in Husky, and the ensign had not been pleased. "Your mission was to mark the beach," he had said harshly at one point. "Not to indulge in your personal taste for heroics. Not to blow up bunkers or get into gun battles with the enemy. It took a lot of guts to get in there under that machine gun and set up your light, Rand, even if it was a damn-fool stunt. I recommended one of the others for a Silver Star for coming up with the same idea in his zone. But I don't know if I should be putting you in for a medal for bravery or recommending your transfer back to the Philadelphia Navy Yard to get you and your damn-fool hero complex out of my unit!"

Rand had come away from that session shattered. They'd just received word that the occupation of Sicily would be followed in the fall by another amphibious operation, probably into Italy, but Bucklew had made it clear that he was reconsidering Rand's suitability to take part in the next attack.

Sitting in front of the ensign now, Rand wondered if his sudden change of attitude might have come with a decision to ship him out of the unit. Was this Bucklew's way of breaking the news to him gently?

An awkward silence dragged on for long seconds before Bucklew spoke again. "There's no easy way to break this to you, son, so I'll have to be blunt."

"You're ordering my transfer, sir," Rand said flatly.

Bucklew looked up at him sharply, surprise written plain on his face. "Transfer . . . No. No, that's not it, Frank." He looked away. "Hell, I know I was rough on you, but I was just trying to beat some sense into that head of yours. You're still on the team, even though you'll miss out when we hit Italy."

Rand didn't know whether to be elated or depressed. He wasn't leaving Scouts and Raiders, but . . . "Miss out, sir? Why?"

Bucklew cleared his throat. "I'm sorry to have to tell you this, son, but I got a telegram from the Red Cross this morning. Your mother was in an automobile accident. I'm afraid . . . I'm afraid she died Saturday afternoon. You're being granted a short period of leave to go home to be with your family. I'm afraid you won't be back to duty in time to join in on the training for Italy. You'll probably be posted to Fort Pierce as an instructor, at least until we see where you'll be most useful . . ." He trailed off.

The full impact of the words didn't sink in right away. His mother in an accident? What . . . ?

Then it hit him. His mother was dead. *Dead.*

"Easy, son," Bucklew said quietly. "Easy. I'm sorry I had to be the one to tell you."

Rand closed his eyes, trying to blot out everything, trying

to recall her as he'd seen her last. She'd been worried about the danger he'd be in with Scouts and Raiders, but she had been the one to die.

How could she be dead? It didn't make sense.

"I've already cut your orders, son," Bucklew said quietly. "You'll head home by military transport plane. Should be home before the end of the week. Take anything you can't bear to be parted from, and I'll have Havlicek gather up the rest of your gear and ship it to you later. Okay?"

Rand nodded vaguely, hardly hearing him.

"Look, son, this won't make things any better, but I've also had word from Washington about you. When you come back from leave, you'll be getting a promotion, and my recommendation for your Silver Star's been endorsed, too. You pulled a silly-ass stunt back there on Beach Yellow, but it was the kind of silly-ass stunt that turns know-nothing kids into genuine war heroes."

"Thank you, sir," Rand said quietly. He struggled inwardly to get control of himself, then stood up slowly. "Will that be all, sir?"

Bucklew nodded. "Yeah. You're dismissed." As Rand started for the door, the ensign spoke again. "And look, Rand . . . Frank. I wish . . . I wish you were going into Italy with us. It just won't be the same without a damn fool to help get us ashore." He mustered a thin smile.

Outside the office, with the door safely closed behind him, Rand slumped against the wall. His mind was a whirl of conflicting emotions.

He could hardly accept the idea that his mother was dead, that he'd never see her again. The memory of how she'd broken down and run from the room after he'd told her about his Scouts and Raiders assignment gnawed at his conscience. Except for the last stiff good-byes when he had boarded his train that same afternoon, that had been his last time with her. Rand had promised himself that he'd make it all up to her, but now he'd never be able to.

And the bitterest irony of all was the fact that he was up for the Silver Star for his part in Husky. That should have been his crowning moment. Instead it had left him feeling empty and confused. His mother would have wanted everyone in Marine City to know ... but now she wouldn't get the chance to brag about her son.

Rand tried to rein in his emotions and get control of himself. But though he stood straight and put on an impassive mask to disguise his feelings from the world, nothing could hide them from himself.

Friday, 30 July 1943

Port Huron, Michigan

Frank Rand adjusted his seabag on his shoulder, stepped down from the train, and looked around, frowning. The platform was almost empty, and for a long moment he thought his telegram with his arrival time must not have gone through.

Then he realized that Christopher Brown was coming toward him, waving. "Frank!"

He was thrown off his stride for a moment. He'd expected Sue to meet him in the Studebaker. . . .

Then he realized the car had probably been wrecked in the accident, and that brought back the whole reality of his mother's death all at once. He'd been able to keep it at arm's length during the trip home, with the novelty of flying in a Navy Douglas R4D transport, Bizerte to Casablanca, then on to London, Cork, Iceland, Newfoundland, and New York. And Rand had caught up on his sleep on the rail journey from there to Detroit. He had come to accept his mother's death in his mind, but from time to time something fresh would hit him from out of nowhere, like now.

Brown shook hands with Rand as he came up, his grasp firm and warm. "You're looking good, Frank. Damned good." He stepped back, studying him. "Another stripe, eh?"

Rand glanced down at the First Class insignia on the sleeve of his dress whites. "Yes, sir. I passed my test just before I went to the Med, and my name was on the list this month."

"Looks like you're really moving up." Brown's smile faded suddenly. "Son, I'm sorry about your mother. It was a rotten shame. She just lost control of the car on a bad curve, hit a tree ... it should never have happened, that's all. I wish there was something I could have done."

"Yeah, that's the way I feel. Thanks. ..."

Brown led him to his car and helped him stow his seabag in the trunk. "You came alone, Mr. Brown?" Rand asked as the other man started the engine and guided the big Oldsmobile out into the road.

"Nancy wanted to come, but I thought it would be better if you didn't have to make a lot of small talk on the way. You need some time to yourself." Brown glanced at him, smiling thinly. "Feel free to stare out the window and ignore me if you want to, son. I'll understand if you'd rather not have to make a lot of polite conversation."

"Thanks," Rand said quietly, grateful to the man for understanding. Had he been saddled with the need to make small talk with Nancy—or worse yet, with Mrs. Brown—he probably would have ended up saying something he'd have regretted later.

Rand took Brown at his word as they headed toward Marine City. The older man respected his silence almost all the way but finally spoke up again as they were taking the turn-off that led to the old Victorian house at the edge of town where the Rands had lived for three generations.

"Frank ... it's not my place to get into the middle of a family mess, but I think I ought to tell you. Your dad's taking your mother's death pretty badly. Nancy went over to see if she could help Sue out before the funeral Wednesday, and according to her your dad's having a hard time getting through this. I know you two haven't exactly got on over the years, and this'll probably make things worse. But if you don't mind me sticking my nose in where it doesn't belong, I'd suggest you cut him some slack. You're hurting ... but so is he. Try to remember it, son."

Rand nodded slowly. "I'll try, sir. Dad and I have always had a talent for getting under each other's skin." He looked out the window for a long moment. "But thanks for everything you've done. And said. It's nice to know *someone* cares."

His sister met him as he stepped up on the porch. She looked tired and drawn, and her eyes were red, but she somehow managed a smile. "Frank . . . oh, God, I'm glad they let you come home, Frank. It's so good to see you. . . ."

He dropped his seabag to hug her. "I wish I could've made it in for . . . for the funeral. Mr. Brown said it was Wednesday."

Sue Rand nodded. "We couldn't be sure when you'd make it. Or even if you could. I mean, we had your telegram, but Dad . . ."

He let her go. "No doubt Dad said I couldn't be relied on, or some such," he said bitterly.

His sister looked away, the forced smile gone completely now. "Don't start, Frank. Please. He said we couldn't be sure the Navy wouldn't cancel your orders if something came up. Give him *some* credit, won't you?"

He thought of Brown's words. "I'm sorry, Sue. You're right. Old habits are hard to break."

"Well, you just came out of one war zone. The last thing any of us need is for you to open another one here. Promise me."

"I'll behave," he said. "As long as *he* does. Where is he?"

"In town, right now. He's in charge of the local scrap metal drive, and there was a meeting of the committee tonight. They would have let him miss it, but I made him go. It's best when he has something to keep his mind off Mom."

Rand nodded. "I know. And I'm glad. I'll get settled in before he comes back. Maybe that'll make it easier to keep my promise."

Saturday, 31 July 1943

Marine City, Michigan

His father stayed late at his meeting and came home after Rand had gone to bed. Saturday morning, when Rand went down to the kitchen, he found Sue there alone, cooking him breakfast. Their father, she told him, had walked down to the diner for his morning meal. Frank couldn't help but assume that his father was deliberately avoiding him, though he couldn't imagine why. They'd never gotten along very well, but his father had never treated him like this before.

Nancy Brown stopped in as he was finishing the Saturday paper. Rand was immediately surprised at how much more serious she seemed now. Had seven months changed her so much? Or was she just being sensitive to his mother's death?

"Sue says you were in Sicily," she said. "What was it like?"

He hesitated. He hadn't actually been ordered not to discuss the doings of the Scouts and Raiders, but he knew Bucklew and others were reticent about what they did. Certainly if the Germans learned how the S&R units operated, they might tighten up their own security and make it rough the next time Bucklew and his men had to scout out a beach somewhere. Nancy wouldn't reveal anything deliberately, but still . . .

"It was tough," he said at last. "But I got through it okay." He didn't elaborate.

Rand almost chuckled as he considered his decision to keep his exploits to himself. Less than a month ago he'd been angry at missing the chance to attract a war correspondent's attention with some heroic deed. Now he had an attentive audience of one actually asking him for his story, and he was sure that his tale would be the perfect way to impress Nancy Brown. A lot of servicemen could get a girl into bed with lies a lot less dramatic than the true story he could tell of infiltrating an enemy-held beach and being right under the guns of a pillbox. Yet instead of taking advantage of a perfect opportunity to play up his heroism, he'd decided to stay closemouthed about it all.

It was ironic . . . and it also struck him as entirely unfair.

"Is something wrong, Frank?" Nancy asked. Then she colored. "I'm sorry . . . I should have thought . . . your mother . . ."

He shook his head. "Don't be sorry," he told her. "You didn't say anything wrong. I was just trying to think how to answer your question about Sicily best. There's a lot of stuff about it that I really shouldn't talk about, Nancy. You know, military secrets." He saw the look on her face and held up a hand. "It's not like they let me in on anything very important. But my outfit does some pretty dangerous work, and the less it gets talked about, even with you or Sue or anyone

here in town, the better. I mean, I don't think there are any
enemy spies in Marine City, or anything, but . . ."

She laughed. "Dad claims the government's convinced
half the people in town are spies trying to find out about the
boats he's working on. You know, all those nickel wetbacks
from Sombra. Obviously dangerous Nazi agents, every one
of them."

That made Rand laugh. Sombra was Marine City's sister
town, located just across the Saint Clair River in Canada.
The ferry that connected the two towns cost five cents, and
a nickel wetback was a Canadian who worked at a job on
the U.S. side and paid the ferry fee every day. The thought
of enemy agents slipping into the country by way of sleepy
little Sombra was about as silly as the picture of Nancy
Brown spilling important secrets to the Nazis.

"Well, whoever might be spying, it's best I don't go into
details. Don't take it personally or anything."

"I won't. And I won't ask any more questions." She
looked serious. "But I *am* interested, Frank. Really. I used
to think the war would never touch us here, but I know better now. First you went away, and got yourself wounded and
all. And then Eddie Lustman . . ."

He nodded. Eddie had been in his class in high school,
and like Rand he'd signed up soon after Pearl Harbor. He'd
joined the Army and died in the fighting at Kasserine Pass.

"I know, Nancy. You go along thinking nothing can really
touch you, not even the war, and then someone you know
buys the farm. Or you leave them safe at home and find out
they died when you were away."

"I never knew Eddie that well," Nancy said softly. "But
when he died, all I could think was that it could have been
you just as easily. I mean, you said you were joining such
a dangerous unit. And when Sue told me you were going to
the Mediterranean, well, the war seemed a lot closer than it
did before."

He looked into her eyes. There was a depth of feeling
there he'd never seen before, not even when they'd been
high school sweethearts. Nancy had always claimed to love
him, and she'd certainly spent enough time describing what
their life together would be like once they got married, but
it had always come across like some kind of light-hearted

game. Now, for the first time, Rand thought he could see some genuine feeling in her eyes.

She'd grown up a lot since he'd seen her last.

They talked for a while longer, skirting around his experiences and his mother's death. Then she had to go, and she left Frank Rand with a lot to think about.

He was still sitting and thinking when his father came home a few hours later. The elder Rand hobbled into the parlor with an unpleasant scowl on his face and sat down awkwardly in his favorite chair by the fireplace. "So," he said, voice quavering a little with ill-suppressed emotion. "So, you came home. A little late, but you came home."

"Ensign Bucklew, my CO, gave me leave as soon as the Red Cross telegram came in, sir," Rand said, instantly defensive. "I came as fast as I could. Flew halfway around the world. And I did let you know I was coming."

His father acted as if he hadn't heard a word. "You missed your mother's funeral. Maybe that was just as well."

Frank's frown deepened. "What's that supposed to mean? I wanted to make it in time. And you could have held it another couple of days so I could have been there."

"I didn't think that would be a good idea." His father fixed him with a harsh look. "You did enough as it was."

"What are you saying, Dad? What do you mean, I did enough?"

The elder Rand leaned forward in his chair, clutching his cane and jabbing it toward Frank. "You don't get it, do you, boy? Don't you know yet why she died? She wasn't paying attention to the road because she was upset about you."

"About me? But—"

"Not a single letter from you after Sicily got started up, and a lot of talk about all the tough fighting around Gela and all. She was sure you'd been killed or wounded and we just hadn't been notified yet. And she wouldn't listen to anything I said. So when she left for the market she was half blind from crying and she ran right off the damned road."

Rand looked at the floor, wincing under his father's words as if they were physical blows. "Dad . . . Dad, I'm sorry she was upset. I didn't write because . . . well, because I thought they were about to kick me out of S&R, and I didn't want to say anything one way or the other until I heard. I thought anything I did say would just upset her."

"Your precious Scouts and Raiders. Your ticket to being the big hero. You knew how upset she was when you joined. And she knew as soon as she heard about the invasion that you were in it. But you couldn't take the time to write and let her know you were okay because you were sulking over the idea of being kicked out." He had never heard so much anger and hate in his father's voice before. "Well, as far as I'm concerned you're the one who killed her. It's just that simple. You've got a right to use the house while you visit, I guess, but the less I see of you right now the better. You hear me, boy?"

Rand stood up, fists clenching at his sides. "I hear you," he said. His throat was so constricted he could hardly breathe. "I hear you. But I won't cause you any more trouble by staying here, that's for sure. Damn it, I would never have hurt Mom. Not for anything. *She* was always behind me, Dad. *She* never treated me like dirt. So don't lay her death at my door. You're the only one I ever wished would die!"

He stormed out of the room and out the front door, blind with anger and tears.

Sunday, 1 August 1943

Marine City, Michigan

It was dark, as dark as it had been off the Sicilian coast that night when Husky had started. Rand wasn't sure what time it was, wasn't entirely sure where he'd been or what he'd done in the hours since he'd slammed the front door of his house behind him after the fight with his father. He had a vague memory of sitting in Kelso's Bar, ordering one beer after another and staring down at the tabletop as if he might find the answers to all the riddles of life and death in the grain of the wood or the pattern of old gouges and stains.

He looked around, squinting into the darkness, his senses dulled from too much to drink on an empty stomach. Somehow his feet had carried him to Ward-Cottrell Park, the place where he'd led the Saint Stephen's High School Mar-

iners to their big win in the championship game just eighteen months ago.

The field and the bleachers were empty now. He was
alone, with none of the cheering crowds he remembered
from those glory days as quarterback of the football team.

His most vivid memory of the big game, though, was of
how his father had decided at the last minute not to come
and watch them play. His mother had done her best to explain it away, telling Frank his father's leg wasn't up to all
the walking they'd have to do. She and Sue had been there,
of course, but for Frank they weren't the same. He'd played
his heart out all year, led the team to the finals, all to make
his father proud. And it had all been for nothing.

All for nothing. . . .

What was the use in trying anymore? He could come
back from the war with the Medal of Honor and his father
would still push him away. Now the man even blamed
Frank for Elizabeth Rand's accident, and that burden was
more than he thought he could carry.

"Frank? Frank, is that you?" A flashlight beam blinded
him for a moment, so that he could hardly make out the two
figures coming across the field toward him.

"Frank, we've been so worried!" Nancy Brown rushed up
to him, threw her arms around him. She recoiled an instant
later. "You've been drinking. . . ."

"Yeah. So what?"

"We damn near tore this town apart looking for you,
Frank," his sister said, coming up alongside the other girl.
"If Nancy hadn't thought of how you used to hang around
the park to sort out your problems, we'd still be looking."

He looked up at her, his head swimming. "I didn't ask
you to come looking for me. Leave me alone. Just leave me
alone, for Christ's sake!"

Sue Rand exchanged a quick glance with Nancy. "I'll go
get the car. You stay with him." Then she was gone.

"Well, you're really a mess tonight, aren't you, Frank?"
Nancy said quietly, sitting down beside him. "Or is this how
all you Navy boys spend your free time?"

He didn't answer.

The silence stretched out awkwardly. Then Nancy tried a

new sally. "What happened to set you off anyway, Frank? Your dad?"

He looked up at that. "Did he send you? No, of course not. He probably didn't even know I left!"

"He knew, Frank," she retorted. "He didn't say much when Sue found out you were gone, but she said he was pretty broken up about it."

Rand shook his head. "Yeah, right."

"For heaven's sake, Frank, let it go! You can't keep punishing yourself because you weren't the son he thought you should be."

"And when did you find out so much?" he challenged. He'd never told anyone outside the family about his problems with his father.

"Sue told me. After you went to Florida. I had to know why you were so set on putting yourself in danger, and I pestered her until she told me all about it."

"Then you know he's never given me a chance. He's hardly admitted I'm really his kid! And tonight . . . tonight was the worst." Rand looked away, fighting back tears again.

She put her arm around his shoulders. "You can't change any of that now, Frank. But the way you're going you're just going to destroy yourself. And him, too. Maybe even Sue. Don't you understand? The only one who can change your father's mind is your father. You don't have to keep pushing so hard."

He laughed grimly. "Oh, I don't plan to anymore. I'm through trying to please him. I'm through with everything."

"Everything? You're even dumber than I thought you were. You need to put your fights with your dad behind you, Frank, but not like that. You've got to stop pushing for *his* sake and start doing a little bit for *you*. Look, just look at what you've done with your life already. You were a scrawny little kid once, but you grew up to be a high school sports star. And the Navy accepted you for one of their toughest jobs. Sue told me you're even up for a medal. You did all those things trying to please your father. Think how much more you could do with your life if you set out to do things because they mattered to you."

Rand looked at her. Though the light from her flashlight

had wreathed her face in shadows, her eyes were sparkling. He'd never heard Nancy speak with such intensity, such certainty, about anything. "You really think so?" he asked. "You really think I could do something that would make a difference? Nothing I've ever done has amounted to much of anything yet."

"Maybe not where your father's involved. But that's not the goal you should have. Isn't it about time you grew up and stopped trying to play the perfect son? You've got your own life to live . . . and maybe if you do that, and quit pushing yourself and everyone else so hard with impossible goals and expectations, maybe someday, your father'll come around on his own. And if he doesn't, Frank, it's not because you didn't try hard enough. Sometimes nothing you can do gets through to some people."

He didn't answer right away, but her words had set him thinking. Maybe he hadn't been meant to be a hero in Africa or in Sicily. And if he had come back with decorations and newspaper accounts and a batch of war stories as long as his arm, would any of it have made a difference in the way his father treated him? Probably not.

Nancy was right. He had to start living for himself, not for some forlorn hope of praise from his father. But that didn't mean just rolling over and dying, either. Frank Rand could still make a mark . . . for himself.

"When did you get so smart, huh?" he asked.

She shrugged. "Maybe when I found out the guy I was in love with wanted more than a doting little wife and a bunch of kids underfoot. I never really understood what it was that pushed you, Frank, maybe because I didn't want to see it. But the more I found out from Sue, the more I figured out about you. All the empty-headed little-girl tricks my mother told me would win me the man of my dreams just drove you away. So I grew up."

"And now you're telling me to."

"Somebody has to," she said softly. "Somebody has to show you the way."

He put his arm around her and pulled her close, and this time she didn't recoil. Their lips met.

They were still kissing when Sue got back with Nancy's car.

Wednesday, 4 August 1943

Port Huron, Michigan

He was back on the railway platform again, waiting for the train that would start him on his way to Fort Pierce once more. Nancy's father had driven them out, but Nancy and Sue both came along as well this time.

Frank hadn't seen his father since their fight. He'd slept in a cot at Brown's Marine and taken his meals with Nancy and her family. Except for a trip to the cemetery to visit his mother's grave, he had avoided thinking about family problems or the rift with his father. Nancy had been right to urge him to put all that behind him.

"I wish you were staying longer, Frank," Nancy told him. Her father and Sue had already said their good-byes and withdrawn, but Nancy remained at his side. "There's so much to plan . . . so much to talk about . . ."

"No plans yet, sweetheart," he said, shaking his head slowly. "I know a lot of guys get married right before they rush off to the war, but that's not for us. I want us to get married when we know we'll have a life together. It wouldn't be fair to you if I was sent overseas again and you ended up a war widow. I don't want anything like that to happen to you."

"So you'll risk letting me run around with all the local boys while you're away, is that it?"

"Half the local boys are nickel wetbacks," he said with a smile. "And I don't think your mother would approve of your running around with one of them. She barely handled the idea of me as a son-in-law!"

"Mom doesn't know you the way I do. And she still thinks the only way to trap a boy is to act like a complete idiot about everything except clothes and jewelry." She looked away. "You're not going back to the war? You're sure?"

"Not for a while, anyway. I'll be at Pierce for at least a few months. Then, who knows? I still don't want to miss out on the war, Nancy. It's important, and I've got an important job to do in it. Maybe my father will never be very proud of me, but I want you to be."

"I already am, Frank. And I want you to come back to me. Don't throw your life away on some empty gesture. I know you want to do your best, and you will. But there are more important things than medals or glory. Things that take more bravery than any heroics on the battlefield. Like doing the right thing . . . and doing it for the right reasons."

"I'll try." The distant whistle of the approaching train made them both look down the tracks. "I'll try," he said again. "I promise I'll come back when I can. Then we'll set a date."

"That's one promise you'd better keep. I love you, Frank. I love you. . . ."

Chapter 15

Monday, 16 August 1943

NCDU Training Center
Fort Pierce, Florida

"All right, ladies! Show a leg! Move it! Move it! Fall in! Line up right here. I said *move!* Atten—*hut!* Dress right—*dress! Front!*"

The big man in neatly pressed greens stalked down the lines of NCDU recruits, staring into each of the young, intense faces as he passed. Gunner's Mate First Class Steven Vincent Tangretti stood at attention, keeping his point of focus on the center of a palm tree thirty yards beyond the clearing where they'd been mustered. It was only barely light, the sun not yet above the horizon. Nameless things peeped and keeked and chirruped in the jungle around them. The air was still cool, though Tangretti knew full well that it would be blistering hot well before noon.

"Good morning, ladies," the big man said. He didn't raise his voice, but the words reached every one of the forty-two men standing at attention before him. "I am Chief Machinist's Mate Wallace, and this is the Navy Combat Demolition Unit Training Course. For the next several weeks, I will be your senior instructor. Lucky, lucky you. . . ."

It felt like Navy boot camp all over again, and that griped Tangretti. Why the hell did he have to go through this nonsense again? Across from the line of trainees, beyond the formidable figure of Chief Wallace, three men in combat fatigues and field caps stood with crossed arms and menacing grins. Only one of them, Tangretti noticed, had the globe and anchor stenciled above the right pocket of his olive drab shirt, but all of them looked like Marines—lean, hard, and very tough.

Tangretti wondered why they were here. He could think of several possible answers and he didn't much like any of them.

"You have volunteered to take part in an exciting new concept in warfare. That concept, the Navy Combat Demolition Unit, emphasizes teamwork . . . teamwork above all else. The NCDU will succeed if, and only if, each and every one of you is dedicated to the success, the survival, the *idea* of the team. This course will teach you to act and think as a team."

He gestured at the three men waiting behind him. "These gentlemen here are Navy and Marine personnel from just up the beach. Gunnery Sergeant Drake, Boatswain's Mate First Class Rand, and Gunner's Mate Chief Harrison. They are the class instructors. They are here to help you learn how to function as a team. Whatever you may think of them along the way."

A mosquito whined at Tangretti's ear, and he resisted the impulse to slap at it. This was suddenly distinctly un-funny. Who could he see to get a transfer out of here?

Except that he didn't have a lot of choice in the matter, did he?

"Starting on the right," Wallace bellowed. "Sound off by twos!"

"One!" "Two!" "One!" "Two!" "One!" . . .

Down the lines the counting went When the last man had

sounded off, Wallace continued. "Very well, you miserable swamp rats. Each of you ones, look at the two on your left. Twos, study the one on your right. Take a good, hard, long look."

Tangretti was a two. Looking to his right, he saw a small, blond-haired man with a wisp of a yellow mustache, and the healing scar of a recent cut just above his right eye. A full six inches shorter than Tangretti's lanky six-one, he had to look up to meet his eyes.

Tangretti didn't much like the looks of the little guy. He had a mean, hard look to him.

"Eyes—*front!* People, the man beside you is your partner, your buddy. You will look out for him. He will look out for you. You will eat together, sleep together, exercise together, and you will work your little tails off together for me and for the gentlemen behind me. If one of you screws up, you will both be punished. If one of you succeeds, it will be because both of you were working together. Am I understood?" There was a smattering of halfhearted yes-sirs. "I said, *am I understood?*"

"Yes, sir!"

Wallace paraded along the line again. He stopped in front of Tangretti. "What's your name? Sound off!"

"Sir," Tangretti snapped in his best parade ground manner. After a year with the Seabees, he'd almost forgotten how. "Gunner's Mate First Class Tangretti, sir!"

"Seabee?"

"Yes, sir!"

Wallace looked down at Tangretti's partner. "You?"

"Sir! Ensign Henry Elliot Richardson, sir!"

"Officer, huh?"

"Yes, sir!"

"Annapolis?"

"No, sir!"

"Civil engineer?"

"Yes, sir!"

"This here your buddy?"

"Yes, sir!"

"Well shit, you two look more like Mutt and Jeff."

There was a titter of laughter in the ranks. "Belay that!"

The laughter died away. Wallace continued to pace down the line.

"Some of you are enlisted men," he said. "Some of you are officers. For the duration of the next few weeks, there will be no rank here, no officers, no enlisted men. No saluting one another, no 'yes, sir' and 'no, sir,' unless, of course, you are addressing one of your instructors. You are, all of you, combat demolition trainees. The first four men down here, including the commanding officer of this unit, Lieutenant Commander Coffer, were all U.S. Navy officers, and they all went through this course. Just as I did. Just as you will.

"People, today is your first day of NCDU training. Many of you are here either from the Seabees or from the Bomb and Mine Disposal School. You are professionals, and you are very good at what you do. If you weren't, you wouldn't be here."

Right, Tangretti thought to himself. *Tell me another one! Some of us don't even want to be here. So much for volunteers!*

"As professionals, I'm sure you're sick to death of chickenshit. You enlisted guys who went through boot camp five, ten years ago, you're probably asking yourself what the heck you're doing going through that petty, ass-ragging torture again. You don't need it. I don't need it. So why the hell are we here?

"I'll tell you. When we get done with you here, you are going to be a *team,* an elite, highly motivated unit that can infiltrate an enemy island in a rubber boat, plant explosives on beach obstacles that haven't even been invented yet, blast a gap through a coral reef, mark a safe lane through the opening for our incoming invasion boats, and not even work up an honest sweat. You will be swift! You will be silent! You will be deadly!

"And how, you may ask, are we going to teach you all of this? Once again, I will tell you. Your instructors, Drake, Harrison, and Rand, are Navy/Marine Scouts and Raiders. They have been at this facility for some months now, perfecting ways and means of infiltrating an enemy island for the purpose of reconnaissance and to prepare the way for invasion forces. It has occurred to some of us here that the physical demands of our missions and need for teamwork are similar.

"First and foremost, we have asked them to boil down their eight-week fitness and conditioning course into a single week. We have tailored this course on the premise that a man, *any* man, properly motivated and with a good mental attitude, is capable of *ten times* the physical output normally thought possible. And you, ladies, are going to prove it, starting today.

"That week begins now. We call it 'Indoctrination Week.' Hit the deck! I said hit it! Push-up position!"

Startled, the trainees dropped full length on the ground, balanced on toes and hands. *"One!"* Wallace snapped, and the line of trainees lowered themselves to the ground, noses just above the pungently moist Florida soil. "Two! *One!* Two! Keep it going, ladies, keep it going!" Up, down, up, down, the line of straining elbows and sweat-soaked backs kept pumping as the early morning light grew steadily stronger.

"Ladies," Wallace added with a malevolent grin, "welcome to Hell!"

Wednesday, 18 August 1943

"Indoctrination Week?" Richardson snorted, trying unsuccessfully to wipe some of the mud off his face with an already muddy hand. "Hell Week is more like it!"

Richardson hated NCDU training from that first, memorable day, hated the course, hated the instructors, and, most of all, he hated this stinking, muddy, bug-infested swamp.

With the other men in his six-man boat team, Tangretti and four others, he was stumbling along through water that ran anywhere from ankle- to knee-deep, a broad, weed-clogged inlet tucked in behind the south end of North Hutchinson Island. The mile-and-a-half-wide stretch of sluggish, muck-bottomed salt water between the Florida mainland and the long barrier island stank of marsh and decaying vegetation. Mangroves, their bark gnarled and slick with slime, their branches drooping ponderously under the weight of vast green sheets of Spanish moss, towered overhead, blotting out the sky.

That was okay. Richardson and the others couldn't look at the sky now even if they'd wanted to. They were carrying a black, seven-man inflated rubber boat, balancing it on head and hands, struggling to remain upright as mud and tangled weeds and the clutching twists of mangrove roots conspired to drag the lot of them down into the brackish water.

"Watch it . . . damn it, *watch!*" a pipefitter named Grover just in front of Richardson shouted warning, then stumbled. A clump of Spanish moss dragged across the boat, slapping wickedly at the men underneath. Grover almost pulled them all down, but he managed to recover, then push ahead through the veil of wet, green strands.

"Aw, for cryin' out loud, Grover!" Richardson snapped. "Watch where you put your big feet!"

"And you'd better pick up your load, dickhead," Tangretti, struggling along at his side, told him. "I think you're just hanging to the bottom of this thing and letting us carry you along!"

"Funny, Tangerine. Very funny! What's the sound made by a flat tire? Wop-wop-wop-wop—"

"Shaddup, dickhead," Lieutenant Hadley snarled from a couple of feet behind him. "Save your breath for walking. And lay off that 'wop' shit. Tangretti's your partner and he's a member of this team."

Yeah, right. Like they all wanted to be here, pulling together, part of one big happy family. It was agony working with the taller men this way. He was so short that he couldn't take some of the weight on his helmet the way they could, and the effort to support his share of the life raft's bulk with just his arms left not only arms but back and shoulders in a white-hot agony after just a few hours.

Somewhere overhead, a bird shrieked and gibbered, a sound like hysterical laughter.

What in the steel-hulled hell made the psychopathic sadists running this circus think they could pack eight weeks of physical conditioning into one? It couldn't be done. It just couldn't! It had to be a plot, an attempt to kill the lot of them from exhaustion.

He wondered if Admiral Cartwright was behind this thinly veiled attempt at slow murder. Would the admiral kill twenty-four men to get at one? It didn't seem likely, somehow. There were surer, more personal forms of revenge. But . . . oh, *God!* He slapped a mosquito on his cheek, then looked in disbelief at the mix of blood and mud that came away on his fingers. Then the uneven motion of the men around him threatened to send the rubber boat toppling, and he reached up to steady it with both hands again.

Shit. They grew mosquitoes in these swamps the size of fucking vultures.

Mud clung to his pants and boots, dragging at him like wet concrete. As always, during these days that ran twelve to sixteen interminable hours each, he was in full combat gear: green fatigues that clung unpleasantly to his skin, combat boots that weighed a ton apiece after he'd squelched through a swamp knee-deep in mud, a steel-pot helmet that was wearing bare patches into three different spots on his scalp, and one of the bulky and uncomfortable inflatable vest harnesses suggestively nicknamed Mae Wests. The day had begun with reveille at 0430 hours, "zero-dark-thirty," with enthusiastic instructors rolling the men out of their tents with shouted choruses of "On your feet! On your feet! Show a leg! Move-move-move-move-*move!*"

. . . all to the amelodious accompaniment of someone pounding on a shit can lid with a billy club. There'd followed one solid hour of calisthenics—all of the usual toe-touching, knee-bending, push-upping, duck-walking, jumping-jacking nonsense he'd endured at OCS and Solomons Island and more, a *lot* more. Day by day, the load had been getting worse, with the instructors piling on more and more, as each day the trainees' fatigue-burned muscles had shrieked for relief. In the first two days so far, five men had dropped out—"DOR," they called it, "Dropped On Request." Richardson never heard what had become of those who'd quit. Scuttlebutt had it the S&R bastards ate them for breakfast.

After calisthenics, their instructors herded them into a three-mile march, double time all the way. Their route went east from the training camp, then doglegged south at the coastline, running south for almost a mile and a half through sand that dragged at boondocker-heavy feet and made thighs and calves ache like nothing Richardson had ever been forced to endure in his life. A mile and a half out. A mile and a half back. *Then,* with the sun just working its way high enough above the horizon that it could begin filtering through the dense vegetation surrounding the camp, breakfast—K rations, usually, though the men were generally so hungry by that time they didn't care much what it tasted like.

There'd been times when Richardson dreamed of thick, juicy, Porterhouse steaks, medium rare . . . with baked potato, and maybe a nice rosé.

What he did *not* dream about, very much to his surprise, was sex. During those first days, he had rarely even thought of girls. He was too damned tired, pushing too damned hard to think about much of *anything* except staying on his feet.

Of course, he would not be in this God-forsaken jungle forever. The word was, those who survived Indoctrination Week would get liberty in Fort Pierce. Watch out, girls, because Hank Richardson is about to hit the beach!

The question was, though, whether he was going to last the rest of the week—and whether he would have any strength left at the end of it. At the moment, just being able to take a hot shower and then sleep for a month on clean sheets seemed like sheer heaven. A girl, no matter how enthusiastic she might be, would just be in the way.

After the run and breakfast, most of the team's time was spent in, on, or under their black, bulbous-nosed, inflated rubber boat. They'd started out with seven boat crews of six men each. As men had dropped out along the way, teams had been consolidated and redistributed, until now there were six teams, four teams with five men and two with six.

Ideally, there were six men for each seven-man boat. The seventh man's place was occupied by 150 pounds of explosives, and with this load, the team launched their craft in the pounding, thundering Atlantic surf, paddled out against the waves for an hour or more, turned around and paddled back, beached amid the crashing waves, then portaged their laden rafts for miles across sand, across rock, across coral reefs, through jungle-thick mangrove swamps, through weed-choked inlets always, always fighting, racing against the

clock. The boat teams competed against one another, with
rewards and punishments meted out to winners and losers.
The teams carried names based on their leaders' names, like
Margrave's Mosquitoes and Ferguson's Frogs. Boat Team
Three, Richardson's team, was Hadley's Hurricanes, under
Lieutenant j.g. Victor Hadley.

Richardson was surprised that the other officers all
seemed to take the chickenshit harassment of NCDU training in stride. At OCS, Richardson had been taught that there
was an inseparable gulf between officers and enlisted men.
Officers ate at a proper officers' mess, off a good service
laid out according to protocol on white tablecloths. They
were served by respectful black or Filipino stewards and
mess mates, and they were expected to use the proper fork
at the proper time, to properly dab the corners of their
mouths with their cloth napkins.

*God, what I wouldn't give to eat off a tablecloth, with
napkins, again,* Richardson thought. *What I wouldn't give to
be* clean *again!* This mud and sweat and stink was for commandos and fools. A swarm of gnats buzzed angrily about
his face. He tried to shoo them away but the effort nearly
made him lose his grip on the raft.

"Steady there, Richardson," Hadley snapped. "Watch
what you're doing!"

"Get off my back, Lieutenant," Richardson replied in a
low, menacing voice that would have been louder if he'd
been able to drag in a deeper breath. "I've just about had it
with—"

A plop among the weeds to his left, a slithering, liquid
movement glimpsed out of the corner of his eye grabbed his
attention, interrupting him. Jerking his head left, he saw a
snake, coal-black, longer than his arm and nearly as thick,
swimming on the surface directly toward him with long, undulating twists of its body. As it came closer, its ugly, flat
head split wide, revealing a cotton-white mouth and fangs
as long as a fingernail.

"Ah! Snake!" Richardson screamed. "Snake! *Snake!*"

He stumbled backward, colliding with Tangretti. Unbal-
anced, the rubber boat tipped over, and all six men collapsed into the muddy water in a thrashing tangle of arms
and legs

Tangretti broke the surface, spluttering. "*Jesus*, Richardson!"

Richardson was still trying to scramble backward through the water, splashing wildly. He collided with the raft, lost his footing and went under. When he splashed his way up to the surface again, the snake was twisting straight toward his face.

A brawny arm snapped out, grabbing the snake behind its head and yanking it from the water. Tangretti flicked his wrist, and the snake was gone, arcing away over the reeds into the swamp.

Slowly, his knees trembling, Richardson rose to his feet. He was breathing hard, and he could still feel his heart hammering away beneath his breastbone. "My God, Tangretti . . ."

"Water moccasin," Hadley said. "Cottonmouth. They're deadly. The one poisonous snake that'll actually come after you."

"Sure looked like he took a liking to Richardson," Engineman First Class Jarvis said. A Navy Scout who'd transferred to train with the CDU team, he had, inevitably, picked up the nickname "Jarhead" from his previous close association with the Marines.

"You got a real good pitching arm, there, Tangretti," Hadley said. "I think you threw that thing halfway to Africa."

"How about you, Richardson?" Grover asked. "You okay? You get bit?"

"Naw," Richardson said. He felt his cheeks burning. He'd acted like a squirming coward in front of the others, and he was ashamed.

"Bet it scared him out of ten years' growth," Jarvis said, grinning.

"Okay, okay, guys," Hadley said. "We're way behind sched. Let's get this raft airborne again and make some distance."

Working together, they manhandled the rubber boat and its load aloft once more and began slogging through the swamp toward the southeast edge of the inlet. Already the water was shallower, the mud a bit firmer beneath their boots. Soon they were scrambling up a slippery bank held together by weeds and mangrove roots, then finding their feet on the solid ground above, where Wallace was standing with a whistle and a stopwatch, urging them on to the next mark in their run. Five more minutes brought them out of the trees and over the top of a ridge, an old sand dune anchored by beach grass. Beyond, the ocean sparkled from horizon to horizon, an impossibly bright, metallic blue sparkling in the sun.

"Man," Jarvis said, panting hard after the climb over the dune. "Are we first? Did we beat 'em?"

"Don't know, Jarhead," Hadley said. "And we won't know until we get there. C'mon, let's get a move on."

For whatever reason—gods of fate, the stupidity of supply officers, or the capriciousness of commanding officers—their rubber boats were supplied with only two paddles apiece. The men had fashioned four more by whittling down pinewood planks of the appropriate size. These worked well enough but still left a lot to be desired, raising blisters on the men's hands that almost immediately broke. The sores stung and smarted with the constant immersion in seawater. The expedition culminated with a wild surf ride into the beach, with the men struggling to keep the boat and its load of explosives from overturning, and then a long, soggy march back to camp, with the rubber boat carried overhead.

That day they came in third out of six boats.

Later that night, Richardson and Tangretti were standing watch together, patrolling the camp perimeter on a four-hour stint of fire and disaster watch. Stars glittered in impossible profusion overhead. After their first couple of circuits, they found a tree, leaned against it, and conversed in low whispers.

"Hey," Richardson said. "I've been meaning to say thanks for getting that snake today."

"No problem. That's what buddies are for, right?"

"I thought you were a city kid. How the hell'd you learn about snakes?"

"Hell, I grew up in New York City. I don't know nothing about snakes. Now if it'd been a rat . . ."

"New York, huh?"

"Yeah, but I got out as quick as I could. I ended up in California with my own business."

"Then the war came, huh?"

"Yep. Then the war came."

After an uncomfortable silence, Richardson decided to press ahead. "So how 'bout it, Tangretti?" he asked. "How'd you wind up in this chickenshit outfit?"

Tangretti shrugged in the darkness. "Basically, they gave me a choice. This or some hard brig time."

"Oh, Christ. Not you too?"

Tangretti looked across at him. Richardson could sense his grin in the darkness. "Same old story, eh? What'd you get caught for?"

"Banging the admiral's daughter."

"No shit?" His eyebrows arched higher. "Who caught you?"

"Who else? The admiral. In flagrante delicto, as they say."

"Man, oh, man, Richardson. That sounds like one shit-headed stunt."

"Well, it seemed like the thing to do at the time. So they packed me off to Sicily, and that was such a cakewalk I thought this would be easy duty. Boy, was I stupid. Your turn. What'd you get caught doing?"

The other man spread his hands. "It was all a perfectly innocent mistake. Could have happened to anybody."

"Right."

"It was! I was with the Seabee detachment at Bora Bora. The Bobcats?"

"I heard about them. Good outfit." Bobcats was the code name for the first big Seabee construction job, building ship-fueling facilities and a runway at Bora Bora, one of the remote Society Islands three thousand miles south of Hawaii.

"Yeah, but that was a real fucked-up operation, let me tell ya. The cranes we had to use for unloading cargo from the barges onto the beach were buried so deep in the transports' holds we had to unload by hand for three weeks before we could get to one. The dumb-ass jerks in the supply depot back in San Diego had loaded wheelbarrows without wheels, welding torches but no masks, forges but no coke, and the wrong fuckin' kind of trucks. We didn't have enough nails, we didn't have spare parts for the trucks we did have, and we didn't have enough shovels."

"Sounds typical for the Navy."

"You got that right. Well, anyhow, I was working with the detachment assigned to setting up a machine shop at Bora Bora, see, and there we are without a bench press, without drill bits, without a band saw, without tin snips, and without welding masks. Now, back before I joined up, I worked with a machine parts company out in California, y'know? And I used to have some pretty good customers over in New Zealand and Australia.

"So I cumshawed a ride down to Auckland. Gave a PBY pilot a bottle of scotch and half a dozen pairs of silk nylons to fly me over. Then I got in touch with some of my old customers in Wellington and Christchurch. Sure enough, the war had left 'em pretty much high and dry. All the young men had gone off to fight with Monty in North Africa, and a lot of the equipment I'd sold 'em was sitting around idle, gatherin' dust.

"So I looked up a supply officer at the U.S. Navy repair depot back at Auckland, and I gave him three bottles of scotch, a case of Coca-Cola, a dozen pairs of nylons, two pounds of coffee beans, some ladies' frillies, and a half-carat diamond engagement ring for his signature on a requisition officially purchasing the stuff I needed from, quote, local civilian sources, unquote."

"Shit, where'd you get all that stuff?"

"Oh, different places. Anyway, for another bottle of scotch, a chief I knew at the base was willing to go collect the stuff, crate it, and load it aboard a freighter that was due back in Bora Bora four weeks later. I hitched a ride back with another Catalina. Four weeks later, hey! The ship comes in and our machine shop's in business!

"That was just the start of things, though. See, with the only functioning machine shop on the island, we could do lots of extra little jobs for other Seabee outfits. Pretty soon we were doing stuff for the regular Navy, the Marines, pretty much everybody who came along. If the gyrenes had some piece of equipment we had a better use for, well, we'd offer to do some special work for 'em on our own time, see ... like rig 'em up a windmill-operated washing machine, or cut, polish, and engrave a commemorative plaque they were giving to their CO. After a while, we had the best-equipped machine shop in the whole damned South Pacific."

"Hell, it sounds like you had it made."

"Yeah, well, it couldn't last. See, my main stock in trade was scotch, bourbon, stuff like that. We had a still goin', of course, for drinkin' liquor, but you just can't beat twelve-year-old Dewar's, right? 'Specially when it's some major or commander you've got to grease. My supply was runnin' kind of low by then. So I traded some special shopwork to the sailors aboard a stores ship in exchange for a couple crates of oranges. Then I traded the oranges to a guy I knew over in Espíritu Santo for a case of scotch."

"And they caught you."

"Christ, not only that, but the guy who traded me the scotch didn't tell me it came from some admiral's personal stores. A snoopy adjutant type caught me unloading the stuff from the B-17 after I landed back in Bora Bora. Hell, they thought I'd *stolen* it, and they were threatening to court-martial me.

"Well, my CO was an understanding kind of guy. He knew I hadn't stolen the stuff, and he knew I wouldn't rat on the sailor who had. So he cut me a deal. I could volunteer for this new outfit they were putting together in Florida, or I could face the admiral at Espíritu Santo and his charge of grand theft. If I volunteered, my CO figured he could tell the brass that I'd already been shipped out, headed for dangerous, secret, and distant duty, and the injured party wouldn't pursue the matter." He spread his hands again. "And here I am."

"Sounds to me like they gave you the short end of the stick."

"Nah. It ain't so bad, the streets couldn't break me and these guys won't either. Of course, I feel kind of fenced in right now. Out of touch, you know? I can't get to my usual sources of supply to arrange for all the finer things in life."

"You know, Tangretti," Richardson said speculatively. "Seems to me there's a pretty decent source of supply right over there at the S&R joint. I understand their HQ used to be a casino."

"What happened? Not enough paying clients attracted to this here island paradise?"

"Maybe the snakes and alligators got too discriminating. Anyway, bet we could find some good stuff over there."

"What'd you have in mind, Richardson? Booze? We get caught with shit like that and—"

"Actually, what I was thinking of was *paddles.*" He held out his hands, palms up, showing the broken, raw-fleshed blisters on the webbing between his thumbs and forefingers. "Those makeshift paddles we've been using for the rubber boats are tearing my hands to hell. Maybe we could find something better over there."

"Hmm," Tangretti eyed the smaller man, then looked down at his own cracked and blistered hands. "Y'know, Richardson, you just might have something there. . . ."

Thursday, 19 August 1943

No one seemed to notice when, the next morning, there was a full complement of six oars to each of the six rubber rafts. The instructors, even the S&R personnel, ignored this magical appearance even when a lieutenant from the Scouts and Raiders School came by looking for some missing equipment. The paddles were all carefully stowed by that time, and the missing gear was never recovered.

Three more men DORed before the midday meal, however. Grover was pulled from the Hurricanes to fill an empty slot with the Mosquitoes. That left the Hurricanes with five men.

Richardson wasn't certain what had changed between him and the other men in his boat crew, but somehow he felt closer to them now. Maybe, he thought, it had to do with him and Tangretti exchanging their life stories. Or maybe it had something to do with that damned water moccasin. By next morning, everyone in the NCDU class, including the instructors, was calling him "Snake." He didn't like it at first, but he soon got used to it. Hey, he reasoned, it was better than "dickhead," which had been on the way to becoming his permanent moniker in this outfit.

Receiving the new nickname was, in some sense, a rite of passage for Richardson. Until then, he'd thought of little save how he could escape from NCDU training—without having that escape brought to the notice of Admiral Cartwright. Now, though, it felt as though he'd crossed some kind of invisible, even mystical barrier. His thoughts focused now simply on lasting out the week.

And after that? Well, he'd think about later, after he'd beaten Hell Week. If Tangretti was going to make it, the Snake wasn't going to quit either.

The next day, during another march through another swamp, this one in the marshy savannah on the mainland south of Fort Pierce, an eight-foot alligator had slipped off a rotten log with a gurgling splash and started moving toward the team. This time, it was Tangretti who screamed and pointed and backpedaled, while Hadley yelled to the others to drop the raft and climb aboard. Whether that was a sound strategy for escaping alligators or not was never tested; Richardson, tired of swamps and tired of mud and especially tired of the damned arrogant wildlife, had snatched up one of the new boat paddles and smashed it across the beast's snout with a lung-tearing roar. The alligator, unused to prey that could actually fight back, vanished with a white-water lash of its tail.

For the rest of the day, the team had experimented with a new nickname for Richardson, "Gator," using it on him as though they were trying it on for size. Before long, however, they decided that "Gator" was better for Tangretti, a name that lent itself to being twisted into "Tan Gator." So far as Richardson was concerned, they all went back to calling him "Snake."

That name did seem to fit him best.

Chapter 16

Saturday, 21 August 1943

NCDU Training Center
Fort Pierce, Florida

They called it "So Solly Day."

On Saturday, the last day of Indoctrination Week, there were twenty-nine men left out of the original forty-two, organized now into four boat teams with six men apiece and one team with five. That day began earlier than usual, with the men awakened from an exhausted sleep by shrilling whistles and thumping garbage can lids and a steady barrage of bellowed orders. Before the sun was up, they'd embarked in ramped Higgins boats, which chugged their way in line ahead out through the Fort Pierce Inlet, around the southern hook of North Hutchinson Island, then up the coast a mile beyond the surf line. The sun was just peeking up through a low-lying bank of red-and-purple clouds at their backs when the boats swung their noses toward the land, lurched forward through the booming surf, and ground up against the beach.

The men, dressed as usual in boondockers, helmets, fatigues, and Mae Wests, pounded down the ramps toward the sand. Before the first man hit the water, however, the entire beach ahead of them vanished in a solid sheet of orange flame and the ground lurched beneath their feet. Smoke and sand whipped through the morning air, and the shock of the detonation slapped at them like a living thing.

Instructors were right there, chivying them on, herding them, driving them. "Go! Go! You want to die here? *Go!*"

Crawling now, the men advanced up the beach as more explosions thundered and boomed around them, each blast seemingly closer than the one before, their faces raw now with the sandblasting of wind-borne grit.

They'd known this was coming, but it was a shock nonetheless. "So Solly Day" was the culmination, the climax of Indoctrination Week, a testing of courage and spirit and toughness that none of them had ever faced before in his life.

Over the top of the dunes behind the beach and down the other side into the muddy swamp beyond. Here the explosions continued as instructors tossed half-pound blocks of TNT at the trainees. The word was that they weren't supposed to drop those improvised grenades closer than ten feet to any of the men, but Richardson was amazed at how tiny a distance ten feet really was, when that was all that separated him from the ear-ringing crack of high explosives.

"Move it, Tangretti! Move your ass or get it blown off! Move! Move! Come on, Snake, you look like a tired old woman! *Hump* your ass! *Move* it! *Move* it!"

Richardson moved, elbows and knees flailing, pushing ahead through a foot-deep scum of swamp mud and dead vegetation. The smell was appalling, a mix of the now-familiar stench of living mud and the stinging, caustic stink of TNT. Each explosion now brought a fine spray of water and mud as twenty-pound charges thundered and roared, hurling huge geysers into the sky about him and the other team members. Out of the mud now, they rose and charged ahead, as Wallace and Rand stood on either side of a trail, waving them on.

"Move your goddamn ass, Snake. Go! Go! *Go!*"

Just in time he saw the slender stretch of a tripwire across the trail and leaped over it. Turning, he waved at Tangretti, who was coming just behind, flagging him down, pointing out the wire, guiding his partner past the trap. A moment later, another trainee hit the wire, triggering a small charge off to the side of the trail that must have left the poor guy's ears ringing for an hour.

"Over here! Move it, move it! Over here! Into the pit!" God, that was Coffer himself waving them on, and the son of a bitch actually seemed to be enjoying this!

Before the morning had turned to afternoon, all of the trainees' ears were ringing. The explosions were incessant as they ran, as they crawled, as they lumbered ahead through a makeshift obstacle course of ropes and tires and a cargo net strung fifty feet up in the air. Much of the course consisted of nothing more than mud; the rope climbs and swings and log bridges all had a pool of thick, clinging, wet mud waiting underneath, ready to catch each trainee who fell.

And still the explosions were going off, a steady background of raw, thundering noise. Richardson reached up and grabbed a four-inch hawser that had been strung across a lake of mud, hauled his legs up high enough to hook them over, and began to painfully hitch himself across the gulf. An explosion in the mud to one side slammed at him and he clung desperately to the hawser. "Keep going, Snake! Go! Go! You're holding up the parade!"

Another explosion, closer this time. Hand over hand, he dragged himself along, dangling upside down like a muddy, demented tree sloth. He *felt* like a sloth, heavy with mud, lethargic with exhaustion, but they wouldn't let him stop, wouldn't let him even slow down.

Wham!

He fell, landing on his back in a two-foot pool of mud. He rose, spitting mud, scraping the black stuff from his eyes and mouth. "This way, Snake! Keep going! *Run!*"

He waded from the pool, then broke into a stumbling, foot-heavy shamble. Others crowded along with him, as cold, as wet, as muddy as he.

The trainees, those who were left, ended up in a muddy pit, shivering with cold and exhaustion, huddled together as blast after blast after ringing blast went off around them, a hell of noise and shock and muddy rain.

The first few hours of steady detonations scraped Richardson's nerves raw. He was jumpy; he twitched and flinched at each new blast and felt like he was perpetually balanced on the balls of his feet, ready to leap in any direction at an instant's warning. After a time, however, he began to get used to it, to think of it as a game. The instructors were trying to get to him, trying to make him quit. All he had to do was last it out, to last *them* out, and he would win.

The trainees ate their midday meal together, sitting in the mud as their instructors continued to toss half-pound charges around them. Sometimes there would be pauses in the explosions and Richardson dared to think that perhaps the worst was over, and then the explosions would continue again. Afterward, there was more marching, more crawling, more running through the obstacle course, and an endless crawl through the mud beneath coils of barbed wire, as a Marine gunnery sergeant fired bursts of live ammo from a water-cooled .30-caliber machine gun a foot above their heads. Finally they ended up jumbled together in yet another muddy pit, digging themselves water-filled foxholes with their helmets as the blasts continued to bang and ring and roar around them.

Four more men quit. One of them, a guy from the Mosquitoes, stood up suddenly, hurled his helmet down in the water, and stumbled away with tears streaming down his face. For Richardson it was no longer a game. The steady, grinding ordeal dug and twisted at the very core of his being, trying him, testing him, forcing him to bend until he broke. . . .

"Atten-*hut!* Fall in! Fall in! Everyone, fall in at attention!"

There was something missing. Richardson couldn't quite place what it was, but something was definitely wrong. He looked around stupidly, trying to decide what it was. The other men around him, the other members of the team, all looked as shocked and bedraggled as he felt, as black with mud and grime as some oil-covered survivor of a torpedoing at sea. They looked dazed, not all there. It was difficult to stand upright, and none of them even approached the erect posture of attention. The mud pit was wreathed in stinking gray smoke.

It was quiet, that's what it was. For a moment, he wondered vaguely if his hearing was gone . . . but he could still hear the instructors calling the men to attention, heard the splashings and squelchings of the other men in the class rising from the mud like shambling, prehistoric beasts.

Coffer was there at the edge of the pit, looking impossibly pressed and clean and neat. So were all of the instructors.

"Men, the purpose of So Solly Day is to weed out any among you who has an inherent fear of explosives. As members of the Navy Combat Demolition Unit, as Demolitioneers, you will be expected to carry out your assigned tasks in the face of fire every bit as intense as what you have experienced here today. You men, *all* of you, can go on from here certain in the confidence that you *can* carry on, no matter what the odds, no matter what the conditions.

"NCDU Class One-E, secure from Indoctrination Week!"

"Secure from Hell Week!" someone yelled in echo, and then the men were cheering, laughing, pounding each other on the back. Some simply collapsed where they stood, too exhausted to cheer, slumping back again into the mud from which they'd just risen. Some helped each other stagger from that field. Twenty-five out of forty-two had made it, an attrition rate of forty percent.

He'd made it. It took Richardson several long, dazed moments to comprehend that blunt, simple fact. He'd *made* it! Tangretti, barely recognizable beneath his mask of mud, grinned at him, pounding his shoulder so hard that Richardson nearly fell. Staggering, Richardson opened his arms wide and the two men hugged, tired and battered and jubilant.

One-Eyed Jack's
Fort Pierce, Florida

There was not a lot to Fort Pierce, a sleepy, tiny town hemmed in against the sea by the flat, vast, fetid sprawl of the Florida Everglades. Since the Navy had arrived, of course, parts of the town had begun to liven up, as restaurants, bars, tattoo parlors, and less decorous establishments sprang up to take advantage of the military trade.

Liberty had been granted to all of the Class One-E survivors of Hell Week. Ten of them, too exhausted by the previous week's activities to even think of doing anything but luxuriating in a hot shower and then hitting their racks, had elected to remain on base. The rest, exhaustion forgotten at least for the moment, had gone ashore—a term which by long tradition referred to leaving a Navy base as well as a ship. Freshly shaved and showered, wearing clean uniforms

of various types, the NCDU trainees had caught the liberty
bus that shuttled back and forth across the bridge connecting Fantasy Island, as the trainees called it, with Fort Pierce.
Descending from the bus, they streamed into town on foot,
whooping and howling and, in general, noisily alerting the
local population to the fact that *real* men had just arrived.

The fifteen NCDU trainees were not the only servicemen
ashore, of course. Men from the Scouts and Raiders School
were in town too. For the moment, the two groups kept a
cool but courteous distance from one another as the newcomers began to disperse. In small, tight knots of happy
men, they divided themselves among the various bars and
eating joints that lined the Fort Pierce waterfront.

One-Eyed Jack's was a seedy-looking bar on South Indian River Drive, a dimly lighted, typically shabby servicemen's hang-out with heavy cedar rafters and pillars, fish
nets and hawsers draped from the walls, and cane-backed
chairs that showed signs of numerous past repairs. The pro-
prietor, a beer-bellied giant who really was named Jack and
who indeed did have only one eye, kept the peace with a
black-painted billy club kept stashed behind the bar.

Richardson and Tangretti, Grover and Jarvis swaggered
into Jack's with what they thought were appropriately salty,
rolling gaits. The other three were all resplendent in their
Navy whites, complete with square-knotted black necker-
chiefs. Richardson had been uncomfortable with the idea of
going ashore wearing his ensign's uniform. He was hitting
the beach to celebrate with his fellow trainees, after all, and
he didn't want to find himself segregated from them by the
gold ensign's stripe on his shoulder boards or damping their
fun. He'd seen nothing in the published regulations about
not being allowed to wear fatigues, so long as they were
neatly pressed and clean, so that was what he'd worn, with
a green field cap as his cover.

Cigarette smoke hung beneath the rafters in a thick, blue
fog only slightly stirred by the big-bladed twirl of a large
ceiling fan. There were a handful of people already there,
including, Richardson was delighted to see, several good-
looking girls.

He'd been pleased to discover that, despite some doubts
during the past week, he retained his enthusiastic interest in

the opposite sex. Still, first things first. Walking up to the bar, he ordered a whiskey, neat, which he downed fast and hard, savoring long-missed sensations, the heat of liquid fire searing down his throat and the pleasant roaring in his ears.

Only then did he turn to survey the local talent.

Most of the women in the place appeared to be already spoken for. There were several Marines in the place, freshfaced youngsters, most of them, probably from the S&R school. One Marine was sitting at a table toward the back of the place, next to a stairway leading to the upstairs rooms Jack reputedly kept for the girls who worked there. He had a pretty, young, dark-haired woman on his lap. She was sitting with her legs tucked up off the floor, and her skirt had ridden up high enough that the backs of her thighs were exposed. Richardson could just glimpse a pretty triangle of sheer red lace beneath the skirt's hem.

"Hey, Gator," Richardson said, nudging the man beside him. "Get a load of that."

"Pipe those gams," Grover said.

"Yeah," Jarvis agreed. "Nice legs."

"I like the red panties," Richardson said. "Wouldn't mind havin' them for ... for my collection."

"Collection?" Jarvis asked. "What collection?"

"Never mind, Jarhead. Ancient history. Bartender? Another one. Leave the bottle, okay?"

There was music coming from somewhere, and two couples were slow dancing in the corner. The Marine and the girl were kissing. She had her arms locked around the back of his neck, while one of his hands was restlessly exploring her nylons.

"Y'know, Gator, I sure wouldn't mind havin' me a piece of that. How 'bout you?"

"Looks like she's taken, Snake."

"Aw, she just ain't seen the competition yet." They drank a while longer, working their way down through the bottle. Grover advanced the opinion that they ought to get something to eat, but Richardson was a lot more interested in the girl.

"This presents us with a facsi ..., with a fascinatin' problem in tactics," he explained carefully to the others. He was surprised at how clearly he was thinking, at how

sharply his mind was working. Hell Week and half a pint or
so of whiskey on an empty stomach hadn't slowed him up
at all. He held up another glass and examined it critically.
What was it the Marines were always saying? *"Gung ho!"*
Down the hatch.

"Aw, just wait a bit, Snake," Tangretti told him. "It's
early, yet. There're bound to be some more girls come in
soon."

"Yeah, but I like *that* one."

"Grover's right," Jarvis said. "Let's go get somethin' to
eat."

"You guys just don't think I can do it, do you?"
Richardson said. "Well, for your information, I am an expert
on women. I could walk over there, and in fifteen minutes
I could have her eatin' outa my hand, or any other designated part of my anatomy."

"Yeah, yeah," Jarvis said. "I've heard all this before."

"Bet you," Richardson said. "Bet you twenty I make it
with her. Tonight."

"Shit," Tangretti said, squinting at the couple. "If you ask
me, she's the kind you *pay* twenty for the privilege. So
what's the point?"

"What, her? She just looks like a nice, local girl. Think
I'll go talk her up."

"Hey, we don't want no trouble, Snake," Grover said.

"No trouble at all, Grove." He set his empty glass down
with careful deliberation. "Okay, gentlemen," he said.
"Lemme show you how it's done . . . how an *ex*pert does
it . . ."

Turning from the bar, he strode with precisely controlled
steps to the table where the girl and the Marine were still
holding a passionate embrace. "Excuse me," he said. "I was
just wondering if you'd care to dance."

The couple stopped kissing and looked up at him. The
girl frowned. The Marine looked him up and down, then
grinned broadly. "I don't think so, sonny. You're not my
type."

Ignoring the man, Richardson leered down at the girl.
Through a thin, alcoholic haze, she looked really, *really*
good. She was wearing a light, floral-print blouse, and he
didn't think she had a bra on beneath it. Her nipples were

standing up like bullets, straining against the thin material stretched across her breasts. "C'mon, baby," he said. "How about it?"

"Get lost, jerk."

"Gosh, ma'am, I don't think you know who you're talking to. You owe it to yourself to enjoy only the very best!"

Gently, the Marine disentangled himself from the woman and stood up. He topped Richardson by a full head, and there was something dangerous lurking behind those hard eyes. "You think kinda highly of yourself, don't you, asshole?" the man growled. "The lady is with *me!* Now shove off."

Richardson looked up at him and briefly wondered if he was making a mistake . . . but decided that it was too late to back down now. "Why don't we let her be the judge of that?" He started to turn toward her, but the Marine's left arm shot out, the hand clamping shut on the collar of his fatigues.

For a blurry moment, Richardson considered reminding the Marine that he was an officer, that to touch him was a mast offense at the very least. Then he remembered that he wasn't wearing any emblem of his rank.

Somehow, he doubted that the Marine would have cared much one way or the other. He held Richardson at arm's length, right fist cocked behind his ear, a dark smile on his face. "Who the hell *are* you?"

"Navy CDU," Richardson replied. He wondered if he could block that fist when it struck.

"Buddy," the Marine growled, "you done picked the wrong guy to fuck with!"

The fist rocketed forward, swelling in Richardson's vision until he saw nothing else. An explosion went off somewhere behind his eyes, and the next thing he knew he was lying flat on his back, his feet entangled in the rungs of a chair.

"You CDU assholes think you're pretty hot stuff," the Marine said, advancing with clenched fists. "Maybe you need to be cut down t'size!" As he reached down to pluck Richardson from the deck, Richardson doubled up his knees, planted his feet on the surprised man's chest, and kicked as hard as he could. Arms pinwheeling, the Marine sailed backward, crashing into a table which, unfortunately, was occupied by two more Marines and several empty or half-empty glasses.

"Navy!" someone yelled. Richardson thought it was Tangretti. Coming up off the deck he collided with a khaki blur that was probably a Marine. He threw a punch and sliced through empty air. A moment later, he was airborne, striking the front of the bar with a shock that jarred his teeth.

"All *right!*" A billy club came down on the top of the bar inches from Richardson's head, the crack hammering through his already rattled skull like a blast from the last trump. One-Eyed Jack raised the club again, a menacing, potbellied giant. "That's enough! You assholes wanna brawl, take it outside!"

Richardson struggled to his feet, shaking his throbbing head. A Marine stumbled backward into his arms, propelled by a right hook from Jarvis. Richardson turned the man, lined him up, and let fly. Pain arced through his right hand, but he had the satisfying experience of watching the Marine spin twice before falling over a chair. The next thing he knew, without planning it, without even thinking about it, he found himself back to back with Jarvis, Grover, and Tangretti as the khaki hordes closed in.

Someone was blowing a whistle, a high, piping, evil sound. An empty beer stein sailed past, smashing against the wall. "I think the time has come for a tactical retreat!" Tangretti yelled. A Marine lunged into their perimeter; Tangretti hit him behind the ear, while Richardson grabbed his collar and shoved him back. The woman who'd first caught Richardson's eye was standing on a chair in the back of the room, screaming obscenities. Her blouse was torn and Richardson saw that his guess had been right; she wasn't wearing a bra.

He had no time to admire the view, however. Another Marine waded in close, throwing a left cross that connected with Richardson's already painful jaw. He sagged to the deck, then felt someone grabbing his arms.

"C'mon, Snake. Let's beat it!"

He was still seeing stars and had no clear recollection of how they got out of Jack's. The next thing he knew, the four of them were running down the street toward the waterfront.

More whistles were shrilling behind them. "Jeez," Grover said. "It's the S.P.s!"

At the waterfront, they pulled up short. The liberty bus was gone, and it was half a mile across the bridge to Causeway Island. Behind them they could see the headlights of a jeep, coming closer.

"Can you guys swim?" Richardson asked the others.

"We all qualified, didn't we?" Jarvis asked. "Of course we can swim."

"Don't know about half a mile, though," Tangretti looked nervous.

"We'll buddy it," Richardson said, pulling off his shoes and knotting the laces together. The others started following his example, hanging their shoes around their necks. "No sweat!"

A Shore Patrol jeep pulled up at the mainland end of the bridge with a chirp from its brakes. "Hold it, you!" one of them called.

"Swim for it!" Richardson leaped into the black water in a half-jump, half-dive that cracked against his belly when he hit, driving the wind from his lungs. As he surfaced, gasping for air, three more splashes sounded around him. Throwing his left arm forward, he started stroking for Causeway Island.

Damn. The sudden shock of the cool water seemed to have left him sober, or nearly so. What the hell had possessed him to challenge a *Marine*, of all creatures on God's earth, for that girl?

NCDU Training so far had not stressed swimming at all. One of their qualifying tests had been to swim two hundred yards, but that had been merely to demonstrate their physical conditioning and was not thought of as a prerequisite for the Teams.

But the four men were in good shape, and there was very little current, fortunately, between the mainland and the island. The half-mile swim in the dark took them nearly forty minutes, and they emerged on the beach at the other side cold, waterlogged, and as tired as they'd been at any point during the past six days.

Tangretti was in the worst shape of all. As they dropped

into the sand on Causeway Island, he rolled over onto his back, arms flung wide, and groaned.

"You okay, Gator?"

"Damn, I hate swimming," Tangretti said. He was panting, too weak to get up. "Damn, I hate the *water!*"

"Then why the devil did you join the Navy?" Jarvis asked.

"Because I hated the idea of living in foxholes, too. Besides, the food's better."

"Yeah," Grover said. "So here he is digging foxholes and eating K-rats by day, and going for long, moonlight swims by night. Go figure."

"Well, I think that we'd better call it a night," Richardson said. His jaw was swollen, and his hand was so painful he winced when he rubbed it. "This liberty didn't turn out quite the way I thought it would."

"Screw it," Tangretti said, sitting up. "At least we made it through Hell Week."

Chapter 17

Thursday, 2 September 1943

NCDU Amphibious Base
Fort Pierce, Florida

Indoctrination Week was over; the real training had begun. Coffer had laid out a schedule that called for four to six weeks more of training in such specialized skills as infiltration tactics, hand-to-hand combat, and reconnaissance skills. A range had been set up on Hutchinson Island, and there the trainees spent time familiarizing themselves with various weapons, including the M-1 Garand, M1918A2 BAR, M-1 carbine, the M1928A1 Thompson submachine gun, and the brand-new M-3 SMG, which had already acquired the nickname "grease gun."

Every morning began with an hour of calisthenics, and the classes, joined together now that Indoctrination Week for each was past, extended their endurance by taking progressively longer runs in the loose sand of Hutchinson Island's Atlantic side. Swimming was still not emphasized as a basic skill, though the classes continued to practice working with the rubber boats. Added to their repertoire, now, were techniques for approaching jetties, piers, and landings, as well as daily practice in preparing and placing demolition charges while clinging to a lifeline aboard a small and pitching rubber boat.

Lieutenant Commander Coffer, however, continued to press for new and innovative techniques. He was interested in the results coming in from DOLO, the ponderously named Demolition of Obstacles to Landing Operations Committee, set up in August. Among the new ideas being proposed was something called a Stingray, an unmanned, radio-controlled, explosives-filled drone that could be steered by remote control to an obstacle and detonated from a safe distance.

Of even greater interest to Coffer, however, was the research being carried out into an entirely new line of equipment for combat swimmers. While most CDU work was still expected to require men working from small boats on the surface, or ashore above the low-tide line on an enemy beach, Coffer was anticipating a much wider range of work that would be possible if only his men could be truly free to move and work in the water.

There'd been discussion for years, of course, on the possible future development of a self-contained air supply, something that would allow combat swimmers to work underwater for perhaps an hour at a time without the bulky steel helmets, cumbersome air hoses, and clumsy canvas suits of hardhat divers. Such units had already been tested in other countries, but they were strictly in the experimental stage in the United States. Other equipment, however, to extend the range and the mobility of free divers carried tremendous promise, and Coffer wanted to exploit it. Inquiries by Coffer, Galloway in Washington, and others had resulted in several shipments of experimental underwater free-swimming gear being sent to the Fort Pierce Amphibious Base for testing and feasibility trials. The first tests were carried out by members of Coffer's own staff.

Soon afterward, some of the advanced NCDU trainees got into the action as well.

NCDU Amphibious Base
Fort Pierce, Florida

They'd paddled the rubber boat to a point about one hundred yards off the inland side of Hutchinson Island, in the calm, sea-brackish waters of the Indian River. Richardson and Tangretti, Lieutenant Hadley, and Chief Wallace were all in the raft, stripped down to swimming trunks. It was mid-morning, and the sun-dazzle beneath the long, low, tree-ragged shadow of Hutchinson Island was so intense it was difficult to look at.

Richardson and Tangretti examined the new equipment that had been issued to them early that morning: a pair of large, black, flexible rubber swim fins, and oval rubber face masks with glass faceplates designed to strap over their heads and cover their noses and eyes. These strange-looking devices, they'd been told, might well be the real future of the NCDU. Richardson flexed the tip of one fin and wondered. He'd heard about a few crazy people who used things like this for sport swimming, but it had never been considered for a serious military application.

Could the idea possibly work? Some of the NCDU staff members, Wallace, the S&R people, and some others, had formed what Coffer called an "experimental and research detail," specifically to test any device or technique that might be of use to the combat swimmers. Masks and fins were less crazy than some of the weird things they'd been experimenting with lately. Some of those radio-controlled boats, for instance . . .

"How do they feel?" Lieutenant Hadley asked. The gentle swell in the river, the movements of the men, gave an unpleasant rocking to the boat. They were all used to that by now, however, with as much time as they'd spent in these craft in the early phase of training.

Tangretti grimaced. "Tight, sir. They chafe pretty bad behind the heel."

"They'll probably feel better in the water," Hadley pointed out. "You two ready?"

Tangretti appeared uncertain as he fumbled with the rubber mask, but he nodded. Richardson adjusted the strap on his mask, pulling it tighter, then gave a thumbs-up.

"Okay," Wallace told them. "Remember the drill. All you have to do is swim to the beach over there. We'll follow you in the raft. Remember what you've been told about using the flippers. Hard, even kicks. Try to stay underwater as long as you can before you pop up for air. The idea is to test whether or not you could swim up to an enemy beach in daylight without being spotted. Okay, ready? Right then. Over you go!"

Tangretti rolled off the edge of the raft, splashed in the water, and was gone.

"Next up! Go!"

Richardson took several deep breaths, squeezed his mask tight against his face until he felt the suction gripping his forehead and cheeks, then rolled off the side. There was a cool splash, a cloud of bubbles, and he was adrift in another world.

It was amazing, dazzling and spectacular. The glass faceplate of his mask seemed to have a magnifying effect under water; when he held his hand up before his face, it appeared larger than it would have otherwise, and his surroundings stood out with a crisp, wavering clarity that faded into murkiness with distance. He could see the black bottom of the rubber boat over his head, the surface around it like a sheet of rippling, silver light alive with the interplay of shadow and sun-sparkle. The bottom was perhaps ten feet below . . . or was it farther? Distance was hard to judge. The rules of perspective and of sensing distance by its clarity in atmosphere seemed to have been abolished. Just ahead, a few feet beneath the surface and already moving toward the beach, was the long-legged form of Steve Tangretti.

Richardson began swimming after his partner. The task set for them was simple enough, a hundred-yard swim to the beach. Since they were in the Indian River, safe behind the protective shelter of Hutchinson Island, there was no surf to deal with, and only a little current. He kicked his legs, and the big fins propelled him forward.

Almost from the start, Richardson knew that something was wrong. They'd told him to kick hard, and he was straining with each stroke, but he felt as though he were fighting against the flippers, not using them. The hard-kicking crawl he'd been taught was draining energy from him at an alarming rate. Already he could feel the muscles of his calves and thighs starting to tighten up.

It looked like Tangretti was experiencing the same thing. He hadn't even covered a third of the distance to the beach yet, and he was already slowing down.

Richardson drew up alongside his partner just as Tangretti began moving toward the surface, his air exhausted. Tangretti broke the surface just ahead of Richardson, gasping for a deep breath. "Lord!" Tangretti called as Richardson surfaced next to him. "That's tough going!"

"Man, there's gotta be an easier way," Richardson replied. He took a couple of deep breaths and submerged again. Tangretti followed.

The bottom was silk-smooth, a layer of fine silt. Richardson could see small fishes, bright silver and as long as his fingers, turning and darting in the shimmer of light from above.

Suddenly, a hand grabbed his leg, clutching, dragging at him with urgent purpose. Turning, Richardson saw Tangretti just behind him. Water had leaked through the seal around his mask, had three-quarters filled his mask and blinded the swimmer. Richardson could see Gator blinking his eyes behind the faceplate, trying to clear them.

As Tangretti stopped, his feet drifted down, his body assuming an upright position. His feet kept kicking, however, and suddenly the crystalline water was filled by a churning, brown fog. The movements of his flippers were stirring up the silt on the bottom. In seconds, Richardson was as blind as Tangretti.

Easy, Richardson told himself. The weightlessness of underwater swimming was disorienting, but there was still a clear "up" and "down." Both men were buoyant from the air they had held in their lungs. If they didn't panic, everything would be all right. They could simply float to the surface.

But Tangretti was snatching at his face mask, tugging wildly first at it and then at Richardson. Through the swirling murk, Richardson could see him starting to lose control, his eyes wild and staring. His mouth opened as if for a scream, and silvery bubbles of air spilled out. Finally, Tangretti managed to tear the mask off and drop it, but he seemed confused and disoriented. His hands closed on Richardson's arm, and they wielded the hysterical strength of raw panic.

Panic! Richardson knew that Tangretti could easily drown both of them. The rubber boat was a long way off, and the men in it could not see what was happening beneath the surface. Tangretti grabbed Richardson's shoulder, his nails biting against his flesh.

Richardson swung his right leg up, planting the flipper against Tangretti's chest and pushing hard. The kick broke Tangretti's hold and the two men drifted apart. Mud swirled around them, and Richardson heard a gargled, strangled shout muffled by the water.

For a moment, he was tempted to head for the surface. His exertions had drained the oxygen in his lungs, and he was fighting an overwhelming need to breathe. But Tangretti must be in even worse shape, and Richardson could not leave his partner.

Kicking hard, he closed in on the struggling man, swinging around behind him to stay out of the reach of his wildly thrashing legs and arms. Grabbing him in a hammerlock from behind, Richardson then began kicking wildly, willing the balky flippers to propel the two of them together to the surface.

They broke into the light and the air explosively, Richardson gasping down a great, sweet draft of air, Tangretti sputtering and gagging in Richardson's grasp. Richardson twisted around, trying to spot the boat. There it was! He waved, frantically signaling. Tangretti was in trouble. Damn, it would take too long for them to paddle the boat over. Grabbing the choking man across the chest, Richardson struck out toward the beach, their original destination, struggling along in an awkward, one-armed crawl. The fins on his feet seemed to give him more power, but his legs were so tired it felt like each kick would be his last. Brackish water flooded his throat and mouth, gagging him. He gulped it down and kept swimming. Then his flippers touched bottom, and he was able to stand up, splashing clumsily ashore with Tangretti under his arm.

He dropped him facedown on the beach, positioning him so that his head was toward the water, lower than his feet, with his elbows out and his hands beneath his throat. Kneeling astride Tangretti's hips, Richardson pushed both hands into the man's back just below his shoulder blades, then grasped his elbows and pulled them back. *Push . . . back . . . push . . . back . . .* The boat had nearly reached the shore, but Richardson was scarcely aware of it. "C'mon, Tan-Gator," Richardson muttered, willing him to breathe. *Push!* "You're not going to quit on me. C'mon!"

Damn it, Tangretti wasn't breathing at all! His skin felt as cold as death. "Breathe, you fucking wop bastard, *breathe!*"

Explosively, Tangretti expelled a mouthful of water onto the sand. Richardson pushed again, and Tangretti started choking, spilling more water from lungs and bronchial tubes. When he drew in a breath on his own, it was ragged and harsh, but then his chest was heaving and his eyes were fluttering open. He choked again, then vomited.

The rubber boat grounded nearby and Wallace hit the beach, splashing the last few steps to shore. "Christ, Snake! What the hell happened?"

"Gator swallowed some water, that's all." He slapped Tangretti a couple of times between the shoulder blades. "No problem."

Weakly, Tangretti rolled over onto his back. His breathing still sounded ragged. "Thanks . . . Snake. . . ."

"Hey, don't mention it," Richardson said, grinning down at him. "That's what buddies're for, right?"

Tangretti recovered, apparently with no permanent damage. The incident pointed up, however, the increasing problems the staff's experimental and research detail were having with the swimming gear they'd been asked to test. Tangretti had been only a fair swimmer; expert swimmers among the Scouts and Raiders had reported the same difficulties, however, and more. The rubber face masks filled with water whenever their seal with the face was broken, either through the swimmer's movements or if he accidentally let some air out of his nose and into the mask. The swim fins, so promising at first, had also turned out to be a failure. The powerful crawl-kick used by long-distance swimmers was simply unsuited for the rubber fins. The men tired quickly, and their legs cramped in painful knots after they'd swum only a few dozen yards. Besides that, the straps that held the fins in place tended to chafe the men's feet, causing blisters and raw patches inflamed by salt water that quickly became infected.

"Well, gentlemen," Coffer said. He was disappointed, and trying not to show it. "Now we know. The swim fins and masks just aren't going to fly."

Coffer had gathered his senior officers together in his office, along with several of the senior Scouts and Raiders men. A folding card table had been set up, and a mask and a pair of swim fins laid on it.

"It really was a nice idea," Chief Harrison said, reaching out and picking up one of the fins. "Right now, one of the biggest problems in the whole NCDU program is how to get our people in close to shore. If they could have swum in using these . . ."

Gunnery Sergeant Drake took the fin from Harrison and flexed the tip. "You know, sir, there are a few guys who use these things. Out in California. For sport."

"California's where guys use masks when they have to go swimming deep, too," Warnock pointed out. "For abalone. Maybe they could tell us what we're doing wrong."

"What makes you think we're doing it wrong?"

"I don't know. Just a hunch that there ought to be a better way to get some distance out of this stuff."

Drake shook his head. "The problem is that these things are toys. They're not designed for combat."

"There's another problem, too," Rand pointed out. "Our boys will be doing a lot of work on coral reefs, and up on the beach, too. You ever seen a guy try to run in these flippers? Or even walk? On a hostile beach, he'd be dead . . . unless maybe the Japs laughed themselves to death first. I'd have to say that the flippers are a total washout. They're clumsy, ineffective, and just plain useless. Now the masks could be useful, if we could figure out how to keep them from flooding."

"And fogging up," Harrison added. "We've had a lot of trouble with that. Rinsing them out with seawater doesn't help."

"Those California abalone divers use goggles," Coffer said. "I already checked on that through Lieutenant Galloway back in Washington." Coffer picked up the mask, then tossed it back on the table. "As far as I can find out, nobody uses these damn things. And small wonder why. They fill up with water too easily when you use them, and there's no way to clear them afterward. I guess our people could surface each time they get water in their masks and clear them on the surface, but that kind of seems to counter the whole point, doesn't it? Useless, for our purposes."

"We might want to check into getting some of the goggles," Harrison suggested.

"Why?" Lieutenant j.g. Wetzel asked, genuinely puzzled. "The NCDU's primary mission is going to be blowing up obstacles and stuff above the low-tide line. You don't need goggles for stuff like that."

"Well, both the Japanese and the Germans have devised landing boat obstacles that are completely submerged, even at low tide," Coffer said. "An underwater capability would let us go after them. Masks and flippers would extend our range as well as increase our stealth. Good God, men, think of the possibilities! A small team, dropped from a boat a mile at sea. They swim all the way in. No motor noise to give them away. They could work all the way up to the water's edge, even move inland to blow up bridges or scout out enemy defenses, and the enemy would never even know they'd been there! It would be ideal. I've been doing some research lately into some of the new underwater breathing gear. You know, rigs that allow a man to rebreathe the air over and over again."

"People have died trying to breathe with those things," Drake put in.

"Yeah, I won't dispute that. The biggest problems involve pressure. As the diver goes deeper, water pressure starts building up, adding one atmosphere of pressure with every thirty-three feet of depth. Oxygen quickly becomes poisonous much past thirty-three feet of depth. Convulsions and unconsciousness underwater can kill a man just as fast as an enemy bullet.

"Anyway, the Italians have done a lot of work in that field. You know, all we've been talking about is finding a way for a man to swim farther and faster. Now, if we could give him a way to *breathe* underwater too—"

"Sounds to me like you want to come up with something like that Italian guy, de la Penne," Drake said. "That's pretty crazy stuff."

"Hey, it worked, didn't it?" Coffer said. "Our underwater swimming capabilities are still way behind the Italians, but hell, if they can do it, we can. Someday we should be able to duplicate what they pulled at Alexandria."

Everyone in the room had seen the top-secret briefs from Washington and knew exactly what Coffer was talking about. On December 18, 1941, three odd, undersea craft called Chariots had been lowered from the deck of an Italian submarine a mile off the entrance to the protected British harbor at Alexandria, Egypt.

The Chariots were little more than drivable torpedoes with places for two swimmers to ride astride them like men on horseback. The men, under the command of Lieutenant Luigi Durand de la Penne, had worn bulky rubber suits, goggles, and carried their own air supply, letting them breathe underwater as they steered their unwieldy craft toward the harbor. A pair of passing British destroyers had given them their chance to slip past the antisubmarine nets outside, following the destroyers' wakes; inside the harbor, de la Penne and his undersea commandos had split up and approached three anchored ships, a tanker and the two 32,000-ton battleships *Valiant* and *Queen Elizabeth*.

Working alone—his mechanic had been swept off the Chariot's saddle—de la Penne had maneuvered beneath the keel of the monstrous *Valiant*, floating just four feet above the harbor bed. There, he'd planted his Chariot's warhead, a six-hundred-pound charge of timer-detonated high explosives, on the bottom directly beneath the *Valiant*'s keel. Afterward, too exhausted to make his escape, he'd surfaced and, before long, been captured.

All three of the charges had gone off; all three ships had been badly damaged. Fortunately, superb British seamanship and damage-control work had kept them from turning on their sides. The ships had settled gently to the bottom, and aerial reconnaissance photographs showed them still apparently riding safely at anchor in Alexandria Harbor. All six of the Italian Charioteers had been captured, so their success was still a closely guarded secret. Only a few men in Washington, besides Coffer's team, had been let in on the story.

The idea that a handful of men equipped to work and travel underwater could put two of Great Britain's battleships out of the war for months excited Coffer. This was the sort of special mission that would be tailor-made for the NCDU, *if* they could get the equipment to carry it out.

"Well, it still sounds like something out of one of Harrison's crazy magazines to me," Drake said, shaking his head, and the others chuckled. Chief Harrison was an avid reader of *Amazing Stories* and some of the other, less reputable science fiction magazines.

"And we're sure as hell not going to make it real," Rand added, dropping a flipper into the pile on the table, "unless we get something better than this crap."

"It's useless, Commander," Drake said. "The masks won't stay sealed and the flippers give swimmers leg cramps. I think we're stuck with boondockers and coral shoes."

"You're probably right." Coffer looked longingly at the gear in front of him. There *had* to be a way to make it work! "Okay. Until we get something new along those lines, something that works, we stick to the published guidelines. The men go ashore in boats. For deep-water work, they stay aboard the boats and work with a lifeline." He looked at Warnock. "Jim? Get rid of this junk. The rest of you, back to the real world.

"Now, I want to go over with you people again what we can expect when we hit a defended Pacific island, one surrounded by a coral atoll. . . ."

Friday, 10 September 1943

NCDU Amphibious Base
Fort Pierce, Florida

The news of the Allied landings at Salerno and Taranto, coming close on the heels of Italy's surrender, had no effect on the NCDU training schedule. Work continued—practice with small boat handling, seamanship, and rigging explosives from their pitching decks; firearms training; communications with field telephones, with "cracker-box" hand-held walkie-talkies, and with the full-sized shortwave sets; silhouette recognition, both of ships and of installations and terrain features ashore; depth charting, using the age-old method of sounding with a lead weight on the end of a string; and always, always, the daily regimen of running and calisthenics.

They'd started working hard on hand-to-hand combat, too, with the idea that a team sneaking onto an enemy beach might well have to deal silently with sentries. The high point in this phase of their training came with the arrival of Major Richard Fairbairn of the Royal Engineers, an experienced British officer loaned to the Fort Pierce school by Combined Operations to teach infiltration, commando, and hand-to-hand combat techniques. The NCDU trainees were especially fascinated by the slender, black, tapering blades developed early in the war by Major Fairbairn and another officer. The commando knives, known as Sykes-Fairbairns, would be deadly in combat, though the practical-minded demolition team members preferred the more utilitarian K-Bars and Mark I Navy knives.

Since they were primarily a combat *demolition* unit, they worked with explosives every day, practicing demolishing everything from concrete walls to tank traps. Their unofficial nickname of "Demolitioneers" stuck, and even their rivals at the Scouts and Raiders school had to admit that nobody could knock things down as fast or as efficiently as the "shootin', fightin', dynamitin' men of the CDU."

They also tested new demolitions explosives, equipment, and techniques.

Composition-2, the newly developed "plastic explosive,"

was one of the most important. It could be kneaded like putty into any desired shape and was so stable it could be dropped or hit without exploding, but when it detonated, it yielded something like twenty percent more energy than an equal weight of TNT. They developed new techniques with primacord, also known as "det cord," a flexible, woven rope with an explosive core. Primacord, which looked exactly like yellow clothesline, had been developed as a near-instantaneous detonator for conventional explosives like dynamite or TNT. Several separate satchels filled with TNT set in widely separated spots—say, along a fifty-yard stretch of sea wall—could be joined by lengths of primacord in such a way that, when one satchel blew, the primacord set off all of the satchels at once.

Inevitably, though, the Demolitioneers' unique blend of Bomb Disposal School familiarity with explosives and the Seabee talent for invention quickly found numerous other, unexpected applications for primacord. It could be wrapped around and around a tree or telephone pole or pier piling and used as a cutting charge; it could be used to tie a satchel charge filled with TNT to a steel and concrete boat obstacle; and it could slice through loops of barbed wire a lot faster than a man with wire cutters could.

By the end of the summer, a race had developed between the Demolitioneers and a team of Allied engineers. The scientists and engineers worked at developing new and fiendishly contrived beach obstacles and traps—devices that the Japanese and Germans *might* think of themselves and emplace on their beaches. The NCDU teams worked at finding means of destroying those obstacles with the minimum amount of explosives, destructive radius, and exposure to hostile fire.

The engineers never even came close to keeping up with the Demolitioneers.

"Fire in the hole!"

The old dynamiter's cry rang across the beach, and five men dropped flat at the edge of the surf near their rubber boat, hands folded protectively over their helmets. A sixth, Ensign Richardson, yanked at the T-wire of a waterproof fuse igniter, then raced back across the wet sand to the other men, dropping prone in the water. The fuse had been cut for a one-minute delay, necessary here to observe the safety regs concerning time and distance.

Tensely, they waited for the blast.

For Richardson, finding the NCDU was like finding a family he'd never known he had. The sense of camaraderie with other men who'd made it through Hell Week, like he had, gave him a sense of purpose and of belonging that he'd never known in his own family. By the end of August, his weight had gone up from a skinny 138 to a better-proportioned 144, a gain reflecting an increase in his muscle mass due to regular meals and constant, strenuous exercise. After one ugly and painful encounter with a case of Florida sunburn, he developed a deep tan. Eventually, he'd even shaved off the Clark Gable mustache. With the tan emphasizing his pale blond hair, he didn't look that much like Clark Gable anyhow.

Besides, he was the Snake now. There wasn't as much reason, it seemed, for make-believe.

"Shit," Wallace said as white sea foam surged past the prone men. "Another dud."

"Give it another minute," Tangretti warned. They hadn't lost anyone to a hangfire . . . yet. One reason was their careful adherence to the demolition safety rules.

"It's the fucking igniter again," Wallace said after another minute ticked past.

"Yeah," Hadley added. "The first law of explosive ordnance: waterproof fuse igniters aren't."

When they were sure that it was safe, Richardson, Tangretti, and Hadley returned across the beach to the charge they'd hung at the nexus of a large welded crisscross of three steel I-beams, a beach defense obstacle known as a hedgehog. They checked each component: eight one-pound blocks of TNT in a haversack, each wired with an explosive detonator and wrapped together with several feet of primacord; the sixty-second length of fuse; the cylindrical, pull-wire igniter crimped to the end of the fuse.

M-1 fuse igniters had been developed as a fast and easy means of detonating explosives, one that didn't require cumbersome reels of electrical wire, batteries, or crank-charge detonators. Best of all, pull-wire igniters were advertised as waterproof. Theoretically, at least, a Demolitioneer could plant explosives on an obstacle underwater, yank the T on the end of the wire, and the device would ignite the waterproof fuse and set off the charge.

Unfortunately, even the mild soaking the igniters got on a wet beach—or in the canvas pouches of an NCDU beach party—seemed to be enough to soak through their seals and ruin them.

"Shit, Lieutenant," Tangretti said, ripping the igniter from the end of the fuse and tossing it away. "How are we supposed to blow a hole in the enemy's beach defenses if we can't even light the fuse?"

"Damfino, Gator," Hadley said. "Waterproof matches'd work better than this shit."

Richardson was studying the fuse. The failure was definitely in the igniter; the end of the fuse wasn't even singed.

"We got any more dry igniters, Lieutenant?"

"Sure," Hadley replied. "Back at the cache, still in their wrappers."

"Won't do no good," Tangretti warned a few minutes later, as they returned to the charge with a fresh igniter. "Damn thing'll soak through just from layin' on the wet sand."

"I got me an idea," Richardson said. He reached down under his uniform blouse, opening the waterproof pouch attached to his web belt. Though they were designed to keep necessary items like first aid kits, electrical tape, and matches dry, the men had long since taken to using them to hold personal items as well. Richardson removed a pack of cigarettes, fished deeper, and finally produced a small flat, square packet. "Never fear," he said, tearing open the paper wrapper. "The Snake is here."

"Snake," Hadley said. "What are you doing with that out here?"

Richardson extracted a flat ring of flesh-colored latex from the wrapper and shook it out. "The Boy Scout motto," he said. "Be prepared!"

"Yeah, but a *rubber* with your field gear?" Tangretti said. "Shit, Snake, which one of us were you figuring on getting friendly with?"

"Don't worry, Gator. You're not my type." Carefully, he

crimped the end of the fresh igniter over the end of the fuse, then slipped the igniter into the condom. The thin sheath of rubber was flexible enough that he could stretch the open end out, then tie it off tight, sealing in the igniter.

"That gives a whole new twist to the expression 'Fire in the hole,' " Hadley pointed out.

Tangretti groaned. "Bad, Lieutenant. I think this character's corrupting you."

"Fire in the hole!" Richardson yelled. He grabbed the igniter's T-wire through the tip of the condom and yanked it.

The three men raced back to where the others were waiting, threw themselves flat, and waited. Sixty seconds after the warning, there was a flash and a deep-throated *WHUMP!* Black smoke geysered into the sky, accompanied by a shower of sand. Inspecting their handiwork a few moments later, they found that the three beams of the hedgehog had been ripped apart and knocked down flat.

"Right," Hadley said, surveying the blast crater. "Wait until Commander Coffer hears about *this* one!"

"I'm looking forward to seeing the pharmacist's mate over at the base dispensary," Richardson said. "He already calls me his best customer." Condoms were distributed free to all personnel before they went ashore on liberty.

"Snake, you're just not thinking big enough," Tangretti pointed out. "We're gonna need rubbers by the gross. Hell, we'll need 'em by the *ton!*"

Hadley groaned.

"What's the matter, Lieutenant?" Richardson asked with feigned innocence.

"I'm just trying to imagine what the supply officer's going to say when I tell him I want an order of ten thousand prophylactic rubbers . . . just for a start!"

"Not to worry," Richardson told him. "Just explain that the NCDU is headed into Fort Pierce again, on maneuvers."

Chapter 18

Monday, 1 November 1943

The Pentagon
Washington, D.C.

"I'm sorry, Commander Coffer. In my estimation, your teams are not ready. There is simply too much riding on Operation Galvanic to commit untried men, untested techniques, at this late date."

Admiral King closed the folder on the desk before him and handed it across to Coffer. Lieutenant Galloway, at Coffer's side, could feel the older man's frustration.

"Some of the classes have been training for four months now, Admiral," Coffer said. "Since the end of June, in fact. They're ready."

"I'll tell you frankly, Commander," King said slowly, "that there is still considerable debate going on as to just what part these Demolitioneers of yours can play. And there's a lot of confusion over just what they're supposed to do. Reconnoiter beaches for invasion? Blow up beach obstacles? Lay down safe lane markers for incoming landing craft? Disarm mines?"

"My boys can do all of that, Admiral. And more."

"Admiral Nimitz and some others out in the Pacific have been talking about the need for some kind of beach commando," King said. "What they're looking for is a team trained in hydrographic reconnaissance. Where are the coral reefs? How deep is the lagoon behind the reefs? What are the tides like? The currents? Is the sand between the low- and high-tide marks heavy enough to support tracked vehicles? Aerial reconnaissance, even reconnaissance by submarine, can't give them all of those answers. And we're going to need those answers when we start taking islands back from the Japanese in the central Pacific.

"CINCPAC is looking into establishing a school in the Pacific," King continued. "A course to train men in the kinds of reconnaissance and beach-mapping procedures we're going to need out there. Possibly we can fold some of your Demolitioneers into that program."

Galloway watched Coffer from the corner of his eye. His face was impassive now, his expression under rigid control. "Very well, sir. May I suggest, however, that some of my people at least be incorporated into Galvanic as observers. It would be extremely helpful to my command if we had some people out there, getting impressions first-hand."

King considered this, then shook his head. "I'm afraid, Commander, that that simply will not be possible. Admiral Turner is already en route from Hawaii, his TO already set. The addition of a party of men outside the regular chain of command would only complicate things in what is already an extraordinarily complex operation."

In other words, the CNO was trying to stay out of Turner's hair. Every flag-rank commander in the field had to deal with the problems and distractions of Washington continually looking over his shoulder. King didn't want to add to Turner's problems by assigning yet another observer team to his entourage.

"Begging the Admiral's pardon," Galloway said, seizing the opportunity. "But I have a suggestion."

"Well?"

Galloway swallowed. "Sir, it is customary to assign liaison officers to field operations as observers."

"True. My planning staff already has a team with the Fifth Amphibious Force."

"Then assign me to that team."

"What . . . you?"

Galloway felt a gallop of excitement. He'd been chafing under the spit and polish of his Pentagon assignment for the better part of nine months; his only relief had been his infrequent flights down to Fort Pierce to confer with Coffer.

"Sir. I've been working closely with Commander Coffer

and the NCDU project since its inception. I know what he wants to do with his teams, and I know something about what his men are capable of. I could serve as staff liaison officer between Admiral Turner and Commander Coffer. There shouldn't be any political problems with more outsiders looking over Admiral Turner's shoulder then, since I'd be just another Pentagon staffer with your liaison team."

King looked thoughtful. He glanced up at Coffer. "That okay with you, Commander?"

"Most satisfactory, Admiral. At least it would give my staff something to work on, as we finish up with your first CDU classes."

"And you, Galloway. You want to give up the Washington night life for assignment aboard ship?"

Galloway grinned. King knew how he felt about the D.C. social whirl, and about how little patience he had with both military and social politics. "It'll be tough, Admiral, but I'll manage somehow."

"Very well. I'll have my people cut your orders this afternoon. Dismissed."

"Aye, aye, sir," Coffer said.

"Thank you, sir," Galloway added.

"Oh, Galloway. One more thing."

"Sir?"

"You keep a low profile out there. Don't try to reorganize Turner's entire set-up. It would not be appreciated, there or here."

"The idea never even crossed my mind, sir."

"Get out of here."

"Aye, aye, sir." He got.

Coffer caught him outside the CNO's office suite. "You sure you want to do this, Joe?"

Galloway gestured, a sweep of his arm that took in the endlessly dwindling corridors to either side. "Commander, anything, *anything* to get me out of this madhouse! I think it's going to be fun!"

Saturday, 20 November 1943

U.S.S. *Maryland*
Fifth Amphibious Force
Gilbert Islands

Galloway stood on the open bridge wing of the U.S.S. *Maryland,* leaning against the portside splinter screen and staring into a darkness that was just beginning to show the promise of dawn. It had been sweltering below decks, but up here, in the air, it was cooler, with a fresh breeze rising. Lieutenant Dennis Schumann, of Admiral Harry Hill's Battle Staff, was with him. He'd met Schumann soon after coming aboard, discovered the man was a fellow Bostonian, and the two had swiftly become friends.

By the dim light spilling from the bridge behind him, he could just make out the face of his watch. Zero-five-zero-one hours, a minute after five A.M. It seemed as though the night would never end.

Galloway raised the binoculars he was carrying to his eyes, scanning the darkness. Nothing. "So how much longer is it going to be?" he asked. He could sense, could *taste* the pent-up excitement, the fear, the tension of the tens of thousands of sailors and Marines in the night around him. From the sea around them came a far-off, muffled growling, the engine noise of hundreds of landing craft and small boats gathering for the assault. General Quarters had been sounded hours before, at 0215 hours; the first Marines had begun going down the cargo nets of their transports into the waiting landing craft at 0330.

The island, the target of the assault he'd flown halfway around the world to see, was barely visible now, a smudge of shadow against a slightly lighter sky. Several times during the night already, a searchlight ashore had probed the darkness, trying to find the armada lurking there. Galloway had stared at that light, and it had come to him then with a small shiver of anticipation that that was the *enemy* over there.

"What's the matter?" Schumann asked. "Afraid you'll miss something?"

"Nah. I just don't like the waiting."

"That's mostly what war is," Schumann said with the air of a man of vast experience. "Waiting, waiting, and more waiting . . . with a few minutes of stark terror thrown in to liven things up."

Galloway felt the deck tremble slightly as the huge forward gun turrets of the *Maryland* began swinging away from fore-and-aft positions, training on the unseen island. He tried to fold his arms across his chest, but the unfamiliar embrace of the Mae West he was wearing stopped him. The air of tension, of expectation, aboard the *Maryland* had reached a pitch so high Galloway could imagine the whole ship coiled like a titanic spring, ready to hurl itself at the enemy.

He was a long, long way from Washington.

Galloway's long journey to this predawn rendezvous had begun a week before with a commercial flight from Washington to San Francisco, followed by an Army C-47 hop to Wheeler Field on Oahu. After that there'd been a quick succession of hops across the Pacific, to Howland Island, to Nanomea, to Guadalcanal, and finally to the seaplane base at Tulagi. The last leg of his trip had been taken aboard a Navy PBY Catalina, flying northeast from Tulagi, and catching up with Admiral Harry Hill's Task Force 53 just six days out from a little-known speck on the map called Tarawa.

Strategic policy for the Pacific war was still being set, but a growing consensus among Navy officers supported the idea of a broad, hammering assault on several different fronts. MacArthur had already begun his campaign of battling up through New Guinea on his way back to the Philippines; U.S. Marines were still fighting in the Solomons in the aftermath of Guadalcanal; General Turnage's 3rd Marine Division had landed on Bougainville on 1 November. As a parallel strategy to these operations in the southwestern Pacific, however, the U.S. Navy and the Marines would spearhead an island-hopping offensive up through the central Pacific. This thrust was aimed at taking or isolating such Japanese strongholds as the Marshall Islands; Wake, Guam, and the Marianas; the bastion at Truk; and—ultimately, it was hoped—islands close enough to the Japanese homeland that U.S. forces could begin launching the same sort of punishing air raids that the Allies had been employing over Germany for the past year.

Astride the equator two thousand miles southwest of Hawaii, the Gilbert Islands were first in this chain of island stepping-stones leading across the central Pacific toward Japan. A cluster of tiny islands, each with its own necklace of coral reefs ringing a central lagoon, it included such unknown places as Tarawa, Butaritari, Abimama, and Makin.

On the charts, Tarawa Atoll had the overall appearance of a crudely drawn right triangle enclosing a vast, deep lagoon; the north-south side was a line of submerged coral reefs, while the west-east side and the hypotenuse of the triangle were both comprised of dozens of islands of varying sizes, each closely surrounded by its own guardian reefs and shallow lagoons.

Key to Tarawa was the island of Betio, westernmost of those islands strung along the triangle's base. A narrow, triangular sliver of sand and coconut palms two miles long measured east to west and barely six hundred yards wide at its broad, western end, Betio was nowhere more than nine feet above the high-tide water level. Its chief attraction was the airstrip built there by the Japanese.

The Navy planners of Operation Galvanic had plenty of intelligence to work with. Planters and traders who had fled the Japanese occupation almost two years before reported that the reefs surrounding the islands were normally covered by four or five feet of water during high tide, more than enough to allow landing craft to cross the reef, traverse the lagoon, and drop their ramps directly onto the sands of Betio only a few feet below the island's sea wall and barricades. Just before the invasion force's arrival, a U.S. submarine had probed the atoll and its approaches, taking photographs of the beaches through its periscope and sounding the bottom. Aircraft had flown overhead, photographing everything and making use of a new, split-image process that allowed Naval Intelligence to construct 3-D images of the island's defenses and terrain.

In some respects, however, the Navy's intelligence was still deficient. Some of the most important charts and tables of beach approaches and reef depths were derived from oceanographic data gathered by the Wilkes Expedition in

1841. Still, everything that could be taken into account *had* been taken into account.

In the early hours of 20 November, the American invasion force closed in on Tarawa. Rear Admiral Raymond A. Spruance was in overall command, with Rear Admiral Richmond Kelly Turner in command of all amphibious forces and General Holland A. "Howling Mad" Smith in charge of the landings. In order to increase the speed and efficiency of the operation, Turner had divided his forces. Task Force 52, with General R. C. Smith's 27th Infantry Division, approached Makin Island to the north. In the south, Task Force 53, under the command of Admiral Harry W. Hill, was set to assault Betio with 18,600 men of the 2nd Marine Division.

Task Force 53 included a bombardment group composed of the *Maryland*—resurrected from the mud of Pearl Harbor—plus two other battleships, four cruisers, and air support from four escort carriers. Although it was a close contest, the beaches on the northern, lagoon side of Betio were chosen as the least difficult of three very tough approaches. Starting outside the main reef to the west, they would have to penetrate the main Tarawa lagoon through a gap in the coral three and a half miles north of Betio, then turn sharply south for the final run into the beach, a total journey of nearly ten miles. Four to five hundred yards short of the beach, they would have to cross a submerged barrier reef for the final run into the island.

The first three waves of Marines would go ashore in amtracks, amphibious tractors properly called LVTs, for Landing Vehicle, Tracked, and more popularly known as "alligators." These were rugged, boxy, open-cockpit machines originally developed before the war from swamp-traversing vehicles used in Florida's Everglades. On land they rumbled along like open-topped tanks on steel tracks; in the water they churned ahead at a slow but steady four knots. Their chief advantage came with their ability to roll right over coral heads or shoals concealed beneath the water and, when they reached land, to keep moving out of the sea and up the beach without stopping.

Succeeding waves of Marines could go ashore in more conventional landing craft—Higgins boats, LCIs and LCMs, and LCVPs. Four feet of water above the coral heads surrounding Betio would be more than enough clearance for the flat-bottomed boats, even fully laden. The plan called for putting more than five thousand Marines ashore at Betio in the first few hours of the operation.

Galloway turned his binoculars on the island once again. He guessed that the range was about eleven thousand yards. "That island just doesn't look that big," he said. The light was growing steadily stronger, and he could make out the shadows of the other ships of the Task Force around them. "Five thousand Marines going ashore all at once could sink it."

"Hell, there are already five thousand Japs there," Schumann said. "Actually, to be precise, forty-eight hundred."

"Aw, c'mon. How the hell can you know exactly how many Japanese there are?"

"That's what Navy Intelligence reports say."

"Yeah? And how do they know?"

"Easy," Schumann said, smirking. "They counted privies."

"Beg pardon?"

"S'truth! I got a buddy with G-2 who gave me the straight dope. The Japanese went and built outhouses along a pier extending over the reef, see? The Navy Intelligence boys know Jap doctrine as well as they do: so many outhouses will be built for every so many men, okay? Photo recon planes shot pictures of the reef; the intel boys counted the privies, and that gave them the final number. Five thousand men, give or take an outhouse or two."

"I guess that would make it privy-leged information," Galloway ventured.

Schumann closed his eyes and groaned, shaking his head. "Another stinker like that and you can walk home, Lieutenant."

Galloway laughed. Despite the tension, the thrill of actually being here where history was being made, the smell of sea and ship and island, all combined to make this what he was certain would be the most exciting moment of his life.

With startling suddenness, one of *Maryland*'s main guns roared, loosing a flare that lit up the night with a glorious, blinding flash of orange-red fire. Galloway had been turned to face that direction when the gun had gone off, and for a moment he blinked at the spots floating in front of his eyes. His ears rang from the concussion. He looked at his watch again: 0505 hours. Another of *Maryland*'s eight sixteen-inch guns flashed and thundered, and this time, to his surprise, Galloway found that he could actually *see* the shell, a fierce-glowing red spark that arced slowly into the darkness to the southeast.

Other guns joined in from the surrounding water, *Maryland*'s huge consorts answering her call to battle. Soon, the eight-inch guns of the cruisers chimed in, and then the six-inch guns of the destroyers, salvo after salvo lighting up the sky in a day-brilliant glare of red-orange-white light, the thunder a continuous roar that at each given instant could not possibly grow louder and then, inconceivably, did. The concussion of *Maryland*'s guns slapped at Galloway, a painful, physical blow with each salvo, and further conversation became impossible.

Flashes popped and flickered against the island as shells struck home. Several minutes into the bombardment, a blast flared up from Betio like the eruption of a volcano, a sheet of flame five hundred feet high marking the detonation of a powder magazine. The sight raised cheers from the sailors watching on *Maryland*'s decks and from the waiting Marines packed aboard their landing craft, audible even over the steady roar of the guns.

"Sweet Jesus," Schumann yelled above the thunder, grinning from ear to ear. "*This'll* teach the little yellow bastards! We're gonna walk right over 'em! It's gonna be a piece of cake!"

And Galloway agreed. American land-based bombers had been dumping their deadly loads on Tarawa every day since 13 November, and now the bombardment force was pouring some three thousand tons of high explosives onto a strip of sand and coral rock just 291 acres in extent.

The Japs were never going to be able to resist *that* kind of firepower. Schumann was right.

Tarawa would be a piece of cake.

Off Betio
Approach to Beach Red Three

Lance Corporal Howard V. Barnes was one of thirty-six men crowded into the well deck of a ramped, wood-hulled Higgins boat in what was supposed to be the fifth wave. He'd gone down the cargo nets at 0635 hours, but it was nearly 0900 before his landing craft reached its assigned rendezvous and began circling, waiting for its turn to go in.

Throughout that time, the noise, the crash and thunder and bark of the big Navy guns, was indescribable, and, at first, comforting with the suggestion that nothing could possibly survive on that tiny island after so intense a bombardment. In the sky, Navy aircraft darted, turned, and wheeled; at one time, Barnes counted over ninety planes within the span of a few moments, all of them American.

But at 0855, the big Navy guns had all but fallen silent. H-Hour, postponed once already, was drawing near, and the bombardment threatened the first waves of Marines already approaching the beach. It was then that Barnes and the Marines with him in that small, pitching boat began to realize that something had gone horribly, bloodily wrong.

As the landing boat motored closer to the atoll, bouncing now in the chop of waves breaking on exposed coral heads, they began to hear the flat crack of antitank guns firing from hidden positions on the beach, the shrill whistle-*WHUMP* of incoming mortar rounds, the incessant chatter of machine guns. If sheer volume of fire was any indication, the Navy had dumped three thousand tons of high explosives onto that tiny triangle of coral and sand to absolutely no effect.

Crouched below the Higgins boat's gunwales, Barnes could see little of the approaching shoreline, but he saw the black pall of smoke already blotting out the morning sun and the brief, towering geysers of green and silver water to either side as the Japanese mortars and artillery pieces blasted away at the lines of approaching landing craft.

"Aw, *shit!*" Private Bob Marcinko, balanced forward where he could look out past the Higgins boat's bow ramp, dropped back into the well deck and turned to face the others.

Gunnery Sergeant Ralph Holmes, their squad leader, steadied Marcinko with a beefy hand. "So? What's the word?"

"It's a royal fuck-up, Sarge. Shit, it looks like boats're piling up all along that inner reef. Ain't no boats got all the way to the beach at all that I could see. Just alligators! I thought they said that fuckin' reef was 'sposed to be under four feet of water?"

Holmes stood upright then, bracing himself against the slap and jolt of the boat, peering ahead as he studied the situation for himself. When he dropped back to his haunches with the others, he could only shake his head. "Well, leathernecks, no one ever told ya it'd be *easy*, did they?"

Barnes cradled his rifle and tried not to think about what was coming. He was nineteen years old and had never been in combat. He was afraid, but he'd found he could draw strength from the men—all boys like himself—who were packed into the Higgins boat around him.

He tried to recall the memorized words of his girl's last letter, and failed. That failure bothered him. He'd wanted to lose himself in Jeanie's words, shutting out the Olympian conflict raging across the water just ahead. When he couldn't, it felt like a kind of betrayal. *I'm sorry, Jeanie!*

Seconds later the Higgins boat collided with the reef, a wall of jagged coral lurking inches beneath the ocean's swell. Barnes heard the hard coral grinding along the boat's keel, felt the shudder that knocked him and the others off balance. Machine gun bullets whined and snapped across the water; a spent round shrieked from the boat's forward davit cleat.

"That's it, gyrenes!" Holmes shouted. "Hit the fuckin' beach!"

With a shrill clatter, the boat's bow ramp came down, splashing into the shallow water over the reef. Barnes trotted down the ramp, his M-1 Garand held high. Expecting shallow water, he was startled when he stepped off the ramp and splashed in up to his chest.

A sea surge picked him up and carried him forward several feet. Around him, the other men from his section were floundering as they came off the ramp; the Higgins boat had grounded on the coral but been carried just far enough forward that its ramp had opened over the deeper water of the inner lagoon beyond.

Everywhere Barnes looked was stark, chaotic nightmare. The coral reef ringing Betio five hundred yards off the beach was littered with landing craft of every description, many of them broken and burning. Across the inner lagoon and along the narrow strip of sand beneath Betio's sea wall, Barnes could see at least fifty knocked-out amtracks, some blazing furiously as gasoline or ammunition aboard them burned. Everywhere he looked, the sea was black with struggling Marines; for the Marines stranded on the atoll when their landing craft went aground, there was no option save wading ashore through water that was waist- or shoulder-deep in most places. Japanese fire swept those bobbing heads and packed, struggling bodies like a deadly, invisible scythe. Smoke boiled into the sky above a green lagoon already stained in patches with oil and blood.

Struggling to get his feet beneath him, Barnes kept clinging to his rifle. He glanced back, noticed Chip Conners hesitate on the grounded landing craft's bow ramp, then saw him twist backward as machine gun fire from the beach chopped into him and the boat. Splinters snapped and spun; Conners made a strangled sound as his chest opened in a bloody, ragged hole, then fell back into the boat. Other Marines pushed past, leaping into the water. Bullets striking the water sent geysers and white spray six feet into the air. A mortar shell struck the water of the lagoon fifty yards ahead with a thunderous roar that sent a fine spray drifting back across the struggling Marines. Six feet from Barnes's position, Paul Wainwright, a good buddy of his since boot camp, stumbled and sank from sight.

That spurred Barnes to action. Wading forward, fighting to keep his rifle dry, he reached the spot where Wainwright had vanished. Holding the nine-and-a-half-pound Garand aloft with one hand, he reached into the water, fishing about for the other Marine. His hand closed on something, a strap for a field pack. Hauling back with all his might, he dragged Wainwright to the surface.

"Oh . . . *fuck!*"

A bullet or a shell fragment had sliced through Paul's throat. Blood was streaming into the ocean in a steady, pulseless flow, spreading across the surface of the water like a scarlet dye marker. His eyes were glassy, unseeing. Barnes didn't know whether Paul had been killed instantly or had been wounded and drowned in the chest-deep water.

"C'mon, Marines!" Holmes was shouting from just ahead. "C'mon! We can't fight the Japs out here!"

Still shocked by his friend's sudden death, shocked by the noise and carnage and smoke and sheer terror, Barnes let Wainwright's body slip away and started wading after his squad leader.

Anything like an orderly formation was impossible, of course. His boat section, what was left of it, had already become mingled with a dozen others. He saw Bob Marcinko, ten yards ahead, thrashing in the water, trying to keep his head above the surface. Barnes hurried as fast as he could but by the time he got there, Marcinko was gone. Had he stepped into a shell hole? Been wounded and dragged under? Barnes began to wade forward more slowly, cautiously testing each step, wary of unseen holes beneath the water.

Better still . . .

Pausing, he clung to his rifle with one hand as he wiggled free of his pack and web belt with the other. In boot camp, he'd been hammered incessantly with the Gospel according to the Corps, that his rifle was his friend, his salvation, his single hope of survival. He would hang on to the Garand and his helmet, but he could ditch the rest. Burden relieved, he moved forward again. Damn? Where was the sarge? Where were any of the others? Suddenly he felt lost, completely and terribly alone despite the hundreds of other men struggling through the water around him. Nearby, an LCM had off-loaded a tank after stranding on the reef. The tank had ground forward in four feet of water, then stalled, its engine drowned. Its crew scrambled from its open hatches, only to be cut down one after another by the storm of gunfire from the beach.

Despite dropping his pack, Barnes was tiring fast. He'd been half-wading, half-swimming for what seemed like an hour, and the beach looked no closer than it had when he'd begun. It was with immense relief that he saw an amtrack chewing its way slowly across the Betio lagoon, pausing here and there to pick up small groups of wet Marines. When the LVT rumbled close, he handed up his rifle, then lifted his arms as a half dozen men aboard hauled him dripping from the lagoon.

"Hiya, hiya! Tighman's Taxi, at yer service!" a jaunty Marine sergeant at the alligator's tiller shouted. "Always room fer one more! Give that man a hand, there!"

The vehicle was one of those from an earlier wave that had made it to shore, dropped off its load of Marines, and was now shuttling back and forth across the lagoon, picking up scores of other Marines stranded on the reef and carrying them in to the beach. According to one of the Marines who'd hauled Barnes from the water, Sergeant Tighman had made three trips already.

At four knots, the vehicle churned and rumbled toward the beach. Designed to carry twenty-five men, it currently held at least forty Marines. They were packed in so tightly that Barnes could not clamber down into its well deck but had to ride on the gunwale with his legs dangling over the starboard side. He felt terribly exposed there, as artillery shells continued to crash and thump on either side of the slow-moving craft, as bullets snipped and zinged overhead, as spurts of seawater erupted into the air in rapidly running chains, lashed to fury by automatic fire from the shore. He was also disturbed by the sight of so many bodies floating in the lagoon, bobbing gently until the alligator's wake knocked them aside. One body, floating on its back, was missing its head and left arm, and the gore had spilled from the open chest cavity like scarlet ribbons on the water.

Barnes battled against a desperate nausea, trying not to be sick.

Jesus Christ, what had gone *wrong?* The predawn bombardment and the steady air attacks were supposed to have knocked out the Jap guns and bunkers. The alligators were to have stormed the sea wall in the first wave, the landing craft were to have reinforced them in strength, and instead everything was falling apart. Hell, while they'd been waiting out there in the predawn darkness, Marcinko had joked about hoping the Navy left some Japs for the Marines to deal with.

Poor Marcinko. He hadn't even made it onto dry land.

They were a lot closer to the beach now, close enough that the Marines manning the amtrack's two machine guns were firing them, at targets Barnes could only guess at. He could make out the sea wall through a haze of white smoke. Most of the island's palm trees had been splintered by the shelling, but a few forlorn specimens remained, their fronds drooping dejectedly from their crowns or missing entirely. On the beach beneath them, hundreds of Marines crouched in the shelter of a coconut log and coral block sea wall four or maybe five feet tall.

From fifty yards out, he could see a few Marines shooting across the barricade at unseen Japanese positions, and once one stood up, almost defiantly in the teeth of the enemy fire, cocked his arm, and let fly with a grenade. The vast majority of the invaders, however, could do nothing but crouch in the sea wall's shadow, tending their wounded and waiting for orders that might well never come. The water's edge was littered with equipment, with crates, with splintered chunks of coconut logs, with broken radios and jerry cans and packs, with the broken and burning wreckage of shattered LVTs, and everywhere, horribly, the obscenely twisted bodies of dead Marines.

If anything, the incoming fire was fiercer, more concentrated, than it had been on the reef. Mortar shells were dropping into the water just below the beach with a savage one-two-three regularity. Dozens of obstacles protruded from the water, with gaps in the defenses serving to channel the invaders into tightly concentrated killing zones. The sheer volume of enemy fire was devastating, an incessant hammering that filled Barnes's universe and threatened to swallow him whole. An explosion roared five yards off the alligator's port side, and the vehicle rocked ominously in the chop. They were twenty yards from the water's edge, now. Come *on! Come on!*

Something hit the amtrack. Barnes didn't hear an explosion, but he felt the shock and lurch as the vehicle's tail dipped sharply, then rebounded. Somehow, clinging to a cleat, he managed to hang on. Turning, he saw that the entire aft half of the LVT was a seething wall of flame.

The fire raced through the stricken amtrack, consuming men in a savage conflagration. Barnes saw Sergeant

Tighman, still at the LVT's conn, his skin blackening under the fire's searing, relentless caress. Dozens of Marines, their clothing aflame, leaped shrieking into the water. Barnes followed, landing clumsily in waist-deep water, stumbling, then coming up spitting salt water. Behind him, a gasoline tank beneath the amtrack's decks blew, and the concussion knocked him under again. With his ears ringing louder than the crash and thunder of the battle, he staggered toward the shore.

His rifle! He didn't have his rifle! Oh, God, where was his rifle? Damn, damn, *damn*—he'd left it on the amtrack. His weapon's loss devastated him as much as had losing the rest of his squad. Somehow, planting one foot in front of the other, he splashed from the water and onto the beach. He felt a swelling surge of triumph. He'd made it! He'd waded that bloody lagoon of blood and fire and death and he'd made it! With so many dead, he would be able to find another weapon and finally, *finally* get to shoot back. . . .

Jeanie would be proud of him.

He'd taken four steps onto the beach when a Japanese machine gun hidden in a pit covered over with logs, sandbags, and palm fronds opened fire, the burst cutting down Barnes and two nearby Marines.

He never even heard the shot that killed him.

Flag Plot
U.S.S. *Maryland*

Galloway stood with the other officers in a semicircle about the map table, which showed Betio, the surrounding reefs, and the neatly squared-off lanes and holding boxes for the landing craft. The clock on the wall read 1335 hours; the Marines had been ashore for over four hours now, but at last report they still held only three tiny pockets along the beach.

"It is clear now," Admiral Hill's Chief of Staff was telling the others, "that the so-called 'dodging tides' were more severe in their effect than anticipated. Apparently, at neap tide in this area, unusual combinations of wind and current can cause the sea level to fluctuate unpredictably during a six-hour period. Rather than being four or five feet deep over the inner reefs, the water was less than two. While the amtracks of the first three waves were able to make it through to the beach, the landing craft in the following waves grounded in shoal water.

"Unfortunately, the full extent of the disaster was not appreciated until after the first waves were already ashore. Succeeding waves piled up on the reefs and added to the confusion, while most of the men were forced to wade across five hundred yards of open water four feet deep. Worse, the Japanese apparently have spent most of their time on Betio strengthening the fortifications. The reports we've had from the beach tell of a tremendously intricate network of trenches, tunnels, beach obstacles, pillboxes, and fortified gun emplacements. While the largest shore batteries appear to have been knocked out by our bombardment, the vast majority of the defenses remain intact. The Japanese are defending their positions ashore with a tenacity that can only be described as suicidal."

A sailor with a messenger's brassard appeared at the door. "Admiral Hill?"

Admiral Hill, a genial man who was known throughout the task force as "Just Plain Harry," waved him in. "Here, son."

The messenger handed him a flimsy. As Hill read it, Galloway could hear the distant crump and rumble of the battle still raging on Betio.

At last, Hill looked up. "Gentlemen. This is a radio intercept. At thirteen-thirty hours, General Julian Smith, on the beach, radioed the *Pennsylvania,* off Makin. He has requested the release of the reserves. His message ends, 'Issue in doubt.' "

Galloway closed his eyes. "Issue in doubt!"

They were teetering at the brink of disaster. It was entirely possible that the Marines would be forced to evacuate their slender beachhead.

A new thought occurred to him. *Could* the Marines be evacuated? At last report, fifteen hundred Marines were already ashore, pinned down behind Betio's sea wall. Perhaps 90 of the 125 amtracks available for the landing had already been knocked out. To bring the men off, they would have to wait for the tide to rise enough for boats to get in across those deathtrap reefs.

In the teeth of that sleeting fire, that savage mortaring, it was possible that the invasion's leaders would be forced to write off the men already ashore. Unthinkable! The Marines *never* abandoned their own!

But what other alternative was there?

Chapter 19

Saturday, 20 November 1943

Tarawa

Ultimately, the fate of the Marines already ashore on Tarawa was determined by the Marines themselves. Throughout that first long and bloody afternoon, Marines continued to straggle onto the beach singly or in small groups, brought ashore by the handful of surviving amtracks or walking all the way in, sometimes across distances of as much as a mile and a half.

On Betio, officers rounded up ad hoc squads and led them across the sea wall. Pillboxes were sealed one by one by tossing half-pound blocks of TNT through the firing slits, by covering them over with sand scraped up by bulldozers, or by burning them out with flamethrowers. Along one stretch of beach, Japanese snipers had been positioned every ten feet; many waited until after the American line had passed before revealing themselves with a single, well-placed shot. In many places, half-buried pillboxes and blockhouses could be subdued only by dozens of Marines swarming up their walls and onto their roofs, then firing down through the openings on top or dropping in satchels loaded with high explosives.

By nightfall, however, five thousand men were ashore, at a cost of fifteen hundred killed and wounded. Individual actions by squad-sized units had expanded the initial beachhead to a pocket three hundred yards wide. Somehow, they hung on through the night, while Turner and his officers discussed whether or not they dared attempt an evacuation.

The next morning, one battalion of the divisional reserve fought its way ashore, losing 13 officers and 331 men in the assault but reinforcing the desperately slender perimeter. By noon, the treacherous tide had turned, finally, and for the first time landing craft began bringing Marines, heavy equipment, tanks, and ammunition all the way to the beach. New landings took place on Betio's western side, as well as on the neighboring island of Bairiki.

With the turning of the ocean's tide, the tide of battle turned as well. By 22 November, the Japanese had been pushed back into three small pockets, and a series of fanatical banzai charges were cut down almost to a man.

By the time Galloway was able to bum a ride ashore, early on the afternoon of 23 November, Tarawa had been declared secured. The bodies had been evacuated already, but the sick-sweet stench of death still clung to the sweltering, naked island. Galloway picked his way across the shell-torn beach and past a pillbox that had been scorched black by a flamethrower and was still smoking. Nearby, Marines and Seabees were busily unloading construction equipment from a beached LCM, while a bulldozer rumbled its way up a crushed-coral embankment that bridged the sea wall, passed beneath the burnt-match remnants of topless coconut palms, and connected with a brand-new road leading to Betio's airfield. Navy planes were already taking off from that field; he could hear the clattering whirr of their propellers as they taxied onto the runway.

A few yards away, three grim-faced Marines were leading a prisoner down to the beach. The PW had been completely stripped of everything save a breechclout and a dirty bandage on his right ankle. He limped ahead, arms high, a look of sullen anger on his face as his captors prodded him from behind.

"Some of his buddies've surrendered with dynamite strapped on under their clothes, Lieutenant," one of the Ma-

rines said when he saw Galloway staring at the procession.
"We like t'make sure, know what I mean?"

"Damn," Galloway said. "What went wrong?" The Marine, a gunnery sergeant in torn and smoke-blackened combat fatigues, wore a tired, almost glazed expression on his
face, but he seemed willing to talk. Galloway wanted to
know what the men who'd fought here felt.

"Shit, what didn't go wrong?" The Marine slung his M-1
carbine as his buddies led the prisoner on down to the
beach. "Gotta light?"

Galloway handed him half a pack of Camels and told him
to keep them. The Marine took them with a grin that did not
quite reach his eyes, then accepted fire from Galloway's
lighter.

"Ah, that's good," he said, drawing the first puff.
"Thanks, Mac."

"Don't mention it."

After a moment's silence, the sergeant seemed to arrive at
some decision. "What went wrong? Look, Lieutenant. I
ain't the brass. Maybe you should talk t'them."

"You think they know more about what went on here
than you guys?"

"Ha! No, I guess not. Well, if y'ask me, someone fucked
up with the intel. The first wave got ashore okay in the
'tracks, but the second and third waves ran into trouble
when the Nips woke up. Then everything went to hell when
the landing craft started piling up on that fuckin' reef. Shit,
my boys were walkin' targets out there, wadin' in from the
boat. Out of my whole squad, I'm the only one I know of
who made it ashore. We shoulda had decent charts of those
reefs, and we shoulda had some kind of reconnaissance on
the Jap obstacles, especially the ones in the water. A longer
bombardment woulda helped, too." He sucked down the last
quarter inch of the cigarette, its tip a brightly glowing coal.
Then he tossed the butt on the sand and shook his head.
"But I'll tell ya one thing, Lieutenant. A hell of a lot of
good men—boys, most of 'em—got thrown away on this
beach the other day. It was a fuckin' waste, and I for one
don't want to see it happen again."

Galloway glanced at the man's breast pocket, where the
name HOLMES was barely legible in faded stencil ink. "Nei-

ther do I, Gunny." He wanted to add something else, something like "Good job" or "You guys did a hell of a job," but words seemed so pathetically inadequate here on this blood-purchased sand. Impulsively, he lifted his fingers to the bill of his hat, saluting the Marine in a breach of the military protocol that required the junior man to salute the senior. Holmes seemed startled, then returned the salute, touching his hand to the rim of his camouflaged helmet cover.

Galloway returned to the *Maryland* that afternoon. By the next day, he was winging back across the Pacific aboard an Army C-47.

He was already composing his report to Admiral King.

Monday, 29 November 1943

The Pentagon

"TERRIBLE TARAWA!"

The week-old newspaper lying front-page-up on Admiral King's desk seemed to scream its headline. Much of that front page was devoted to accounts of the slaughter. There was a photograph, too, of dead Marines lying at the edge of the surf. The War Department had only recently lifted its censorship of such pictures, and the images were still shocking both in their intensity and in their newness. Galloway had to remind himself that similar images had first been captured almost a century before, during the Civil War. Somehow, their display as part of a newspaper headline carried an impact that was unsettling. He had actually *been* there, had seen some of those bodies and the rows of white body bags, and still he could not look at that simple black-and-white photo without feeling a stab of pain.

Coffer had returned to Washington and was sitting in a chair to one side of King's desk. Also present was another Navy officer, Captain Tom Hill—no relation to Task Force 53's Just-Plain-Harry. Coffer, Hill, and King all listened in silence as Galloway told them about what he'd seen at Tarawa and gave them his conclusions.

"My recommendation, Admiral," he said, wrapping up his verbal report, "would be to start folding NCDU teams into our amphibious operations out there just as quickly as is possible. Small units, working from boats or from rubber rafts, could have surveyed the beach approaches to the island. They also could have marked or blown up some of the obstacles in the Betio lagoon. The Japs had those planted to funnel our landing craft into plotted fire zones."

"Hmm." King shifted in his chair. "Possibly. They couldn't have predicted those dodging tides."

"Maybe not. But they might have found and marked gaps in the coral. And if there weren't any gaps in the coral to begin with, they could have blasted some. If there'd been Navy demolition teams along, we might have had landing craft going ashore at Betio by mid-afternoon of the twentieth, instead of at noon the next day. How many lives would have been spared if we'd done that, Admiral?"

King sighed. He looked worn down, and there were circles under his eyes, as though he'd not been getting much sleep during the past week or two. "I really don't know, Lieutenant. I do know that we can't go second-guessing ourselves. We pick up from right here and get on with it."

"We also learn from our mistakes," Captain Hill said quietly. "Sir."

"Yes." There was an uncomfortable silence. He glanced up at Galloway. "Admiral Turner has already written a long report," King said finally. "He's also endorsed the idea of what he calls 'beach reconnaissance forces.' "

Galloway nodded. He'd seen an unclassified extract of that report already and discussed it at length with Tom Hill during the flight across country to Washington. He'd first met Captain Hill, Admiral Turner's Operational Readiness Officer, during his layover in Pearl. Hill had told him of a meeting with himself, Turner, and Captain Jack Taylor, Turner's Staff Gunnery Officer, after Tarawa where they'd discussed the lessons learned in the costly operation. Turner had assigned Hill the task of convincing both CINCPAC and the CNO of the urgent need for Navy reconnaissance teams. Planning had already begun for the invasion of the Marshall Islands, and something would be needed by then.

"I'm still concerned about the men's level of training," King said. "From what I've been given to understand, they've been trained to operate in small boats. Won't that be suicide, sending them up under the enemy guns in the open like that?"

"Not necessarily, sir." Commander Coffer leaned forward in his chair. Galloway heard the eagerness in his voice. "At Tarawa, the Japanese didn't really start to fire back until the second wave reached the beach. We think it likely that their troops won't open fire on a small group of men, because that would give away the number and the position of their guns. For all they know, that's why we're going to be out there, trying to tempt them into taking potshots at us while we write down the location of their strong points."

"I don't see any guarantees there, Commander."

"Hell, who said anything's guaranteed in wartime, Admiral? We have to take risks or we risk losing everything."

"It's also possible that a lot of the work could be done at night, Admiral," Galloway pointed out.

"That's right," Coffer said. "At Fort Pierce, we've been training the men hard in night operations."

"Very well," King said at last. "Commander, Admiral Turner has suggested that he set things in motion by setting up a training school in Hawaii. Someplace to teach reconnaissance personnel what they need to know about mapping, beach survey work, and so on. Could you have some of those people ready to go to Hawaii in, say, two weeks?"

"Abso-damn-lutely, Admiral."

Galloway smiled. He'd clearly heard the unspoken "and it's about time" in Coffer's reply.

"Captain Hill has orders to begin selection for such a class," King continued. "He can go with you, perhaps help you with the details."

"Yes, sir."

"We're also going to need teams for assignment to England. I want to see your TO&E for that as quickly as possible. Any questions, gentlemen? Very well. Dismissed."

Coffer seemed positively buoyant. "Aye, *aye*, sir!"

Galloway felt that same buoyancy himself. After all of these months, the training at Fort Pierce, the blundering at Tarawa, at last, perhaps, Coffer's NCDU teams were about to prove their worth.

He was convinced of it.

Fort Pierce, Florida

An insistent pounding on the door brought Richardson blearily awake. Now what the hell?

Beside him in the bed, a naked girl stirred, murmured something in her sleep, and snuggled closer. The knocking sounded again, louder this time, and faster.

"Hey! Snake!" The words were a hoarsely shouted whisper, loud enough to penetrate the door, quiet enough that no more than ten or twenty of the other guests in the hotel would be awakened. *"C'mon, man! Show a leg!"*

Damn. It was Gator. Now what the hell did *he* want?

The girl was already showing plenty of leg, Richardson thought. He could just make out her form in the moonlight spilling through the window. Her bare left thigh lay across his hips, her head was cradled on his left arm. He searched a memory fuzzy with sleep. What was her name? He remembered meeting her in town on liberty earlier, remembered checking into one of Fort Pierce's small resort hotels, then sneaking her up the back stairs.

She was a delicious redhead, he remembered, not much in the chest department but with a lively enthusiasm on the sheets that reminded Richardson of what's-her-name, the admiral's daughter, back in Norfolk. But what the hell was her name?

The next round of knocking at the door was loud enough to rattle the hinges. Gently, so as not to wake her, he extracted himself, freeing his arm first, then sliding out from under her leg. She moaned and stirred, then rolled onto her stomach. He reached down and patted her buttocks.

"Snake!"

It was a cool night and the hotel window was wide open, but he didn't stop to retrieve his clothes. Naked except for his wristwatch, he padded across the floor to the door and threw it open. Tangretti was standing in the hallway, wearing his dress whites.

"Gator!" he whispered fiercely. "What's with all the damn racket!"

"Drop your cock and grab your socks, buddy boy," Tangretti said. He looked past Richardson, and his nostrils flared slightly as he saw the girl in the bed. "Oops. Sorry to interrupt. But this is important."

"What," Richardson said with great deliberation, "could possibly be more important than getting laid?"

"We gotta get back to the base, and I mean now!"

"How come?" He held his wrist up and squinted at his watch. "Christ, Gator! It's only twenty-three-hundred! Liberty's on till oh-seven hundred tomorrow!"

"One word, Snake. Hawaii!"

"Huh? What are you talking about?"

"Friend of mine over in Personnel just gave me the straight dope. Coffer himself just phoned in the orders. They want to put together some guys for a special team. They'll be calling for volunteers at morning formation. Then it's off to Hawaii for a quick class in beach survey work, followed by assignment to the fleet."

"Fine. I volunteer. I'll see you in the morning." He started to close the door.

"Hold it, Snake! Don't you understand? They'll be asking for volunteers at zero-seven hundred. Every guy on the base who's even halfway through training's gonna be screaming for a place on this unit. We'll have a chance in a hundred of getting picked."

"So what's the angle?"

"The angle is we get back tonight. I happen to know that Chief Wallace has the duty. We'll get to him first, convince him to put us down on the list tonight."

"Why should he?"

"Because we asked nice. Because we asked first. Because we used our superior reconnaissance skills to uncover this intelligence. Because of our special experience during training."

"Shit. What special experience?"

"Hell, do I have to think of everything? Think of something!"

Despite his initial reluctance, Richardson found himself nodding, then agreeing enthusiastically with Tangretti. "Okay," he said. "Okay. I need time to get my shit together here. You go ahead back and put in both our names. I'll be along as quick as I can."

"Don't fail me, buddy. This is what we've been working

for ever since last summer!" He looked past Richardson's shoulder again, appreciatively studying the naked girl asleep in the bed. "Nice," he added. "You sure you have enough rubbers?"

Richardson and Tangretti both had become a constant source of in-jokes and ribald humor within the teams ever since the idea of using condoms as waterproofing for the so-called waterproof fuse igniters had been adopted. Snake was targeted, naturally enough, for the number of rubbers he supposedly used, and because it was rumored he'd come up with the idea only to insure that he had an adequate supply. Gator was ribbed because on several occasions, when the amphib base supply officer had been unable to get enough cases of prophylactics shipped to Fort Pierce, it was Tangretti who'd made the necessary contacts at Norfolk, the Navy Yard, and elsewhere to cumshaw enough to see them through.

"As you were, sailor," Richardson said, stiff-arming Tangretti in the chest and knocking him back a step away from the door. "I'll let you know."

Gently, Richardson closed the door and threw the bolt. He could hear Tangretti whistling as he moved off down the passageway outside.

"Hank?"

The girl was sitting up in bed now, rubbing her eyes. Her long red hair spilled in a glorious tangle over her bare shoulders.

"Hey, babe. Sorry to wake you."

"S'okay. Who was that? What time is it?"

"A little before eleven. Go back to sleep."

He walked over to the side of the bed. Gator's news had excited him, provoking a rather dramatic and uncontrollable physical response. As he leaned over the bed, the girl reached out, took him in both hands, and began gently fondling him. "Gee, we don't *have* to go to sleep, do we, Hank? I mean, as long as we're already awake and everything . . ."

Well, hell, Richardson told himself. He could spare another thirty minutes or so before catching the liberty bus back to the base. He let her guide him down on top of her. After she was asleep again, he'd gather up his stuff and quietly slip out. It was better that way, quick, clean, and no hard good-byes.

Katie! *That* was her name!

Tuesday, 30 November 1943

Georgetown

"God*damn* it, Joe! Why didn't you tell me you were going over there!"

Galloway took a step back, his hands raised before him as if to ward off a blow. "Hey, easy, Ginnie! I'm sorry, but things happened so fast, I just didn't have time. Besides . . ."

"Besides, what?" Her eyes were dark with her anger.

"Well, I just didn't want you to worry, that's all."

They were standing in Galloway's apartment early on Tuesday morning. This was a definite improvement over Mrs. Dilmore's two-rooms-and-a-bath. It was larger, located closer to the Pentagon, and it had real hot water. He still didn't have kitchen privileges, but the landlady had no objection to his bringing women into the apartment—as long as there were no loud parties and no *obvious* hanky-panky at night.

It suited Galloway perfectly. Virginia had wanted him to stay at the Lewis house indefinitely, but he'd felt more comfortable with a place of his own, out of the reach of her father and his prejudices against Catholics, Jews, and Republicans. Galloway was neither Jewish nor Republican, but one out of three had been enough to convince him that sooner or later he would say the wrong thing.

And then Virginia's father might well forbid her to see him again.

He had no doubt that Virginia would find a way around such an obstruction. She was a determined, even a willful, young lady, and he doubted very much that there was anything she couldn't or wouldn't have if she set her mind on having it. But he didn't want to be the cause of hard feeling between her and the rest of her family. Besides, he savored the privacy his apartment afforded him.

Having Virginia show up on his doorstep at six A.M., however, was showing signs of becoming a habit. This was the second time since last May she'd awakened him with a knock on the door, though this time, at least, she was wearing a skirt-and-blouse outfit instead of slacks, with a black leather pocketbook slung over one shoulder. He did hope that, if Mrs. Carmichael was on the prowl, she'd seen Virginia arrive. Even if his present landlady was more accepting of the modern-day collapse of American morals than the last one, apartments in Washington were still damned hard to find, and he had no wish to press his luck.

Just as he had no wish to face Virginia's anger.

"You head off for the South Pacific without even saying good-bye! You get back yesterday and you don't even tell me! I ought to knock a knot on your head!"

"Virginia, please!" He wished she would keep her voice down. "I was tied up with Admiral King all day yesterday. I never even made it down to Metzel's office to say hello. I was going to look you up first thing this morning."

Was that really true? There were a lot of feelings he would never have admitted to Virginia, partly because he didn't want to admit them even to himself. He was undeniably attracted to her, and from the depth of her anger, he had a pretty good idea now that she felt the same way about him.

But he couldn't become involved with a woman, not *now*.

"A likely story," she said, her arms folded across her breasts, but she didn't sound as angry now. Her lips twitched back, the ghost of a smile. "I think you're just like every other sailor I've heard about. A girl in every port, a port in every girl."

"Ginnie!"

"Oh, damn it, Joe! I'm sorry. I just don't want anything to happen to you! I . . . I don't think I could stand that."

She came into his arms. Self-consciously—once again, he was wearing only his skivvies and a rather tattered old bathrobe—he gave her a gentle hug.

Somehow, the gentle hug became a passionate one, and they were kissing. Her pocketbook dropped to the floor by their feet, and her mouth opened wide beneath his. His robe had fallen open, and he could feel her soft breasts straining against him through the thin material of her blouse. The smell of her filled his nostrils, intense and erotic. Thoroughly aroused now, he could not hide the erection swelling in his shorts. The bulge was acutely embarrassing, a dead giveaway to how much he wanted her, how much he *needed* her.

He started to draw back. Virginia slipped her left hand between them, touching him lightly. "You know, Joe," she said softly, "you haven't been working in my office for a *long* time now."

"What . . . what about your father?"

Her expression hardened for a moment. "Do you think I'm going to march to his drum for the rest of my life? I'm twenty-six years old, Joe. I'm a grown woman and I've got my own life to live." She touched him again, harder, more aggressively. He could see the invitation in her dark eyes. For a dizzying moment, he was ready to sweep her up off her feet and carry her back to his bed. . . .

"I think," he said, his mouth gone dry, "I think maybe you'd better leave."

He read the quick, successive flashes of disappointment, of hurt, and of anger in her eyes. She stepped back, and he hastily closed his robe. "Look," he said. "I didn't mean—"

"I'm sorry I bothered you, Lieutenant. Good-bye." She started to reach for her pocketbook.

"No, Ginnie!" Reaching out, he grabbed her arm, pulling her back. "Wait! Don't go!"

"Obviously, you don't want me here," she said, the faintest tremble evident beneath the control she was imposing over her words. "Let me go."

He released her. "Ginnie, please. I didn't mean it that way."

"How am I supposed to think you meant it? I practically throw myself at you and you push me away!" She turned from him, her eyes on the floor. "You must think I'm awful. A . . . a slut. . . ."

"Oh, God. Not at all. I . . . please. Can I explain?"

She didn't answer, didn't even seem to hear, but he plunged ahead, speaking quickly. "Ginnie, I care a lot about you. I have for a long time, I guess. I think maybe I'm just now starting to find out how much. But at the same time, I'm starting to feel like if I don't get out of this damned town I'm going to go crazy. I don't know how much longer I can take this."

It was true. Since Coffer had set up the headquarters for the NCDU in Fort Pierce, Galloway had felt like some kind of castaway, isolated in an office of his own buried in the labyrinthine depths of the Pentagon. He even had a staff of his own now—a civilian secretary, a Navy chief, and an Army sergeant who served as messenger and all-around errand boy. His official title was Pentagon Staff Liaison Officer, which, roughly translated, meant he was Coffer's link to Admiral King's staff, seeing to it that the NCDU's needs and goals were not lost within the vast chaos of Washington's military bureaucracy.

Hell's Bottom. That described Galloway's opinion of the Pentagon perfectly. The place was a kind of five-sided maw that swallowed men's careers and lives and never let them go. He'd chosen to make the *sea* his career, damn it, not the sterile passageways and treacherous personal politics of Fort Fumble.

He'd requested reassignment several times and been denied each time. His work, his experience with Coffer and with the NCDU staff, was too valuable, he'd been told. But now that the first teams were about to be sent overseas, he thought, that could very well change.

"You know how much I need to get out of here," he told Virginia. "To get a ship, *any* ship, somewhere out where the action is, where every request doesn't have to be typed up in triplicate and politics is just another sport to be argued about, like baseball. Damn it all, I can't spend the rest of my Navy career telling other guys to go fight and maybe get killed while I sit on my tail here shuffling papers!"

"What does that have to do with . . . with us?" Tears were trickling down her cheeks, one after the other, leaving crinkled wet trails in her makeup.

"Ginnie, if I get what I want, I'll be leaving. Going overseas. Maybe even for the invasion."

Invasion. The word had been on people's lips more and

more of late, used specifically for the creation of a new
front in Europe. The Allied invasion of Italy, begun with
such promise in September, was rapidly bogging down
among the razorback ridges, the mountains, and the narrow,
muddy roads of that country. Clearly, the next step in the
liberation of Europe would be *another* invasion, probably in
France. Everyone knew it was coming. The only question
was when.

Galloway wanted to be a part of that, wanted it so badly
he could taste it. Damn it, it was *his* turn!

He looked into Virginia's wet eyes but saw no comprehension there. "Don't you see?" he asked her. "In the Pentagon, the worst thing that can happen to me is an infected
paper cut. Or maybe getting lost. Over there . . ." He
shrugged. He'd had one ship torpedoed out from under him.
He knew how slender his chances were if that should happen again.

And Virginia had already lost one man to this war. "Anything could happen. I can't—can't—make any promises
now that I might not be able to keep."

"I understand all of that, Joe," she said. Her voice was
very low, the words almost inaudible at first but growing
stronger as she spoke. "You say you want out of Washington? Well so do I! My God, do you have any idea what it's
like being the daughter of Howard Lewis, gray eminence to
the Secretary of War? Or how hard it is for a single girl to
get out and live on her own in this damned city? To even
find an *apartment* that will take her?"

"I know it must be hard—"

"You're damned right it's hard! Most people think that a
girl trying to live on her own is a prostitute."

"I—"

"What I wanted, Joseph Galloway, was *you*. And maybe,
I suppose, the freedom to make one adult decision for myself for a change." For one brief moment, he thought she
was going to melt into his arms again and he reached out
for her. But she stepped back with a small shake of her
head.

"You know," she continued, "the worst part of it is, now
you're standing there thinking that I tried to seduce you be-

cause I'm looking for some goddamned white knight on
horseback to come and carry me away from all this. A prostitute trades sex for money. Is trading sex for security any
different?"

"I don't think that at all, Ginnie."

"Maybe not. But I do. I don't ... I don't know what
came over me, Joe. I've never done anything like *that* in my
life. Maybe ... maybe I just didn't want to lose you. Like
I lost Bernie."

"Ginnie—" He stopped, confused. He was pretty sure he
loved this girl ... and that she loved him. But it still
wouldn't be fair for him to love her and leave her, rushing
off to battle, quite possibly never to return.

On the other hand, if two people needed each other, did
anything else in the whole world matter?

He reached for her again ...

... and she stepped aside, shaking her head. "Joe, this
isn't going to work."

"We can make it work. . . ."

"No." She almost smiled. "You sailors have one of those
salty expressions ... about having all your shit in one seabag?"

He nodded. The vulgarity on Virginia's lips surprised
him, left him unsure of what to say.

"Well, I think we'd better keep each other at arm's length
for now. Until you have your priorities worked out. And until I've worked out mine. Especially ... I've got to know
I'm not *using* you to get away from my father. Or to get
back at him for Bernie."

Stooping, she picked up her pocketbook from where it
had fallen on the floor. She fished inside for a moment, extracted a lady's handkerchief, and dabbed at her eyes. Closing the handbag again, she looked up and gave him a
cheerful imitation of a smile.

"So. Give me a call sometime, when you ... when you
have all your shit in one seabag. Okay?" Turning abruptly,
she walked quickly to the door. He thought she might be
trying to hide the new tears that were continuing the de-
struction of her makeup. He wanted to go after her, but his
indecision left him rooted to the spot, not knowing what to
do or what to say.

Then she was gone, and Galloway took a deep breath.
Damn it all. Why did life have to be so complicated?

Chapter 20

Wednesday, 1 December 1943

Waimanalo Amphibious Base
Hawaii

Richardson made it . . . just barely. He'd gotten to the Fort
Pierce headquarters an hour after Tangretti had already gone
in to talk to Wallace, arriving just in time to clinch the argument. "Look at it this way, Chief," he'd said happily. "At
least this way, you can tell the supply officer that the guy
who needs all those rubbers has shipped out!"

"It might be worth it, Snake," Wallace had replied, "just
to have you out of my hair!"

The two of them were on a C-47 bound for the West
Coast, and Hawaii, the next afternoon.

From that extended first class of Seabees and bomb disposal experts recruited and trained at Fort Pierce throughout
the summer and fall of 1943, some eleven Navy Combat
Demolition Units were organized and shipped overseas. The
first one, the six men of NCDU Number One, had left before the other teams finished training, bound for the
reoccupation of the Aleutian Islands. Foul-ups in orders, and
the fact that no one else in the Navy quite knew what to do
with the new unit, resulted in the team's being stranded in
San Francisco, having literally missed the boat.

NCDU Numbers Two and Three ended up in the Southwest Pacific, serving with General MacArthur's forces.
Since some of the Army staff officers thought the new units

were a kind of specially trained Seabee unit, and because MacArthur himself preferred to use Army engineers rather than Navy Construction Battalions, those teams were never used as Coffer had intended, as reconnaissance and demolition units ahead of American invasion troops.

Two more NCDUs went to North Africa, where they began training more teams; another was transferred to England, where it was to begin preliminary work preparing for the invasion of France; two were sent directly to the South Pacific, where they were assigned to Amphibious Force Three under Rear Admiral Wilkinson; and three ended up in Hawaii, where they reported to Admiral Turner.

Turner, excited by what Captain Hill had told him about Coffer's NCDUs, was busily creating his own organization. The men from Fort Pierce were happily accepted; so too were volunteers from the Pacific. The Pacific teams already included Navy Seabees, Army personnel with demolition experience, and U.S. Marines fresh from Tarawa.

There also was a brand-new name for the organization; from now on, Turner's people would be known as the Underwater Demolition Teams.

So far the volunteers, old hands and new recruits alike, had been organized into two teams. The TO&E called for each to have a strength of one hundred men, formed up into four operating platoons of twenty men apiece, plus a headquarters platoon. UDT-1 was under the command of Lieutenant Edward D. Breucort, a Seabee officer stationed in Hawaii who'd volunteered for hazardous duty and been reassigned to the new team as a result. UDT-2 was given to Lieutenant Thomas C. Chapman, a lanky, soft-spoken Seabee from Texas. Richardson and Tangretti, insisting that they were partners and didn't want to be separated, were both assigned to UDT-1.

Neither Tangretti nor Richardson much liked the changes. They'd volunteered for this duty under the impression that the Fort Pierce gang, as they called themselves, would serve together in their own unit. There'd been a sense of camaraderie with their own people, all the more when they knew that every man in the team, from the lowest-rated enlisted man to the most senior officer, had been through the same training.

Hell Week, it seemed, had forged a sense of belonging among those who'd survived it.

"I dunno, Snake," Tangretti said as the two men walked toward the headquarters building for the Waimanalo Amphibious Base. "I think we got ourselves dealt a bad hand here."

"What do you mean 'we,' Gator? I seem to recall it was you pounding on my hotel door the other night. 'One word,' you said. 'Hawaii,' you said. Well, fine! We're in Hawaii! Wonder-fuckin'-ful!"

Tangretti's doubts about staying in the NCDU had vanished sometime during the training at Fort Pierce. He loved the teams, so long as he had the freedom to make his contacts and swing his deals. Before he'd been forced to volunteer, he realized now, most of his efforts had been directed at making his life—his own personal niche within the service—as comfortable as possible. He still liked his comfort—after a day of exhausting hard labor in wet clothes, salt water, and burning sun he liked to arrange all the comforts he could manage—but most of his efforts now were devoted toward the *team*.

Since arriving on Oahu, though, a lot of those doubts had returned.

Waimanalo was located just across the Koolau mountain range from Honolulu, just down the coast from Bellows Field. East, the morning sun sparkled from the azure waters of Waimanalo Bay. Headquarters was a Quonset hut built just above the beach. Jungle-clad Konahuanui towered three thousand feet overhead, beneath an impossibly deep and blue, cloud-puffed sky.

"Yeah," Tangretti agreed after a moment's silence. "I know what I said. But damn it all, I don't think they know what they're doing out here, Snake! They got a fuckin' *Seabee* in command."

"You're a Seabee."

"Not anymore I'm not! I'm NCDU!"

Richardson shook his head. "Nope. Sorry to have to break it to you, pal, but you're a bluejacket. And that means you're whatever the Navy says you are, that you follow orders and like it."

"But . . . but *Jesus,* Snake! A Seabee in charge!"

"Hey, that just means we'll have all the comforts of home, right? Cumshaw liquor. Cumshaw fresh fruit. C'mon, Gator. Let's go take the measure of this new CO."

An hour later, the members of UDT-1 were sitting in a semicircle under the palms behind the headquarters, listening to a tall man in green fatigues with the silver "railroad tracks" of a lieutenant on his collar address them.

"You boys're going to be learning a lot of new stuff here," Lieutenant Breucort was saying. "You people from the East Coast can forget all the shit you learned out there about German explosive devices, because the Japanese have their own bombs, mines, and booby traps. While we're here, we'll be going over all the devices we encountered at Tarawa, plus some new wrinkles we think they may be working on up in the Marshalls.

"We have been given four weeks for this training. In this course, you will be given training in hydrographic reconnaissance, in demolitions, in mapmaking, and in landing craft seamanship. Since most of you are already familiar with standard demolition techniques, we will emphasize what we've learned about Japanese obstacles and mines. You men from Tarawa know what I'm talking about.

"Boat drill will include measuring water depth and planting explosives from landing craft and from rubber boats. In deep water, personnel will wear standard fatigue uniforms, helmets, and Mae Wests. You will remain attached to your boats with a safety line at all times."

"Same drill as at Pierce," Tangretti whispered in an aside to Richardson.

"I think they're afraid we might get lost," Richardson replied.

"We will not emphasize hand-to-hand techniques here," Breucort continued, after shooting a hard glance at Richardson and Tangretti. "You men are considered too valuable for the Navy to risk you in direct engagements with the enemy."

"See?" Richardson added in a whisper just loud enough to carry to some of the nearer UDT men. "They don't want to lose us! I'm touched!"

If Breucort had heard the comment, which raised a small

titter from part of his audience, he ignored it. "We will also be familiarizing you with the operation of some of our new secret weapons."

Mention of the "secret weapons" caused a stir among the men. There'd been considerable speculation, based on the scuttlebutt that had been floating around the base since the UDT personnel had begun arriving there.

One man in the audience held up a brawny arm.

Breucort nodded at him. "Question, Chief?"

Chief Howard L. Schroeder stood up, tucking beefy hands into the front of his dungaree trousers. Schroeder was already something of a legend within the UDTs. Known as "Red Schroeder" for his extravagantly bushy, bright red beard, he was an old Navy China hand who claimed to have fought as a mercenary against the Japanese in China before Pearl Harbor.

"Yessir," Schroeder said. With his feet planted apart, with the piratical beard and a hard squint to his eye, all he needed was a cutlass to look the part of a modern-day buccaneer. "I was just wonderin' if this here secret weapon of yours is the Stingray."

Breucort stared at Schroeder for a long moment. "That information is classified, Chief."

"That's okay," Schroeder replied. "We're all friends here." That raised a laugh.

"I'd like to know where you got that information, Chief Schroeder."

"That wouldn't be a good idea, Lieutenant," Tangretti called out. "*That's* classified information. If he told you, sir, we'd have to shoot you."

"Hmm." Breucort considered that. "Looks to me like this group has some excess high spirits. A little run down the beach ought to redirect some of that energy into useful channels. Let's fall in!"

Tuesday, 21 December 1943

It was a few days before Christmas, the second after Pearl Harbor. The sky was crisp and blue, the temperature pleasantly in the mid seventies. Both UDT teams had been as-

sembled on the beach facing Waimanalo Bay for a
demonstration of the Stingray. On a table set up on the
beach was a complex-looking assembly of shortwave set,
gasoline generator, and control panel, all breadboarded together with electrical wires, power cables, and alligator
clips.

"Looks like Dr. Frankenstein's lab," Richardson commented. Tangretti and Schroeder were beside him, watching
the proceedings get under way.

"Can't be," Tangretti said. "We need a dungeon for that.
All we have here is sand and that landing craft."

"Is *that* what that thing is?" Schroeder said. He nodded
toward the boat drawn up onto the beach, an old Higgins
LCP(R) that had obviously been extensively modified. A
complex tangle of struts, wires, and tubes had been mounted
on the boat's well deck, extending above the gunwales. It
looked a little like a cluster of organ pipes, canted toward
the boat's bow. "I thought some mad cumshaw artist might
have been at work."

"More like a mad scientist," Richardson said. "Uh-oh.
Here comes the brass."

"The brass" included Captain Hill, of Admiral Turner's
staff, and several other Navy staff officers.

"Captain Hill," Lieutenant Breucort said, speaking loudly
enough that the entire group could hear. "Gentlemen. Welcome to our demonstration this morning. It is my pleasure
to introduce Commander Finch of the Navy's Special Weapons section, who will tell us about Project Stingray. Commander?"

"Thank you, Lieutenant." Finch was a small man with
glasses and a rumpled khaki uniform. His unmilitary presence and manner led Richardson to suspect that the man
was a scientist—or a bureaucrat—first, a naval officer second. "Good morning, everybody. The device you see on the
beach behind me is Stingray, a weapon that we feel confident will change the course of the war in the Pacific.

"What we have here is an ordinary, wood-hulled landing
barge, loaded with five tons of high explosives and radio-
controlled detonators. Controls have been rigged to allow
the craft to be operated, by remote control, as an unmanned
drone." He walked over to the table and rested his hands on

the large radio set there. "We can steer the craft from here across a range of several miles." Reaching across the radio, he touched the makeshift control panel. "This panel lets us operate one or two drones slaved off of a single unit. This switch scuttles the Stingray in the desired position. This one arms the explosives, and this one detonates them." He turned to the group of officers standing nearby. "Lieutenant Chapman? Would you care to demonstrate?"

"Aye, aye, sir."

Chapman took his place at the controls, flipped several switches, and turned a knob. The single engine on the landing craft coughed, sputtered once, then roared into life, accompanied by billowing clouds of blue smoke. Slowly, its bow scraping sand, the landing craft backed itself off the shelf, pivoted in the shallow water as the surf broke around it, then began puttering through the chop toward the open water of the bay.

"The idea, you see," Finch continued in his class lecturer's tone, "is to allow the new Underwater Demolition Teams to deploy their explosives over key spots in a barrier reef and detonate them by remote control. We can get larger amounts of explosive to the target this way, with far less risk to valuable personnel."

"Ah, Commander," Captain Hill called out. "What is that contraption mounted above the deck?"

"Ah! That's a special little something extra one of the 'Bees rigged up for the demonstration today, Captain. That is a battery of rockets, fired by remote control. They can be launched at the touch of a switch on the master panel. The idea is that the Stingray could actually participate in a naval bombardment en route to the reef it was assigned to blow."

"You know," Richardson said, whispering to Tangretti. "Chief Harrison, back at Pierce, would love this. Push-button warfare, right out of *Amazing Stories!*"

"It's amazing, all right," Tangretti said. "And a few other things I'm too polite to mention."

"I sense some overengineering here," Schroeder added. "You boys hang on to your hats."

The landing craft was chugging along perhaps one hundred yards offshore now. Finch pointed to a small, rocky island half a mile off the coast. Whitecaps and breakers surged above the coral heads, visible as a light green patch in the water against the ocean's deeper ultramarine.

"For the purposes of our demonstration, Captain, gentlemen, we will direct the test Stingray against that island. Lieutenant Chapman will demonstrate the rocket-launching feature, then direct the Stingray into the coral, where he will blast a channel through to the enemy beach! Mr. Chapman?"

The landing craft turned, swinging its bow toward the distant island as if by magic. Chapman flicked a switch, arming the rockets and, at a nod from Finch, closed one more switch.

Smoke and flame billowed from the framework mounted on the boat and then, almost too fast to follow, darts of orange flame streaked off from the landing craft's hull, arrowing through the sky on contrails of white smoke. The sound of the rockets, a rushing *shoosh-shoosh-shoosh*, reached the watchers on the beach an instant behind the launch.

Someone raised a cheer, and it was taken up by others in the audience, mingled with a patter of applause. The rockets arced down out of the sky well beyond the island, missing the target by a generous margin but providing a spectacularly wonderful show.

Tangretti was not watching the rockets. His eyes were glued to the landing craft. "Oh, shit. . . ."

"What?" Richardson couldn't see anything wrong.

"There's smoke coming out of the well deck. I think those rockets—"

The landing craft vanished in a white flash and a towering pillar of black smoke; water surged upward with the smoke and raced out from the detonation like a tidal wave. A thunderclap sounded an instant later. Every man on the beach dropped as one, lying full-length in the sand as the green column of water began to fall.

The wave reached the shore, racing high enough to slosh past the table where Lieutenant Chapman was staring at the controls, wondering what could possibly have gone wrong. A spark jumped from one of the cables lying on the sand, and the electrical generator died with a tired wheeze and a small puff of smoke. A fine mist rained from an otherwise clear sky, dampening the beach and its occupants and, out in the bay, bits and pieces of the landing craft, some of them afire or trailing smoke, dropped back into the water.

Slowly, with multiple echoes off the mountains at their backs, the roar of the explosion died away, leaving a stunned silence over the beach. The explosion had come far too soon, at least half a mile away from the target.

"Anybody hurt?" Schroeder called. "Everybody okay?" The audience had been entirely too close to the detonation of five tons of high explosives.

The assembled personnel rose to their feet again. Finch, the front of his crisp khaki uniform now coated with wet sand, brushed at his trousers ineffectually. "Mr. Chapman! I told you not to arm the explosives until—"

"Sir! It wasn't me! It was . . . I think those rockets set fire to the explosives, sir!"

"Oh, *shit!*"

The UDT men watching the show broke into whoops and gales of laughter, pounding each other on the back, tossing handfuls of sand in the air, pointing at the floating wreckage and miming the explosion with their hands.

"So much for push-button warfare!" Tangretti said, laughing.

"I guess that settles that!" Richardson said. "I hope we've seen the last of that kind of stupidity!"

"Ah, don't count on it," Schroeder said. "Your typical Navy officer's mind shows an amazing capacity for generating stupidity!"

Richardson, who, like the other UDT men, was wearing his combat fatigues, refrained from reminding Schroeder that *he* was an officer. Such fine distinctions had been lost a long time ago in the swamps of Fort Pierce.

"I think it's obvious there are still a few problems with this system," Captain Hill observed. His uniform, too, was wet and clotted with sand.

"We'll have them worked out in time for Operation Flintlock, sir," Finch said. "I promise!"

"See?" Schroeder told the others. "We'll be running into those devil boats again. The Navy's *never* convinced something's a bad idea after only one fuck-up! It takes at least three, plus a board of inquiry, a congressional investigating committee, and even then they might keep the idea because by that time it's a part of Navy tradition!"

"Christ," Tangretti said suddenly, pointing out into the bay. "You see what I see, Red?"

"Fish. *Dead* fish." He shaded his eyes against the sun dazzle. "*Lots* of dead fish!"

"Tuna."

"How do you know that?"

"Trust me. I know."

"There's a weapons carrier parked up the beach."

"Sounds good."

"What the hell are you two talking about?" Richardson wanted to know.

"Never mind, Snake," Tangretti said, grinning. "You don't want to know."

"Suffice to say Gator'n me've got some real good contacts over in 'Lulu," Schroeder said.

Richardson never asked, but by the following day he'd already heard the story of how Chief Schroeder and MM1 Tangretti had collected several hundred pounds of prime tuna in a weapons carrier and traded it in Honolulu for two cases of Stateside Scotch whiskey. Most of the liquor, Tangretti explained, was for his "business." There were sources and contacts that had to be kept happy, supply officers to be greased, and inspecting officers to be appeased.

Still, there was enough left over for Schroeder, Tangretti, Richardson, and a select few others to have a very warm and merry Christmas.

The extended celebration soon became more of a farewell party, however, for new orders arrived on Thursday, two days before Christmas. Now, after four brief weeks of training, UDTs One and Two were shipping out. Their destination was Admiral Turner's Fifth Amphibious Force, and the Marshall Islands.

Operation Flintlock had commenced.

Chapter 21

**The Better Hole Pub
Falmouth, England**

Rain spattered against the windowpane, and a gust of cold air blasted across Chief William Wallace's back as someone left the pub. There weren't many customers tonight, and somehow that just reinforced the gray mood engendered by the cold and the rain outside.

Wallace took a long swig of ale, draining his glass. He set it back down on the table in front of him and stared down into the dregs like a mystic trying to read the future in a swirl of tea leaves. But there were no hidden messages for him here. None Wallace could read, at least.

He'd honestly thought his luck was finally starting to change when Commander Coffer had signed the orders transferring him to one of the NCDUs shipping out from Fort Pierce for active duty in England. Coffer had finally found a man he grudgingly deemed acceptable to replace Wallace on the Fort Pierce staff, an ensign named Culver who had seen action of a sort with the short-lived Mediterranean NDU. Harold Culver had been part of the same groundbreaking class of NCDU recruits that had included Snake Richardson and Gator Tangretti.

The news that he was bound for England, for the ETO and the upcoming invasion of France, had made Bill Wallace want to hug the scrawny lieutenant commander. Hell Week and the constant demands of turning raw kids into competent Demolitioneers had convinced Wallace, over time, that his concerns about his personal bravery were groundless. An *instructor* at Fort Pierce faced more hazards every day than most sailors on active duty went up against in six months.

Still, Wallace felt the need to test himself, to see if he could truly push past the fear when the bullets and the shells started flying. Orders to join the NCDUs in England had sounded like just the ticket for that back in December. Since then he'd come to know better.

When he'd first arrived, together with five others from the latest graduating class from Fort Pierce, Wallace had been expecting to see preparations for the invasion visible in every corner of the country. He'd assumed that the NCDU teams here would have set up the same kind of ongoing training programs their Pacific counterparts had created at Waimanalo. Instead he'd been shocked to find out that nobody in authority even knew what an NCDU was supposed to do. Apparently the levels of secrecy and security surrounding the invasion plans for France were keeping people in the middle levels of the officer corps from realizing the need for demolitions on the beaches.

Wallace and a first class named Bronson had been split off from the rest of their unit and assigned as guards at an ammo dump near Dumfries in the Scottish border country. Evidently the officer who'd processed Wallace's group through had assumed that this was the sort of job their training as combat explosives men qualified them for.

So Wallace had passed a bleak Christmas season. Not only had he not found any sign of the active assignment he'd craved, but now the brass had cut him off from the work he'd learned to love.

" 'Ere, luv, want another?" Even Wallace's untrained ear recognized that the waitress probably wasn't one of the locals, whose speech tended to be slow and deliberate. She was most likely a Londoner who'd relocated to Cornwall during the dark days of the Blitz.

He shook his head. "I've had my limit," he said.

The waitress flashed him a smile and lingered for a moment as she gathered up his glass. Wallace toyed with the idea of picking her up. A lot of British girls were eager to prove their Allied solidarity with American servicemen, a fact that often stirred up trouble with British men.

But though she was a tempting little piece, Wallace decided he wasn't really in the mood tonight. He was tired and frustrated and angry, and what he really wanted to do was get better acquainted with the new rack he'd been assigned back at the naval base. So he watched her walk away, not without a twinge of regret for lost opportunities.

At least the teams were getting back together again. The arrival of Lieutenant Robert C. Smith, another Sicily veteran, had guaranteed that. Smith had raised a stink from London to Washington and back again, complaining to everybody he'd been able to buttonhole—Coffer, and that Pentagon liaison officer Galloway, and every base commander in England, among many others—until the orders had finally come down recalling all of the NCDU men from their make-work assignments and consolidating them in one of the amphibious training facilities at Falmouth in the very corner of southwestern Cornwall. That was an improvement, certainly. Smith had let it be known that the teams would be starting up exactly the kind of further instruction Wallace had been expecting from the start. They would have been at it already, in fact, except that the past few days had been spent rounding up as many beach obstacles as possible for use in that training program.

Fortunately, beach obstacles were easy to find in England. There were plenty left over from the big invasion scare after Dunkirk back in '40. Wallace had just come back to Falmouth that afternoon, in fact, with a truck, an NCDU detail, and half a dozen assorted heavy obstacles that would be perfect for a little demolitions practice. Other NCDU men had fanned out all over the country in search of more. Any veteran of Fort Pierce knew how fast Demolitioneers could go through obstacles.

He saw the bartender watching him and decided it wasn't wise to linger without ordering another drink. Wallace stood up, gathered up his pea coat, and left the waitress a large tip on the table. Since he'd been paying for his drinks as he went, he headed straight for the door, only pausing long enough to don his heavy coat.

Outside it was wet and raw, though not as cold as he'd

expected. Dumfries had been a lot worse, but someone had told him that the winters in Cornwall were the mildest in England. Some of the Demolitioneers were happier about that than they were about getting free of the silly details they'd been assigned to before Smith had shaken things up.

Wallace stood outside the pub for a moment, his hands shoved deep in his pockets. Even getting the teams back together and starting up the training program hadn't been enough to help him shake his dour mood of late. Somehow the war seemed farther away than ever now that they were in this sleepy little Cornish town. There were rumors of impending action somewhere in the Pacific, and Wallace frequently found himself wishing he'd been able to volunteer back when Snake and Gator had shipped out. Now they were about to have all the fun while Wallace waited in the cold, wet purgatory that was England.

Finally he shook his head. There was no postponing the inevitable. The cold, wet rain wasn't going to lift, and that meant he'd have to put up with that much more discomfort riding his motorcycle back to the base.

She was a real gem of a machine, a fourteen-year-old Brough Superior in absolutely mint condition. The cycle's previous owner was a Tommy who hadn't yet learned not to draw on an inside straight. The Brit had been a fool to put up the motorcycle when his cash ran out near the end of that last hand, especially on a night when the cards were all falling Wallace's way. As it happened, the Tommy had shipped out the next week for Italy, so Wallace didn't feel quite so guilty about keeping the Brough. He lavished attention on it during his off-duty hours and enjoyed the stares it drew from the locals and his fellow sailors alike when he tooled around town astride it. From time to time, out on a stretch of open road, Wallace would open the throttles up all the way and thrill to the feeling of all that power, that *controlled* power literally right in his hands.

Tonight, though, the thought of driving back through the cold and wet on an open motorcycle made him wish he'd won something *useful,* like the deed to a whorehouse.

Wallace mounted the cycle and started her up. Cruising down the narrow, winding streets of the town, he found himself wishing he could open her up and push her to the limit tonight. That was one of the two ways he'd found that always worked to pull him out of one of his black moods. The other was the chance to play with a block of Composition C-2 and a length of primacord.

But the roads were slick tonight. The temperature was hovering right at that point where the rain didn't quite freeze but managed to come as close to liquid ice as it could. Even at his most reckless, after a hell of a lot more drinks than he'd had tonight, Wallace knew better than to play the daredevil when conditions were this bad.

He headed northwest on the main road out of town, squinting to spot the sign that marked his turnoff and praying he'd correctly memorized the route that would take him back to the Amphibious Base. He had the whole weekend free, but there was no point wasting money on a room in town without a pressing reason—say a half dozen or so of Snake Richardson's leftovers. Better to get back to the base, out of the weather, and into his rack as soon as he could.

The rain started to come down hard, lashing his face and obscuring his vision. He squeezed the brakes and felt the cycle start into a skid. Wallace fought for control, trying to hold the motorcycle upright by sheer determination as it slid on the slick, wet road. . . .

Lights flashed in his eyes and a black shape loomed up out of the rain just in front of him. Wallace swerved sharply, and this time he did lose control.

Somehow he was thrown free as the cycle went down. He hit the wet, hard pavement with a solid thud that knocked the breath out of him, but reactions honed in Hell Week helped him take the fall.

Brakes squealed as the car that had almost hit him went into a skid of its own. It ran onto the grass beside the road opposite Wallace, stopping right in the cone of light thrown by the headlight of his fallen Brough. As Wallace was struggling to sit up, the car door opened. Wallace had a good look at a pair of long, shapely legs as the driver climbed out. She paused for a moment, looking shaken up. Then she reached back into the car, produced a flashlight, and switched it on as she hurried across the road toward Wallace.

"Are you hurt?" she asked. Her voice was pleasant, with

an accent that was a lot easier on the ear than the one that Cockney waitress back at the bar had.

He squinted up at her, got a vague impression of an attractive face with a small, upturned nose and brown hair gathered in a severe bun that still managed to look attractive. "I . . . I don't think so," he ventured tentatively. "Give me a minute to take inventory."

"You're American," the girl said, kneeling at his side.

"Guilty as charged," he said. "Bill Wallace. From Oklahoma."

"Army?"

"Please, madam, you insult me," he said in mock tones of outraged dignity. "I am a Chief Petty Officer in the United States Navy."

"The Navy. . . ." A shadow crossed her face. "My hus—my brother is in the Navy." She moved the flashlight back and forth over him, stopping from time to time to study some specific spot. Once her long, slender fingers probed a tender spot on his arm where something had torn through the sleeve of his coat. "I don't think there's anything broken," she said at last.

"Just bumps and bruises, I think," he agreed.

"Well, that's a pretty nasty cut on your arm. More than just a bump or a bruise." She produced a handkerchief from her purse, folded it neatly, and pressed it down on the wound. After a moment's thought she took off her scarf and tied it tight around the arm to hold the makeshift bandage in place. "You should have this tended to. Can you stand? Walk?"

He started to nod, but that made his head hurt. "Yeah. I'm okay. Really." Nevertheless, he let her help him up, and he found he had to lean on her to favor a sore ankle.

He probably would have made it a point of pride to walk without even a hint of a limp if he'd been in front of a batch of NCDU trainees back at Fort Pierce. But there were worse things he could think of than leaning on a pretty girl.

"It wouldn't be a good idea to let you go riding that infernal machine of yours," she said. "We'll shove it off the road into that patch of bushes over there, and I'll have a friend of mine at my garage come out in the morning and collect it for you. Assuming you're still daft enough to want to have anything to do with it after tonight!"

"Th-thanks," he stammered. He managed to wrestle the motorcycle upright and switch off the headlight. Together they pushed it into the bushes. He couldn't see any serious damage, but it still made him angry. He'd worked so hard to keep the machine in top form! "I really appreciate all your help, ah . . ."

"Alice," she filled in the unasked question. "Alice Pascoe."

"Well, Mrs. Pascoe, if someone had to run me off the road, I'm glad it was you."

With her help he made it across to the car. She opened the passenger door on the left side. "If you feel the need to see a doctor, I can give you a lift back into Falmouth, to the hospital. But I can take care of that cut faster and throw a hot bowl of soup into the bargain if you let me take you home. It's only a few minutes away. Which would you prefer?"

He decided he liked her straightforward, no-nonsense manner, neither aggressive nor coy, just matter-of-fact, businesslike. Most girls he'd known back in the States would have either screamed at the sight of blood or turned the whole situation into some kind of seduction scene. Or they would have tried to mother him. Alice Pascoe was something different.

She was also married. She'd started to say that her husband, rather than her brother, was in the Navy, and she'd not corrected him when he called her Mrs. Pascoe. Wallace had a firm rule to steer clear of married women. He appreciated her help, but he had to guard against thinking of her as anything more than a friendly woman helping a distressed cyclist.

"Are you sure your husband won't mind you bringing home strays?" he asked with a smile.

She turned away. "My husband's dead. Has been . . . coming up on two years now, I guess." Her voice was almost inaudible.

"I'm . . . I'm sorry, Mrs. Pascoe," he said, angry at himself. Inwardly, he cursed himself for his lack of tact. So many, here in Britain especially, had lost loved ones to the war. And they didn't need to have bad memories stirred up by strangers.

"No . . . no, I'm the one who should apologize," she said. "I . . . don't usually let it affect me so." She paused, still looking off into the distance. "It's just, well, we used to have such arguments about his motorcycle, and for a moment there you reminded me of him so much. I guess my guard was just down, that's all." Looking back at Wallace, she cleared her throat. "But you still haven't answered the question, Mr. Wallace."

"At the risk of confirming all the worst things you've heard about American sailors, I'd choose your place," he said. As soon as the words were out, he wished there was some way to take them back. Now he sounded like Snake Richardson talking up a date, trying to take advantage of her. "I mean . . . well, I could use something warm to eat or drink, I guess, and I don't really need a doctor to put a bandage on the arm. . . ."

"Relax, sailor," she said with a hint of a smile. "Don't worry. I *did* invite you, after all, and I wouldn't have done that if I hadn't meant to. You needn't worry about accepting." She started to close the door, then paused for a moment. "Oh, yes, and just in case you *are* one of those sailors I've heard about, I live with my mother, and I can assure you we'll be *very* well chaperoned." Her smile, turned on full force this time, made it plain she understood everything that had been going through his mind.

As they pulled out onto the road, she looked across at him. "Are you with a ship, Mr. Wallace? Or at the base here?"

"The base," he said. "I work with explosives, munitions . . . stuff like that. Nothing I can discuss, I'm afraid. And please, call me Bill, Mrs. Pascoe. Unless that violates some deep, dark British tradition of dignity and modesty."

"Well, if we're going to go with this quaint Colonial informality, then, you may call me Alice. But *not* in front of my mother or the vicar, please. They still have standards to maintain and aren't as easily corrupted by you Yanks as I am." She paused. "Explosives, you said? We have something else in common, then. I work at an munitions factory over in Cambourne. I pack powder into shell cartridges. They also made me a driver this month. I run finished ordnance from the factory to some of the bases around here." She smiled. "I'm getting to know these roads pretty well . . . everything but the stray motorcyclists."

He laughed. "You never know *where* we'll turn up next. But at least we speak some of the same lingo. We could really be the life of the party somewhere, talking about grains and velocity, specific impulse and force-to-weight ratios until we make everyone's eyes glaze over. That's what happened the last time I tried to tell a date about what I did back before the war."

"And that was?"

"Roughneck on an oil field. I guess there just aren't that many people who appreciate hearing about such things as fuse lengths and blast areas."

"Well, then," she said with another smile, "perhaps we should promise not to talk shop when we go to a party, hmm?"

"That could be construed as a hint that you might go to a party with me sometime," he said, studying her profile in the dim light.

"Yes, I suppose it could at that," Alice replied. She didn't elaborate.

They drove on in silence for a few minutes, passing through the outskirts of Falmouth and finally pulling up in front of a small cottage. "Here we are," Alice said. "Do you need any help?"

"No, I'm better, now." He *was* feeling better, but also a little shaky as the adrenaline from his spill wore off.

"I really do think they should just ban those beastly machines," she said as they walked up to the porch. "They're totally unsafe. Look at Lawrence."

"Where? Who?" He looked around, baffled.

Alice Pascoe laughed, a musical sound. "Oh, come on, now, even you benighted heathens in the Colonies must have heard of Lawrence? Colonel T. E. Lawrence . . . Lawrence of Arabia?"

"The guerrilla leader? Sure. Any serviceman worth his salt knows about Lawrence of Arabia. *He* knew what to do with explosives! But what does he have to do with unsafe motorcycles?"

As they stepped up onto the front porch and into the circle of light beside the door, Wallace got his first good look at her. Alice looked about thirty, with light brown hair and hazel eyes and attractive, fine-chiseled features. Her heavy coat couldn't completely hide a trim, curvy figure. "You really don't know? You Yanks are really quite provincial sometimes, you know. Colonel Lawrence retired to private life after the war, and then enlisted in the RAF as an ordinary airman under an assumed name. He never explained why, but he seemed quite happy to be Airman Shaw instead of the glamorous Lawrence of Arabia. He collected motorcycles and rode them all over the countryside. Then one day, not too long after his enlistment was up, he was in an accident. It must have been, I don't know, almost ten years ago now. All very mysterious, with talk about strange black cars following him around or running him off the road. He died a few days later. I never really believed all the talk about conspiracies to have him killed, even if people did think the government was afraid he'd support the Fascists. I just thought it was foolish that a great man like that should go about doing something so foolish as riding a motorcycle without any sort of protection from a crash. I guess heroes can be as foolish as anyone else."

"I don't know much about heroes," he said. "But I wouldn't dismiss those conspiracy stories so fast. Black cars *have* been known to run poor defenseless cyclists off the road, after all."

She laughed. "Well, well, so speaks Wallace of Arabia. But I promised you medical attention and something hot . . . and a chance to be interrogated by my mother, of course. I hope you're up to the ordeal. Or perhaps you'd prefer the hospital after all?"

"I'll chance it here. I've been through Indoctrination Week . . . our trainees call it Hell Week. After that, even protective mothers seem pretty tame."

She smiled and reached for the door.

Bill Wallace knew already that he'd found someone special, someone he had to get to know better.

All of a sudden, life in England was starting to look just a little bit brighter after all.

Tuesday, 18 January 1944

U.S. Naval Amphibious and Operating Base Plymouth, England

Boatswain's Mate First Class Frank Rand was amazed at the sheer size and scope of the American facilities around Plymouth. After four months at Fort Pierce, still a comparative backwater as far as naval installations went, the largest U.S. amphibious base in England was an impressive, often confusing place to be. The bustle all around him reminded Rand of Malta before the start of Operation Husky. He could almost feel the rhythm of the place, the sense of purpose, the suppressed excitement of the men and women, military and civilian, working together to mount the greatest invasion in history.

And now he would be a part of it all.

After his mother's death and the final rift with his father, Rand had been content for a time with his new role as an instructor. His CO at the Scouts and Raiders School had loaned him out to Lieutenant Commander Coffer and his Naval Combat Demolition people, and it had been exciting to work with those dedicated, enthusiastic trainees. Rand had not only taught, he'd also learned, monitoring some of the lectures on demolitions and other NCDU specialties. He'd come away with an appreciation for just how much small, elite units could accomplish when properly trained, supported, and motivated.

A team of those NCDU men with weapons and plenty of explosives could, for instance, have silenced the pillboxes above the beaches in Sicily long before the regular troops had started ashore. Rand was convinced that the future of amphibious warfare lay with such small, hard-hitting teams who could scout a beach, destroy the static obstacles blocking a landing, guide in the first assault wave, take out hostile strong points, and hold their own against enemy troops in a stand-up firefight. The Navy was only beginning to grope toward the full array of possibilities, but Rand believed that the service would inevitably develop just such a force.

The interlude at Fort Pierce had been one of the most pleasant periods in Rand's memory. For the first time in his life the need to push harder to impress his father hadn't been dominating everything he did and said and felt, and though his work had been hard he'd also had plenty of time to think, to reflect on his life, his goals, his future. Nancy Brown loomed large in that future. Her letters had helped keep alive his newfound feeling of freedom from the shackles of his own past. Now he was his own man, and he would stay that way.

But Rand had been a man of action too long to be content at Fort Pierce forever. The Allies had followed up their success in Sicily with landings on the Italian mainland. Phil Bucklew, Pete Havlicek, and others from his old S&R gang had led the way in once more, scouting the Salerno beaches and guiding in the armada from the same tiny kayaks they'd used before Husky. Only a few days ago, another landing had gone in just south of Rome to break the stalemate that had gripped the fighting in Italy. And in the Pacific, the Allies were driving the Japanese back on several fronts, in New Guinea, the Solomons . . . at Tarawa.

And now, of course, rumors were flying thick and fast about the next big invasion. France. No one knew where, no one knew when, but *everyone* knew that France would be the long-awaited Second Front.

So Rand had taken advantage of a general reorganization among the NCDU people at Fort Pierce to apply for the Scouts and Raiders command in England, and somewhat to his surprise the new assignment had come through promptly. Now he was here in Devonshire, at the main U.S. amphibious base, trying to figure out where he would find the Scouts and Raiders contingent he'd come halfway around the world to join. It had to be *somewhere* in this madhouse. . . .

"Rand! Frank Rand, by all that's holy! Welcome to Plymouth, son!"

He spun around as soon as he heard that familiar, booming voice, and found himself gaping at the heavyset, powerfully muscled figure of Phil Bucklew. Rand noted the new rank insignia on his collar, the single silver bar of a j.g. "*Lieutenant* Bucklew now, is it? I didn't know *you* were here, sir. I thought you were still in Italy." He saluted almost as an afterthought.

Bucklew grinned as he returned the salute. "Nope. *This* is where the action is now. Italy's just a sideshow." He stepped back and studied Rand critically. "I knew you were on my list of fresh meat, but I wasn't sure when you were due in. Lucky I spotted you here. Lost?"

"Sir, it's a shame to admit it, but this is one place that even the Scouts and Raiders couldn't crack without a map and a ball of twine."

"You'd do better if you could come in at night in a raft," the lieutenant said, chuckling softly. "It's good to get an old Sicily hand in with that mob of new kids they keep sending us. I can use a seasoned hand . . . even a reckless damn fool like you."

"I'd like to think I know a little better now, sir," he said soberly. "I've learned some, I think." Then Rand smiled. "But I sure as hell want to be in on the action, sir. That's why I kicked and screamed and held my breath until they let me come."

"Ah, the professional way to ask for a transfer. I'll have to keep it in mind next time I want to go somewhere."

"Any of the other guys here, sir?"

"A few," he said. His smile faded. "Did you hear about Havlicek?"

"No . . . what happened?" Rand felt his stomach twisting. He knew the answer from the look on Phil Bucklew's face.

"I just saw the report on it on my desk this morning, Frank. I'm afraid Havlicek bought it. At Anzio. One of the LCIs got out of the safe lane and hung up on a sandbar, and his scout boat was trying to maneuver in close to help them. They got caught by an HMG on shore."

Rand nodded sadly. "God, what a waste. I never expected Pete to be the one to go. He was always so damned careful when he was working a beach."

"Yeah." Bucklew was silent for a moment. "Hey, Rand, why don't you come down to the harbor with me? I'm heading out on a run tonight, but I'll show you around before I go."

Rand fell into step beside him. "Tonight? Any chance I could get in on the fun?"

"Whoa, there, son. Thought you said you were cured. Before we start letting you go out, you're going to have to get acclimated, just like everybody else. I'm not taking any kid fresh off the boat out on an op, Silver Star or not. You read me?"

"Sorry, Lieutenant. Force of habit, I guess. . . ."

"Anyway, you've got to go to school first."

"School, sir?" He tried to keep the disappointment out of his voice.

Bucklew looked at him with an expression that said the older man could read his mind perfectly. "Yeah, school. Another one. Evasion and Escape, this time. How to keep secrets if you're captured. All that cloak-and-dagger stuff."

"We never needed it in the Med. . . ."

"This ain't the Med, son." Bucklew laughed. "The brass really screwed up big-time when they brought Scouts and Raiders in. Just think about it, Frank. The details of Operation Overlord are the biggest secret of the war to date. We don't want the Krauts to know when we're going to hit, and we sure as hell don't want 'em to know *where*. So the boys at the top have really clamped down on the security. Hardly anybody knows anything he doesn't have to."

"Sounds like a good idea to me, sir," Rand said. He was thinking about the story he'd heard in Sicily of a French harbor pilot from Tunis steering one of the ships bound for Operation Husky out of port to join the armada, which was doing its best to keep its course and destination a secret. The Frenchman had walked down to the deck to board a small boat to take him back to shore, but stopped at the rail, lifted his hat, and called out a cheery "Good luck in Sicily, *monsieurs*." He'd been taken into custody by military police back in Tunis to keep him incommunicado, but of course no one knew how far the information had spread. It sounded like Overlord was going to be kept under wraps a little bit better than that, at least.

"Yeah, well, some bright boy realized they'd need to scout the beaches in advance and brought us in," Bucklew said. "My whole gang here, in one big meeting. So they unroll all the maps and charts they've got of the invasion zone—the actual, honest-to-god, Hitler-would-give-his-only-ball-to-know-it *invasion zone*—and start asking us for advice on scouting the beaches."

"Oh *shit!*" Rand said, suddenly horrified. "But if our boys know the plans . . ."

"Yep. Makes it kind of risky to send 'em in to scout the beaches. One guy gets caught and the whole damned Overlord cat is out of the bag."

"You could bring in men who haven't seen the maps. Like me, for instance." Rand held up his hand. "No, I'm not trying to go looking for the glory, sir. But you could send men who don't know the plans in to lots of different beaches, including the real ones. That would confuse the issue if someone was caught. . . ."

Bucklew shook his head. "Not enough manpower. Not enough time. You remember how many missions we needed for Sicily. Well, this Overlord plan makes Husky look like a pup. We need soundings. Beach gradients. Sketches and maps of the landing zone, with landmarks. Plots of all the new obstacles and hardpoints the Krauts are starting to put up." He laughed. "Hell, now some staff whiz kid is asking me, with a perfectly straight face, mind you, for samples of the sand on the beaches so they can figure out if it'll support the weight of our tanks."

"I can see them wanting it," Rand commented. "Remember how our heavy stuff kept getting bogged down on the beach in Sicily?"

"Yeah. Well, the point is, we couldn't *train* enough Scouts and Raiders to give every beach that kind of treatment, but if anyone saw a pattern of us favoring one sector over another, that'd be as good a tip-off as if one of us from that damned meeting was captured and spilled his guts. So instead we set up these new regs. Everybody goes through E&E training with the Brits, same kind of stuff their commandos get. And everybody in the outfit gets to study the real beaches. You're gonna have to learn that coast backwards, forwards, and upside down, son. 'Cause some day, pretty damn soon, you're gonna be leading a few hundred thousand men in to hit those beaches."

Rand met his eyes and nodded slowly. "Then I guess I

can put up with another damned school in the meantime, sir. If it means I'll be in on the kill."

"Good!" Bucklew grinned. "Now look here, Rand. That bit about you being too reckless—"

" 'Reckless damned fool' was the way you put it, I believe, sir," he said blandly.

"Yeah. Look, the kind of stuff we'll be doing in France calls for stealth. I don't need someone who wants the CMH for single-handedly capturing a panzer division or some shit like that. If you have to go in and scoop up buckets of sand to satisfy some staffer up at SHAEF, then by God I expect you to do it without stirring up a hornet's nest. Sneak in, sneak out, and don't call attention to yourself. Do your job . . . and do your duty. That's the only kind of heroics we have room for in this outfit."

"Yes, sir," Rand said. "Like I said before, Lieutenant Bucklew, I've learned a few things." He looked away. "I won't lie to you, sir. I wanted to get into that fight in Sicily so bad I could taste it, and maybe when it gets hot and heavy the next time out I'll *still* want it. I've spent so much of my life trying to show that I've got what it takes, and I don't know if that's something you can just walk away from any time you want to." He looked back at the j.g. "But I will promise you this, sir. I'll be a part of the team. No more glory hound. No more of that John Wayne stuff."

"That's what I wanted to hear, son." They had reached the waterfront, and Bucklew pointed to the sleek gray shape of a torpedo boat tied up at the pier in front of them. "Come on, let's see if the gear they've been stowing on board bears any relation to the stuff I actually requisitioned."

As Rand followed him to the boat, his mind was preoccupied with the promise he'd given to Bucklew. He wasn't running after medals or news stories or glory to impress his father anymore. He was sure of that.

But would he still give in to the lure of excitement and heroics when the bullets started to fly? Maybe not for his father, but for himself. . . .

Rand hoped he'd be able to keep his promise. He owed it to Bucklew to try, at least.

And to himself.

Chapter 22

Monday, 31 January 1944

Kwajalein
The Marshall Islands

Operation Flintlock was the code name for the American invasion of the Marshall Islands. If Tarawa had been the first step toward the Japanese homeland in the central Pacific, the Marshalls would be the first time Americans would be fighting for territory the Japanese considered to be their own. The Marshall Islands, lying between Wake Island and the Gilberts, were part of the Japanese territorial mandate, awarded to them after they seized the islands from Germany in World War I. Betio had demonstrated the Japanese willingness to fight to the death; it was expected that their defense of the Marshalls would be even more desperate, even bloodier, than Tarawa.

For this reason, the American commanders of the task force approaching Kwajalein Atoll were willing to try any expedient, any tactic, that would let them seize the targets while minimizing American casualties. While Admiral Turner had publicly expressed more confidence in the Stingray drones than in the two UDTs accompanying them, the fact that the UDTs were being used at all reflected the Navy High Command's willingness to try anything to avoid another "Terrible Tarawa."

Kwajalein Atoll, the largest coral atoll in the world, was key to the American occupation of the Marshalls. On the charts, Kwajalein had the appearance of an enormous, leaping dolphin outlined by a line of coral reefs and occasional islands, sixty-six miles long and in places up to twenty miles wide. To the southeast, at the dolphin's pointed snout, was boomerang-shaped Kwajalein Island, occupied by nearly five thousand Japanese under Rear Admiral Akiyama, dug into a complex of pillboxes and bunkers more forbidding than the one at Tarawa; north, at the tip of the dorsal fin, were the Siamese twin islands of Roi and Namur, joined by a slender sand spit and a man-made causeway. Roi-Namur together comprised a tiny area a mile and a quarter long and only three quarters of a mile deep, but packed into their defenses were another thirty-five hundred troops. Both Roi-Namur and Kwajalein possessed airfields; Kwajalein's was large enough for four-engine bombers, while Ebeye Island, just to the north, possessed a heavily defended seaplane base.

Two naval task forces had been detailed for the assault on the atoll. Once again, Admiral Spruance was in overall command, though, aside from providing the naval bombardment, he would involve himself and his Fifth Fleet only if the Japanese fleet sortied out from their fortress at Truk. In tactical command of the landings was Admiral Turner, who had again elected to divide his forces. The Northern Forces, under Admiral Conolly, would take Roi-Namur; the southern Force, under Turner, and including the U.S. Army's 7th Division, would assault Kwajalein Island.

UDT-1 was assigned to Turner's Task Force 52, while UDT-2 sailed with Conolly. Despite the month's training in Hawaii, there was still little in the way of solid operational planning for the deployment of the UDTs. The original plan for UDT-1 had called for a midnight reconnaissance of the submerged reef stretching from Kwajalein to the neighboring island of Enubuj, a mile-long strip of coral sand lying two miles to the northwest, but at last report that plan had been scrapped. Turner, reportedly, had worked out five alternate plans for utilizing the teams at Kwajalein, even though he did not expect them to be that useful. Most of his enthusiasm for the UDTs was focused on the cranky but promising Stingrays, which, it was still believed, would blast holes through the coral in advance of the approaching landing craft.

Task Force 52 reached Kwajalein at dawn on 31 January.

At first, the men aboard the transports thought a thunderstorm was brewing, but that proved to be part of an intense bombardment that had been going on for most of the past three days. Just the day before, seven battleships had pounded the islands, and over four hundred bombing sorties had been flown off the task force's carriers. D-Day for Kwajalein Island would be the next day, 1 February; today, landings were being carried out on Roi-Namur, and on Enubuj, which would provide an ideal platform for American artillery, which would lend support to the man landings on Kwajalein tomorrow.

One of the lessons of Tarawa was the need for extended naval bombardment. For three days, Admiral Spruance's Fifth Fleet had been pounding the islands with salvos from what for a battleship was point-blank range, and the bombardment continued now, booming and thundering as the sun rose slowly above the eastern horizon. And aboard the transport *Callahan*, the UDT personnel began to prepare for their first operational mission.

"Okay, you boys remember what to do?"

"Sure thing, Lieutenant," Ensign Richardson called to the officer on the deck opposite. He and Tangretti, wearing life jackets and helmets and hanging on to lifelines, were standing in the well deck of a Higgins LCP, suspended from a pair of crescent davits off the starboard side of the naval transport *Callahan*. Naval gunfire thundered and boomed in the background, making even shouted conversation difficult. "Let's get this show on the road!"

The lieutenant nodded to the boatswain's mate at his side, who turned to the sailors standing by to slack the falls suspending the swaying wooden landing craft. "Lower away!"

The Higgins boat dropped smoothly down the *Callahan*'s side. "Hold her for'ard! Hold her aft!" There was a slight lurch, and the LCP(R) hung suspended just above the water.

"Start 'er up," Richardson told Tangretti.

There was an ominous thud, followed by a clicking sound from the engine hatch. Tangretti, muttering dark imprecations, left his position at the helm and vanished headfirst into the engine compartment. "Snake!" he called, his voice muffled by the hatch. "Hit the starter, will ya?"

Richardson left his place by the aft fall and moved forward to the coxswain's position. He threw the switch and was rewarded by a grinding sound, an explosive cough, and finally the thuttering rumble of the Higgins boat's 150-horsepower engine.

Tangretti reappeared, his face and forearms streaked with oil. "Damn piece of shit," he muttered. "Okay, sir. We're ready."

Richardson returned to the aft boat davit fall, bemused. Tangretti, forced by circumstance back into his original role as machinist's mate, had reverted to the use of "sir" when addressing a boat's officer. Thinking back, Richardson could not remember a single time when Tangretti had ever called him "sir." They'd been trainees together at Fort Pierce, and after Hell Week there'd been no point to the courtesy. Ever since those two memorable incidents in the Florida swamp, they'd always been just "Snake" and "Gator" with each other.

The Higgins boat's engine was running now, dirty and rough, but serviceably. Tangretti still had the clutch out, however, and the single screw was not yet turning.

When he was sure the engine wasn't going to quit on them, Richardson waved to the boatswain's mate watching from *Callahan*'s deck. At a command from the BM, lowering was resumed. The boat's stern kissed the water a second before the bow. "Up behind!" the boatswain called.

Richardson took Tangretti's place at the wheel, acting as coxswain. He held the rudder over to keep the LCP(R) clear of the transport's side while the other man scrambled aft to unhook the after block, then made his way to the bow to release the hook forward.

With the boat falls unhooked and hauled clear, the landing craft was trailing alongside the transport on a single sea painter forward. There was a gentle swell on the sea. *Callahan* was under way, but slowly, barely moving. Waves slapped and thumped along the Higgins boat's hull. Richardson checked aft to make sure there were no lines, no "Irish pennants," trailing near the screw, then engaged the boat's clutch. An uncomfortable shudder ran through the small craft's length, but the screw began to bite and the painter slackened. "She's got way!" Richardson called, and

Tangretti cast off the painter, which was rapidly hauled up the side of the *Callahan* by a lighter line attached to its end.

They were under way now and on their own. Gently, Richardson fed her more throttle. Blue-gray smoke billowed alarmingly from the engine hatch and from the exhaust vents astern, but their speed increased steadily. With a heavy slapping motion as they cut through *Callahan*'s bow wake, they drew slowly ahead of the larger ship.

Richardson tried not to think about their cargo. Three tons of cratering explosive would make a very, *very* large bang, and it could be set off by almost anything . . . a shell, a fault in the detonators, a stray signal at the wrong radio frequency intercepted by the boat's touchy remote-control equipment. If the stuff went off now, there would not be enough left of him or Tangretti to mop up with a sponge.

They both had volunteered for this job, of course, though he still wasn't sure why. The long-standing popular wisdom that enjoined naval personnel to never volunteer had no place in the UDT, where the men were *expected* to be gung-ho, and the guy who hung back became the butt of jokes and yellow-stripe humor. At the time, during their passage from Oahu to the Marshalls, it had seemed like the right thing to do.

Still, piloting one of the Stingray drones, driving it in toward a hostile beach under the fire and fury of a covering naval bombardment, *especially* after witnessing the debacle during the test demonstration at Waimanalo the previous month, did not exactly seem like a sane or sensible course of action. With a loud thud, the boat's bilge pumps kicked in, running with a steady *thumpa-thumpa-thump*. There must be a fair amount of water in the bilges. That was strange; the ocean swell was pretty stiff this morning, but they weren't taking any spray over the bow. Where was the water coming from?

Standing up on his toes to see over the Higgins boat's bow, Richardson could see the low-lying strip of land ahead. The mile-long island of Enubuj sported what sailors aboard the *Callahan* were calling a "Spruance haircut," the splinters, stubs, stumps, and naked trunks of what once had been forests of coconut palms. To the east, Kwajalein, half glimpsed beneath a pall of smoke and dust, had been just as roughly handled. South, some of the battleships and cruisers of Spruance's Fifth Fleet armada could be seen as low, gray shadows on the horizon, the muzzle flashes of their guns twinkling and flaring in death blossoms of livid orange. Kwajalein was getting most of the attention at the moment. Gouts of water erupted off the beach; ashore, flashes and fireballs barked and thumped, hurling splintered trees and mountains of sand aloft, while steadily adding to the storm-gloomy pall of black smoke shadowing the southeastern corner of the atoll. High overhead, a single aircraft circled, spotting for the battleships' big sixteen-inch guns.

Richardson tried to imagine what the Japanese defenders of those islands must be going through after three days of intense shelling and aerial bombings, and failed. It seemed starkly impossible that anyone could even be alive on those islands after such a god-awful hammering.

Half a mile to port, a lone Higgins boat identical to the one he was in plowed ahead through the ocean swell. A mile astern was a third landing craft, the Stingray control boat. The plan called for Stingrays One and Two to be piloted in to within a couple of miles of the coral reef sheltering Enubuj. Their two-man crews would then set them on automatic and go over the side in rubber boats, while the control boat steered the explosive-laden landing craft to designated points above the Enubuj reef, sink them, and set off their charges. A spare drone accompanied the control boat. Astern, the landing craft carrying troops of the Army's 7th Division, veterans of the recent Aleutian campaign, were filling up to the line of departure, ready to move in on Enubuj.

Perhaps the worst part of the whole operation, to Richardson's way of thinking, was the fact that the Kwajalein invasion didn't *need* a hole blasted through the Enubuj reef. Nobody in authority had said so, in so many words, but it was well known that the reefs sheltering Enubuj lay under more than enough water at high tide to permit the passage of landing craft. The operation this morning was nothing more than another test of Terrible Turner's beloved high-explosive toys.

Something was wrong with the Stingray to port. She appeared to have slowed . . . no, she'd gone dead in the water.

She was pretty low, too, and seemed to be settling by the stern.

Jesus, she was *sinking!*

"Hey, Snake!" Tangretti called from the engine hatch. "Looks like we're losing Jack and Fitz!"

"I see 'em," Richardson yelled back. Chief Jack Lacey and EN1 Ronald Fitzpatrick were the UDT men operating the second boat. "There they go, over the side!"

At this distance, he could just see the black speck of the rubber boat as Lacey and Fitzpatrick launched it. The landing craft was a lot lower in the water now, the waves beginning to break over her bow.

"Shit!" Tangretti yelled. "What the hell happened?"

In seconds, the Stingray was gone, with only the rubber boat and two crewmen left on the surface to mark its passing.

"Looks like they're firing up the spare," Richardson said. He was worried now. The *thumpa-thumpa-thump* of his own Stringray's pumps was growing louder and more labored, a cacophony of mechanical noise that nearly drowned out the harsher roar of the engine. The feel of the landing craft was different too, heavier, more sluggish. He turned the wheel experimentally, felt the dullness of the boat's response.

"Hey, Gator!"

"Yeah, boss."

"Better check the bilges. I think we're taking on water."

"Christ. Hang on a sec." He vanished aft but was back a moment later. "Bad news, Snake. We got a good foot, foot and a half of water, and more's coming on fast."

"Damn. What happened? Someone leave a seacock open?"

"I checked all seacocks and bilge plugs myself, Snake. I think the damned boat is a pile of crap. There's so much rust in the bilge I think that's all that's holding her seams together."

"You think she'll make it as far as the reef?"

Gator shrugged. "Fifty-fifty, I guess. If we don't breathe real hard or look at her cross-eyed, she might just do."

Richardson had a growing, unpleasant suspicion. Whoever had had charge of releasing Higgins boats for Turner's Stingray project must have figured they were in for a one-

way trip in any case and turned over the most worn, dilapidated, or badly repaired craft in their inventory. Possibly
they saw it as a way to rid themselves of junk; possibly they
simply didn't believe the UDT/Stingray project could possibly work and figured old and beat boats were good enough.
Whatever the reason, the Higgins boat was in danger of
foundering under Richardson and Tangretti long before they
reached the coral reef.

"Gator! Put the raft over the side. Get ready to abandon
ship!"

"Aye, aye, Snake!"

Richardson throttled back; if the boat was moving more
slowly, there'd be less stress on her joints and seams. Looking about, he could tell that they were at least a foot deeper
in the water now than they had been at the beginning. They
were still about six hundred yards from the island, and perhaps half that from the beginning of the reef.

A moment later, Tangretti heaved the inflated two-man
rubber boat over the starboard side, where it dragged along
in the water on the end of a single painter. Richardson took
a last look around at his small command—his *first* command, he realized with a start—then threw the switch that
put the craft onto remote control. Damn. Half an hour into
his first command, and it was sinking already.

It was time to leave.

Tangretti swung over the side, dropped feetfirst into the
rubber boat, then steadied it as Richardson followed. When
they were both in the raft, Tangretti cast off the painter, and
the LCP(R) wallowed on past them, its movement heavier
now as it settled lower into the water.

Each man took one of the paddles stored in the bottom of
the raft and began stroking, making their way slowly back
toward the control boat. The third Stingray was passing
them now, about two hundred yards to the north.
Richardson could see its two-man crew deploying their life
raft and preparing to go over the side.

"Push-button—*uh!*—warfare, that's what this is,"
Tangretti said at Richardson's back. "Revolutionize the
whole—*uh!*—science of war. . . ."

"Shut up and paddle," Richardson told him. "Uh-oh. . . ."

The stuttering roar of the Stingray's engine had just died

with an ominous clunk. Turning in the raft to look back over his shoulder, Richardson could see the LCP(R) drifting powerless, broaching to in the gentle swell.

"Goddamn," Tangretti said. "She went and quit on us!"

"Pumps are out, too," Richardson said. "Shit, Gator. We're gonna have to go back."

"I don't know if that's gonna do any good, Boss. I think the engine on that thing is a relic from the Spanish-American War."

"That's okay. The hull's left over from the War of 1812. Hard about, Gator. Let's see if we can give her a kick."

"Kick her too hard and we'll sink her."

"Well, we've got to do something. The invasion force is at its jump-off line by now. We don't want an LCP(R) loaded with three tons of explosives adrift in the beach approaches." Even with the explosives aboard unarmed, the Higgins boat was a floating bomb.

"You got that right."

Bending their backs into it, they paddled back toward the slowly drifting landing craft. Richardson looked critically at the hull. She still carried about two feet of freeboard—the distance between the water and her scuppers. Glancing back to the north, Richardson was amused to see that the spare Stingray had conked out as well, and that its crew, too, was paddling back to reboard her.

Leaning far forward, Tangretti was able to grab the painter, which had been left trailing over the starboard side, and secure it to an eye on the rubber boat's bow. Richardson steadied the boat alongside the LCP(R) as Tangretti hauled himself over the gunwale and back into the well deck.

"Kinda wet aboard, Snake. Watch your step."

Water was ankle-deep inside the landing craft now. Tangretti moved aft to the engine and again plunged his head and shoulders into the darkness of the engine access hatch. Richardson checked the satchels of explosives and safed them by pulling the detonators. That didn't eliminate the danger—a stray round could still detonate that deadly cargo at any moment—but at least it cut down on the risk that the remote-control device would trigger something accidentally. He had no wish at this stage of the operation to have a stray radio signal from the control boat blow the two of them to pieces. That urgent task complete, he assumed the coxswain's position once more.

To the south, behind them and beyond both the control boat and the *Callahan,* he could see a clutter of small gray shapes on the horizon, the transports and landing craft of the invasion force. "Better step on it, Gator. We're about to have company."

"Okay, Snake. Crank her up."

He turned the switch. There was a grinding sound from below decks, but not the hoped-for explosion of firing cylinders. Tangretti swore softly and kept working.

"Hit it again."

And again, nothing. The control boat was coming up astern now, less than fifty yards away. *"Ahoy, there, the Stingray!"* sounded from the control boat's deck. It was an LCVP, a larger landing craft than the sinking Higgins boat.

Richardson cupped his hands to his mouth and shouted back. "Ahoy! Our engine's dead!"

"Stand by to be taken in tow!"

"Okay, Gator," Richardson told Tangretti. "Leave it. I guess the world's not ready for push-button coral blasting."

"Never will be, if you ask me, boss. Blowing holes in things, that's a man's job!"

The LCVP passed close aboard the Higgins boat's port bow; a sailor on the control boat's stern tossed a monkey fist—a piece of heavy, tightly knotted cable attached to a length of light line—across the LCP(R)'s hull. Tangretti snatched up the line and hauled it in, bringing across the heavier cable it had been bent to. With the tow cable yoked to the LCP(R)'s bow, the LCVP was able to bring the smaller landing craft under tow, gently coming about and slowly hauling the Higgins boat clear of the beach approaches. Apparently, the third boat's crew had managed to restart their vessel, but the engine was choking so badly—Richardson and Tangretti could hear the ragged misfiring and sputtering from three hundred yards away—they evidently decided to return to the *Callahan* rather than attempt to carry out the mission.

Twenty minutes later, the Stingray was being hauled from the water. Tangretti pulled her bilge plugs after she'd been swayed aloft and pointed to the filthy, rust-stained streams pouring from the outlets. "See what I mean, Snake? I think the bilges're about rusted out."

"We'll put that in our report, Gator," Richardson told him. "Frankly, I think this whole operation was a god-damned royal fuck-up from start to last!"

"Amen to that!"

Aboard the U.S.S. *Callahan*

Later that morning, Tangretti and Richardson were on *Callahan*'s forward deck. They'd helped off-load the explosives and store them, but now there was little to do. Mail call had been announced, so Richardson was sitting now on a hatch coaming on the *Callahan*'s forward deck, reading the one letter he'd received. Many of the transport's sailors could be found in odd corners of the ship now, reading letters from their loved ones at home.

There'd been nothing for Tangretti. His parents were both dead, and his wife, at last report, had vanished to parts unknown with a guy with a defense worker's deferment. It had been over a year since his last letter from Deborah, and it still hurt.

He banished the gloomy thought. "Okay," he said, sidling over to Richardson. "Which one is it?"

"Huh?" Richardson looked up over the top of the letter. "Which one is what?"

"That letter. It's gotta be from one of your girlfriends. Which girl is it? That admiral's daughter? The redhead you were laying in Fort Pierce? Is she pregnant?"

Richardson smirked. "You've got a dirty mind, Gator. It just so happens this is from Bill Wallace."

"No shit? He's pregnant?"

"Asshole. No. He's in England."

Tangretti sobered. "Oh, yeah? Since when?"

"He went over in December. He was assigned to an NCDU team that's been there since the first of November. He says he can't talk about what he's doing in the mail, but he does say that it's plenty exciting."

"Yeah, I'll just bet it is," Tangretti said. He stared off at the horizon for several long beats. The naval gunfire continued in the distance, a steady, throbbing pulse in the air.

"You know what he's getting into if he can't talk about it, don't you?"

"Sure. France." The long-awaited, long-promised, long-dreaded-and-hoped-for invasion of France could not be very far off. For months, American, Canadian, Anzac, Free French, and other Allied troops had been gathering in camps across southern England, until it seemed that the ancient fortress isle could not support the weight of one more man or rifle. And the aircraft, the ships, the landing craft, all of the supplies and equipment necessary to organize and launch a successful invasion across the English Channel . . .

Richardson was still reading the letter from Wallace. "Aw, shit!"

"What? What's wrong?"

"Wallace is talking about the English girls."

"What's the matter? You wish you were there with him?"

"Don't I ever. Wallace says he's found a girl."

"Uh-oh. Sounds serious."

"Yeah, it does. Her name's Alice, he says. He says they've been seeing a lot of each other."

"Somehow, I can't picture Bill getting serious with a girl. He doesn't seem like the type."

"What, Bill Wallace? Aw man, Gator, he's definitely the type. Serious. Not much to say. Always thinking. Girls eat that stuff up. That's the kind of guy you really have to watch."

Tangretti walked to the rail, staring out across the crisp, blue water of the Pacific. The thunder of the Navy bombardment rolled across the sparkling sea, the rumbling, muffled sound of a distant storm. "Well, girls sure as hell are in short supply around here. I wonder . . ."

"Hold it, Gator. You've got the cumshaw look about you again. What've you got cooking in that little Eye-tie brain of yours?"

"Oh, nothing. I'm just looking at some of the angles, that's all."

"Well, count me out. The last angle you worked, I ended up in Hawaii."

"You wanted to be in Hawaii. Anyway, the last angle I worked, you got to share in a bottle of scotch."

"Yeah, that's right. I forgot." Richardson carefully folded

up the letter, replaced it in the envelope, and slipped it into a pocket. "Did I ever thank you for that?"

"Yes, Snake. You did." Tangretti walked back to the hatch coaming and slumped down alongside Richardson. "You were lying flat on your back at the time, swearing me your undying love and fealty. Whatever the hell that is."

"I don't remember that."

"I'm not surprised. It was just before you made the big play for that cute blond WAVE."

"You're shitting me."

"I wouldn't shit you, buddy. She had great tits. Out to here."

"I don't remember that, either."

"Now *that* surprises me. You told me you were going to marry her. You probably told her that, too."

"Doesn't count if I don't remember it. Was she good-looking?"

"Hey, Richardson! Tangretti! Front'n center!"

The two men sat up. Lieutenant j.g. Breucort was coming toward them across the deck. With him was Ensign Lewis F. Luehrs, a young UDT officer Tangretti remembered from Fort Pierce. "Oops. Vacation's over," Tangretti said, rising to his feet.

"You wanted us, Lieutenant?"

"You boys like to go for a little spin?" Breucort asked. "We're about to muster the team for the recon."

"Sounds good to me, Lieutenant," Richardson said. "I hope the equipment's in better shape this time around."

Luehrs pulled a lopsided grin. "Don't sweat it, Snake. They've got an engineman tearing your Higgins boat apart now. He just told me he's never seen such a piece of shit in his life. A real clunker. Same for the other boat. Looks like someone tried to pass off some shoddy merchandise on the admiral."

"Oh, he'll just love that," Tangretti said. Admiral Richmond Kelly Turner was not known for his easygoing disposition. In fact, his dour attitude and caustic temper had long ago earned him the sobriquet "Terrible Turner." Someone, Tangretti thought, was going to get hung from the highest yardarm of the admiral's new command ship over that affair.

"Well, you boys are in the clear, anyway," Breucort said. "Some of the guys working on that engine are wondering how you two got it to run as long as you did! So, ready for another boat ride? Let's go saddle up!"

"That's right," Tangretti agreed. "Let's show 'em what *men* can do when the machines break down!"

As they walked across the deck toward the davits where a deck party was readying more landing craft, Luehrs nodded toward the crowd of people standing by, then shook his head. "You boys getting the same bad feeling about all this that I am?" He kept his voice low, so Breucort, walking ahead of them, couldn't hear.

"I haven't been impressed with the setup so far," Richardson said. "I'm still not too clear on what this mob is supposed to accomplish."

The personnel now climbing aboard the four waiting LCMs included their Navy crews, machine gunners, radiomen, leadsmen to measure water depth, intelligence specialists, mapmaking experts, photographers, and, of course, the UDT men themselves.

"Me neither." Luehrs slapped the sides of his fatigue trousers, at the hips. "I figure they're going to be getting in each others' way. Me, I'm wearing my swimming togs underneath. Chief Acheson and I think we might just go for a little swim if we get bored out there."

"Right," Richardson said. Clearly, he thought Luehrs was joking.

Tangretti didn't think he was.

Chapter 23

Monday, 31 January 1944

Kwajalein
The Marshall Islands

At 0930 hours, Tangretti and Richardson scrambled aboard another davit-swung landing craft with a small crowd of other Navy personnel and clung to safety lines as the ugly little craft was lowered into the water. The LCM wasn't big, and after the earlier mission, where just the two of them had been knocking about in a boat large enough for twenty-five, seemed crowded.

Ensign Luehrs gave them a cheerful wave from the *Callahan*'s deck, then walked off to board his own LCM. There were four other UDT men aboard with Tangretti and Richardson, none of them alumni of Fort Pierce. Three were former Seabees, while the fourth, to the amused and friendly derision of the others, was a Marine who'd volunteered for Turner's UDT program in December. The landing craft's cargo, besides the various Navy specialists, included a number of satchels filled with explosives, tagged lines for measuring distances, buoys for marking channels, and so much other equipment that Tangretti wondered how anything was going to be accomplished.

They were certainly getting a splendid send-off, Tangretti thought. Earlier, a spectacular breakfast, which some of the men, with dark humor, insisted on calling their "last meal," had been laid out in the ship's mess. Tangretti and Richardson had missed the meal, which had been served while they'd been bobbing around chasing the broken-down

Stingray. Now, a large portion of the ship's company had lined the rail to watch the four landing craft of the reconnaissance party slowly lowered into the sea. After several confused moments while the crew tried to sort things out, the boat's skipper, a lieutenant j.g. named Whitehead, gave the order to get under way. Slowly, one after another, the LCMs pulled away from the transport.

This was what the Fort Pierce and Waimanalo training had been all about, Tangretti thought. He would have been happier if only UDT personnel had been along, and happier still if the team had been composed solely of Fort Pierce alumni. He didn't know these people, didn't know how they would perform in a tight spot.

And combat was not the place to find out. Still, this seemed to promise more than had those damned Stingray drones.

The lead boat of the four reconnaissance LCMs was under the command of a j.g. Tangretti didn't know, but the senior UDT officer aboard was Ensign Luehrs. The plan called for the LCMs to motor in toward the edge of the reef as far as they could go, spreading out in a line between Kwajalein and Enubuj and taking depth readings along the coral wall.

Tangretti looked up at the sky, clear blue with puffy white clouds. It occurred to him that this mission really was suicidal. As much as they all hoped that the bombardment had wiped out every Japanese on the island, everyone knew that that wouldn't be the case. And here they were, going toward the beach in broad daylight.

Actually, the operation was not quite as crazy as it seemed. At 1000 hours, according to the plan drawn up by Turner and his staff, the battleships *Pennsylvania* and *Mississippi* would draw in close to Kwajalein and begin pasting it with point-blank salvos. The theory was that the Japanese would be too busy taking shelter from the close-in bombardment to bother with such comparatively minor nuisances as four landing craft puttering along the edge of the reef.

Knowing what was *supposed* to happen, however, carried small comfort in a pitching, open boat drawing close to an island fortress that might well make Bloody Tarawa look like a picnic.

Richardson slapped him on the shoulder, then pointed. "There go the big boys," he said. Turning, Tangretti could see the huge gray hulls of the two battleships as they drew in closer to shore, their weather decks bristling with guns, their superstructures like cathedral spires against the cloud-dotted sky. A moment later, there was a brilliant orange flash from the lead ship. Seconds later, the thunder of the shot reached the LCMs, a deep, hollow boom. Another shot . . . another . . .

Then both battlewagons were firing full salvos rather than single guns. Shells crashed into Kwajalein, now a mile and a half to the south, piling thunder upon thunder, plowing up sand already tossed and blasted by the earlier bombardments, splintering already splintered trees, and, occasionally, finding some more substantial target hidden beyond the treeline, marking it with the uncoiling blossom of a fireball.

"Yeah, yeah, yeah!" a nearby sailor was chanting, pumping his fist for emphasis. "*Give* it to the slant-eyed sons of bitches! *Yeah!*"

Tangretti had never seen such hate and joy mingled in a single face at the same time.

The channel the four boats had been ordered to survey was two miles wide, a stretch of shallow water overlaying a broad, flat-topped reef that joined the neighboring islands of Kwajalein and Enubuj. By this time, landings had already begun on Enubuj; tomorrow, the plan called for landings on the western end of Kwajalein, with the landing craft crossing the reef under covering fire from American troops on the smaller island. Admiral Turner's battle staff wanted to know what the reef was like between the two islands. Of particular interest were the defenses on the west side of Kwajalein, facing Enubuj. Aerial reconnaissance photos taken late in December had shown the Japanese hard at work on some sort of fortification there, possibly a sea wall of the type that had held up the Marines on Tarawa. Turner's people wanted to know what that wall was like, what it was made of, and whether there were any other defenses, obstacles, or mines on the beach or in the approaches.

No one wanted a repetition of Tarawa, with landing craft grounding five hundred yards from the beach.

As the reconnaissance boats drew closer, the battleships gradually shifted their aim farther and farther to the east. They were quite close to the beach now, with the *Pennsylvania* steaming slowly four thousand yards off the southern coast of Kwajalein, and the *Mississippi* pressing in to a range of two thousand yards, accompanied by several greyhound-lean destroyers.

Abruptly, the LCM swung its bow ramp away from the island and began wallowing heavily in the swell. Leaning over the side, Tangretti could easily see the bottom sliding slowly past the LCM's keel. The water was shockingly clear, like aqua-tinted crystal. It almost seemed as though the landing craft was floating in the air, with the coral beneath its hull forming a magical and mysterious landscape just a few feet below. He could see the boat's shadow rippling across a patch of white sand, exactly like the shadow of an aircraft seen from the air. Schools of fish drifted and darted among shadowed forests of living coral.

"What's the matter?" he asked Richardson. "Why're we turning back?"

Richardson pointed. Fifty yards farther in, waves broke across a slender ridge of sun-bleached coral protruding a few inches above the surface. "We're pretty close to the edge of the shoals," he said. "I guess the coxswain doesn't want to play amtrack in this thing."

Two sailors lowered an inflated rubber boat over the starboard side, securing it with lines bent to cleats on the LCM's gunwales. One of the leadsmen scrambled down into the raft and started paying out a length of depth-tagged line attached to a lead weight. "Three feet!" he called back.

"A quarter twain," Richardson added, keeping his voice low, so only Tangretti could hear.

"What the hell's that?"

"Leadsmen aboard a river steamer used to sing out with formulas like that to let the helmsman know how deep the water was. 'Quarter twain' meant three feet. 'Mark twain' meant two fathoms of water under the keel, deep enough for safe passage."

"Mark Twain . . . like the writer?"

"That's the one. Clemens took that as his pen name. What's the matter? Why are you looking at me that way?"

"I'm just surprised you know something about a subject other than pussy."

"The benefits of a classical education in a private school. I learned a lot about pussy at school too."

The LCM continued its explorations along the edge of the reef, but the UDT men aboard found themselves at loose ends. The raft alongside wasn't large enough for more than four men at a time, and it was generally occupied by the leadsmen. When the UDT men managed to take a turn, they found there was little they could do. They'd been issued twelve-foot poles marked off in six-inch increments, but these proved only marginally more effective than the clumsy lead-weight-and-string approach. Tangretti could tell just by watching that the information gained by this method was going to be slim to nonexistent. The mapmakers were trying to plot the location of each sounding by taking careful compass sightings off landmarks ashore. Unfortunately, after the extensive bombardment, there were remarkably few landmarks left standing on either island, fewer, in fact, with each passing moment as the pall from the naval shelling thickened overhead. That kind of plotting from a pitching, open boat was almost useless in any case. A particular coral head might be placed with an accuracy of to within fifty yards or so . . . useless when trying to mark safe lanes for landing craft.

Besides, this method told them absolutely nothing about the coral farther in, squarely between Enubuj and Kwajalein, and lying beneath the paths the landing boats were expected to take the next day.

"Hey, Coxswain," Tangretti called to the man at the wheel, frustrated by the lack of organization in the mixed party. "Can't you take us in any closer?"

"Hell no," the sailor replied. "You want me to pile up on that reef?" He pointed to another LCM in the distance. "*They're* not going in any closer, so I don't see why I should!"

Tangretti stared at the other landing craft. It was the lead boat, Luehrs' LCM, moving parallel to the reef about seven hundred yards to the west. There appeared to be some sort of activity in the water alongside. "Shit, Snake," he said. "What's going on over there?"

Richardson had a pair of binoculars to his eyes. "Man overboard? Hell, it looks like someone's in the water. I can't quite make it out."

"Maybe they gave up and decided to go swimming."

Richardson stared at Tangretti for a moment, the binoculars held tightly in front of his chest. "You know, Gator? That's not a half bad idea."

At first Tangretti didn't know what Richardson was getting at. Then his eyes widened. "Snake, you're not thinking what I *think* you're thinking . . ."

"Why not? Look, we're not going to be able to tell shit from here." He gestured over the side, where a pair of leadsmen were bobbing in the small boat, trying to retrieve a line snarled somewhere below. The heavy swell was giving them problems, too, producing wildly varying measurements. "You know, Lew said something about wearing his swim trunks under his uniform. I thought he was kidding."

"Snake, it's against regs. 'In deep water, no personnel will be allowed to enter the water unless wearing flotation jackets and equipped with a suitable lifeline secured to the boat.' Remember?"

"Gator. You? Worried about regulations? I'm surprised at you!"

"Regulations have their place. If there's a reason for 'em." He eyed the water uncertainly. "You know, Snake, I still don't like the water. Deep water, I mean."

Richardson shrugged. "Well, I could go in alone, I guess, or ask one of the Seabees to come along."

"Damn you, Snake!" Tangretti flared. "*I'm* your fucking partner!"

"Well, I'd rather have you, of course. But if you don't want to . . ."

Tangretti pulled off his helmet, then started untying his life jacket. "Who says I didn't want to? I just think you're an asshole, and I'm crazy to let you talk me into things. What are we going to use for swim trunks?"

Richardson blinked. "Actually, what do we need swimsuits for? Who's to see?"

"Everybody else aboard this landing craft. Not to mention the Japs."

"I doubt they'll care. Besides, I don't intend to get that close to them."

Tangretti started shucking off his trousers. "I just know I'm gonna regret this."

"What the hell's going on here?" Lieutenant j.g. Whitehead walked up to the two men as they continued to strip off their uniforms. He was a quick, intense man with crew-cut hair and a square jaw.

"Hi, Lieutenant," Richardson said. "We're going for a swim. Want to come along?"

"Like hell you are, Ensign. Orders are for all personnel to stay in the boat."

"Look, Lieutenant," Tangretti said, facing the man. "We're not accomplishing shit out here, right? We can't get in closer because of the coral, and the swell is too heavy to let the leadsmen work from the raft. Either we turn around, right now, go back to the ship, and tell Admiral Turner that we can't do a fucking thing out here, or you let Snake and me go over the side and do it our way. Okay?"

Lieutenant Whitehead took a step backward, his hands raised. "Okay, okay. I heard you Fort Pierce guys were tough, but skinny-dipping off an enemy-held island is a new one on me. You sure you guys know what you're doing?"

Tangretti looked at Richardson, who returned a maniacal grin.

"Hell, Lieutenant," Tangretti said. "We *always* know what we're doing!"

The costumes they elected to wear in the end were little short of ludicrous: their white undershorts, more as protection against the possible touch of various small, stinging creatures than out of any sense of modesty; goggles, drawn from a store of the things shipped aboard from California for UDT operations; web belts, fitted with a Navy Mark I knife and scabbard in Richardson's case, and a Marine K-Bar for Tangretti; and white canvas shoes, "coral shoes" that had also been brought along for offshore survey work and, fortunately, had been included in one of the canvas bags of equipment for the reconnaissance party. Those shoes would be clumsy in the water, but the two men intended to penetrate the reef as far as they could, and coral could slice a man's bare feet to ribbons in seconds. Lightweight canvas shoes would let them stand on those razor-edged branches without crippling themselves ... or attracting sharks with their blood.

Tangretti thought about sharks and shivered a little, but it was too late to change his mind now.

They also carried waterproof grease markers tucked into their belts. Since the whole point of this exercise was to bring back data on the reef, they decided that they would need some means of keeping records. The markers would write under water; with nothing else available, they would use their own bodies as notebooks.

When all was ready, Tangretti and Richardson clambered down into the raft. They sat for a moment on the side, adjusting their goggles. Then at a common signal, they rolled over the side with a double splash.

The water was warm and crystal clear, much the same as it had been that time in the Indian River when they'd tried out those newfangled masks and swim fins. With the goggles in place, Tangretti's view of the undersea landscape was only slightly distorted; it gave him the feeling of flying. Coral loomed up out of emerald depths—towers, mesas, castles, mushrooms, shapes out of wild fantasy. Near the top, most of the coral was dead and bleached white. At slightly greater depths, and along the flanks of the coral ramparts, living corals grew in astonishing varieties of colors and shapes. Fish darted, swarmed, and floated in magic profusion; Tangretti, who had never had more than a passing interest in fish unless he could trade them for something else, could not begin to name them or even to guess at the number of species.

Perhaps what was most astonishing, though, was the peacefulness of the scene a few feet below the surface of an ocean torn by war. Even down here, though, he could hear the distant thud of the ongoing barrage.

He felt a touch on his shoulder and looked up. Richardson hovered just above him, his goggles giving him an unearthly look as he pointed in the direction of the reef. Tangretti interpreted his signal: *Let's go.*

They swam underwater for several yards, keeping one an-

other in sight. Then, as Tangretti's lungs began signaling an
increasing need for air, they moved toward the surface, a
shifting pattern of sky and silver rippling above their heads.
Tangretti's head broke through into the air, chill after the
warmth of the water. He took several breaths, then began
swimming on the surface with a long-armed crawl. As he'd
expected, the shoes dragged at his feet somewhat, but the
long runs in the sand at Fort Pierce had strengthened his
legs to the point that they didn't bother him that much.

The swell carried him forward, lifting him bodily as each
wave passed beneath him with a rapid surge. It made the
swim in toward the beach easy but left him wondering how
hard it was going to be to get back. He couldn't see much
of the undersea terrain from the surface, so after a time he
took in a deep breath and submerged again. Richardson followed.

They appeared to be in a kind of canyon between sheer
walls of jagged white coral. As Richardson swam on ahead,
Tangretti stopped, estimating the width of the passage.
Thirty or forty yards, it looked like, though distances were
hard to guess. Next he tried to estimate depth by standing
on a block of coral at the bottom of the passage. At first he
had trouble getting his feet under his body; he was buoyant
enough that he fought a tendency to bob back to the surface
like a cork. Finally, he got the trick of expelling enough air
from his lungs that he could stand upright, with his arms
raised over his head and breaking the surface. Eight feet, it
looked like, or near enough. Taking the grease pencil, he
noted the depth and approximate location on the back of his
arm. If this sort of thing was to become routine for the
UDTs, he thought, it would be imperative to develop some
means of writing and keeping records underwater. Possibly
a slate of some sort.

One thing was quite clear. While there were passages
through the coral, they would have to be marked and
buoyed if landing craft were to find them. As at Tarawa,
amtracks would be better, giving the invasion force a clear
path into the beach without having to worry about finding
the deep channels.

He kept swimming, sometimes underwater, more often on
the surface. He found that a gentle breast stroke gave him

the best distance without using up a lungful of air too quickly.

Tangretti was especially and pleasantly surprised to find that he was not afraid in the water, as he'd thought he would be. Being able to see helped; had the water been ink-black, he was certain he would have panicked. Visibility was splendid, however, offering an unobstructed view of the bottom whenever he chose to duck his head under. After swimming for perhaps two hundred yards more, he caught up with Richardson, who was standing on a coral block with his head above water.

Tangretti joined him, stepping onto the coral and cautiously poking his head out of the water. He was astonished to see how far he'd come in the past few minutes. The landing craft was a good three hundred yards away, bobbing in the swell just outside the reef wall. Turning in the water, he studied Kwajalein Island. They were a lot closer to the beach now. Tangretti could easily make out the sea wall that so concerned Turner and his staff.

"Let's move in closer," Richardson suggested. "I want to get a good look at that wall."

Tangretti scanned the beach. There was no sign of life. Beyond the straggling remnants of palm trees above the high-tide line, perhaps a mile inland, battleship shells continued to crash and rumble. To the right, perhaps three hundred yards away, was a Japanese gun emplacement, a truncated hill of concrete with a six-inch gun mounted behind sandbag parapets. Evidently, the bombardment hadn't nailed all of the defenses on this end of the island. "Okay. Not too close, though. And let's move over that way, clear of that emplacement."

They made the final part of the approach underwater, examining the way the bottom shelved and checking the depth all the way in. They searched for underwater obstacles or mines but found none. The Japanese hardly needed them. The entire area was peppered with coral heads, blocks of coral ranging from the size of a jeep to the size of a house, rising irregularly from the shoaling bottom to within a few inches of the surface. Navigating a small boat between them at low tide would be a nightmare.

Where was Richardson?

Carefully surfacing, Tangretti spotted his partner fifty yards ahead, almost at the water line. Quickly, he swam toward the beach.

"What the hell are you doing, Snake?" he demanded. The surf here was gentle, a foot-high swell breaking in the last few yards before splashing up on the white, coral sand. Richardson was on his hands and knees in water two feet deep, clinging to the wet sand as each wave broke past him.

In answer, Richardson pointed. Just beyond the shelf of sandy beach, the Japanese sea wall was plainly visible now. He could see that it was massively thick, heavily reinforced with concrete and stone. Logs like sections of telephone poles had been planted in front of the wall, pointing out to sea. It was now just past high tide; Tangretti guessed that at high tide, the water must wash over the feet of those stakes. They would make a formidable obstacle to landing craft trying to get all the way up to the sea wall. Craters pocked the beach everywhere, evidence of the fierce bombardment that had brushed across this end of the island earlier.

Richardson grinned, a wild look in his eye. "Let's do some sightseeing, Gator!"

"What, are you crazy? C'mon! Before the Japs come!"

"Ah, there ain't a Jap within two miles." Rising suddenly, he broke through the surf and trotted up onto the beach.

Tangretti looked left and right. They were far enough up the beach to be out of sight from the gun emplacement they'd spotted earlier. The bombardment had scoured this end of the island of vegetation, leaving only the bedraggled ruin of a Spruance haircut. Except for the wall itself, which on this part of the beach appeared to be shoring up a crumbling sand embankment, there was no cover at all. If there were Japanese pillboxes or gun emplacements on this part of the beach, he couldn't see them. He was more concerned that the *Pennsylvania* and the *Mississippi* might suddenly decide to start pasting this end of Kwajalein again.

Sprinting after Richardson, he caught up with him at the water's edge, just below the line of log obstacles. "Snake!" he said, his voice near hiss. "You are insane! Certifiably insane!"

Richardson picked up a handful of wet sand, squeezing it

in his fingers. "Yeah, but look at us, Gator! We're first ashore!"

"Somehow, I don't think we ought to include this in our report. Come on. Let's get the hell out of here!"

"Uh-oh. Hold it!" Richardson, already on his knees, dropped prone, hugging the wet sand. Instinctively, Tangretti copied him.

Fifty yards down the beach, a man was climbing down over the seawall. It was a soldier . . . no, *two* soldiers. Japanese. They wore mustard-khaki uniforms and carried rifles slung over their shoulders. They were close enough for Tangretti to see that one was wearing round-framed eyeglasses. They stood on the sand for a few moments staring out to sea, apparently studying the distant line of American ships. One pointed, speaking. The other nodded.

Then Tangretti realized that it was not the battleships that had captured the soldiers' attention but the four reconnaissance landing craft, still moving slowly along the edge of the reef some five hundred yards beyond the surf. Suddenly, possibly impulsively, one of the soldiers slipped his rifle off his back, raised it to his shoulder, and aimed it at one of the LCMs.

Tangretti stifled an impulse to yell, to rush forward, to try to attract the enemy's attention and divert them from the landing craft. Somehow, he kept himself still.

The soldier fired, the rifle's bark a flat crack that echoed across the beach. He worked the bolt, took aim once more . . . and fired.

Richardson laid a warning hand on Tangretti's shoulder. When Tangretti looked at him, he raised his index finger to his lips: *Keep quiet.* Then he made a contemptuous gesture, as though throwing something away: *Besides, they can't hit the side of a barn.*

At this range, Tangretti couldn't tell whether the Japanese soldier had hit his target or not. He doubted it. Five hundred yards was pretty long range for one of those bolt-action rifles, and the guy wasn't even firing prone or bracing it on a log or tree trunk.

He touched Richardson's shoulder, then jerked a thumb over his shoulder: *Let's get out of here.* Richardson nodded agreement. Carefully, the two men backed down off the beach, inching their way feetfirst into the surf. The Japanese, laughing, turned away from the water and started moving up the beach, kicking at the sand as they walked.

Toward the two UDT men.

They kept backing into the water until only their heads were showing, then began swimming away from the beach. Tangretti turned to look over his shoulder just in time to see one of the soldiers, now thirty yards away, grab his companion's arm and point.

"Tomare!" the second soldier shouted, loud enough that Tangretti could easily hear him over the thunder of the distant bombardment. *"Mibun shomeisho o misero!"*

Tangretti didn't speak Japanese, but he had no doubts about what the soldier was shouting. Extending his arms forward, he dove beneath the next ocean swell coming toward the beach, lunging into the emerald clarity of the sea.

He heard something in the water close by, a kind of sharp, metallic chirp. He kept swimming, kicking as hard as he could. There it was again! Sound traveled astonishingly well underwater, and he wasn't sure what the noise was.

Several feet in front of him, a white streak of bubbles appeared as if by magic, accompanied by that chirp and a sharp hiss. Bullets! He was hearing bullets striking the water just above their heads! They seemed to slow within a couple of feet of the surface, so he arched his back and dove deeper, Richardson close by his side.

Another chirp, and this time, an instant later, he saw the coppery glint of the bullet itself, sinking through the water a couple of feet in front of him, its speed spent. Tangretti reached out and snatched the round with his hand. What a good-luck piece *that* was! Or could he sell it to some shipboard sailor? Back at Oahu, one of his contacts in Honolulu had told him about the market for souvenirs—especially Japanese swords, pistols, and battle flags. What would some sailor or rear-echelon desk jockey pay for a Jap rifle bullet?

That presumed that the guy believed his story about where the bullet had come from. And that he would live long enough to make the deal. Clutching the trophy in his fist, he kept swimming.

When his lungs felt as though they were about to burst, he surfaced briefly, gulped in a fast breath, then dove once

more. After six more quick surfacings, he dared to linger in
the air long enough to look back at the beach. The soldiers
were gone, and that gave Tangretti an eerie, uncomfortable
feeling. Had they gone to tell their commanding officer? To
get a boat? Maybe they would start mortaring the water
where they thought the swimmers might be lurking.
Tangretti had no desire to try to catch mortar shells in his
bare hands.

The return trip was exhausting, but otherwise uneventful.
The tide had turned and was well into the ebb, and that
helped carry them along. There was no further sign of the
Japanese soldiers, and no further attacks. Back at the landing craft, Whitehead and a couple of sailors helped drag the
two men from the water and into the rubber boat. By that
time, Tangretti's legs were so tired he could scarcely clamber the rest of the way up into the LCM.

Moments after they were aboard, however, they were motoring back out to sea. At Richardson's suggestion, they
bypassed the *Callahan* and made instead directly for the
Monrovia.

At Tarawa, Admiral Turner's flagship had been the U.S.S.
Pennsylvania. Unfortunately, every time the battlewagon's
main guns fired, the ship's communications system was
knocked out, sometimes for minutes at a time. The same
problem had been noted aboard the *Pennsylvania*'s consort,
the *Maryland*.

For the Marshalls operation, however, Turner had shipped
aboard a new concept in amphibious warfare, a command
ship. Once an attack transport, or AKA, of 14,247 tons
named the *Delargentina*, she was now the *Monrovia*, and
she served as Turner's flagship . . . without the irritating and
possibly dangerous communications blackouts.

On their way to the *Monrovia*, Tangretti and Richardson
got a sheet of clean paper, torn from the pages of the boat
coxswain's operational log, and roughed out a map based on
what they remembered and on the cryptic smudges of
marker still visible on their arms and stomachs. Half an
hour later, dressed again in their fatigues but wringing wet
in the absence of any towels aboard the landing craft, they
scrambled up a Jacob's ladder to *Monrovia*'s deck, then
were led aft by a couple of smirking sailors. Their unautho-

rized swim, it seemed, had attracted some notice back in the fleet.

Turner was in *Monrovia*'s Combat Center, along with several of his staff officers. Still dripping after their long swim, Tangretti and Richardson reported to the man known as Terrible Turner.

"Well?" Turner said, his dour face showing disapproval. "Don't tell me you two have been swimming too?"

Tangretti and Richardson exchanged glances. " 'Too,' Admiral?" Richardson said. "I'm afraid I don't understand."

"Two of your compatriots decided the LCM couldn't get close enough in to get decent measurements of the coral," one of Turner's officers explained. "Ensign Luehrs and Chief Acheson, in Boat One."

Tangretti suppressed a grin. That sounded like Lew Luehrs, all right. The guy had a lot in common with Richardson, in fact.

"As a matter of fact we did go in the water, sir," Richardson said. "We got pretty close to the beach on the west end of Kwajalein."

Pretty close? Tangretti shook his head.

"And?" Turner said gruffly.

Richardson took a deep breath. "As the aerial photographs showed, sir, the Japs have built a solid-looking wall across that part of the island. Concrete, coral rock, and log. There are also what look like seasoned hardwood posts along the wall, pointed seaward. Looks like they may have been set up as a barricade to fend off boats or amtracks at high tide."

"Go on."

"There was no sign of mines on the obstacles or the wall, Admiral. We thoroughly searched the waters right off the beach. There were no underwater obstacles that we could find, no sea mines, and nothing that looked like low-tide beach defenses.

"The bad news is that the water offshore is heavily strewn with coral heads." Richardson held out the paper on which he'd drawn the survey map, showing passages and estimated depths. One of Turner's officers took it, looked it over, then began comparing it with a large map of Kwajalein on a nearby chart table. "We were there at just past high tide, and it looked like boats could probably pass over most of them. But then they'd then have to contend with those log obstacles. At anything less than high tide, landing craft would ground on the coral heads three, maybe four hundred yards out.

"Our recommendation, sir," Richardson continued, "would be to send the troops in aboard amtracks if at all possible. If you send them in aboard conventional landing craft, the troops are going to have a real tough time getting to the beach. Just like Tarawa."

Richardson continued describing their swim, including everything except the part about how they'd actually gone onto the beach, and about how they'd been shot at afterward.

"I see," Turner said after Richardson had completed his slightly edited report. "Young man, you've both done a remarkable job. My compliments to you, and to your partner here. In fact, you've confirmed what Luehrs and Acheson reported in this room half an hour ago. They actually got all the way up to the beach itself, or pretty close, measuring the depth of the water like you did, with their bodies. You'll be pleased to know we've already made the decision to send the invasion force in aboard amtracks."

Tangretti could see the slight stoop to Richardson's shoulders at the news. It *was* disappointing; here they'd thought they were bringing in one-of-a-kind information, crucial to the success of the invasion, and it turned out that they'd been also-rans by a good thirty minutes.

Still, they had provided confirmation, a separate source of information to Turner's staff. And they'd also confirmed the usefulness of this new technique, using swimmers to probe the approaches to an enemy beach. Possibly, the UDTs' repertoire of tricks could be expanded now to include combat swimmers.

Whatever happened in the future, though, one thing was certain. They'd been the first on the enemy beach, wearing nothing but shoes, goggles, shorts, and a knife. The whole damned 7th Division could come storming onto Kwajalein tomorrow, but that couldn't change one essential fact.

The men of UDT-1 had been there first.

Chapter 24

Monday, 31 January 1944

Kwajalein
The Marshall Islands

At 1600 hours that afternoon, at low tide, a second reconnaissance was made of Kwajalein's western end, this time in amtracks. Though a heavy rain started falling, the recon teams were able to further confirm the earlier reports made by the swimmers and to identify more gun batteries untouched by the earlier bombardments. As a result, Admiral Turner decided to bring the battleships back to the west side of the island.

Early on the morning of 1 February the battleships came to virtually point-blank range and slammed shell after shell into the sea wall and the strong points sighted the previous day by the recon teams. From 0618 hours to 0840 hours that morning, and then again from 0905 hours to H-Hour twenty-five minutes later, explosions gouged and tore at the beach, smashing at the sea wall, pulverizing the defenses, and ripping up the dunes beyond until one observer suggested that the entire island looked as though it had been picked up, turned over, and dropped back into the sea. For added measure, an air strike was flown off of Tarawa's hard-won airfield, flinging two-thousand-pound bombs into the flaming, churning hell of Kwajalein. Turner was determined that the sea wall would not pose a barrier to his forces.

The sea wall was pounded until there was virtually nothing left but a splintered, broken ruin. As the UDT swimmers had suggested, the first waves of Army troops went in aboard eighty-four amtracks, armor-plated and mounting three machine guns apiece, churning ahead through emerald waters on curling rooster tails of white foam. They rumbled onto the beach behind a line of amphibious tanks. The sea wall posed no obstacle at all; there wasn't enough of it left to serve as much more than a ramp leading up off the beach. Within twelve minutes after H-Hour, twelve hundred troops were ashore without a single casualty.

The hard fighting came later, as the Americans moved into the island's interior. There, perhaps half of Admiral Akiyama's garrison was still alive, dug in within a network of pillboxes, trenches, and air raid shelters. As at Tarawa, the Japanese were determined to fight to the last man, and they very nearly did. In the end, only 35 of them surrendered, and most of those who did were wounded. Kwajalein Island was not declared secured until 5 February. Roi-Namur had fallen three days before that, after some hard fighting, but it was 7 February before the entire atoll was in U.S. hands, including Ebeye and several of the smaller, outlying islands. Total American causalities numbered 372 dead and another 1,500 wounded—stiff losses by any standards, but a far cry from the slaughter-pen of Tarawa.

On 1 February, Tangretti and Richardson had been summoned back aboard the *Monrovia* for another interview with Admiral Turner. The normally sour Turner had seemed positively jovial. "How would you gentlemen like a visit Stateside?" he'd said, leaning forward on a chart table. The map there showed all of Kwajalein Atoll, with inked-in blocks showing task force elements and units already ashore.

"Back to the States?" Richardson had asked. "I don't understand. Did we do something wrong?"

"Not at all, son. If you had, I sure as hell wouldn't reward you with a ticket home. Someone in Washington wants a report, in person, from someone who took part in that beach reconnaissance yesterday. In particular, they want to talk to some of the idiots who were crazy enough to ignore orders and swim to an enemy-held island."

"You're *sure* we're not in trouble, Admiral?" Tangretti had said. He tried to make it sound like a joke, and failed.

"Aside from your sanity, which I seriously doubt," Turner

said, "you're in good shape. Washington wants someone—preferably two—and they don't much care who. Ensign Luehrs and Chief Acheson are on an assignment right now. So you boys are it." He turned away then and walked over to a desk set against one bulkhead. Picking up a sealed envelope, he returned and handed it to Richardson. "As long as you're going to Washington, you can be my personal couriers and take them that."

Richardson turned the envelope over in his hands, curious. "Aye, aye, sir."

"It's my final report on the Stingray Project."

Monday, 7 February 1944

The Pentagon

Six days after their talk with Turner, Tangretti and Richardson were in Lieutenant Galloway's office in the Pentagon, just down the hall from the office of the CNO himself. Tangretti felt uncharacteristically subdued by the immensity of the building, its bare white walls, its endless echoing corridors. Certainly, nothing in his background, not even the skyscrapers of New York, had ever prepared him for a building that enclosed so much sheer space. He'd heard a rumor to the effect that after the war the government planned on housing the entire U.S. Army here.

He could well believe that.

Galloway had invited them to be seated. Sitting across from Galloway in front of his desk, Tangretti unobtrusively held his new good-luck piece in his right hand, nervously slipping it back and forth between his fingers. The lieutenant listened without expression as Richardson described their attempt to employ Turner's Stingray boat at Kwajalein.

"We finally abandoned the attempt, sir," he finished. "The landing boats were on the way, and we didn't have the time to screw around with them. Fortunately, they weren't really needed."

"Indeed," Galloway said. He paused, studying the two men. "Tell me. What was your impression of the Stingray project?"

Tangretti laughed. "Sir, I really don't think you'd care to

hear our comments. You wouldn't be able to repeat them or include them in a report."

"That bad, huh?"

"Sir," Richardson said, "the Stingray project was the most colossally screwed-up operation it's ever been my privilege to witness and, believe me, I've witnessed a few in this man's Navy!"

Galloway picked up the envelope that Richardson had handed him at the beginning of the interview. He'd read it in their presence but told them nothing about what it said. Tangretti had wondered frankly if Turner's letter had been about them.

"This is a brief on Admiral Turner's report on Operation Flintlock," Galloway said. He scanned the letter. "Ah. Here. 'Overemphasis of certain problems which experience at Tarawa had exaggerated in the minds of those concerned . . .' ah, here '. . . caused general doubt regarding the effectiveness of our weapons and tactics, and much time and effort was expended on dubious and fruitless schemes.'" Galloway dropped the letter on his desk. "'Dubious and fruitless schemes.' A suitable epitaph to the Stingrays, don't you think?"

"Very much so," Richardson said. "Was Turner trying to cover his ass with that?"

Galloway frowned. "I don't think I should comment on that, Mr. Richardson. Certainly, Rear Admiral Turner was a strong proponent of the Stingray project from its inception. However, it is obvious that he's changed his mind. The key part of this letter stresses his enthusiastic support of the UDT program. Specifically, he is now interested in the human element, using men to do what has to be done rather than machines. The era of push-button warfare, it seems, is not yet here."

"Thank God," Tangretti said. "I didn't trust those drone boats from the moment I first saw them."

"For your information," Galloway told them, "they were less than successful at Roi-Namur. Did you hear?"

They shook their heads no.

"UDT-Two was at Roi-Namur, of course, under Admiral Conolly. Lieutenant Chapman and several other UDT personnel tried controlling a Stingray from an amtrack. They set it on its way, and it vanished into a smoke cloud. They armed it, then pressed the firing switch. Nothing happened. They were still trying to figure that out when the damned thing reappeared, coming straight back at them. Then it started going in circles. Two UDT men managed to reboard the drone. Turned out the arming circuits were good and the fuses already fired. They disarmed the thing seconds before it would've blown."

"God," Richardson said.

"I think he had a hand in it," Galloway said simply. "Later, they tried sending off another drone. It went out of control, circled around, and rammed the amtrack. As Lieutenant Chapman's report put it, 'being rammed by ten thousand pounds of dynamite is not a pleasant experience.' "

"Shit," Tangretti said. "It didn't go off?"

"Nope. Fortunately. At the time, everybody thought the Japanese had come up with some sort of electronic jamming wizardry. The final report, though, indicates it wasn't anything that dramatic. It seems that salt water was short-circuiting the remote control receivers.

"Oh, and Admiral Turner's Stingrays? The ones that kept sinking out from under you? Seems some supply officer decided that junk was good enough for boats that were going to get blown up anyway." He shook his head. "You should have seen Admiral Turner's report on *that* one!"

Richardson and Tangretti exchanged knowing looks at that. Richardson's eyes were laughing. *What'd I tell you?*

"Okay. That takes care of the damned drones," Galloway said. "Now. About your little swim."

Uh-oh, Tangretti thought. *Here it comes.*

"Sir?" Richardson said, his best innocent look firmly in place.

"I'd like you to tell me about your reconnaissance of the Enubuj-Kwajalein passage."

"Well, it's all in our report—"

"I'd like to hear about it from the two of you. Please."

Reluctantly, Richardson again launched into the story of their highly unauthorized swim in the sea of Kwajalein.

Again, Richardson did not mention their sortie onto the beach.

"I see," Galloway said when Richardson had finished.

"You men did well." He seemed to read the relief in their faces and smiled. "No, no, you're not in any trouble. I've been known to bend a regulation or three in my day, too. You two used daring, resourcefulness, and inventiveness to carry out a mission which could not possibly have succeeded as originally conceived. You are to be commended, both of you."

"Thank you, sir," Tangretti said. Richardson seemed too surprised to answer right away.

Galloway leaned forward, clasping his hands together on the top of his desk. "I'd like you to tell me one thing. Off the record, man to man, no recriminations. I just want to know, firsthand."

"Sir?"

"Just how close did you boys get to that beach? I mean, how close *really*?"

Richardson and Tangretti exchanged glances. "Well, sir . . ." Richardson began.

Tangretti stood up, reached out, and dropped the Japanese bullet onto Galloway's desk. It landed with a small thump on the desktop blotter. "Actually, sir," he said, "we got just a bit closer than we mentioned in our official report. . . ."

Galloway picked up the bullet and held it up, looking at it closely. "Arisaka Rifle Type thirty-eight," he rapped out, as though reading the words from a reference book. "Two-five-six-caliber, bolt-action repeating weapon firing from a five-round box, first adopted by the Japanese Imperial Army in 1905. You want to tell me about it?"

Richardson took the lead then, describing how they'd actually left the surf and gone up on the beach, close enough to touch the log obstacles the Japanese had installed in front of their sea wall. He assumed the responsibility himself, saying that he'd left the water first and that Tangretti had followed only because he was trying to get his partner to return to the safety of the sea.

"We were getting ready to go back when we spotted two Japanese soldiers," Richardson continued. "We hugged the sand at the edge of the water line while one of them took a couple of potshots at the boats offshore. Then they gave up and started coming in our direction, so we moved off the beach and back into the water. We were about thirty or forty yards out when they spotted us and took a couple more shots."

"They missed," Tangretti added, smiling hopefully. He nodded at the bullet in Galloway's hand. "That was the closest they got."

"Remarkable." Galloway reached out, handing the bullet back to Tangretti. "Thank you for telling me."

He looked almost ... wistful. *It almost seems as though he wishes he could've been there,* Tangretti thought. He had trouble believing he was reading the lieutenant right. This building was the very center of power in military Washington, the hub of all the action, all the contacts. Ever since he'd enlisted in the Navy, Tangretti had sought that place in the military with perfect access to people who could make things happen, to sources of goods and information, to *power.* It seemed strange that an officer assigned to Washington duty could want anything else.

And then again, on second thought, maybe it wasn't so strange after all. Tangretti could understand the feeling of suffocation an officer might feel in a sterile concrete hive like the Pentagon. He felt it after less than an hour in the building. And from what he'd heard, Galloway had been working here for almost a year.

"I'll tell you the reason I wanted to hear your story personally," Galloway said. "As I'm certain you're both very much aware, the Allies are building up toward the invasion of Europe. We don't know when it will be." He read their expressions again and smiled. "No, not even us Pentagon types know when it'll be. Not yet. Or where. But we can be damned certain that it's going to be soon. Best guess is late this spring. Possibly as early as mid-May."

The room seemed to grow quieter, a silence stretched out by the ticking of a clock on a wall behind the desk. Tangretti and Richardson said nothing, their attention totally focused on Galloway.

"I needn't remind you boys to regard everything said here as classified."

"No, sir."

"Absolutely not, sir."

"The Germans," Galloway continued, "have created something of a science out of building impressive and sophisticated beach defenses. We've been keeping pretty close track of their beachfront properties, as you can imagine."

Leaning back, he opened a desk drawer and pulled out a manila folder. Inside were a number of black-and-white photographs, frames taken from a fighter's gun camera. Each showed an oblique stretch of beach, the sand and surf clearly distinguishable, though often blurred. Dotting the sand or protruding from the water, in photo after photo, was a bewildering variety of shapes: posts, concrete blocks, steel spikes, welded constructs that looked like nothing so much as a huge gate without the fence.

"The Germans have been improving them steadily since last year," Galloway went on. "Field Marshal Erwin Rommel . . . you've heard of him? I thought so. He's been sent to France to make recommendations on improving coastal defenses, and he has been going about it with ruthless Teutonic efficiency. They're building obstacles. Tank traps. Boat traps. Mines. Hedgehogs. Tetrahedrons. Dragon's teeth. Believe me, gentlemen, when I say that nothing, *nothing,* we've encountered so far in the Pacific even comes close to the sophistication and the efficiency of the German beach defenses in France.

"Since November, we've had one of Commander Coffer's NCDUs in England. More have gone over since. We are attempting to organize a new type of unit, one composed of a Navy CDU force teamed with an Army squad of engineers. The idea will be to land these teams either just in advance of the main landings or with the first waves, ideally during low tide. They will plant explosive charges on the German obstacles and blast paths through them right up the beach. As the tide comes in, we will have cleared and buoyed channels for the later boat waves to navigate."

"That sounds exciting, sir," Richardson said. "It sounds like the original mission of Commander Coffer's teams."

"Yes, it is. You're absolutely right. The commander's original concept was for a unit that could move in with an invasion force and blow up enemy beach defenses. The teams operating in the Pacific have had to adjust their strategy, to adapt quite a bit. Out there, coral is a bigger obstacle to landing on the beach than anything the Japs can build. They need reconnaissance teams to check out the beach approaches, and maybe demolition guys to knock holes in it. In Europe, though, we're still definitely thinking more in terms of a combat demolition unit, people who can deal with these things." He tapped the photographs.

"How would you two like to be a part of it?"

The question caught both of them completely by surprise. On the way back from the Pacific, Tangretti and Richardson had talked endlessly about their chances of getting reassigned to their old unit, the NCDU. Chief Wallace's letter had gotten both of them thinking. Admiral Turner's UDT seemed to have great potential, but nobody in the Pacific was using that potential, at least not yet. They'd heard about NCDU-2 being used as Seabees by MacArthur. They'd seen the excitement of the brass over those damned Stingray toys, and even if Turner had changed his mind about them, the *thinking* in the Pacific command still emphasized the gimmick over the man.

Besides, most of the men Richardson and Tangretti had served with in UDT-1 had never been through Hell Week. That peculiar brotherhood, forged in that first week of training at Fort Pierce, counted for a very great deal with everyone who'd survived it.

"Well?"

It took a moment for Tangretti to realize that Galloway was waiting for an answer. "We've talked about that a lot, Lieutenant," he admitted. "It would be awfully good to be back in our old unit."

"I think we can arrange that," Galloway said. "While we're reorganizing the NCDUs in England, we're also putting them through additional training. Commando tactics. More bomb disposal work, to catch them up on some new wrinkles the Germans have come up with recently. Infiltration. It's a whole different kind of war over there, gentlemen, from what you experienced in the Pacific.

"You two have had the experience of actually crawling onto an enemy beach. We're trying to do some of that along the French coast, but it's not easy . . . not least because some of our own people have trouble thinking in terms of sneak raids, reconnaissance, and combat intelligence. You follow me?"

"I think so, sir," Richardson said.

"So you'll be assigned to teams. And you'll be asked to talk to the men about your experience in Kwajalein. Tell them, especially the officers, that it can be done. Get them thinking along new lines." He pointed at Tangretti's hand. "You can show them your trinket."

"I've been wondering if anybody would believe me, sir."

"When do we go, Lieutenant?" Richardson wanted to know.

"Immediately. Or damn near. That soon enough for you? I'll have my people cut your orders this afternoon. Oh. One more thing, speaking of orders. Mr. Richardson? I have something here for you." Reaching again into his desk drawer, he produced a box, which he handed to Richardson.

Inside were two separate silver bars, the insignia of a lieutenant j.g.

Richardson's eyes widened, his eyebrows crawling toward his hairline. "Uh . . . sir?"

"Just came through. In fact, the paperwork won't be down until tomorrow." Galloway reached out and took his hand in a firm handshake. "Congratulations, *Lieutenant* Richardson!"

"Gosh! Thank you, sir!"

"Hell, don't thank me. You've had time in grade. Mostly, there's a serious shortage of j.g.s and lieutenants out there, and I guess they're willing to snatch up anything they can get." He shook his head. "Just don't let a certain admiral find out about that, okay? Or we'll both be in trouble!"

Richardson opened his mouth, then clamped it shut. "Aye, aye, sir."

For almost the first time since he'd known him, Tangretti saw Snake Richardson at a complete loss for words.

In the passageway outside Galloway's office, Richardson shook his head. "Damn. I thought I was going to be an ensign for the rest of my life."

Tangretti punched Richardson in the arm. "Yeah. You gotta start acting like a real officer and a gentleman now, Snake. Not like some wet-behind-the-ears punk ensign!"

"You'll have to treat me with more respect, son."

"When you earn it."

"Damn!"

"What's the matter?"

"How the hell did he know about that admiral's daughter?"

"Hell, the way I read it, Lieutenant Galloway knows just about everything that's going on in the Navy. So. You going to celebrate your promotion properly? I think tradition calls for the promoted officer to buy the drinks."

"Shit," Richardson said. "And I thought you were going to supply the scotch!"

Chapter 25

Saturday, 19 February 1944

Falmouth, England

They were part of a shipload of eight new Combat Demolition Units arriving fresh out of training from Fort Pierce. The word was that all of the demolition teams coming out of the NCDU training center for some time to come would be heading for England.

Tangretti and Richardson checked in at the Navy CDU base just outside Falmouth a little past 1400 hours. There, they met Lieutenant j.g. Scott Franklin, a short, skinny, red-headed kid who claimed to have started out as a powder monkey in a West Virginia coal mine before joining the Seabees and, later, the Navy demolition teams. Spotting the two of them as "new fish" as soon as they'd walked into headquarters, he'd walked up and introduced himself. "Welcome aboard, gents," he'd told them. "Scotty Franklin. You boys have the Fort Pierce look."

"Yeah?" Tangretti said. "What look is that?"

"Hell Week."

Richardson grinned. "Class number one."

"Really? Old-timers, then. I was in number two. How ya doing, upperclassmen?"

"Just fine." They shook hands, a firm and knowing clasp. "I'm Hank Richardson. My friends call me Snake."

"Good to meet you, Snake."

Tangretti lowered his seabag from his shoulder. "You can call me Gator."

"Okay, Gator. So. Where are you boys from? The scuttlebutt is you two've seen some action."

Richardson wondered at the speed of Navy rumor. Sometimes personal information about Navy personnel seemed to travel faster than bad news. "Yeah, I guess we have. A little, anyway. We were both at Kwajalein."

The youngster's eyes opened wide. "Kwajalein! Oh, man! What unit? Team One or Team Two?"

"UDT-One," Richardson said. "Breucort's team."

"What was it like? Did you see any Japs?"

"Yeah," Tangretti said easily. "A couple."

"No shit?"

"No shit."

"How's life in England?" Richardson asked, changing the subject. He was still a little uncomfortable with their escapade in the Pacific, if only because most people had trouble believing it.

"Well, the girls are friendly," Franklin said with a grin and a wink.

"Yeah?" Richardson liked the sound of that.

"The Brits are nice enough, most of 'em, though there's some resentment against the Yanks, as they call us. You have to remember they've been on the front lines here for four and a half years, now. And I don't think they care much for the competition with their girls."

"I can imagine. Listen, we're all checked in here. How about showing us the town?"

"Can do," Franklin said, using the Seabees' favorite motto. "Stow your gear and we'll go for a walk."

Richardson plucked at the dress blue uniform he was wearing. "How 'bout waiting until I get into something a little more comfortable? Is undress okay in town?"

"Well, you're supposed to get dolled up for going ashore, but nobody'll say nothing if you're in fatigues or dungarees.

We've got guys coming and going from field exercises and details all the time, and how do you ride herd on all of them?"

Both men changed into their fatigues. The only emblem of rank Richardson wore were the unobtrusive silver bars of a j.g. on his collar.

Falmouth was an ancient town, rising from the shore of one of the best harbors in southwestern England. The oldest part of town stretched along the eastern side of Pendennis Peninsula. On the rocky promontory at the end of the peninsula, overlooking the gulf of water known as Carrick Roads, a squat and grim-looking castle dominated the approaches to the harbor. Pendennis Castle, Franklin told them, had been built in the 1540s by Henry VIII, with additions by his daughter, Elizabeth I. "Shit," Tangretti said, staring up at the brooding gray stone walls. "Doesn't look like nothing a good Demolitioneer couldn't take apart inside twenty minutes or so."

Before long they found themselves walking a narrow sidewalk into Falmouth's waterfront district. "So how's the demolition training going with your bunch, Lieutenant?" Tangretti asked Franklin.

"Shit, call me Scotty. Us Hell Week grads've got to stick together—right, Gator?"

"Okay, then, Scotty. What's it like over here?"

"Some chickenshit. Mostly, we've been practicing blowing things up."

"Any problems?"

Franklin laughed. "Well, the biggest problem is taking all the new guys and breaking them of their good habits."

Tangretti blinked. "Excuse me, 'good habits'?"

"That's right. Most of our people are old powdermen, you know. Seabees. Construction engineers. Bomb and mine disposal."

"Sure," Richardson said. "That's where the whole Fort Pierce gang came from originally."

"Well, we've got lots of new kids coming in. Same backgrounds, but they haven't had as much time to knock off some of their safety habits. You know the drill. In a commercial firm, you wear safety shoes with rubber soles, right? Nonsparking tools. Explosives stored in special containers, under regulated temperatures. No cigarettes, matches, or inflammable materials allowed anywhere within a set hazard radius. The safety cards call for, what? Nine hundred feet of safety radius for one to twenty-seven pounds of explosives for personnel in the open, right?" They nodded. "Nine hundred ten feet for twenty-eight pounds, and so on, up to twenty-four hundred feet of distance with a quarter-ton charge. Over here, well . . ." Franklin shrugged expressively. "Look, we're training to go into *combat*, for chrissakes. We've been drilling for weeks under combat conditions. Carrying high explosives in satchels slung over our shoulders, bouncing around inside pitching landing craft, piling the stuff up on a beach without even bothering to break it into small lots or store it in a proper bunker. As for safety distance, well, we take what we can get. Usually lying on our faces in the surf with a big charge rigged and primed just up the beach. These new guys've gotta learn how to let the safety rules slide a bit, y'know? That's hard for some of these kids."

"I can imagine," Richardson said. He was mildly amused by Franklin, who himself seemed as raw and as new as the newcomers to the unit he was describing. "I've found myself doing things this last year or so that, well, if my father had ever caught the powdermen in his company doing shit like that on the job, man, they'd have been fired in no time flat, then blacklisted clear from Bangor to San Diego."

"You had anybody killed in your teams?" Tangretti asked, curious.

"A few. Not from safety violations, though. At least, not so far. Last month, we were carrying out an exercise on a practice beach down in Fowey. Practicing puttin' together a Bangalore torpedo, you know?"

Richardson nodded. The Bangalore torpedo was a simple if somewhat cumbersome demolition tool consisting of a number of sections of pipe, each packed with explosives and interconnected by lengths of primacord. The sections could be carried onto a beach separately, then threaded together piece by piece into a single long tube. As it was assembled at one end, the other end was pushed ahead little by little through or under any soft target—barbed wire, a culvert beneath a wall, even across a minefield, so long as care was taken not to hit a mine during the process. The fuse at the end was fired either by an electrical wire hooked to a battery and a detonator down the beach, or by using a measured length of fuse and a pull-wire igniter. The entire length of pipe exploded and a narrow path was blasted through the obstruction.

"Well, this guy was fitting together the pipes and shoving the torpedo ahead underneath a stretch of barbed wire," Franklin went on. "Near as we could figure it later, he managed to hit an old British mine that had been planted there on the beach way back in '41, during the big invasion scare, and then been forgotten. The torpedo went off in his hands. Killed him and another guy with him, and wounded four others. Blinded one guy I'd known ever since Fort Pierce."

"Damn. Bad luck."

"Yeah. The worst part of it, though, is thinkin' about those guys killed or torn up, and they never even had a chance to get at the Germans, you know? Never had a chance at taking the Krauts' beach defenses apart. *That's* a bitch."

There was an uncomfortable silence for several moments. Richardson glanced up as a flight of four aircraft passed overhead with a threatening growl. They were American B-24s with their odd, narrow wings and twin-stabilizer tails, and they were heading south, toward France.

And pretty damned soon, we'll be heading that way too, he thought. He found he didn't like thinking about guys like Franklin's friends, killed before they could even come to grips with the enemy.

"So where do you go around here to wet down your throat?" Tangretti asked, breaking the momentary silence.

"C'mon. I know a place right down this street."

The place was the Crown and Bull, a pub that had witnessed a full-blown invasion by the military units stationed in the area, American and British alike. Inside, it was dimlit and smoky, with all of the usual English pub accoutrements, including a dart board on one wall and a piano against another. Glasses clinked and clattered, voices mingled in a steady background murmur. Most of the customers in the place were men in uniform, of course, but there were a number of women there too, and, except for the waitresses, most of them were in uniform. Richardson saw one very pretty, black-haired girl near the back, wearing a WAC corporal's uniform and talking to a U.S. Army private. Though she was seated, she looked like she was even shorter than Richardson, but finely, exquisitely formed.

Seeing so many women in uniform was a new experience for Richardson, who was used to the Victory girls back in the States. Franklin led the way through the crowd to an empty table in the back.

Eventually, an attractive girl in a white apron and a nicely filled green blouse with the top three buttons open arrived to take their orders. "Three beers," Franklin told her.

"Baby, I think I'm in love," Richardson said. He reached out and put his arms around her hips. "Is there somewhere we could go and get better acquainted?"

"Sorry, Yank," the girl said with a saucy wink and a slick twist-and-shift that pulled her beyond Richardson's reach. "This 'ere beach'ead's already been spoke for. An' the major wouldn't like it t'know you been 'oldin' maneuvers on it!"

Richardson spread his hands. "The sad story of my life."

"Behave yourself, Snake," Tangretti said. "For once in your life, try to act like a reasonable facsimile of a civilized human being."

"What? What? What'd I do?"

"Acted like a sex-starved idiot, is all. Keep your pants buttoned for a change, okay? *Sir?*"

"But I think she likes me! Did you see her wink at me?"

Tangretti lowered his voice to a rough whisper. "Take my advice, Snake. If you want to see any action over here, stay the hell out of trouble, keep your mitts off the local talent, and keep your cock to yourself! Except by express invitation!"

Nearby, several men in British army uniforms were gathered around a battered upright piano rolled back against the wall. One was at the keyboard, throwing everything he had into a rusty and missed-note rendition of a popular song. His companions had linked arms beside the piano and were swaying back and forth as they sang.

> *Bless 'em all! Bless 'em all!*
> *Bless the long and the short and the tall . . .*

"So, gentlemen!" Franklin said, tilting back in his chair. "Let's swap war stories. Tell me about Kwajalein." He sounded eager. "You know, when I first heard that some of our NCDU guys were in Kwajalein, I sat down and wrote a long letter back to Fort Pierce. Asked 'em for a transfer to the Pacific."

"Shit, you're kidding!" Richardson said.

"What's wrong with that?"

"Hell, Scotty," Tangretti said. "We were *at* Kwajalein. We drove suicide boats and we went swimming off a Jap-held beach, and the first thing we did after we left the place was to wangle a transfer back here! Felt damn lucky we managed it, too."

"Good God. You guys *wanted* to come here? How come?"

"Because we figured this is where the real action is," Richardson said. The waitress reappeared, expertly clutching the handles of their three tall beer glasses in one hand. Franklin paid her, and after she'd left, Richardson saluted the others with an upraised mug. "To action!"

"Action!"

"Hell, yes!" Franklin downed a gulp that left a white foam mustache on his upper lip. "Shit," he said, dropping the glass to the table and scowling. "Still can't get used to this Limey piss."

Richardson chugged a swallow, then made a face. "Maybe that's why they call the stuff 'bitters.' "

"Christ, this ain't bitters, Snake," Tangretti said. "Bitters is a tonic. Something you put in your cocktail."

"Yeah, a Molotov cocktail," Richardson replied. He raised the glass, examining it against the light. "And this here is the stuff you put in the bottle to give it its kick. *Gah!*"

"Pretty bad, huh?"

"How come *you* drink this stuff, Scotty?"

"More to the point," Richardson added, wiping his mouth, "why do you make *us* drink it?"

"Well, they say you get used to it if you drink enough. I'm still working on gettin' the hang of it."

"I'll bet you like banging on your head with a hammer,

too." Tangretti took another swallow. "Actually, you know, for mule piss this stuff ain't half bad."

At the piano, a man in U.S. Navy uniform, a first-class gunner's mate, had crowded in close to the Britisher at the piano.

" 'Ey there, Yank! What'cher think yer doin'?"

"Shove off, chum," one of the gunner's mate's buddies called. "Let Chuck get in there and we'll hear some real music!"

"Yeah! If I hear that old 'long and the short and the tall' chestnut just one more time, I'm gonna puke!"

The British army contingent protested vocally but appeared to be outnumbered at the moment by the U.S. Navy. The gunner's mate took his place on the stool as several of his buddies hooted and clapped. After holding up his hands and waiting for the applause and the catcalls to die down, he interlocked his fingers, cracked the knuckles loudly, then began banging out a tune that, in a quiet room, might have been recognizable as the old Georgia Tech engineer song, the one that started out "I'm a ramblin' wreck from Georgia Tech." At some point during the preceding months, the NCDUs had appropriated the tune as their own. As frequently happened in such cases, the verses had been proliferating ever since, some of them suitable for polite company, most of them not. Several of the Navy demolition men standing around the piano started bawling out the first verse. Other Demolitioneers began joining in.

> *When the Navy gets into a jam*
> *They always call on me*
> *To pack a case of dynamite*
> *And put right out to sea.*
> *Like every honest sailor*
> *I drink my whiskey clear.*
> *I'm a shootin', fightin', dynamitin'*
> *De-mo-li-tion-eer!*

The British soldiers in the audience booed and shouted ribald comments, but the Americans kept singing.

"So c'mon and tell me about Kwajalein already," Franklin said, raising his voice to be heard over the increasing background noise. He laced his fingers around the beer stein on the table in front of him, as though fearful that it might slip away. "I want to hear all the good stuff. I heard it was really hot out there, that the teams were trying out a lot of new gadgets."

> *Out in front of Navy*
> *Where you really get the heat,*
> *There's a bunch of crazy blasters*
> *Pulling off some crazy feat.*
> *With their pockets full of powder*
> *And caps stuck in their ears,*
> *They're shootin', fightin', dynamitin'*
> *De-mo-li-tion-eers!*

"Oh, it got hot enough, all right," Richardson said, grinning. He looked across at Tangretti. "Didn't it, Gator?"

Taking up the cue, Tangretti reached into his uniform blouse pocket and pulled out his keepsake. "Yeah, some unpleasant people were shooting at us on the beach, just before the invasion boats went in," he said. "I managed to snag this. Water slows a bullet down to nothing, y'know, in just a couple-three feet."

> *Oh, they sent me out to Italy*
> *To clean the Fascist up.*
> *I put a case of TNT*
> *Beneath the dirty pup;*
> *And now they're rushing madly*
> *Straight up into the air.*
> *I'm a shootin', fightin', dynamitin'*
> *De-mo-li-tion-eer!*

Franklin's eyes narrowed as he examined the bullet critically, weighing it in his hand and then holding it up close to his eye. "You're shittin' me, right? What, I'm supposed to think you guys're Superman'r somethin', catching bullets in your bare hands?"

"Hell, no!" Tangretti said, hurt. He held out his hand and Franklin dropped the bullet back into his palm. Tangretti tucked it back into his breast pocket. "C'mon, Snake. Let's blow."

> *Some day we'll hit the coast of France,*
> *Put Jerry on the run.*
> *We'll wrap a roll of primacord*
> *'Round every goddamn Hun.*
> *Goebbels and Herr Göring*
> *Can blow it out their rears.*
> *We're the shootin', fightin', dynamitin'*
> *De-mo-li-tion-eers!*

"Hey, Gator, I'm sorry," Franklin said, putting his hand on Tangretti's arm. "No offense, okay?"

"None taken, Scotty," Richardson said. He pulled a pack of Camels from his blouse pocket, offered one to the others, then lit up. Leaning back, he took a deep drag, then stifled a cough. "So what is it you wanted to know about Kwajalein?"

"Shit, everything! Mostly, I just want to know what it's like bein' in action. You sure as hell don't get much around here! You just sit on your asses half the time, and the rest is training and lectures."

> *When our Marines reach To-ky-o*
> *And the Rising Sun is done,*
> *They'll head right for some Geisha house*
> *To have a little fun.*
> *But they'll find the gates are guarded*
> *And the girls are in the care*
> *Of the shootin', fightin', dynamitin'*
> *De-mo-li-tion-eers!*

"You're gearing up for France," Tangretti pointed out. "The invasion. Hell, that's something."

"Shit, some of us've been sitting on our asses over here for three months. Listen, you know what they've been having us do? Do you *know?*" The others shook their heads. "I'll tell ya. When we first got to this goddamn hole, the brass didn't know what the hell to do with us. British or American. Nobody'd told 'em, see? They knew we had something to do with demolitions, from our name, so what'd they do? Put us to guarding munitions dumps, that's what! Here I'd spent months back at Fort Pierce learning how to blow up beach obstacles, and they have me with a rifle on my shoulder, standing guard over a bunch of blasting caps!"

> *When the war is over,*
> *And the WACS and WAVES come home,*
> *We'll swim back to the U.S.A.*
> *And never more shall roam.*
> *All the local maidens*
> *Will get the best of care,*
> *And we'll raise a bunch of squallin', bawlin'*
> *De-mo-li-tion-eers!*

The crowd broke into ragged cheers, mingled with catcalls and boos from the British. Empty beer glasses thumped and pounded on tabletops.

"Cor, mates," a thick Liverpool accent called out. "Let's 'ave us a proper song!"

Another minor scuffle broke out near the piano as the gunner's mate at the keyboard was shoved aside by a short, powerfully built Britisher with a sergeant major's stripes on his arm. "Hold it right there, Limey!" someone shouted, and then there was the meaty sound of a fist colliding with flesh. Someone tumbled backward into a crowd of onlookers, arms pinwheeling as he fell.

"Right then, Yank! You been bloody askin' fer it!"

Tangretti had been surveying the action. "I think maybe we should—"

"Fire in the hole!" a Demolitioneer shouted from the press beside the piano. "Fire in the hole!"

"Let's go, Gator!" Richardson called, rising. "That's our dance they're calling!"

"Aw, shit." All three men waded into the fray, answering the battle cry of their fellow Demolitioneers. If anyone noticed the j.g. bars on the battledress collars of the two officers, no one admitted to it. Richardson got one good swing in against a British private, then went to his hands and knees as a hard-driven fist slammed into the side of his head.

The room whirled around him. He shook his head to clear it, then wished he hadn't. In the background, someone was blowing on a whistle, a shrill, hard, endlessly repeated piping that carried all of the urgency of an air raid siren.

Richardson felt someone's hands on his arm. Struggling upright, he took a groggy swing and missed.

"Easy, Snake, easy! Time to make a tactical withdrawal."

"Aw, shit. Again?" Glass shattered near the bar, and a woman screamed. Gator dragged Richardson to his feet.

"The S.P.s're gonna be here any minute."

"Where's Scotty?" Richardson looked around the chaotic scene, where American sailors and British soldiers were assaulting one another with positively joyful glee. A woman screamed again, and Richardson spun, seeking the source.

Eight feet away, in a corner next to the pub's rear exit, a British corporal, a man mountain standing at least six foot two and sporting a shaved skull and droop-ended handlebar mustache, had just grabbed an American WAC from behind, closing huge hands around her waist. Richardson felt a pang of recognition. The girl was the tiny, black-haired beauty he'd glimpsed earlier when he'd first come in. Her male companion was nowhere to be seen.

With a powerful heave, the Brit corporal plucked her up off the floor, laughing as he hoisted her into the air. Her fists, tiny compared to his huge hands, pounded furiously but ineffectually against his forearms. Her legs kicked wildly. "Put me *down,* you big ox!" she yelled.

Another soldier, a sergeant, closed in from the front, grinning widely. " 'Ere, now, Smitty. Let's give 'er wot th' Yanks been givin' our birds, right?"

"Right yer are, Sar'nt! We'll tyke 'er pretty knickers fer a souvenir!"

The sergeant pinned the WAC's thrashing legs together with one arm, putting a stop to her kicking. With the other he reached out and grabbed her left breast through her uniform tunic, twisting it like a doorknob.

Richardson, buoyed by a surging tide of red fury, leaped forward, grabbing the sergeant from behind and yanking him back off his feet.

" 'Ere, now!" The corporal dropped the woman on the floor, then advanced on Richardson, his huge hands curling into fists. "Wot's this now?"

"Why, it's one o' them pansy Yank sailor fairies," the sergeant said, rising from the floor. "Let's 'ave us a piece of 'im!"

Richardson had never thought much about the commando hand-to-hand fighting classes the demolition teams had endured back at Fort Pierce under Major Fairbairn and others. The high command had always seemed reluctant to allow the highly trained demolition units to actually mix it up with the enemy, as proven by the concern about their swimming off Kwajalein, and the chances of actually using any of the holds, kicks, throws, and punches they'd been taught had always seemed remote.

As the sergeant threw his first punch, however, Richardson stepped back with a fluid, almost effortless grace. The right hook sailed past his face and he helped it along with a shove to the man's elbow; at the same time, he pivoted hard to the left, bending, snapping his right foot up and swinging it into a roundhouse kick that slammed into the sergeant's exposed kidney with the solid thud of shoe leather against meat. The sergeant *oofed* and collapsed, clutching his side.

The big corporal closed in with a wordless growl. Richardson reached up with his left hand and grabbed the dangling end of the guy's mustache, yanking down, hard. His right hand, folded back, fingers curled out of the way and the heel exposed, snapped straight up in a satisfying collision with the giant's bulbous nose.

By this time, Tangretti had joined the fray, clenching his hands together and bringing them down like a sledgehammer on the back of the sergeant's neck. Another soldier coming to his buddy's rescue grabbed him from behind, fumbling toward a full nelson. Tangretti brought his right foot up, then slammed it down on his attacker's instep. The man yelled, then jackknifed himself as Tangretti's elbow rocketed back through eight hard-driven inches and buried itself in his diaphragm.

The giant, his nose oddly twisted to one side and sprinkled with blood, shook his head, splattering crimson droplets across the floor. "You *bugger!*" he screamed. "You filthy *bugger!*" He picked up a bottle by the neck, then smashed the end down across the edge of a table in a sharp spray of liquid and glass. The jagged ends of the bottle protruded from his fist, gleaming in the pub's smoke-hazy light. He advanced slowly with the improvised knife held high.

Richardson crouched, eyes not on the broken bottle but on the hollow of the corporal's throat, a point of focus that allowed him to be aware of his opponent's entire body. He was still feeling a little groggy from the punch in the head he'd taken earlier, but the giant was slow. He should be able to take the guy . . . though if the corporal managed to land even one good punch, Richardson knew he was done for. Watching the giant's throat, he sensed the bunching of muscles in shoulder and back that telegraphed the coming move. The corporal lunged with the bottle . . .

. . . and staggered beneath a splintering crash and a small storm of wooden slats, rungs, and fragments. The small WAC stood just behind him, a wild look on her face, her uniform disheveled, the broken shards of the back of a chair still clutched in both of her tiny hands. The broken bottle skittered from his grasp as the corporal dropped to hands and knees.

Richardson stepped up to the WAC. "Excuse me, miss." He plucked a three-foot-long chair leg and upright from her grip. "Thank you so much," he said. "This is exactly what I've been looking for!" He turned then and brought the club down on the back of the bald giant's head. The club broke in two; the giant slammed facedown to the floor.

"Are you okay, Corporal?"

The girl nodded, tugging various parts of her uniform back into place. "Damn big lummox," she muttered, retrieving her pocketbook and uniform jacket from the floor nearby.

"You've got a great overhand pitch," he told her. "What's your batting average?"

The rest of the battle in the pub appeared to be breaking up, though the whistles were still shrilling. Franklin was nowhere in sight, but many of the combatants were crowding out the front door. Suddenly, the tide at the door reversed itself, as soldiers and sailors began crowding back in. Then the doors banged open wide and several uniforms wearing military police armbands burst through, billy clubs very much in evidence.

"It's the snowdrops, everybody!" someone sang out. "Snowdrops" referred to the white helmets worn by American M.P.s. A police siren wailed in the near distance.

"Let's haul ass, Lieutenant," Tangretti said, "before we spend the rest of the war in the brig."

Impulsively, Richardson reached out and took the WAC's hand. "Come on, Corporal!" he snapped.

The pub's rear exit was unlocked and unguarded. The three of them plunged through to an alley in the rear. Outside, the sky was clear and chill, and already growing dark. The air was cold enough to make their breath visible as puffs of white vapor.

"Well," Richardson said as they hurried down the alley. "Can we show you the town, Miss . . . Miss . . . ?"

"Corporal Stevens, sir," the WAC said.

"Please, no ranks," Richardson said, looking about, then shrugging his collar up in a conspiratorial fashion. "Us Americans have got to stick together. I'm Snake. This here is Gator."

She dimpled. "Okay. I'm Veronica. Veronica Stevens. And my date is still back there somewhere."

"We can't very well go back in after him," Tangretti said reasonably.

"That's right," Richardson said. "I'd say, either the M.P.s'll take care of him or he must've scrammed before they arrived, and *that* means he abandoned you, lovely lady, leaving you to fend for yourself. Ah, you *were* the lady in distress back there? Were you not?"

"I was indeed."

"Actually," Tangretti said, "she seemed to be doing pretty well all by herself. She swings a chair the way DiMaggio swings a bat!"

"She does indeed." Richardson stopped, backed off a step, and looked her narrowly up and down. "Tell me, Veronica. What do you weigh?"

She drew herself up a bit taller. She was still at least three inches shorter than Richardson's five-seven. "One-oh-five, if you *must* know."

He shook his head. "And here you took down a gorilla at least twice your weight. Not bad!"

"Well, I really did need your help at the start, sir, when they were ganging up on me. So thank you!"

"Ah! Ah! Don't call me sir! Tonight, at least for the moment, I am one of the little people."

Tangretti groaned, his eyeballs rolling up in their sockets. "Oh, brother!"

"Don't pay any attention to my friend, here. He caught a bullet with his teeth at Kwajalein, and he hasn't been the same since. So! Since your boyfriend's missing, would you care to spend the evening with me?"

She looked at him doubtfully. "There are rules against enlisted personnel fraternizing with officers, you know."

Richardson grimaced, then reached up and unpinned the rank bars from his fatigues. "These damned things are nothing but trouble."

"You can't do that, sir!"

"Sure I can! To be permitted to spend a few brief hours with you, my lovely lady in distress, I would do anything!"

Tangretti muttered something under his breath. Richardson shot him a warning look.

He tucked the rank insignia into his pocket. "There. That's that. Where would you like to go? Dinner? Dancing?"

Veronica seemed to consider her choices. "Well, the USO has taken over a theater in town, and they show American movies there. Right now they're running *Guadalcanal Diary*. With Anthony Quinn?"

"I'm more a Clark Gable man, myself," Richardson said.

"I don't care that much for Gable," Veronica replied. "He was okay in *Gone With the Wind*, but I really can't understand what girls see in him."

"Yeah?" Richardson rubbed his bare upper lip thoughtfully with his forefinger. "I know what you mean."

"There'll be a lot of Army guys there, though. *Our* Army."

Richardson looked at Tangretti. "Gee, Gator. What do you think? I don't mind taking on the British army now and again, but now this lady's got us infiltrating the American army too."

"We can handle it, Snake. No sweat."

"That's what I thought. Well, Gator, I guess we'll be seeing you."

"Aw, c'mon, Snake. Let me come too. I haven't seen a movie in months, and I've been wanting to see that one."

"Gator . . ."

"You can *both* come," Veronica said, stepping between them and looping her arms through both of theirs. "Believe me, I'll feel *much* safer!"

"You know, miss," Tangretti said, looking at Richardson and getting a dark scowl for reply. "You just might have a point there."

The show led off with a Popeye cartoon, the one-eyed sailor taking on a Japanese submarine attacking an American battleship. Each time the sub launched a torpedo, a caricature of a Jap sub skipper, complete with round glasses and impossible buck teeth, poked his head out of the torpedo tube, lifted his cap, and announced, "So solly!" This quickly reduced both Richardson and Tangretti to near hysterics.

"Don't you think Popeye looks like Chief Wallace?"

"No, I think Chief Wallace *is* Popeye! See the squint?"

"Unmistakable!"

Soon, Popeye had downed his spinach and was taking on the sub with his fists at the bottom of the sea, accompanying each punch with a heartfelt "So solly!" He snagged the sub with a hook from a crane aboard the battleship, reeled it onto the deck like a flopping, beached fish, and gave it one final, crushing right hook. The rising sun flag ran up a flagpole atop the dead submarine, fluttered for a moment in the breeze, and then magically changed to white. Richardson and Tangretti cheered and applauded wildly.

"Hey, pipe down in front!"

"Quiet down, swabbies!"

"What is *with* you two?" Veronica asked. Sitting between them, she'd intercepted most of the comments and blows traded back and forth during the feature.

"Sorry, Veronica," Richardson told her. "It isn't every day you see one of your old instructors on the silver screen!"

Richardson saw little of *Guadalcanal Diary*. He didn't care much for Anthony Quinn, and when he did watch he kept catching them in little technical errors.

Instead, he spent most of the first half of the movie talking in whispers with Veronica Stevens. He learned that she was twenty-one years old and had been born and raised in Milwaukee, that her father worked at a brewery, that she'd joined the Army early in 1943, that she worked in 1st Division's G-2, and that the guy she'd been with at the Crown and Bull was nobody serious, a friend from camp. Halfway through the movie they slipped out together, leaving an engrossed Tangretti in the middle of a Japanese banzai charge.

Dinner was spent at a café in Falmouth, where they tried something called a "pasty," a pastry shell filled with chopped meat, onions, and potatoes. The waitress told them that it was something of a specialty in Cornwall, that it had once been a way for Cornish miners to carry their lunch with them to work. They also sampled something called "scrumpy," a locally brewed dry cider that was both quite refreshing and deceptively mild.

Richardson decided that he much preferred scrumpy to English beer, and Veronica agreed with considerable feeling. Her brewer father, she claimed, would shoot her if she ever tasted a drop of what the British claimed was beer.

They ended up walking along a spit of sand below the rocks of Pendennis Castle. It was a chilly evening, and he had his arm about his shoulders, just for the warmth and the closeness.

"Can I see you again?"

"Sure, Hank," she said. "It might be a little difficult, though. The Big Red One's headquarters is at Weymouth."

"Weymouth? Where's that?"

"In Dorset. East of here."

He was still bewildered by English place-names. Geography had never been his strong suit. "Is that far?"

"Oh, depending on the military traffic on the roads, it's a three, maybe a three-and-a-half drive. I just came out here with George to look up some of his old family friends. I wasn't expecting to come back."

"Will you?"

"Yes. I guess I will."

"I'll come see you in Weymouth. I really do want to see more of you."

"I'd like that."

They walked a little farther. "Can I take you home?"

She looked at him. "I thought you just got here today. You don't have a car, do you? Or a gasoline card? Or a *pass?*"

He waved his hand. "Mere formalities. I've got a friend who can do absolutely magical things when it comes to getting what you need."

She laughed, a delightful sound. "Your friend back at the theater?"

"That's the guy."

"Tell you what," she said after a minute. "I really do owe it to George to at least find him. I'm staying in a hotel here in town. So is he." She caught Richardson's alarmed glance. "In separate rooms, if you please. You see what arrangements your friend Gator can make, and I'll see if George got back to the hotel in one piece. Maybe we can work something out. Deal?"

"Deal. Absolutely."

"We could meet tomorrow. At the Crown and Bull?"

"Hmm. If that guy we clobbered is a regular, that might not be such a good idea. How about the USO place? About noon?"

"Do you have tomorrow off?"

He shrugged. "It's Sunday. If I don't, I will have."

"You sound awfully sure of yourself, Lieutenant Richardson. Do you always run the whole U.S. Navy just for your personal benefit?"

"No. It's my partner who does that. I'm just along for the ride. But if I could arrange just a little of it, I'd make sure I had a chance to see you. Every day."

Her eyes gave him all the invitation he needed. He drew her close, enfolded her in his arms, and they sank together into a long, deep kiss.

He didn't get her back to her hotel until nearly ten, and he had three separate run-ins with the curfew wardens on his way back to base.

By the time he checked back in, Lieutenant j.g. Henry Richardson knew that he was in love.

Chapter 26

Wednesday, 8 March 1944

Falmouth, England

Chief Wallace sat in a folding, wood-slat chair with several dozen other Navy officers and senior enlisted men in Falmouth base headquarters lounge, listening to the men who were giving the day's briefing. Major Richard Fairbairn, British Royal Engineers, stood to one side at the front of the room, a tall, hard-looking man whom many of the Fort Pierce graduates in the audience remembered from the days of their NCDU training. Fairbairn was now the British Liaison Officer of the Eleventh Amphibious Force, and a frequent instructor/lecturer at the demolition team base. He'd taught many of the men commando infiltration tactics and hand-to-hand combat techniques, both in Florida and, more recently, here at their Falmouth base.

With him was an American naval officer, Lieutenant j.g. Carl P. Hagensen, a pleasant-faced youngster from Pennsylvania who'd graduated from the University of Maine, then joined the Navy just before Pearl Harbor. Lieutenant Smith and most of the officers and senior enlisted men of the CDUs had gathered here in one of the common rooms of the base's HQ for another in a series of training lectures on German beach obstacles and the latest in ways to deal with them.

"We call this monster Element C," Hagensen was saying. He held up a large poster on which had been drawn a massive, flat-faced structure, showing it to the assembled demolition men. Composed of angle irons welded together in a complex, upright latticework, it looked like a cutout of a building with a peaked roof, constructed out of three massive uprights, plus numerous crossbeams, vertical posts, and diagonals. The entire affair was held upright by a tapering framework of braces extending to the rear. Hagensen placed the poster on an easel that had been set up at the front of the room where everyone could see it, then used his pen to point out key points on the drawing.

"This upright section faces the sea," he told them. "It measures at least ten feet high by ten feet wide and, as you can see, is constructed of angle iron beams ranging in size from three and a half to five and a half inches thick. These irons may be bolted, welded, or riveted together and can be expected to be strong enough to resist ramming even by a landing ship. The supporting tail extends to the rear for at least fourteen feet."

Wallace jotted the dimensions down in the notebook he held in his lap. Hagensen continued talking.

"Large numbers of these obstacles have been spotted under construction in Belgium, hence their common name of 'Belgian gates.' Most of them are built on rollers to facilitate placement. They are rolled into place on the beach between the low- and high-tide lines. Their great weight causes their bases to sink into the sand, and they are strong enough to withstand the roughest surf or even a full-blown Channel storm. Once these babies are planted, gentlemen, they're here to stay."

Wallace glanced up, looking about the room at the faces of the others at the briefing. Two months ago, even one month ago, he would have expected to hear some wiseass crack from the audience, something to the effect of "Until we get at them!"

Now, though, the listeners were silent. Some looked sullen or resentful. All looked tired and drawn. Their silence, their lack of banter and humorous back talk, bothered Wallace. It was an indication of just how far morale had fallen in what was supposed to be an elite and eager-to-go volunteer outfit.

"So far," Hagensen continued, "we've only seen Element C in Belgium and in several regions around the Pas de Calais. Recent intelligence, however, suggests that the Germans have begun extending them to the west, to the Normandy coast clear up the Cotentin Peninsula."

Well, Wallace thought, *so what?* Everybody knew the landings, when they came, would be at the Pas de Calais. With only twenty miles separating the French coast from Great Britain at that point, where else could so massive a cross-Channel invasion possibly be launched?

"Large numbers of Belgian gates," Hagensen continued, "can be set up close alongside of each other, welded together by heavy steel cables, chains, or iron bars to create one huge beach obstacle hundreds of yards wide.

"The nasty thing about the Belgian gates is that when you set off your usual demo charges under the thing, what you get is a twisted mass of jagged steel that's nearly as rugged a barrier to tanks or landing craft as the original obstacle. If you load on the TNT, pile on enough to completely demolish the structure, the explosion will be so powerful that chunks of steel will be hurled across a hundred yards of beach, and on a crowded landing beach that could be more deadly than a heavy machine gun.

"We have, however, found a possible solution. Major? If you please?" He held out his hand, and Major Fairbairn came forward carrying an olive-drab canvas satchel. It had a steel eye on one end, a cord with a hook on the other. A length of yellow primacord dangled from beneath the flap.

"This pack contains two pounds of C-2," Hagensen said. "The tail, here, is primacord and is used to connect with a ring main or with a trunk line. Our initial tests have suggested a way of employing twenty of these charges, emplaced at key demolition points and interconnected with primacord in such a way that the Belgian gate can be knocked flat, with a minimum blast radius."

Fairbairn clapped Hagensen on the shoulder. "Your compatriot, gentlemen, is entirely too modest. Lieutenant Hagensen here is the man who dreamed up this little gem. In fact, some of us have already started calling this infernal device of his a 'Hagensen Pack.' And if we're going to have a chance in hell of breaching Jerry's beachfront fence, it's going to come packaged in these little parcels here."

"It was a team effort, Major. Anyway," Hagensen continued "we've had considerable trouble figuring out how to demolish this particular obstacle, the Element C. The steel shortage has meant that we don't have that much scrap we can use to imitate Kraut constructs for us to practice on. However, we've learned that the key is to place the charges on top of the junction points in such a way that the resultant blast forces the steel beams down, instead of up and out. Performed properly, the demolition results in the gate being knocked flat, allowing easy passage for small craft or vehicles. . . ."

The briefing rambled on, with illustrations on sheets of poster board and with a small-scale model of a Belgian gate. Twenty separate sites on the obstacle had been identified as charge placement sites. The primacord tails on each pack were tied with right-angle knot connections to a loop of primacord, the ring main; the main fed to a primacord trunk line, which in turn could be fired either electrically or from a fuse and an M-1 igniter.

As Wallace continued to listen to Hagensen's lecture, he came to the conclusion that morale in the unit had never been lower. A number of reasons for the slump came to mind. There was little, however, that could be done about any of them.

One big problem was the fact that very few officers in England seemed to know what the Fort Pierce gang was there for, and it seemed fairly clear that no one was making an effort to fit them in to the overall invasion plans.

Their name change was another, a switch in the teams' designation purportedly done for security reasons. Back during Operation Torch, the ad hoc team thrown together to breach the massive boom and net across the Sebou River had been called the Combat Demolition Unit, or CDU. Six months later, Admiral King's directive had called for the creation of a Naval Combat Demolition Unit, or NCDU, and it was under that designation that the Demolitioneers had trained at Fort Pierce.

Not long after the first NCDUs had arrived in England, however, the word went out that for security reasons, the name of the Demos had been changed. From now on, the NCDUs would be known as . . .

Combat Demolition Units, or CDUs.

Not that the name or the letters mattered all that much to

the men themselves. As far as they were concerned, they were still Demolitioneers or, increasingly, Demos. But those who'd actually been there knew that the only people to be confused by the tactic of changing NCDU to CDU would be the brass, the people charged with deciding how the teams were going to be used and where.

And that led to perhaps the most morale-damaging problem of all. Presumably, Eisenhower and Montgomery and the other brass hats at the top knew where and when the invasion was going to be held, at least as a rough, working plan. By now, they might even know which units were going to storm which beaches, where those beaches were, and what sorts of German units, beach defenses, and obstacles were backing them up.

Unfortunately, the invasion plan, whatever it was, was such a closely guarded secret that no one, *especially* enlisted men and junior officers, was being told anything at all about it.

For ordinary troops, Wallace thought with a dark and brooding humor, this was not necessarily a handicap. One stretch of beach, after all, was as good a place to die as any other. For the specialists of the CDU, however, this was crippling, especially now, when they were trying to plan and train for the big event. Damn it all, didn't Ike and his command staff *know* that tides varied from beach to beach, depending on the water depth offshore, the contours of the sea bottom, and the actual slope of the beach? Everyone figured the troops would be going in at low tide, if only because German obstacles were so thick that at high tide the landing craft would not be able to reach the water's edge. Obviously, the CDUs would hit the beach ahead of most of the other troops. How long would they have to plant their charges and clear the lanes for the follow-up waves? How fast would the incoming tide be rising, submerging the very obstacles they were working on? The answers to all of those questions and more depended on where the beaches were, and nobody was talking.

What would the terrain be like? At the Pas de Calais, where everyone assumed the landings would be held, there were chalk cliffs behind the beach, smaller parts of the same geological formation as the more famous white cliffs of Do-

ver on the opposite shore of the Channel. An invasion there
would have to be prepared to scale those cliffs or smash
through the barricades certain to be erected at the various
beach approaches. At Normandy, the beaches were relatively broad and flat but were backed by sheer bluffs and
hills penetrated only at certain points by gaps leading inland, gaps that, again, would certainly be heavily defended.
Between Normandy's open beaches, there were rocky head-
lands, vertical cliffs such as those at Point du Hoc, which
could be assaulted only by men with ladders or grappling
hooks. And farther west still, on the Cotentin Peninsula,
beaches tended to be quite flat, backed by low sand dunes,
but were isolated by swamps and wetlands crossed by easily
blocked and defended roads.

And the beaches would not all be defended the same way.
Some would have one type of beach obstacle, others another, and still others would have a mix. Would they have
mines planted on them? How much explosives would the
CDUs have to carry ashore? How much primacord? How
long should the fuses be cut? Should they carry more Bangalore torpedoes, to blow paths through single rails, concertina wire, and minefields? Or should they carry more
Hagensen Packs to deal with Belgian gates?

The tactics, even the exact mix of equipment and demolitions packs the CDU teams carried ashore, would depend
almost entirely on just where the landings would be taking
place. And, since nobody who knew any of the answers was
talking, there was a widespread feeling that, ultimately, the
high command would simply throw them into battle with
the rest of the invasion force, ignoring their special training
and experience, and expect them to fend for themselves.

There was no question about the bravery of these men,
Wallace thought. Volunteers all, they were here to do a job
that they knew how to do, that they wanted to do, that they
would be very, very good at doing. To have come this far
and discover that no one, from Eisenhower down, knew exactly how to employ the men of the CDUs left the men feeling both abandoned and futile. Among all of the scuttlebutt,
the rumors that spread through the base like epidemics on
an almost daily basis, the most fearful for these men had
been the one suggesting that, when the invasion came, they

would be assigned once again to guarding munitions bunkers right here in Falmouth.

A very few officers, British or American, seemed aware of the CDUs' plight and were trying to do something about it. Major Fairbairn was one of them. American Lieutenant j.g. Lane Blackwell, a technical liaison with the staff of the U.S. Naval Attaché in England, was another. They saw to it that critical intelligence—such as this information on the type C elements—was disseminated among the CDUs, and they'd reportedly been trying to convince their own superiors of the usefulness of demolition-trained beach-assault units.

They'd better hurry and do something, though, Wallace decided. It was now the first week of March. Scuttlebutt from those who claimed they knew held that the invasion was now set for the middle of May. Two months was not enough time to put together an assault plan, even if someone told them today what their actual targets were going to be.

Turning slightly in his chair, he caught a profile glimpse of one of the new arrivals in the CDUs, Lieutenant Richardson. "Snake" had been a wild sort back at Fort Pierce. In the early days, Wallace had never been able to imagine that they could become friends. Training together, though, had forged some unusual bonds . . . like the one between Snake and his partner, MM1 Tangretti. The three of them'd become close enough that he'd kept corresponding with them after their transfer halfway around the world to the Pacific. Now, against all of the odds, they were together again. If anything could be done to pull the CDUs together, it would be through men like Richardson who'd not yet caught the despair, the sense of futility, that seemed to have afflicted most of the old hands.

Strange. Snake had changed a lot since Wallace had known him in Fort Pierce. If he didn't know the young rake better, he'd have sworn the kid was in love. Come to think of it, there were rumors that he was seeing one particular girl, instead of the usual queue from the pages of his little black book. Wallace wondered if there was anything to it.

"Finally," Major Fairbairn said, "I'm afraid I have some bad news."

The words, and the way the young major said them, captured Wallace's full attention. *Uh-oh,* he thought. *What're they going to hit us with this time?*

"Reports from several intelligence sources," Fairbairn said, "suggest that the Jerries are now planning to back up their beach defenses with poison gas dispensers. We expect that these will be relatively static units designed to spray chemical agents, most likely mustard gas, over key beaches. SHAEF is now looking into the possibility of equipping lead beach-assault elements—and that does mean you fellows, whatever you've heard to the contrary—with rubber suits, gloves, hoods, and gas masks."

A loud, collective groan sounded from the assembled officers and chiefs. The mere thought of trying to do any work at all on a hostile beach under fire while wearing rubber gloves and a hot and uncomfortable protective suit was agonizing.

If Wallace knew these people, though, they might wear the suits to the beach . . . and then "lose" them the moment they started to work. The CDUs, with their solid core of Navy ex-Seabees, were not known for their adherence to orders they deemed inconvenient or inefficient.

"And another piece of intelligence," Fairbairn continued, "which is not good news at all. Our sources tell us that Field Marshal Rommel, our old friend the Desert Fox, is now in full charge of the French beach defenses. The German high command brought him in late last year, of course, but it appears that some infighting over there between Rommel and his immediate superior, Von Rundstedt, has been resolved. Von Rundstedt is still in overall command of the area defenses, but Rommel appears to now have a free hand in the implementation of his strategy, which calls unequivocally for stopping any invasion landing force on the beaches. Rommel, gentlemen, as I'm sure all of you are well aware, is one of the best strategists Jerry has, arguably *the* best. We can be very sure he will do everything in his considerable power to make your jobs on the beaches interesting. This new element C is likely his doing. So, too, is the sudden increase we've seen recently in working parties on the French beaches, setting up new lines of obstacles.

"And on that cheery note, gentlemen, we will conclude today's intelligence briefing."

Wallace was on his way back to the Nissen hut that housed the CDUs' chief petty officers when he felt a hand on his shoulder. "Chief Wallace?"

He turned. "Well! Lieutenant Richardson!" He saluted. "What can I do for you, sir?"

Richardson returned the salute. "I need a favor, Chief," he said. He looked mildly uncomfortable. "Can we go somewhere and talk?"

"General mess?" Both enlisted men and officers used that as a common area.

"Good enough. I'll buy the coffee."

Minutes later, seated at one of the long wooden tables in an almost deserted mess area, with mugs of steaming coffee before them, Richarson broached the subject that he'd wanted to discuss with Wallace. "Chief, I don't quite know how to bring this up, but I'm getting married."

Wallace's eyes opened wide. Richardson? The original Prophylactic Kid? *Married?*

"Shit, Lieutenant! I never thought you were the type!"

"Oh?" He grinned. "What type is that?"

"I don't know. The marrying kind, I guess. The kind of guy who would settle down with just one gal."

"Funny you should say that. I wondered about you and Alice the first time you wrote me about her."

Wallace's lips pressed together, a thin, hard white line. He didn't want to talk about Alice just now. She'd been so good for him since he'd met her. And yet . . .

"Anyway," Richardson continued. "I've met someone. She's wonderful."

"A local girl?"

"No, actually. She's American. A WAC with the Big Red One. She's stationed over in Weymouth. We want to get married."

"You hardly need my permission for that, Lieutenant." He was wondering, though, just how Snake *would* go about getting permission. Marriages between personnel in two separate outfits must be, mercifully, relatively rare, but there would have to be an official protocol governing who asked whom for permission, where they shared quarters, even whether or not both of them would stay in the service. The Navy, especially, was touchy about that sort of thing. Ever since the five Sullivan brothers serving aboard a single American ship had been killed during the same battle when their ship was sunk, the Navy made a point of not putting relatives aboard the same ship or duty station. It was considered bad for morale at home to learn that an entire family had been wiped out.

"Oh, we've already got the paperwork under way, Chief, though it might take a couple of months for everything to get straightened out. No, I was wondering if you could see clear to giving the bride away."

"Eh?"

"Steve Tangretti's going to be best man. We're arranging to get married in a little chapel here in Falmouth. Veronica—that's my girl's name—Veronica would like to be as traditional about all of this as we can manage. I've told her all about you, of course, and she was wondering if you could stand in for her father."

"You're making me feel old, Lieutenant." He saw Richardson's eager face fall, and laughed. "Hell, yes. Of course I'll do it. When's the date?"

"Well, that depends on the paperwork, mostly. There's a chance Veronica can get an administrative discharge, 'convenience of the military' and that sort of thing. Then we don't have to worry about her being stationed in the Army someplace while I'm shipped off to God-knows-where with the Navy."

"You could have chosen someone a little less complicated. Tangretti, for instance. You two are practically married to each other now."

"Nope. I love Gator like a brother, but he just ain't my type. Besides, Chief, I likes 'em complicated. You ought to know me well enough to know that by now."

"Affirmative."

"Right now, though, we're shooting for a date sometime in May. Maybe the last Sunday. That's the twenty-eighth."

"You know, Lieutenant, there's just one thing wrong with this scenario of yours."

The grin on Richardson's face vanished as though someone had thrown a switch. "I know. D-Day."

"There's a good chance we'll be moving to new digs before long. Her too. The two of you might end up on opposite sides of England before your permission to marry comes through."

Richardson nodded. "We're well aware of that, Chief."

"And as you say, D-Day could be scheduled for that weekend. Or the weekend just before. Have you two talked all of this out?"

"Yes. We've been talking about it a lot."

"How long have you two known each other, anyway?"

"Almost three weeks. I met her my first day in England."

"I was afraid you would say something like that. My God, Hank. Three *weeks?*"

Richardson shrugged. "We love each other, Chief. That's all that matters, right?"

"Sure, sure. Love is grand. And if your love for each other can't last through a little thing like the invasion of Europe, well, gee, it must not count for much."

Wallace had meant the line as a joke, but he could see that it had fallen flat with Richardson.

"It *will* last, Chief. She means more to me than I can put into words. All we can do is grab the chance while we can, you know?"

"Of course it will. I didn't mean to suggest that it wouldn't. And I'll be happy to stand in for . . . Veronica? For Veronica's dad. Just tell me where and when, and I'll be there."

Richardson's boyishly infectious grin returned. "That's just great, Chief! Thanks!"

"Don't mention it, Snake. I just hope you two know what you're getting into!"

"Hey, no sweat, Chief. The Snake's got it covered! Just like I always do!"

"That," Wallace said, smiling, "is exactly what I'm afraid of!"

As always, of course, the needs of the military took precedence over the preferences, even the needs, of individuals. On Friday, 10 March, all movement and communications on the island were placed under severe restriction, with signed passes necessary for any travel on the highways whatsoever.

Chapter 27

Friday, 17 March 1944

The Pentagon
Washington, D.C.

Lieutenant Joe Galloway settled back in his chair with an audible sigh, glaring at the stack of papers in his In basket with the same wary eye most naval officers reserved for shallow waters or the telltale wake of an enemy periscope. Sometimes it seemed that the more work he did, the more came in to clamor for his attention. Maybe that was why bureaucrats always seemed to do as little as possible. Perhaps they'd discovered some new law of Nature that said incoming problems decreased in direct proportion to a decrease in outgoing workload.

Somehow, Galloway doubted it would work. If he didn't handle these problems, they just wouldn't get handled, and that could spell the end for the whole naval demolitions project.

He picked up a file folder. Here was a good case in point. It seemed Lieutenant Smith, the officer in charge of the CDUs assembling in England for Overlord, was being squeezed out of the picture by Army Corps of Engineers officers who claimed they already had the organization and the manpower to do everything the Navy could do and then some. The Army had brought in some heavy hitters to make their case, and Smith was having trouble fighting back. A mere naval lieutenant didn't have much access to the big boys up in SHAEF. Smith wanted ideas, help, or behind-the-scenes influence—whatever Galloway could offer him—and he wanted it yesterday.

And there were a whole stack of problems just as nasty, just as dangerous to the future of the teams, waiting on his desk if and when he pulled another rabbit out of his hat and solved this one. . . .

Galloway dropped the folder. God, he was sick of this job. The desk . . . the office . . . this soulless Pentagon. Why couldn't someone else take over for a change and let him get out in the field where he could really do some good?

There was a rap on his door, and before he could answer, it swung open to reveal Lieutenant Commander Coffer. "Still hard at it, eh, Joe?" Coffer said, grinning.

Galloway stood up. "Commander! I didn't know you were back in town. Come in, please."

"It's just a quick call," Coffer told him as he shut the door and crossed to one of the chairs by Galloway's desk. He turned slightly before he sat down, brushing at his backside. "Happened to be in town. Is my rear end still intact? I can't see."

"Still there, Commander. It's smoking a little, but it doesn't look serious."

"I have just been the proud recipient of one of the most thorough and professional ass-chewings it's ever been my lot to endure." He dropped into the chair.

"What happened?"

"I have been moving Heaven and Earth lately to get out to where the action is. Of course, you wouldn't know anything about that, would you?"

Galloway smiled. "Hardly. I *like* paper and desks and typewriter ribbons and battling with armies of accountants over fifty cents on a length of wire rope. . . ."

"Well, my ship finally came in." Reaching into the inside pocket of his jacket, Coffer extracted a letter and laid it on Galloway's desk.

Galloway picked it up, quickly scanning the letter. "My God," he said, eyebrows rising. He looked up. "Admiral Turner's asking you to go to his command. The Pacific!"

"That's right. I'll be leaving Fort Pierce probably sometime this spring."

"So why is your ass smoking?"

"Well, it seems that they received *two* requests for my services at the same time. One from Admiral Turner. One from SHAEF. Talk about your pick of duty! Well . . ." Coffer stopped. He looked mildly embarrassed. "Actually, they called me on the carpet to find out why both letters had exactly the same wording. Let it be a lesson for you, though, Joe. Always pull out all the creative stops when it comes to dealing with the bureaucracy!"

Galloway laughed. "So they caught you cumshawing your own orders, eh?"

"I guess. Actually, it looks like I was heading for the Pacific anyway. Admiral Turner is an old friend of the family. He knows my father."

Galloway nodded. The elder Coffer, he knew, was now COMCRUDESPAC, the commanding officer of all cruisers and destroyers in the Pacific, with his headquarters at Pearl Harbor.

"Anyway," Coffer continued, "Turner has been hot on demolition teams ever since Kwajalein, and I guess Dad caught his ear with stories about what I've been doing down at Fort Pierce."

"Man, oh, man," Galloway said. "The Pacific! You'll be running the UDTs out there?"

"That's what it looks like."

"Congratulations, sir." Galloway was happy for his superior, though he couldn't avoid a sharp pang of jealousy. At long last, David Coffer was getting the war zone duty he'd sought for so long.

The duty Galloway had been all but begging for these past months.

Coffer must have read some part of Galloway's thoughts from his expression. He sighed. "Joe, I've got some bad news."

"Yes, sir?"

"I talked to them upstairs about dragooning you as my exec. I thought you might like to go with me."

Galloway felt a quick surge of excitement, followed instantly by disappointment. Obviously, Coffer's request had been turned down, or he wouldn't have called it "bad news."

"They didn't go for it, then."

"I'm afraid not."

"Can't say I'm surprised. I've all but given up trying to bribe my way out of this place. Lately I've taken to trying to have myself smuggled out hidden inside baskets of dirty laundry, but they keep catching me and bringing me back."

Coffer chuckled. "You've done a hell of a job for me up here, Joe. I'd hoped to be able to reward you. But, the fact of the matter is, you're just too damned important to the teams where you are."

"So I've been told. Frequently."

"And I have to agree with them." He paused, studying Galloway critically. "Have you heard about the flap in England over Smith and the Army engineers?"

"Where the Army wants to take over clearing the beach obstacles in France?" He tapped the offending folder on his desk. "I've got it right here."

"Nice little case of interservice rivalry, eh? Any ideas on how to handle that one?"

Galloway thought for a moment. "Well, it strikes me that our problem in SHAEF is that we don't have anybody over in England batting for the teams with a rank above lieutenant. When those brass-heavy SHAEF guys start rumbling about Army engineers clearing the Overlord beaches, Bob Smith just doesn't have the clout he needs to fight back."

Coffer nodded. "Sounds like you've identified the problem. What are you planning to do about it?"

"I hadn't really gotten to the planning stage yet. Of course, it did occur to me that we might talk to Major Fairbairn about this."

"Dick Fairbairn?"

"Yes, sir. He's done a lot of work with the teams already, cross-training, intelligence sharing, that sort of thing. I was wondering if we could approach him to come on board as our representative to SHAEF."

Coffer looked surprised . . . and delighted. "Ha! Great! You enlist a Brit to deal with the Army! I love it!"

"I don't know yet if he'll go for it. . . ."

"Oh, I imagine he will. Major Fairbairn is pretty impressed with what he's seen of the NCDUs so far. And SHAEF will listen to him because he's the best there is. Anyway, you've just demonstrated why I can't have you come with me. You know the system, you know what we need . . . and you are innovative and inventive enough to know where to cut corners when we need to."

"Hell, Commander, anybody could do this job."

"Maybe. Maybe not. I know I want you covering my back here, though. I've been hearing stories . . . Did you know some damn fool in the NCDU down in Italy is talking about another drone like those Stingrays."

"That again."

"Yup."

"And somebody at Intel has a bee in his bonnet about German mustard gas generators on the beaches in France and how our Demolitioneers are going to get wiped out. And an admiral who was at Sicily insisting that the Scouts and Raiders can handle all the preinvasion work without bringing in our boys. It just goes on and on, and I can't shove it off on anybody else and trust it'll all work out right."

He hesitated. "I understand, sir."

"Do you?"

"Absolutely." The strange thing was, Galloway knew Coffer was right. He still wanted sea duty . . . but who would run things when he was gone? Would his replacement know what he did about the teams . . . or most important of all, would he care?

"I do have one small consolation for you. I can't get you out of this hole, but . . ."

"Yes, sir?"

Coffer reached out and took his hand, pumping it. "But I *can* say congratulations on your promotion, Lieutenant Commander Galloway!"

"Promotion . . ." Galloway was stunned. He had put in plenty of time in rank, but he'd been starting to wonder if his name had dropped off the promotion lists entirely.

"I can't claim any credit for that one, unless you count all those 'outstandings' I've put on your ERs."

"I don't know what to say. . . ."

"Then say 'Thank you,' and forgive me for running off to the Pacific for fun and games without you."

"Of course! Hey, I can be jealous and still be happy for you, can't I?"

"Nothing in the regs against it. I'm glad you see it my way, though."

Galloway shrugged. "Hell, sir. The job here's got to be done, and someone's got to be here to do it. For the good of the teams."

"For the good of the teams," Coffer echoed softly.

March–April 1944

England

By the end of March, word had begun to reach the top that the Navy's Combat Demolition Units had an important part to play in the coming drama. Since February, they'd been practicing assaults with the Second, Sixth, and Seventh Beach Battalions, units that had been formed to organize the American beaches after they'd been secured. With none of the officers or men still in the know concerning their actual landing beaches or deployment, several members of the CDUs actually wrote detailed plans describing how the Navy units could be employed. Commander Eugene Carusi, of the Sixth Beach Battalion, showed some of these plans to members of the SHAEF planning staff.

Perhaps it was coincidence, but at the same time the Allied High Command was finally becoming aware of just how extensive the new German beach defenses were. Rommel's labor forces had been going at it full swing for months, adding rank upon rank of new obstacles to the formidable defenses already in place. Belgian gates, sloping ramps, hedgehogs, a bewildering array of geometrical shapes and traps and roadblocks designed to pin an invading force on the beach while the guns on the heights above blasted it to bits. *Festung Europa* was fact, not propaganda, and the walls of that fortress would not be easy to breach.

By the beginning of April, then, things began rolling for the Navy Demolitioneers. A four-day conference between high-ranking Army engineers and some of the CDU's senior officers was held to discuss how the Navy teams could best be employed. Major Fairbairn attended as the senior U.S. Navy representative.

Several critical decisions came out of that conference.

Perhaps most important, it was decided that the CDUs would be integrated with the Army units. Each numbered CDU would be changed from a six-man to a five-man team. Each of these would be integrated with three Navy seamen and five Army engineers into a larger unit, a thirteen-man unit called a Gap Assault Team, or GAT.

. Further, each GAT would be assigned to a twenty-six-man engineer platoon under the command of an Army lieutenant. Two tanks would be assigned to each platoon for fire support, plus either a bulldozer or a third tank with a bulldozer blade attached, while the Navy CDUs would receive rubber boats. In theory, at least, the CDUs would demolish all of the beach obstacles planted between the low- and high-water marks, while the Army engineers handled the obstacles planted between the high-water line and the top of the beach.

Much to the relief of some of the CDU personnel, plans to employ explosives-laden drone landing craft to destroy offshore landing craft traps and mined obstacles were dropped. The Navy teams would take out the beach obstacles by placing their explosives by hand.

Throughout England, the pace of preparations for the coming invasion quickened. There were by this time 1,108 Allied camps, accommodating nearly three million men waiting for the big day. As the time neared, reorganizations took place, and units were transferred to new locations so they could begin working on the final phase of their training.

A giant now, lumbering forward with unstoppable momentum, Overlord began to assume its final form.

Saturday, 8 April 1944

Navy CDU Base
Falmouth, England

Wallace had the evening off. After a day out in the countryside with CDU-12, practicing with the new Hagensen Packs, he returned to the chiefs' quarters, showered, shaved, and changed into his dress blues, complete with jacket and white flat-billed cap. As he'd done numerous times before, he hesitated before pinning on the board that held his ribbons in their ordered places. That blue ribbon at the upper left with the single vertical white stripe—he still felt embarrassed about wearing it. Having been awarded the Navy Cross seemed like such a lie.

Dressed then, he checked out with the base duty officer, then walked along the duckboard planks covering the dirt path outside the Nissen hut that served as CDU-12's headquarters. He turned left at the ramshackle building that served as the base exchange, passed a line of tents that served as barracks, and finally reached the front gate.

He'd asked Alice to pick him up at 1730 hours. There she was, waiting for him across the main road. He checked out with the guard, then trotted across to her.

He still had trouble believing he could have fallen in love so fast. That first night, when she'd helped him after his motorcycle accident, had ended with the two of them staying up late talking in her mother's parlor, sharing an almost instant understanding and rapport. The next day they'd arranged for repairs to the motorcycle and then spent the afternoon seeing the sights in Falmouth. By dinner that evening it had seemed like they'd known one another for years, with the comfortable, warm-shoe familiarity usually shared only by long-time married couples, if then.

Alice Pascoe's husband, Roger, had been a Royal Navy petty officer who'd died with H.M.S. *Hood* in 1941. Her own family, too, had a long and venerable association with the sea. Her brother, Adam, was currently serving aboard the *Ramilles,* and an uncle was now with the British Admiralty.

"Hey, sailor," she called, leaning out of the right-hand, driver's-side window of her car. "Going my way?"

He smiled and waved, then went around to get in the left-hand side. Cars were a relative rarity for civilians in wartime Britain, and rarer still since the virtual shutdown of all civilian traffic the month before. Alice was one of the few exceptions, though; her defense job in Cambourne warranted her a special ration card. That had proved to be a lucky break for Wallace. He'd been able to keep seeing her despite the restrictions.

"So." she said as he slid into the seat beside her. She was

wearing the blue dress he liked so much, the one with the frilly white collar. "Where are we off to tonight?"

"Oh, anywhere you like," he said. For the first time since he'd met Alice, he was not looking forward to their evening together. "You choose."

"The Pandora Inn, then," she said. "I feel like seafood." She looked at him, as though measuring his mood. "And after that . . . the Greenbank?"

"Fine."

Skillfully, Alice edged the car out onto the road in front of the base. She reached over and squeezed his thigh. "And the Greenbank has such a *lovely* view. . . ."

They'd been sleeping together since sometime late in January. Wallace wasn't quite certain even now how it had come about. They'd been at Alice's home, in Falmouth, sitting together on the overstuffed couch in the dayroom. They'd begun kissing, and one thing had led to another. . . .

That first time had been possible only because Alice's mother hadn't been home at the time. Subsequent rendezvous had taken place at various hotels in the area, including the Greenbank. Wallace often wondered if the desk attendants at those places weren't well aware of the polite "Mr. and Mrs. William Wallace" fiction, especially since Alice had lived in Falmouth all her life.

The fact that Alice was a war widow certainly helped, but it was also true that the war had brought about an unspoken but definite relaxation to some of the social strictures governing the relationships between men and women. They could not flaunt their new relationship, certainly, but they didn't need to deny it, either, at least so long as they were discreet. Sometimes they went as far afield as Saint Mawes, across the harbor from Falmouth.

Wallace felt like a thoroughgoing rat. For the past three weeks, he'd not met Alice for anything more intimate than lunch at a local café. She knew that something was wrong, but had been too politic to ask.

He knew that, and he also knew that the charade would have to end tonight.

The Pandora was a thatched-roof pub, with a maritime flavor and a splendid seafood menu, located near the Mylor

Bridge. They parked along Restronguet Creek outside and he walked around to open the door for her.

As he helped her from the car, an army six-ton truck rumbled by, its bed packed with British soldiers. Someone had scrawled DON'T CHEER, GIRLS, WE'RE BRITISH across the truck's tailgate, a wry reference to the fact that English girls seemed to prefer Americans to their own countrymen. There were catcalls and shouts from the soldiers as they recognized Wallace's uniform as American, and not a few hands raised in Churchill's famous "V-for-victory," sign, but with the back of the hand facing out.

It had taken Wallace a while to catch on, though by now he knew the significance very well. That peculiarly British gesture, two fingers, back of the hand out, was called "the fig," and it meant roughly the same as the extended middle finger did in America. Churchill used it when referring to Germany, a subtle insult that most of his American cousins missed.

It was *not* a complimentary gesture.

Many Britishers resented the Americans, who, they claimed, were brash, arrogant, rude, and had entirely too much money to spend at the Navy base exchange or the Army PX on luxuries that most British people—and especially British *girls*—had not seen for four years. British soldiers intensely resented the attention the Yanks got from the English lasses. As some local wags put it, the Americans were overpaid, overfed, oversexed, and over *here.* The American response was predictable: the British were underpaid, underfed, undersexed . . . and under Eisenhower.

"Ignore them, dear," Alice said as the truck rumbled off into the gathering night, accompanied by the laughter and catcalls of the men aboard.

"Oh, I don't mind them," he grumbled. The incident had merely raised the problem he faced tonight earlier than he'd hoped to have to face it. "I do wonder sometimes, though, just what you see in me."

"Oh, lots of things!" she said cheerfully as she took his arm, her voice and the twinkle in her eye bantering. "Chocolate, nylons, tinned hams, all those *wonderful* presents you bring me from your exchange. . . ."

Dinner passed largely in silence, with only occasional

small talk about a girl who'd been fired that afternoon at the plant, or a CDU petty officer who'd been discovered to have a cleverly hidden still in the base motor pool. They'd found they could be comfortable together, not feeling that they had to speak to fill empty air.

But damn it all. When should he tell her?

And how?

The timing was largely decided for him. He didn't want to spoil their dinner together ... and he *had* to tell her before they went to bed.

The Greenbank, built at the side of Falmouth's harbor, had once been the hotel preferred by British mailboat and packet captains. The elegant lounges had large picture windows overlooking the harbor, and many of the rooms had splendid views. They registered at the desk under his name, then followed the bellhop with her one small suitcase up to their room.

By that time, he'd almost decided not to say anything, but she'd picked up on his mood during dinner, and later, during the short drive to the hotel. "Well?" she said, after they entered the hotel room and he'd locked the door. "You've been brooding all evening."

"Brooding?"

"Bill, if gloom has a color, you've been black as a Welsh collier. Want to talk about it?"

"I guess so." He sat down on the bed and she came and sat by his side. She took his arm in hers, but he gently disentangled himself and pulled back.

"Alice ... my orders came through today. I'm ... my whole unit, actually, we're moving out."

She didn't blink, her expression didn't change. "Where are you going?"

"I'm not sure. Somewhere in Devonshire."

"Oh, well, that's not so bad. Devon's right next door to Cornwall. Fifty miles, maybe, by motor. Here I thought you were going to tell me Italy or some god-forsaken place like that."

"Alice, I really think ... that it would be better if we not see each other again."

He'd expected ... well, he hadn't known what to expect.

Rage, possibly. Tears, almost certainly, though he'd never known Alice to cry.

"What is it, Bill?" She reached up with the slim fingers of one hand and touched that damned blue-and-white ribbon on his breast. "Is it this again?"

"Hell, Alice. That thing's a gedunk ribbon. A prize in the Cracker Jack box. There were sixteen men with me on that Higgins boat in North Africa. Every one of us got that goddamn medal. It doesn't mean a thing."

"No, I don't imagine it does. It's not the medal I love, just in case you were under any misapprehensions about that. It's the man."

"You know," he said thoughtfully, "for a long time I wondered if I was a coward, medal or no medal."

"A man who disarms bombs for a living is not a coward, believe me. Neither is a man who volunteers for a unit like what you've described the CDU to be."

"Yes, well . . ." They'd had this discussion, or variants of it, before. Always, her logic stopped him cold. But it wasn't that simple, damn it. "Look. Bombs are, well, they're solid. And they work by predictable mechanisms. If the thing blows on you while you're working on it, it's because you slipped, or you turned a screw the wrong way, or, hell, it's just because the guy that assembled the thing was smarter than you are. Or were."

"Of course. You told me once that you're the sort of guy who always has to be in control of his environment."

"Yeah . . ." But he was beginning to doubt that premise now.

"I *know* you," she continued. "You wouldn't think twice about jumping out of an airplane with a parachute . . . *if* you were the guy who'd packed the parachute in the first place. Am I right?"

He sighed. "I don't know anymore. I used to think so." He thought about it for a moment. "You know, I don't think I'd mind fighting an enemy soldier face-to-face. I mean, it'd be like the bomb. Either I beat him because I'm faster, bigger, better trained, or whatever, or he beats me. Simple, right?"

She nodded.

"But the one time I was in combat, I was terrified. Of being shot. Not because some guy with a rifle was out there aiming at me. I could take that, I think. There'd be a good chance that he'd miss. No, I was scared because most of the bullets whipping around during a battle aren't aimed. They're just ... *there*. If you happen to be in the wrong place at the wrong time, you're dead, or maimed, and there isn't a damned thing you can do about it. If you try to duck out of the way, it's a fair chance you'll end up ducking *into* a round, instead of missing it. Bullets, they can't be outthought. They can't be outfought. They just are. It's the damned *randomness* of them that gets me. Do ... am I making any sense?"

"Of course." But suddenly, Wallace wondered if his original conviction, born of those nights of fire and terror in Morocco, hadn't been the right one after all. By the time he left the States, he'd managed to convince himself that it hadn't been the fear of being killed that terrified him about combat but the sheer, bloody randomness of death on the battlefield.

But fear was fear, cowardice was cowardice, whatever the cause.

Wasn't it? As the long-awaited day of the invasion rolled closer, it had the effect of wonderfully clarifying so much that had been muddled in his mind ever since North Africa.

Maybe he *was* a coward, afraid of death.

Alice leaned closer, placing one hand on his knee. "Bill, what does any of this have to do with you not wanting to see me anymore?"

"I ... well, I'm no good for you. Don't you see? I think about Roger, what you've told me about him, and I'm ashamed."

She reached up with her hand and took him by his chin. Her fingers were cold, her grip as hard as steel. She moved her head forward until her green-brown eyes were staring into his from six inches away. "You listen to me, William Wallace, and you listen to me carefully. That decision, whether or not you're right for me, it's mine to make, and nobody else's. I loved Roger. And now I love you. Clear?"

She released him then, and looked away. "You say you're afraid of random death and you say it as though you expect me to hate you for it. Roger was aboard the *Hood* when she faced the *Bismarck,* you know."

"Yes . . .'"

"You want to talk about random death? One salvo, and a lucky shot—an unlucky one, really—found *Hood*'s magazine and blew her to bits. One thousand, four hundred thirteen men simply . . . died. Ceased to exist in an instant. Out of her whole crew, they pulled three men from the water. Does the fact that Roger wasn't one of those three make him less of a man?"

"But that's not the point. Roger *went*. He was there. He wasn't a coward . . ."

"You didn't know him. Damn it, Roger was a mechanic from Devon before he enlisted in the navy. I always used to think he enlisted only because he wanted to impress me, with my oh-so-impressive naval pedigree right down to the rigging and the yardarms on the family tree. He hated the navy, actually. Hated everything about it. The food. The discipline. The crowding and lack of privacy." She smiled sadly. "I'm afraid he wasn't a very good sailor."

"But he went."

"So? You're here, aren't you? And you were at North Africa, where, incidentally, you won that 'gedunk ribbon,' as you call it, for participating in a mission that had to be done, and from which it was quite likely you would never return. I know a thing or three about fighting men, I think. You're all scared to death. Every one of you. The stupid ones are the ones who won't admit it. The brave ones are the ones who shoulder arms and get the job done, even though their spines are turned to jelly and their knees are knocking so hard they can scarcely hold you up."

He sighed. "You don't understand."

"You think not? Damn you, Bill, do you think I would love you as much as I do if you were half the sniveling coward you claim to be? I think one reason I fell in love with you in the first place was because you reminded me of Roger a little. Something about the eyes, I think, and the fact that you always cared for what I did, who I was. But now I love you for *you*. For what *you* are. And, damn you, you must have a piss-poor opinion of me, thinking I'd fall for a man like you've described after having been married three years to as good a man as Roger!"

"I . . . didn't mean it that way."

"I should hope not."

"There's . . . more."

"You're in love with another woman?"

"No!"

"Good. Because then I would break every bone in your body. Then I would drag you to bed just to show you that I can do anything she could. And, in your condition at that point, what followed could be very painful!"

"Look. We both know the invasion's coming up. I'm going to be in it, and probably I'm going to be in the thick of things."

"This is the man who thinks he's a coward."

"Shit, Alice, let me finish! At the base, they're starting to throw numbers around. Percentages. They're talking about us having maybe—*maybe*—a fifty-fifty chance of coming back at all. I've also heard seventy-five to twenty-five, against." He'd long held the common view that luck was a quantifiable commodity, something issued, then used up. A man, after all, could only have so much luck. "The odds are against my ever coming back. I couldn't do that to you. . . ."

"So now you want to live your life by the numbers? Can't be done, dearest. I know. Tomorrow there could be an accident at my plant. Or an air raid. And I could get blown to kingdom come, and where would you and your precious statistics be then?"

"Devastated." He wasn't sure where she was going with that.

"Damned right. Just like I would be if *you* didn't come back. So, what do we do about it?" Gently, but with a pressure that was irresistible, she pushed him back onto the bed. Then she stood before him and slowly unzipped her dress. "We grab what time we can." She stepped out of the last remaining wisps of clothing, then moved close to him, naked. "*Carpe diem,* seize the day. And the hell with everything else."

Her words startled Wallace. They reminded him of poor Richardson, who'd talked about seizing his chance and mar-

rying his girl . . . days before the military had cracked down
on all travel in England.

He wondered if Snake had been able to see his girl since.
Probably not.

Minutes later, they were naked in one another's arms. As
Wallace drew her tight against his body, she nuzzled his ear.
"Besides," she whispered, "you can't possibly get rid of me
that easily." Then she giggled. "Hell, you're not going to
get rid of me at all!"

"I'm glad."

But he'd already made up his mind. He would not even
think of marrying Alice until after he came back from France.

If, in fact, he came back at all.

Chapter 28

Saturday, 15 April 1944

Female Enlisted Barracks
HQ Section, 1st Division
Weymouth, England

On 10 April, all military leave was canceled and anyone in
khaki outside of the controlled areas across the southern end
of England was assumed by the military police who pa-
trolled its borders to be a deserter.

That didn't stop all nonmilitary traffic, of course. It just
made things considerably more challenging.

"*Hank!* What are you doing here?"

Richardson glanced up and down the street. There was
nobody in sight, no one near enough to hear, anyway. He
looked back at Veronica, who was wearing her WAC uniform, as lovely as he'd ever known her.

"Hey, babe. Are you game? We'll get married now. To-night."

"Are you completely nuts?"

He grinned. "Probably. Did your jail guard deliver my message?" The sergeant at the front desk of the women's barracks had not been exactly cooperative. Or friendly. It had taken all of Richardson's considerable powers of persuasion to get her to even deliver a handwritten note.

Veronica pursed her lips. "She said a gentleman was downstairs to see me on an important mission. I don't think she bought your line about working for SHAEF Headquarters, though."

"Yeah. I wondered if that might not be a bit much. Any trouble?"

"Darlene's a friend. You still haven't answered my question. What are you doing here? And . . . *how?*"

"The how is easy. Gator got me some passes—don't ask how he did it—and a truck with a priority sticker. As for what I'm doing, I'm getting married to you. If you'll say yes."

"But we won't be able to *see* each other!"

"We'll take a room at a hotel."

"No, I mean from now on! I can't leave my post. You can't leave yours. God, if the M.P.s catch you here, Hank, you could be shot!"

"I don't think it'll come to that, Ronnie. And the restrictions'll just be on until after the invasion. After that, we can put in for all the paperwork. Even have a real ceremony, if you want." He stopped, suddenly worried. "You do still want to get married, don't you?"

She grinned up at him. "God, I've never wanted anything so much in my life. You have a justice of the peace in mind?"

"I don't think they're called that here. But yes, I do. Or rather, I have a friend who can perform the ceremony."

"*Not* Gator?"

He grinned. "Not exactly. Here's the deal. I have two passes, signed by General Bradley himself."

"Not really!"

"Well, the guards won't know the difference. I told you, you don't really want to know. Anyway, we drive you out in a truck Gator borrowed for us from the motor pool and head back to Appledore."

"Appledore?"

"Oh, yeah. You haven't heard. It's a place in Devon, up on the Bristol Channel. We got transferred there last week for some last-minute training. Anyway, it's less than a hundred miles from here. Two hours, tops."

"Hank! There's a blackout on! How do you expect to drive one hundred miles at night with almost no light?"

"Okay. Three hours. We get there about oh-two-hundred and check you into a hotel. Tomorrow morning at zero-nine hundred, we get married. You do still have Sundays off, don't you?"

She nodded. "Actually, I didn't as of two days ago, but I swapped yesterday with a friend."

"Good. They've been working us like dogs, but I managed to get tomorrow off too. I'm supposed to be on a working party down in Salcombe, which is why nobody'll miss me."

"Gator is a useful guy to have around."

"I've noticed. I'm thinking of making him my butler when this is all over. *Our* butler."

"Would you trust him around me?"

"No. But we share everything else. Why not you?"

"Rat."

"Flatterer."

"So we're married tomorrow morning. Uh, by who?"

"Lieutenant Kingsbury, the CDU team chaplain. He'll say the words and take care of the paperwork."

"How did you wangle that?"

"Not me, actually. It was—"

"Gator."

"Yeah."

"Tell me. Is Gator going to take part in everything we do together?"

"Well . . ."

"Never mind. How the hell did he bribe a chaplain?"

"Oh, it wasn't a bribe. Not exactly. But, well, Lieutenant Kingsbury does like good scotch, and Gator happened to have a couple of bottles. . . ."

"Never mind. You're right. I don't want to know. So we're married by a drunk chaplain. Then what?"

"We check back into your hotel as man ánd beautiful wife. We enjoy one another's charms until midnight."

"And at midnight, what? You turn into a pumpkin?"

"No, midnight to zero-six-hundred is the time frame written on another stack of passes signed by the kind and generous General Bradley. I drive you back here, drop you off, take the truck back to the motor pool and leave it with a friend of Tangretti's, then return to my bachelor life at my barracks, smug in the knowledge that you are mine forever and ever! So, what do you say?"

Her answer was an enthusiastic yes. Aside from the fact that they took a wrong road in Taunton and got all the way to Exeter before they realized their mistake, then decided to sit it out until daylight, everything went pretty much according to plan. They didn't show up in Appledore until 0750 hours, but there was still plenty of time before meeting Lieutenant Kingsbury at the Nissen hut appropriated as the base chapel.

"You watch out for this guy, Mrs. Richardson," Wallace told Veronica a few minutes after the ceremony. They were standing inside the chapel's entrance, waiting for Franklin to bring up the four-by-four truck Tangretti had appropriated from the motor pool as transport for the wedding party. It was pouring outside, the rain drumming on the steel curve of the Nissen hut's roof with a hollow, metallic rattle.

"Really, Chief?" Veronica said with an affected, wide-eyed innocence. Clinging to Richardson's arm, she snuggled closer. "Whatever do you mean?"

For the first time since he'd known the chief, Richardson thought Wallace actually seemed embarrassed. He looked away, clearly uncomfortable. "Look, Snake, you got yourself a real prize here. You just be good to her, okay? Or I'll take you apart myself!"

Veronica released Richardson's arm and stood on tiptoe to kiss Wallace on the cheek. "Thanks, Chief," she said. "But I think I can handle him!"

"Here's your ride," Tangretti said from the chapel's open door. Outside, the four-by-four pulled up in the muddy river that was the street. He handed Richardson an umbrella. "You two take care. Anything you need, anything at all . . ."

"Thanks, Gator," Richardson said. He accepted the umbrella in one hand, then clasped Tangretti's hand with the other. "Thanks for everything." The handshake became an un-self-conscious embrace.

"Just remember," Tangretti told him, pulling back. "When you two finally get around to having your reception, *I* get to cater it."

It was a short dash to the waiting truck's open door, but they had to pick their way along a narrow walkway of planks in the mud, and by the time Richardson boosted Veronica up the high, high step to the cab, they were both soaked. Tangretti, Wallace, and the handful of other CDU officers and men clustered at the chapel's door cheered and waved and made enthusiastic thumbs-up gestures as he slid in beside Veronica and slammed the door shut.

They said little during the ten-minute drive into Appledore proper. Conversation was necessarily restricted by the roar of the engine and by the hiss of the pelting rain on the cab's roof.

Richardson was astonished to realize, as he picked through his jumbled thoughts and emotions, that he was terrified.

He had never known a girl like Veronica . . . ever. They'd had time during their night-long drive, hours before, to talk, and he was still digesting much of what he'd learned. Veronica came from a big family, and she wanted a big family herself. "At least a dozen kids," she said, "though I'd settle for one who looks like you."

He didn't mind the big family part, though he'd never really given much thought to the idea. What did worry him was the fact that Veronica was still a virgin.

Hell, that wasn't it either. Plenty of the girls he'd bedded in the past had been virgins, and every time he'd been able to worm his way in between their legs with gentle persuasion followed by careful, gentle loving.

No, the problem was that Veronica was what was known as a *nice* girl . . .

. . . while he had the sexual past of an alley tom.

Suppose she found out the truth about him?

It was still raining when they reached the hotel Tangretti had arranged for them, a former Victorian resort on a hill overlooking Bristol Channel. The building had seen better days; steel buckets placed at strategic points in the lobby protected a faded, water-stained carpet that showed threadbare paths along the routes most traveled. A bellhop who must have been at least seventy years old showed them to their room. Richardson was glad they had no luggage with them, for he doubted that the old guy would have made it up the stairs, but the man smiled and nodded as Richardson swept Veronica off the floor for the traditional carry-across-the-threshold, and he refused the proffered shilling tip.

And then they were alone.

In their room, two more buckets collected steady plip-plops of water from a patched and rust-stained ceiling. A large window overlooked the channel through shabby curtains, though nothing was visible now save dark clouds and steady, gray sheets of rain. The bed was a big four-poster with a mattress supported on ropes instead of springs, and the coverlet was thick enough to drown in.

"Would . . . ah, would you like me to draw the curtains?" he said, as unsure of himself as any fumble-tongued schoolboy. "I mean, would you prefer the room dark?"

She stepped close, slipping her arms around him. "I think," she said softly, "that I'd like to see what I'm getting. Besides, I like the rain." She shivered a little, then moved back, stepping out of her shoes and reaching up to unbutton her uniform blouse. "I also think we'd better get out of these wet clothes, don't you?"

The blouse clung to her like a second skin, and he helped her peel it off. In moments, all three chairs in the room, as well as the dresser and an open bathroom door, were festooned with their clothing, hung out to dry.

"So . . . are you sleepy yet?" Richardson asked his bride. Nude, they sat cross-legged on the bed, facing one another. "It's been an awfully long night."

"Well, I'm ready for *bed*," she said, smiling slyly. "Not necessarily for sleep."

Wonderingly, he drank in the sight, the loveliness of her body, slender, small-breasted, delicate, perfectly formed. She had an elfin, girlish beauty that held him transfixed. His gaze traveled down the smoothness of her, lingering at last on the tuft of dark curls that failed to hide the folds of her genital lips.

Memories surfaced, unbidden. The first time he'd ever seen a naked girl had been when he was ten, playing you-show-me-yours-and-I'll-show-you-mine with his eleven-year-old cousin in a barn on her parents' farm in upstate New York. The first time he'd ever had sex, or tried to, had been four years later with a classmate's older sister at that summer camp up on Lake Champlain. *That* had been an unmitigated disaster. They'd tried to go skinny-dipping but the water had been frigid; then he'd gotten so excited rolling around with her in the weeds that he'd disgraced himself with a sticky mess on her hand and thighs before she'd even been able to guide him inside. That bout of poison ivy, plus the discovery a few months later that half of the school had somehow learned about his incompetence, had added considerable insult to injury.

And why, dear God, did he have to remember that episode *now*, of all times? He hadn't thought about Lake Champlain for years. . . .

"Hank?"

"Huh?"

"Are you all right? You seemed a little distant for a moment."

"Uh . . . sorry. I was just . . . I mean . . ."

She dropped her gaze. "You're not . . . not disappointed, are you? In me, I mean."

"Oh, God, Veronica. *No.*" He reached out, brushing his fingers across her cheek, her bare shoulder, the crinkled pink bud of one nipple. Then he brought his hand up and lifted her chin. "You are so very, very beautiful."

He felt shy, and embarrassed, emotions he hadn't felt since Lake Champlain. He wondered if, possibly, all of his conquests since that awful summer ten years ago had been some kind of atonement for that failure—or, worse, revenge. Now, with Veronica, it was as though *he* was the inexperienced one, as though all of those other girls had never existed.

He wondered if he would even be able to perform.

Veronica placed her hands on his knees, then slowly slid

them up his thighs. "I've . . . I've heard that men like this," she said, and then she leaned forward, lowering her face to his lap, kissing him lightly, then drawing him into her mouth. In another few seconds, he had no doubts at all about his performance . . . or hers.

"Let's get under the covers," he told her.

Much later, the rain had stopped, and they could see the cloud-shadowed glitter of Bristol Channel through their window. They'd made love and then slept. When they'd awakened, their clothes were dry; they went downstairs for lunch, then returned to their room, made love, then slept again. Later, they'd watched the sunset, and made love once more as the sky turned a fiery red.

"Happy?" he asked after a time.

"Mmm." She stirred, then opened her eyes. "You still want to wait until midnight to go back?"

He grimaced. "After all the trouble we had last night, maybe we should get an early start. Nobody's going to look at the time discrepancy on the passes. And, much as I want to keep you forever, I don't want to risk getting you back to Weymouth late."

"I wish I didn't have to go back. That we didn't have to."

"It won't be forever." For a little while, the war had been excluded from their warm, close universe. Now, with the knowledge that they might not have many more times like this before the invasion, it had returned.

"I know."

His hand was over her bare back, and he felt the stifled sob. "Veronica? What is it?"

"I'm afraid. . . ."

"It's okay. It's okay. We'll get through this."

"I know."

"Are you sorry you went and married me?"

She raised her head. Her eyes glistened in the near darkness, wet with tears. "Never. Never in a million years. I love you, Hank."

"And I love you. And soon the invasion will be over with and I'll be back and nothing will ever keep us apart again."

"Promise?"

"I promise. And if it looks like anything's going to keep us apart, you know what?"

She turned to face him, her eyes glistening. "What?"

"I'll put Gator to work on it. Believe me, Ronnie. Gator can fix *anything*."

Laughing, she wiped away the tears. "You know, I almost believe you," she said. "But for your information, sailor, I happen to know there's *one* thing Gator can't do."

"Impossible. What?"

Throwing back the coverlet, she rose to her knees in the bed. Again, he luxuriated in the glorious sight of her body. Smiling, graceful, she slid one leg across his hips, taking him in her hands as she mounted him. *"This . . ."*

Friday, 28 April 1944

U.S. Navy CDU Reserve Area
Appledore, Devonshire

On 26 April, all of the troops intended for the first wave of the invasion were sealed in their camps, along with all civilians living within ten miles of the coast. Whole villages, including Sapton and Devon, were evacuated, taken over completely by what could only be called an army of occupation. The military camps became known as "cages," and signs erected on the barbed wire encircling them warned civilian passersby not to talk to the troops.

For the CDUs, late April was a time of vital importance. The teams learned at last which beaches they were bound for and what they were expected to do. By now, the Demolitioneers had new commanding officers, a reflection of the Navy's realization that the operation needed senior men. Lieutenant Commander Joseph H. Gilbert was in charge of Force O, the teams that would assault Omaha Beach. Lieutenant Commander Herbert A. Henderson would command the Utah group.

Yet another briefing had been called for all of the senior naval officers and chiefs of the CDUs assigned to Omaha Beach. Wallace was sitting next to Snake Richardson in the makeshift auditorium in the camp at Appledore. Lieutenant Commander Gilbert was addressing the group. With him, Wallace was delighted to see, was a familiar face from his days as an instructor back at Fort Pierce. He'd heard a few months back that Frank Rand had been stationed at the Amphibious Base at Plymouth, but he'd never had a chance to look him up. Now Rand had shown up to help Gilbert with the day's intelligence briefing.

"Good morning, gentlemen," Gilbert said. "First off, I have some good news for a change. At least, I trust you'll think so. The word has just come down from SHAEF that the invasion, which was provisionally set for mid-May, has now been set back to 5 June."

A groan ran through the room, and Wallace smiled to himself. Morale had improved quite a lot in these last few weeks. All it had taken was the sure knowledge that the men were going to be allowed to do their jobs. The groan was an indication of the improvement. They didn't want to wait another month, practicing on abandoned British beach obstacles; they wanted to *go*.

"I know, I know," Gilbert said, holding up his hand. "However, SHAEF has agreed with us that we need more time for practice, now that we know exactly what targets we're going to have to face. There are other reasons as well, of course, but the important consideration so far as we're concerned is that we have an extra two, almost three, weeks to get ready. In particular, we can practice some more with the DDs."

DD—short for Dual Drive, though most enlisted men insisted it stood instead for Donald Duck—referred to Sherman tanks equipped with canvas skirts and propellers, which allowed them to be released at sea to "swim" ashore. The British had developed an entire menagerie of specialized armor for the invasion, but only the DD tanks had been accepted by the Americans. They would be the first units to come ashore on the American beaches, followed closely by a company of infantry to provide close support for the armor and to mop up snipers. The CDUs would follow close behind, a few minutes past H-Hour.

At least, that was what was called for by the plan developed so far. Wallace knew, however, that in combat, plans rarely bore any similarity to what actually happened.

"The gentleman with me today," Gilbert continued, "is Boatswain's Mate First Class Rand, of the Navy-Marine Scouts and Raiders. Some of you may have heard of them."

A ripple of laughter ran through the room. Not many of the Fort Pierce graduates would ever forget the sadistic S&R instructors from their training session the previous year. "What Rand has to say will be of particular interest to you men of CDU-12. Rand and some of the other Raiders in his team went almost all the way into the beach of Vierville a couple of weeks ago. They brought back some of the photographs he has to show you. Rand?"

"Thank you, sir." Rand stepped forward.

"First, a review of the beach." Rand reached out and accepted a folder from an aide. Inside were black-and-white photographs, some taken from the air, others from the sea. All showed the same general terrain—flat beaches thickly littered with obstacles of many different types, high bluffs backing up the beaches, and several draws or valleys penetrating those bluffs, like natural highways leading to the interior of France.

"You can think of Omaha Beach as enclosed by a crescent of hills," Rand said, "stretching five miles from end to end. The crescent's horns reach the sea, where they become sheer cliffs, a hundred, a hundred-fifty feet straight up. The beach itself ranges from one hundred to three hundred yards deep at low tide. At high tide, the sea reaches nearly all the way up to the foot of the bluffs.

"The Germans have heavily defended the beach, of course, with a variety of obstacles, arrayed in at least three and sometimes as many as four separate layers. Most of the obstacles are rigged with Teller mines, which can rip a small boat—or a man—open on contact. There are conventional minefields in the sand, and, of course, the gun emplacements and machine guns on the hills above have an excellent field of fire over the whole beach.

"One bit of good news in all of this gloom. Intelligence reports that the troops manning the Omaha defenses are simply not that good. They've been identified as members of the 726th Infantry Division, definitely a third-rate outfit that's been overstretched in manning the defenses. Now, then. On to the good stuff."

Rand unrolled a large map and set it on an easel. Lieutenant Henderson helped hold it open while Rand picked up a pointer and began indicating particular areas of the hills.

"The hills behind the beach are penetrated by five ravines or draws," Rand said, pointing each out in turn. "These provide natural highways off the beach and will be of supreme importance on D-Day. Those hills provide an impassable barrier for vehicles and tanks. The only way to get them and our army off the beach will be up those draws. We can expect them to be heavily defended with mine fields, with concrete roadblocks and barbed wire, and with covering fire from the hills. Our aircraft have identified no fewer than twelve defensive positions guarding these ravines, with machine guns, French 75s, and German 88s.

"The ravines have been charted, reading west to east, as D-1, D-3, E-1, E-3, and F-1. The D, E, and F designations, of course, refer to the Dog, Easy, and Fox beaches fronting them. D-1 is the draw leading to the town of Vierville, on the extreme right. D-3 is the Les Moulins draw. E-1, right smack in the center, leads to the village of Saint Laurent. E-3 is the largest ravine. It leads to Colleville-sur-Mer. Finally, on our extreme left, is F-1, which doesn't lead directly to a village, so it's simply known as Number Five Draw.

"Opening the draws will be the responsibility of the Army engineer components of your GATs, of course. However, each of them has a different character when seen from the sea. I'm here today to brief you on the appearance of each of these ravines, along with associated terrain features and buildings, so that when you hit that beach, you'll know exactly where you are and where you'll have to go."

The briefing continued. Wallace was particularly interested, of course, in the area where his team would be landing. His CDU-12, attached to GAT-1, would be going ashore on the western flank of Omaha on Dog Green Beach, opposite the Vierville ravine. Richardson, he knew, was assigned to GAT-4, where he would be leading CDU-5. They would be farther to the east, on Easy Red beach below the Saint Laurent draw. Steve Tangretti, Wallace knew, was also going ashore at Easy Red, but for once he would not be with his old swim buddy. The Army cared little for sentiment, and men were simply assigned to units based on where the military needed warm bodies. Gator the Cumshaw King had been assigned to CDU-6, GAT-5.

Having Tangretti and Richardson split up worried Wallace, and for a time he wondered why. He finally decided that the problem was that so much had been taken out of the hands of the CDUs. They would be going in as detachments in an Army unit, doing their jobs under Army officers. The Fort Pierce training would be valuable, of course, but the unit cohesion that Wallace and his fellow instructors had worked so hard to build the previous year in those Florida swamps would be largely missing.

He wondered if that boded ill for the operation. He did know, now, that Alice was right about him.

Wallace detested not being in control.

May–June 1944

Navy CDU Marshalling Area
Salcombe, England

In mid-May, new intelligence reached the teams. Some of the enemy mines emplaced on the coast were filled with gasoline and were designed to spread flames across the water when they detonated, and there was still a possibility that mustard gas or worse awaited the first men ashore. The assault teams were issued new garb, a hooded, fire-resistant coverall worn over the men's regular uniforms. This, plus the rubber galoshes, gloves, gas mask, and goggles that went with it, was to be carried along with almost ninety pounds of explosives and equipment.

Wearing the new equipment, the men practiced on the Bristol beaches, aching beneath the new and heavy load of uniform and gear. They practiced racing the clock. Now that they knew which beaches they would assault, they knew something of the tides they would face. At Omaha Beach, the tide on the morning of the invasion would be coming in at the rate of one foot every eight minutes.

On 22 May, the teams moved once again, this time to Salcombe on the Channel coast, where they were employed nearly around the clock assembling Hagensen Packs. Sailmakers working in lofts throughout England manufactured thousands of canvas sausages, into each of which the Demolitioneers stuffed two pounds of C-2 explosive.

They also began going over their equipment, piece by piece. Every operating unit would have two sets of gasproof coveralls and one pair of boots for each man, a .30-caliber M-1 carbine and 100 rounds for the enlisted men, a .45-caliber pistol and ammo for the officers, a seven-man rubber boat, ten paddles, an M-2 demolition reel kit, 1,000 blasting caps, 2,000 pounds of C-2 explosive, 1,500 waterproof pull-wire igniters, twenty dozen rubber prophylactics . . . This list went on and on, and every team was repeatedly inspected to make certain that all was in readiness.

On 30 May, a German air raid dropped bombs in an ordnance battalion camp back at Falmouth, killing several men. Wallace was frantic, for he'd heard exaggerated stories about the raid and was not allowed to telephone Alice to see if she was all right. All he could think about for the next several days was the knowledge that she occasionally drove truckloads of munitions to various camps in Cornwall. Had she been there when the German planes went over? Had she been hurt? Was she still alive?

In the end, he convinced himself that she *must* be alive, and that he would go and find her as soon as the invasion was over. To do anything else, to think anything else, meant madness.

And then it was June, and the last few days flickered past and were gone. On 3 June, the Omaha Assault Teams moved a final time, to Portland for embarkation.

The long-awaited invasion of France had commenced.

Chapter 29

Tuesday, 6 June 1944

GAT-1
The Omaha Approaches

They crossed the English Channel aboard an LCT(A), a square-sterned, flat-bottomed, broad-beamed tank landing craft measuring just 114 feet in length overall and with a capacity of 150 tons. There were no accommodations aboard for troops, but the crossing, it was thought, would be so brief that the men would hardly have time to get uncomfortable.

Of course, that was before the worst channel storm in twenty years blew up on 4 June, hours before the scheduled departure of the greatest invasion armada in history, lashing the English coast with rain and gusting high winds. Eisenhower called one meeting . . . then another. The invasion was postponed from the morning of the fifth to the morning of the sixth. There could be no further postponement, the waiting men knew, for the combination of moon necessary for the airborne portion of the assault and the early morning low tide required by the amphibious forces would not be repeated for another month.

In that month, the chances that the Germans would discover the marshaling forces of the invasion were simply too great. That bomber strike at Falmouth, the accidental encounter with German E-boats at a rehearsal landing at Slapton Sands a month ago that resulted in the sinking of two LSTs and the deaths of seven hundred men . . . these and countless other lesser incidents made it clear that the secret of the invasion could not be kept much longer.

So the engineers and Demolitioneers of GAT-1 rode out part of the storm drenched and miserable in their tiny, pitching craft in Portland Harbor. Later, they found shelter ashore in a Nissen hut used for storing uniforms and boots. Wallace thought about the thousands of men already embarked aboard troopships and shuddered. There would be no relief from the constant pitching and seasickness for them, for there were simply too many troops to be off-loaded and quartered on such short notice.

It rained and blew all throughout the day and evening of 5 June, while the Navy men wagered with the Army over whether Ike would take the gamble. At 2245 hours, the word came through at last. The invasion was on.

The Channel seas were still running rough, though the ceiling had lifted somewhat and the rain had stopped. The sensation of being aboard the flat-bottomed landing craft wallowing through those seas was simply indescribable. The motion was made worse by the fact that each GAT LCT(A) was towing a smaller landing craft, a fifty-foot LCM loaded with the team's explosives and equipment. This meant that, in addition to the usual corkscrew motion of the boat as it plowed through the waves, periodically there would be a sudden jolt transmitted through the deck as the tow to the LCM was snapped taut, halting the LCT's forward motion with a sickening, wrenching shock.

Aboard the LCT(A), the thirteen demolition men, the twenty-six Army engineers, and the eleven men of the LCT's crew made the best of it, drenched by spray breaking over the rounded bow, crowded in among the craft's deck cargo: two tanks, one tankdozer, and much of the GAT beach-assault gear. Aviation Ordnanceman First Class Bronson spent the first hour of the crossing taunting the Army engineers of the GAT, remarking on their drawn, gray and green faces. Then they cleared the Bill of Portland and the seas *really* got rough. Bronson became explosively, miserably sick and there was no more talk about "the poor Army pukes who just couldn't hold it."

"So, Bill. How's it feel?"

Wallace was sitting on the lead DD tank, trying to ignore

the queasiness in his stomach by reading a novel under a hooded flashlight. It was a Penguin Wartime Special, but, after struggling with it for twenty minutes, he still didn't even know what the story was about. He snapped off the light. "Beg pardon, sir?"

Lieutenant j.g. Gary Aldershot was a young, long-faced, big-boned farmer from Kansas who'd joined the Navy the previous summer, then volunteered for CDU duty just after Tarawa. Wallace had heard that he'd been to Georgia Tech, but he didn't really know the man that well. He'd been with another CDU until the reshuffling of the teams early in May.

"I was just wondering how it feels, Chief. Being in one of these damned little boats, going into a hot beach the second time around."

That again.

Wallace had been wondering whether the twisting in his gut was from seasickness or from fear.

He shrugged. "No better the second time than it was the first, Lieutenant."

"Yeah, I don't imagine it ever gets any easier." He jerked his helmeted head, indicating the men gathered in clear spots on the deck farther aft. "What's your assessment of our boys?"

Wallace turned on the tank, taking in the wet figures half visible in the darkness. Frazier and Kaminsky were engaged in a heated debate of some sort with several of the Army guys. Al Frazier had been a bomb disposal instructor at Wallace's old alma mater, the Navy Yard, before going on to Fort Pierce. Kaminsky was a "wet-nose," as the British called their unblooded American comrades. He'd been a third-class radioman in a Navy enlisted pool in Scotland before being rushed in three weeks before to bring the CDU to full strength.

"It's a mixed bag, sir," Wallace said carefully. He could feel the beginnings of that old, familiar pounding behind his eyes, the throb of building stress. "I can't really say how some of the newer guys are going to manage." *Or some of the old hands, either.*

He looked back at the lieutenant. "Of course, there's not a hell of a lot we can do about it now, sir."

"No. No, I guess not. But I wish they hadn't shuffled things up so much just before the jump-off."

It occurred to Wallace that Aldershot was not so much calling a conference with his senior enlisted man as he was looking for reassurance. *He's scared too,* Wallace thought. *And damn it, I'm going to have to keep an eye on him once we hit the beach.*

The realization was at once frightening and steadying. The fact that the Navy team's leader was as scared as he was, maybe more so, brought his own fear into clearer perspective.

It also made him realize how much the others were depending on him.

GAT-4
The Omaha Approaches

Lieutenant j.g. Richardson had found a vantage point perched atop the lead DD tank's turret, pleased to know that the vicious seasickness that afflicted most of the Army engineers and some of the CDU sailors didn't seem to bother him at all. He loved the exhilaration of lunging through those cresting waves, of feeling the cool wash of spray breaking past him over the bow.

Come on, come on, come on!

It was as though he was willing the bulky LCT(A) ahead, pushing it faster through sheer effort of will. They were behind schedule already, damn it, and he wanted to make up the lost time. Shortly after leaving the Channel assembly area, dubbed "Piccadilly Circus," and starting for the beaches south, their LCM's tow had parted, and the fifty-foot landing craft, packed with one ton of C-2 and hundreds of pounds of primacord, blasting caps, and other explosive materials, had gone adrift. The situation was made worse by the fact that they were now in one of the German mine fields guarding the French coast. Minesweepers had already swept lanes clear in advance of the armada, but the danger that the runaway LCM would drift out of the lane and strike a mine or—worse—collide with one of the troop transports coming up astern, was appalling. It had taken them almost two hours to recapture the bucking, pitching LCM and secure it astern once more. Richardson had been forcibly reminded of the time he and Tangretti tried to catch up with that drifting Stingray drone off Kwajalein.

He wondered if they were as far behind the other engineering boats as he was afraid they were. Lieutenant Pinkowski, the Army CO of GAT-4, was a decent sort, but he struck Richardson as something of a scatterbrain, full of good intentions and friendly, just-one-of-the-guys affectations, but in a bumbling, puppy dog kind of way. Where was the pup, anyway? Richardson twisted around on the tank turret, trying to see. That looked like the lieutenant, aft by the tankdozer, talking to Lederson, Kline, and some of the Army guys.

He heard a low-voiced droning sound and looked up. Everyone said that every aircraft in the sky on D-Day would be friendly, but Richardson wasn't certain how far he could believe that. He'd heard rumors of an air raid over their old base at Falmouth just a week ago. The sky was overcast, and all but pitch-black, with only the faintest glimmer of gray from a moon somewhere above the clouds. He couldn't see . . .

No! There it was. He could just make out the blacker cross of an aircraft against the black sky. And another. And another.

Bombers, he thought . . . or possibly paratroop transports on their way to France.

Suddenly, with the crisp and astonishing surprise of a falling star briefly glimpsed, a light winked at the side of one of those dark shapes. *Dit-dit-dit-dah. Dit-dit-dit-dah.*

A Morse *V.* V for victory. Someone up there had glimpsed the landing craft on the sea below and was flashing the Morse equivalent of a thumbs-up. Quickly, Richardson fumbled around on the turret top until he found the flashlight he'd taken up there with him. Aiming it at the sky, he clicked it on and off in reply: *Dah-dah-dit. Dah-dah-dah. Dah-dah-dah. Dah-dit-dit. Dit-dah-dit-dit. Dit-dit-dah. Dah-dit-dah-dit. Dah-dit-dah.* G-O-O-D-L-U-C-K.

There was no reply, and he had no idea whether or not his tiny flashlight could be seen from nearly a mile above the Channel. Still, he felt strangely close to the unknown men

overhead, closer in some ways than he felt to the men he'd
been training with for the past month.

He wished Gator were here. He wanted to talk, and there
was no one he knew well among the Navy members of his
team. He knew most of them from the past couple of
months of training, of course, and two guys, Chief Williams
and PO1 Truett, had been through NCDU training at Fort
Pierce.

He found he was most comfortable with them. It was almost as though the others were still outsiders, strangers he
would soon have to rely on, who might prove themselves to
be decent sorts in time but who meanwhile were not quite
worthy of unreserved trust.

Damn, *why* had they assigned Gator to another boat?

GAT-5
The Omaha Approaches

Tangretti wondered where Snake was right now, what he
was thinking. Most likely he was thinking about that pretty
young WAC of his, wondering when he would get to see
her again. He still thought Snake had been an idiot to go
and marry the girl *now*, just before the invasion and at a
time when he couldn't even be with her for more than that
one, strictly illegal, honeymoon afternoon at Appledore.

A shape loomed up in the darkness. "You okay, Gator?"

Lieutenant j.g. Scott Franklin was the senior officer for
the CDU team. "Hi, Lieutenant." In the boat, with the rest
of the GAT team nearby, Tangretti did not refer to Franklin
as "Scotty." Lieutenant Randy Bishop, the Army commander of the engineering platoon, was a straight-laced
West Pointer who insisted on everything being done by the
book. "Yeah, I'm fine. Just wondering how old Snake's getting on without me."

Franklin laughed. "You know, I heard some scuttlebutt
the other day, something about that son of a bitch sneaking
ashore and getting himself married. You wouldn't happen to
know anything about that, would you?"

"What, Snake?" Tangretti's eyes opened wide. Then he
laughed. "You're shittin' me, right, Lieutenant? Snake?
Married?"

Franklin laughed and shook his head. "Yeah, sounds crazy. I just wondered if it was so crazy it might be true . . . and I figured you'd be the guy to know about it if it was."

"Hell, Lieutenant. I'd be the first to tell you if I did."

Franklin turned and started to leave, then stopped. "Oh, and Gator?"

"Yes, sir?"

"I've been meaning to tell you. Thanks for those nylons. Mailed 'em to my wife for her birthday last week, and she really appreciated them. She says they're so hard to get, lots of women are actually painting their legs to look like stockings, seams and all! Where the hell'd you get them, anyway?"

"Oh, a supply sergeant I knew in Appledore had a little business on the side. He let me have some for . . . well, a favor."

"Gotcha. Thanks."

"Don't mention it, sir."

Actually, it had been a Storekeeper First Class in Salcombe, but Tangretti always protected his sources. Always, even from people he knew.

You couldn't trust everyone the way he trusted Snake.

LCC-7
Off Easy Red Beach

BM1 Rand stood in the cockpit of the LCC, the Landing Craft, Control, assigned to guide the lead waves into the strip of beach off the Saint Laurent draw, designated Easy Red. Lieutenant Tomlinson and the coxswain at the wheel stood with him in a tightening silence broken only by the purr of the boat's powerful engines.

Like the others, Rand wore plain, Army-issue fatigues, a helmet, and a Mae West life jacket. Tucked into a boot sheath was a good-bye gift from Major Fairbairn, one of the black-bladed, double-edged knives the major and one of his colleagues had designed, then sold to the British Army in 1941—the Sykes-Fairbairn commando knife.

The LCC was a 75-ton motor launch, 112 feet long and capable of twenty knots. She carried a three-pounder gun mounted on her forward deck, a twin machine gun aft, and a jury-rigged rocket launcher for shore bombardment, but her primary mission was not fire support. She was one of a number of control boats assigned to lead the initial waves ashore at the correct beaches. Aboard were Scouts and Raiders, many of them men like Rand and Tomlinson who'd conducted covert explorations of these beaches during the past few months.

Rand checked his watch: 0530 hours, a half hour before sunrise. The predawn light was bright enough, though, to let him see the beach, still shrouded in a low-lying blanket of silvery fog. The sky was overcast, the water rough and choppy. Astern, the LCTs carrying the first-wave DD tanks were visible as shadows in the mist.

Gunner's Mate Chief Costigan clambered up the ladder to the cockpit, joining Rand and the coxswain at the wheel. "Hey, Skipper? Feels like we're drifting a bit to the east."

"Damned crosscurrent," Tomlinson replied. "Helm, keep her steady!"

"Aye, sir," the coxswain said.

That current, Rand thought, would play havoc with the landing craft if they couldn't stay lined up with the LCCs.

Guns rumbled to the west. Earlier, long before it had grown light, the boat party had been surprised by the flash and rumble of a bombardment and, for a time, wondered if something had gone seriously wrong. Finally, Rand had pointed out that the Rangers were due to assault the German batteries atop the cliffs at Point du Hoc, several miles west of the Omaha beaches, before dawn. Still, the feeling, the *dread*, that this entire, monumental effort was plunging ahead only marginally under the control of those who'd set it all in motion was inescapable.

Some German guns had opened up from the beach ahead, but so far their fire was sporadic and inaccurate.

He looked at his watch again: 0545 hours. The Allied bombardment was scheduled to begin in another ten minutes.

GAT-1
Off Dog Green Beach

This, Wallace thought, was always the roughest part . . . the waiting, knowing that in a few moments more you would be hurled into the teeth of battle but that in the meantime there was nothing to do but wait and pray and wonder whether or not you would come out of this alive.

At zero-two-hundred hours, the Omaha assault force had mustered eleven miles off the beach, a long distance in those rough waters but one calculated to keep them out of range of the deadly German shore batteries reported to be mounted at Point du Hoc, high atop the cliffs to the west.

There, in wildly pitching, corkscrewing seas, the GAT had transferred to the fifty-foot LCM they'd towed astern all the way from Portland Harbor. By the time they were aboard the smaller craft, anyone who hadn't gotten wet and seasick before was now drenched to the skin and looking as green as any of his companions.

The GAT personnel were wearing long underwear and khaki uniforms. They now climbed into their bulky, gas-resistant, flame-resistant coveralls in preparation for the final assault. All that seawater weighing down his cotton underwear made Wallace feel as though he was sloshing when he walked. He wondered how well he would be able to move once he got ashore.

Over the coveralls he wore several canvas bags and a backpack, as well as an inflatable life vest. An M-1 carbine was strapped over one shoulder, and he carried a heavy reel of cable for firing electric blasting caps. He began wondering what would happen if he sank while burdened with all of that gear while he was still offshore. He sure as hell wouldn't be able to swim.

After a few moments of consideration, he started pulling off his gear.

"Shit, Chief," Aldershot demanded. "What the hell do you think you're doing?"

"Travel light, I always say." He slipped off the backpack and carbine, pulled the inflatable vest over his head, and began unfastening the coveralls. The other GAT men watched him with expressions ranging from curiosity to amusement.

Signalman Second Class Daystrom sounded off with a raucous "Dum-dum-dump! Da-dum-dum-dump," mimicking the bump-and-grind of a striptease artist. Kaminsky joined in, clapping in time.

Aldershot ignored the chorus. "Chief, if the Germans use gas on that beach ..." He plucked at his own coveralls. "Shit, Chief, these duds'll be the only things you've got to protect yourself!"

Stripped down to his khakis, Wallace started donning his various pieces of gear again, leaving the coveralls and galoshes in a pile on the LCM's desk. He didn't reply.

"Chief," Aldershot said warningly. "I'm ordering you—"

"Don't," Wallace told him. "Sir."

"Damn you, Chief. You can't do this!"

"With respect, sir. I already did. If the Krauts use mustard on the beach, I won't be any worse off than two hundred thousand other guys, right?"

"But we're different, Chief! We're valuable and we've got to be protected!"

"Bullshit." Wallace reached out and flicked the back of his fingers against Aldershot's coveralls. "You think this monkey suit'll do you a damn bit of good when the bullets start flying? Give me a break! And as far as this goes"—Wallace indicated his carbine—"a demolition man's weapon is explosives. This will just get in the way!"

Aldershot's face turned red, and he appeared to be wavering between two courses of action. Evidently, he decided that it was too late to put Wallace under arrest. Without another word, he turned on his galosh-covered heel and stalked off aft, leaving Wallace alone by the LCM's bow ramp. A few minutes later, though, he noticed that most of the Navy men and several Army engineers as well had removed their own gas suits.

Strangely, Wallace felt a lot better after that. He still could not control the terrible randomness of battle, but he'd just taken one tiny step, made one small decision for his own peace of mind, and with that the growing throb in his head receded. If the Germans used gas or flame weapons, he was dead, but he now had a much better chance of reaching the beach alive.

And the hell with Lieutenant Aldershot.

Eventually, the sky lightened, as the first lines of landing craft reached their jump-off points and started grinding in toward the beach. A heavy blanket of fog lay across the sea, silver-gray in the predawn light.

Thunder boomed, rolling in the near distance and then echoing from far-off cliffs. Scrambling up on the bow ramp, he could see over the LCM's side to port. Far off, on the horizon to the east, the American battleship *Arkansas* had just loosed her first salvo at the German beaches. She was answered, moments later, by a battery on the cliffs ashore.

Then the U.S.S. *Texas*, positioned several miles behind the bobbing LCM, cut loose with flame and thunder against Point du Hoc. A British cruiser, the *Glasgow*, and two French cruisers, *Montcalm* and *Georges Leygues*, added their voices to the argument. The bombardment thundered and boomed and howled, and shell after shell was hurled toward the beaches.

"My God," Aldershot said nearby, the coverall incident apparently forgotten. "We're gonna have it easy. *Nothing* could live through that!"

Wallace decided not to disillusion him.

GAT-4
Off Fox Green Beach

"It's gonna be a cakewalk!" Lieutenant Pinkowski shouted. He dropped down from the LCM's ramp and beamed at the engineers and Navy demolition men crowded onto the deck. "It's gonna be a fucking cakewalk! I can see shells hitting the beach and the hills. The smoke's so thick I don't think the German gunners are even gonna be able to see us!"

"Could you see the Saint Laurent Draw, sir?" Richardson called to him.

"Negative, Lieutenant. The smoke is too thick."

Fucking wonderful, Richardson thought. *That means we don't even know if we're on the right beach.* Theoretically, the landing boats were following carefully designated and buoyed channels al[1] the way in to their assigned landing beaches, but Richardson's experiences at Kwajalein had convinced him that things rarely went as planned in an operation as complex as this.

Hell, Kwajalein had been a Sunday afternoon parade compared with this incredible concentration of ships, aircraft, and troops. He'd heard somewhere—as one of the meaningless bits of trivia associated with any plan as massive as this—that Operation Neptune, the seaborne part of the invasion plan designated Overlord, included something like five thousand Allied ships, carrying two hundred thousand troops in the first wave.

That made Neptune, at a rough estimate, six or seven times larger than Operation Flintlock. There was scarcely any ground for comparison between the two.

Richardson looked at his watch. It was just past zero-six-hundred, which left thirty minutes to H-Hour. Balancing himself as the LCM thumped through a wave, he stood up, leaning over the starboard gunwale so that he could see, looking out over the beach for himself. Pinkowski was right. Much of the beach was obscured by smoke, and he couldn't see a single landmark made familiar by the briefings they'd had back in England.

He also couldn't see the lane markers that the boats were supposed to be following in.

Still, Pinkowski had one point. It didn't look like anything could survive the shellacking those cruisers and battlewagons were dishing out.

LCC-7
Off Easy Red Beach

The roar of the bombardment was deafening, guns booming and pounding and thundering across the choppy waters off Omaha. Rand, still in the LCC's open cockpit, turned and stared aft. "I don't see the DDs, Skipper," he said.

Tomlinson was already holding binoculars to his eyes, scanning the horizon, now thick with the massed vessels of the D-Day armada.

"You're right. What the hell happened?"

"It might be too rough, Lieutenant. Those canvas bloom-

ers might work well enough on paper, or in calm waters off
Slapton Beach—"

"Rand," Tomlinson said, lowering the binoculars. He had
to shout to be heard over the thunder of the shelling. A German 88 exploded forty feet off the starboard bow, sending
a towering geyser of white water into the sky. "Get aft and
tell Kent I intend to come about just off the beach and head
back out to the line of departure. If we can find those DDs,
we can lead them on in. If not, we'll start guiding the engineers in. He should fire the barrage as we come up to the
turnaround."

"Aye, sir."

He slid down the ladder, hands on the steel guide rails,
then trotted aft to where Ordnanceman First Class Kent and
his team were standing ready with the LCC's rocket
launcher.

"Stand by to fire," he told Kent, then repeated
Tomlinson's order. They were less than one hundred yards
off the beach now. Forward, Costigan and his men were at
the three-pounder, engaged in an uneven duel with German
88s ashore.

Quickly, Rand went all the way aft. Where the hell were
the DD tanks?

He never heard the explosion. The next thing he was even
aware of was fighting his way to the surface, spitting sea
water and gasping for breath. His Mae West held his face
above the waves, so for several moments he simply hung
there in the water, trying to breathe.

Rand was surprised to find he wasn't hurt. No broken
bones ... no wounds ... nothing but a dull, overall ache
that felt like he'd been bruised and beaten from head to
foot. There was no sign at all of the scout boat, but apparently he'd been blown clear, unharmed. Either the LCC had
struck a mine or a German artillery shell had made a lucky
hit on the scout boat's rockets. Either way, he was alone
now and adrift off the enemy beach.

Clumsy in the Mae West, he started swimming for shore.

GAT-5
Off Fox Green Beach

It was full light now, and the thunder of the naval bombardment reminded Tangretti forcefully of Kwajalein. Crouched in the well deck with the rest of his Gap Assault Team, he couldn't see the beach. He could hear it though, a steady slam-slam-slam of high explosives. He wondered if there would be any beach obstacles left for his team to take out. It sounded as though the Navy was giving Omaha Beach one hell of a god-awful pasting.

"One thousand yards!" Lieutenant Bishop yelled from the LCM's bow. He was standing behind the high bow ramp, peering over the forward quarter at the beach. Tangretti was with the other Navy men, clustered around the large, black, rubber boat that held much of their explosives and blasting equipment. He felt weighed down by his coveralls and equipment, but the adrenaline was pulsing through him now, generating energy he wasn't aware he'd possessed. Lieutenant Franklin stood in front of them looking at once foolish and heroic, a box of blasting caps perched on his left shoulder, his .45 pistol drawn, cocked, and locked in his right hand. They all wore their clumsy and uncomfortable gas suits, but no one had yet donned gloves, hoods, or gas masks. There'd been no indication yet that the Germans were employing gas, little response at all, in fact, save for a couple of wildly inaccurate potshots from the hills.

A savage, buzzing roar shrieked low overhead, and Tangretti looked up wildly. Aircraft!

Then he glimpsed the alternating black-and-white stripes on wings and fuselage, the special livery of all Allied planes over Normandy that day. They were big, four-engine bombers, Liberators, Tangretti thought, flying in low to pummel the beach ahead of the landing craft. He and the men with him cheered, thrusting clenched fists into the air. The B-24s roared low across the beach. Tangretti waited for them to loose their bomb loads . . . and waited . . . and waited . . .

The cheers of the men in the LCM died away, their excitement replaced by a baffled wonder. Moments later, fresh explosions crashed and rumbled from the shore, but far off, back well behind the dunes and hills.

"Damn Brylcreems," Franklin said, using the footslogger's derogatory term for the glamorous aviators. Then he laughed. "Never send the Air Force in to do a man's work!"

The rest of the team laughed at that, most of them. But Tangretti was scared. Everything in this operation was supposed to be so precisely planned, so precisely timed.

What was going wrong?

Let's get in there and get this business over with!

GAT-1
Off Dog Green Beach

The surf in close to the beach was rough. The landing craft bucked and slapped beneath him, and Wallace was caught up again in the nightmare of North Africa. A shell detonated yards beyond the boat, the concussion ringing against the boat's steel hull with piledriver force. Water spouted thirty feet into the sky, then rained back across the well deck of the boat, a sheet of rain that would have drenched them all had they not already been soaked to the skin.

And the bullets. The bullets were finding the landing craft now. He could hear them peck and chirp as they ricocheted off the hull. The Germans had opened up on them while they were still half a mile out, but so far none of the boats Wallace could see had been hit. He was surprised at how calm he felt. The pounding ... was completely gone. That realization filled him with a kind of wild, savage exultation.

"Fifty yards!" Lieutenant Caldwell, the senior officer in the engineering platoon, yelled back at the rest of them. "Get ready!"

Wallace stood shoulder to shoulder with the other Navy GAT men, the heavily loaded rubber boat slung between them. With one hand, he patted at various pieces of equipment: wire cutters, crimpers, inflatable life jacket, first aid kit, web belt, and canteen.

Another shell struck close by, staggering him. He had to reach out and support himself with a hand on the boat's hull. More water came over the bow. One of the GAT engineers crowded in close behind him gaped at the suddenly raining sky, his eyes wide and terrified. "Christ!" he called. "That was close!"

"Yeah," Wallace yelled back, trying to keep his voice light. "The Met boys weren't predicting fucking rain today!"

That raised a nervous laugh from those men close enough to hear. The engineer seemed to relax a little. *Come on! Come on! Get it the fuck over with!*

He looked at his watch: 0629 hours. Somewhere ahead of them, the DD tanks must just be wading up into the shallows, blazing away at any strong points that had survived the preliminary bombardment. Another shell slammed into the sea, and he reminded himself that no bombardment could be one hundred percent effective. There would always be a *few* survivors. . . .

One minute later, a company of infantry would land, following in close behind the tanks to mop up any snipers on the beach.

Then it would be their turn.

At 0633, just three minutes past H-Hour, Wallace felt the flat bottom of the boat's bow scraping across sand, felt the shudder as it drove hard against the shore and wedged itself in place. "Ramp coming down!" the LCM's coxswain yelled. With a clatter of chains, the ramp dropped, splashing as it struck the water. A stray bullet whined somewhere far overhead, lonely against the steady background roar of artillery.

"Let's go, engineers!" Lieutenant Caldwell yelled, and he thumped down the open ramp and into the water.

"Go Navy!" Wallace cried, and the seven other sailors of GAT-1, carrying the rubber raft between them, charged down the ramp with the engineers close behind.

The water was only about two feet deep here, just knee-high except when an incoming wave sloshed past at waist level. Wallace wondered if he should have ditched his coveralls, since he was obviously in no danger of drowning, but immediately rejected the thought. It was worth anything to be rid of that hot, heavy, cumbersome thing.

The Navy men dropped the raft to the water and pushed ahead, dragging it along between them. For the first time now, as he waded toward the shore, Wallace could really *see*.

He saw a long beach, thickly scattered with rows of obstacles. In the foreground a line of Belgian gates had been planted nearly shoulder to shoulder. The next rows were steel-rail stakes interspersed with dozens of inverted Vs, their narrow ends elevated; these were ramps designed to catch incoming landing craft at mid-to-high tide and capsize them, or destroy them with Teller mines mounted at their tips. Beyond the stakes and ramps were randomly scattered hedgehogs, the three-piece stacks of angle irons that could block a tank on dry land, or tear out the belly of an LCVP at high tide. Finally, at the far side of the three-hundred-yard-deep beach, he could see the heights, partly shrouded in smoke.

And yet the beach looked strangely, deceptively peaceful, despite the noise and the smoke, and it took Wallace a moment to realize why.

There was no one else on the beach. No DD tanks, no company of infantry. *No one!* Through mix-up or the blind confusion of invasion, the leading elements weren't here, and GAT-1 was the first goddamned team to hit the entire goddamned beach! The distinctive, high-pitched chatter of a German Maschinengewehr 42 sounded from somewhere up ahead, followed by the hollow-sounding *whump* of a mortar, and Wallace suddenly felt completely naked.

GAT-4
Off Fox Green Beach

Richardson had the definite feeling that things were going wrong. He leaned over the side of the LCM and remembered guys in the Pacific telling him stories about Tarawa. He wondered if something like this was what had led off that bloody day.

First of all, the German guns above the beach had *not* been silenced by either the offshore bombardment or the last-moment bombing by aircraft. Shells were whuffling in from the beach now, howling overhead to crash astern in vast sprays of white water, or falling short, detonating in a surge of spray, setting the LCM to rocking wildly as it crested the blast surge. He could hear machine guns, too, hammering away with an insistent chatter of promised blood.

Explosions kept going off one after another, some in the water, others among the thickly grown obstacles on the beach, snapping orange flame that was instantly lost in a boiling pillar of smoke.

And the *fires*. He counted a dozen boats and vehicles that had made it at least as far as the water's edge and were now on fire, the smoke of their burning drifting low across the beach, laying down a dirty fog that blurred but could not obscure the enemy-held hills beyond.

Movement caught his eye to the right. The LCM was passing one of the ungainly DD tanks, visible only as a white canvas ring encircling the top of a Sherman tank's turret. Damn. The DDs were supposed to have been launched well ahead of the LCMs, so that they would reach the beach first. It looked, however, as though everything had piled up wrong. Infantry was already on the beach, pouring from a long row of LCVPs. The tanks were still floundering in the water, and they were making slow headway in the rough surf.

Horrified, Richardson watched the DD tank to starboard lurch and shudder as a wave broke over its canvas skirts. Suddenly, literally in the blink of an eye, the tank was gone, sunk beneath the waves, its skirts torn open and its engine flooded.

A moment passed . . . and another. Then a head bobbed in the oily foam marking the DD tank's grave. The head, wearing a tanker's helmet, submerged once, then reappeared. The man was waving wildly, signaling for help.

But neither Richardson's LCM nor any of the other landing craft riding in through the surf could even consider stopping to pick up one man, not with the traffic so thick, not with German shells crashing and booming among them with their deadly, appalling thunder.

In another second, the head was gone.

Richardson looked away. To port, though, it was no better. One hundred yards away, an LCVP had been hit by a mortar shell. The entire landing craft was ablaze, and Richardson could see men burning on her deck. Others were

leaping overboard, some with their clothing on fire, prefer-
ring a long swim to shore to roasting alive.

They were about three hundred yards out from the shore
now. Richardson could see the black heads of obstacles half
submerged just below the water line, each of them topped
by its own deadly Teller mine. Beyond the water line, small
groups of men were beginning to cluster around the bases of
the obstacles, and he could make out several still, dark
shapes sprawled on the open sand, the first Americans to die
on this already bloody beach.

He heard the shrill whine of an incoming round, and
wondered whether this one would pass over or fall short.
The explosion, when it came, was close . . . too close. The
LCM staggered in the water as a waterfall howled down
onto the deck, knocking Richardson to his hands and knees.
Six inches of oily, stinking water were sloshing across the
deck.

Were they sinking? Damn, he should tell Gator to check
the bilges . . .

Only Gator wasn't here.

The next shall slammed into the LCM somewhere astern;
he felt the deck buckle, felt the stern rising, and then he was
hurling against the boat's bulkhead with a painful thump.
Smoke was boiling from the aft end of the boat, and he
knew a sharp stab of fear. Sitting on top of one ton of explosives in a burning LCM was definitely not his idea of a
good time.

Turning, he yelled at the Gap Assault men clustered
around the rubber boat. "Get ready to go! Williams! Release
the bow winches!"

Fire was boiling from the aft end of the LCM, and he
could feel the boat settling lower in the water. Chief Williams yanked on the port winch release, then moved to the
starboard side and loosed the second winch. The bow ramp
started opening, admitting two walls of emerald green water
spilling in past the sides of the ramp. The LCM, which had
been moving ahead at perhaps four knots, shuddered and
went dead in the water as its well deck started filling up.
Some of the engineers clambered over the gunwales and
started swimming. A shattering blast tore through the air
from astern; Richardson didn't know whether they'd been

hit again or whether flames had touched off explosives or gasoline. Fire was spreading across the water as he and the rest of the GAT shoved the rubber boat past the half-open bow ramp, then clung to it as it floated free of the LCM. He could hear someone screaming, a high-pitched wail of terror and pain.

He couldn't stop. None of them could stop. Kicking ahead in their heavy coveralls, the Navy team, plus a number of engineers, struggled forward through the surf, clinging for their lives to the overloaded raft.

GAT-5
Off Fox Green Beach

Tangretti's LCM ground onto a bar, slid for a yard over wet sand, then lurched to a stop. A geyser of white water fountained twenty yards to port, then cascaded back onto a foaming, shot-torn sea littered with floating debris and struggling men.

First the bombers had dumped their loads too far inland. Next, for whatever reason, the initial landing waves had gotten mixed up. The engineer platoons were supposed to have gone in right behind the DD tanks and covering infantry, but Tangretti didn't see any tanks ashore yet . . . only landing craft, some of them burning, and hordes of wet, struggling men.

"Ramp's coming down!" Lieutenant Bishop yelled. He vaulted onto the bow ramp the instant it splashed into the sea, took three steps, then flopped over backward as though jerked by a wire. As he dropped onto the deck, Tangretti saw that the engineer's left eye was gone, replaced by a gaping red hole. Machine gun fire rattled from the drifting banks of smoke hovering above the hills just three hundred yards away.

Tangretti leaped forward, caught in the press of the other Navy and Army personnel in the landing craft all trying to crowd down the ramp at once, hauling the rubber boat filled with explosives along with one hand, clinging to a load of Hagensen Packs with the other. He splashed into the water with a lurch and nearly fell. The water was waist-deep, with a surf that surged past intermittently and lifted him from his feet. Each time, he clung to the rubber boat along with the others, half walking, half swimming, as together they pulled the raft toward the beach.

Obstacles protruded from the water everywhere, rising above the heads of the struggling men. Gouts of water splashed and hissed, stitching a line across the water. One of the engineers grabbed at his helmet, then vanished, swallowed by the sea. Tangretti opened his mouth to call to one of the other engineers, to tell him to see to the fallen man, when with a loud cough the rubber boat began deflating. Bullets had torn through the fabric and collapsed its flotation cells. Another engineer stumbled, clutching both hands over a face suddenly transformed into a mash of blood. A sailor doubled over, then sank in a bloody froth.

"The explosives!" Tangretti yelled at the others. "Get the explosives!" But one of the CDU sailors and two Army men were down, dead or drowning. Another soldier and a Navy engineman second class named Rollins tried to grab the satchels from the boat, but the rubber boat was already going under. More machine gun bullets slashed through the little group. The engineer pitched back, his helmet and half of the top of his head blown away in a bloody spray. Tangretti lunged forward, trying to grab some of the team's precious demolition charges . . .

. . . and felt the bottom drop out from beneath his feet.

The next breath he drew was a strangling gulp of salt water as he sank into blackness.

Chapter 30

Tuesday, 6 June 1944

GAT-5
Off Fox Green Beach

As Tangretti sank beneath the surface, the raw, thundering noise of the battle was muted to a distant throb. He was in wet blackness, sinking into a yawning shell hole of unguessable proportions.

His gear was weighing him down.

For a moment, the old panic, the dread of deep water that he'd thought he'd finally licked at Kwajalein, closed in on him. He struggled, dropping the Hagensen Packs slung from his shoulders, tearing at the straps holding his pack, at his web belt, at the chin strap holding his helmet on his head. He was strangling . . . drowning. . . .

Then, somehow, he forced the panic back. Groping at his chest, he found the pull-ring for his inflatable life vest. With a loud hiss, the vest inflated around his chest and collar.

Instantly he popped to the surface, gasping and sputtering, his feet dangling in the deep water. Spray exploded from an impact two feet to his left, and he felt the shock of the projectile as it seared through the water. Bullets shrieked and hissed, passing inches above his head or splashing into the water. For a horrifying instant, Tangretti felt as though every German gun on that entire stretch of fire-torn beach was aimed directly at him.

Reaching up again, he grabbed the release straps on his flotation vest, tugged them loose, and then with a surge of almost pure joy freed himself from the vest. He sank again, leaving the vest afloat on the surface. Underwater, he pulled off his pack, unzipped his water-heavy coveralls, and kicked his way out of them.

Lighter now, he began to swim.

Fox Green Beach

Rand splashed ashore through the surf, onto the fire-swept beach. Dozens of landing craft had passed him by during his long swim to shore, and the beach was already crowded with men, some making their way up through the tangle of beach obstacles facing the sea, most still huddled at the water's edge.

Bullets cracked overhead or whined off steel obstructions. Explosions roared, on the beach and in the water, sleeting the troops with spray and wet sand. On his knees, Rand stripped off his Mae West, then began looking around for a weapon. A dead sergeant lay on his back nearby, his legs still awash in the surf, an M-1 Thompson submachine gun slung over his shoulder.

Stooping above the dead soldier, who would have no further use for the stuff, Rand pulled off the Thompson, then unbuckled a web belt, which included a canvas pouch stuffed with loaded magazines for the weapon, and two AN-M8 HC smoke grenades.

Now what? Rand studied the chaos of the beach. This was not Easy Red, that was certain. He suspected that the current had dragged him to the east. It might be Fox Green, though with all the smoke and confusion, he couldn't be certain.

All around him, men continued to straggle ashore. The gunfire from the bluffs overlooking the beach was ferocious, but there might be some shelter to be found at the top of the beach, along the sea wall below the foot of those hills.

Clutching the Thompson, Rand started zigzagging up the beach, using the obstacles as cover.

GAT-1
Dog Green Beach

Wallace splashed onto the beach, laden with Hagensen Packs, forty-pound packs of demolition gear, and a backpack filled with other equipment. Glad that he'd ditched the coveralls, he turned to begin directing the unloading of the LCM.

Half a dozen CDU sailors trotted out of the water, the rubber raft slung between them. Lieutenant Aldershot was close behind them, standing in water halfway up to his knees, his arm outstretched, shouting orders to the rest of the Navy men strung out between the water's edge and the landing craft.

The explosion seared Wallace's eyes; Aldershot was engulfed in a fountaining column of smoke and water. Something slammed hard into Wallace's gut, stinging, and for an agonized instant he thought that he'd been hit by shrapnel. Looking down, he saw blood splattered across his khaki shirt ... but no wound. *No wound!* A severed hand, fingers half clenched in an ugly claw, lay palm up at his feet.

Aldershot's hand. The Navy lieutenant's leg and lower torso floated in a pink swirl a few yards away, ropy entrails pilling endlessly into the water. Wallace gagged on rising bile, then forced it down. He would *not* be sick!

"Come on! Move it! Move it!" he shouted. With Aldershot dead, he was senior man in the Navy team. He looked around for the Army engineering platoon leader but couldn't see him. Smoke hung thick on the beach, reducing visibility to a few yards. "Get up that beach, damn you! You want to stay here and get blown to bits?"

Like Aldershot. Bad choice of words. But the men responded, trotting up from the waterline. Wallace led them to the shelter of the nearest Belgian gate, then began directing them in the placement of their Hagensen Packs. Soon, Frazier and Kaminsky were well on the way to having the first gate wired; Wallace ordered Bronson, Daystrom, and a kid named Bosilivic to the next line of obstacles. An Army engineer began unreeling a length of primacord from the gate to the ramp. Ideally, they would wire a number of obstacles together with primacord and blow them all at once.

GAT-5
Fox Green Beach

It was slow going, swimming forward in the blackness, but Tangretti could still sense the surge of the tide moving in toward the beach, and in a moment he was past the shell hole and his boots were again scraping along on the sand. He surfaced five yards closer to the shore, took a deep breath as bullets sighed and snickered past his head, then submerged once more. When he broke through again, he was close to the surf line, and the waves were breaking past his shoulders. He emerged at last on hands and knees, dripping wet and without any of his equipment, but at least he'd made it from the water's black embrace.

By the time he splashed ashore, Omaha Beach was already a shambles. Obstructions, the beach defenses he'd trained for months to destroy, were everywhere, waiting for the engineering teams to go in and clear them out, but the teams were scattered, their equipment missing or sunk, the DD tanks that were to have protected them lost, and the infantry squads that should have provided cover scattered about the beach in small, huddled groups, hiding behind obstacles or still struggling ashore through fire-swept waves. Many were dead. Everywhere Tangretti looked there were bodies, alone or in sad, tiny groups.

Only then did he realize that all of the men in his assault team were dead, wounded, or missing. He was alone on a beach crowded with strangers, while the Germans on the bluffs overlooking the beach tried their best to kill him.

GAT-4
Fox Green Beach

Richardson was sure this wasn't Easy Red Beach, where GAT-4 was supposed to have landed. With all of the smoke and confusion, nothing looked exactly like what it was supposed to look like; certainly it didn't resemble the photos BM1 Rand had shown them back in the safe, quiet confines of their English headquarters.

Straight ahead of him, the bluffs above the beach opened in what was obviously one of the five ravines debouching onto Omaha Beach. But which one? It looked quite large, a wide gap in the hills at least five hundred yards wide, with a massive concrete barrier of some sort stretching from one side to the other. It looked too wide and deep to be the draw leading to Saint Laurent. It might be the Colleville Draw, but if it was, that meant their landing craft had shifted a whole beach to the east, missing their original target by as much as a mile.

He continued to cling to the rubber boat, however, along with five sailors and eight or ten Army engineers. The tide carried them along fairly smoothly, helped along by their weakening kicks.

Then sand scraped under Richardson's boot. He stumbled, nearly went under, then staggered into waist-deep water. Walking, then, the close-bunched crowd of engineers and demolitioneers walked the last hundred yards to the shore as shells and mortar bursts continued to splash and thunder and roar on every side.

Other survivors of their LCM were coming ashore at the same place. Richardson spotted Lieutenant Pinkowski thirty yards up the beach, helping Lederson out of the surf. Chief Williams was closer, lying flat on the sand behind a sheltering hedgehog along with three engineers.

Richardson dropped into the shelter of a Belgian gate close to the water's edge, peering past the crisscross of its steel girders to study the heights beyond the beach. There was a sea wall up there, close to the base of the hills. A hardy handful of soldiers had already made it that far, though most were pinned down among the obstacles right here at the waterline. There were already at least ten men huddled behind this one Belgian gate, and similar groups were gathering at other obstacles all along the water's edge.

The mingled sounds of the shells overhead were fascinating. The big rounds from the warships offshore sounded like tearing canvas. The shrill rasp of the German artillery, especially their 88s, sounded harsher, flatter somehow, and the crack and whump of their detonations were like the unleashing of Hell itself.

Machine guns fired from the gray-green heights, probing, sweeping the beach in clearly defined lanes of fire. Looking back out to sea, Richardson saw four soldiers struggling ashore, their rifles held high to keep them dry. A German machine gun near the big gap opened fire, tracers flicking like yellow fireflies from man to man, raising six-foot spouts of water and cutting the soldiers down, from back to front in a rapid-fire four-three-two-one succession.

He reached for the .45 in its holster dangling from his web belt, then restrained the impulse. Blazing away at those hills might make him feel better but it would accomplish absolutely nothing. Instead, it was time to get things moving here. Most of his CDU had made it ashore. And they still had a job to do.

He turned to the men hiding behind the gate. "You guys better move," he warned. There was no immediate response, and certainly no eagerness to brave the hail of bullets and flying chunks of metal beyond the imagined shelter of the gate. Richardson looked around at the other obstacles. Perhaps they could start the clearing someplace else . . . but by now, every structure on that fire-swept beach had its quota of men huddled in its shelter.

This was as good a place to start as any.

"Williams!" he barked. Then louder, "Chief Williams!"

The chief turned, saw him, then rose to his feet and scrambled across a stretch of open sand. Bullets snapped overhead. An explosion tore at the water fifty yards behind them. Richardson was already on his knees, tearing at the lashings of the equipment in the raft.

"Yes, sir!"

"Help me get this shit unloaded. You! Truett! Yes, you! Get over here!"

Soon, he'd managed to assemble nine of the original thirteen men in his GAT—seven sailors, including himself, plus two of the engineers. Swiftly, with practiced speed, they began unloading two-pound Hagensen Packs and secured them to the key points on the gate. Truett and Richardson began tying together the lengths of primacord, forming the ring main and trunk line.

It was time to move the men sheltering behind the obstacle.

"You guys better move up the beach!" he told them. "Go on! Get a move on! This thing is rigged to blow!"

The soldiers hesitated, then reluctantly broke into small groups and started moving to other nearby obstacles.

The firestorm continued, machine guns yammering, shells booming. The mortars were especially bad, explosion after explosion hurling up thick mushrooms of smoke and mud with a dull crump that was painful to the ear.

As he worked, Richardson saw an LCVP motoring up to the beach, grounding a few yards out. Its ramp came down with a splash and the soldiers aboard stormed out. A German machine gun opened up before the first man hit the water, sending round after hellish round slashing through the closely packed troops, cutting them down in a bloody, tangled mass.

At least ten men out of thirty-six were down, dead or wounded. Their comrades, most of them, pushed on past, dropping into the water and wading for the shore. Others stopped to help the wounded; many of them were hit as they tried to drag a wounded friend to the illusory safety of the beach.

At the back of the Belgian gate, Gunner's Mate First Class Harry Kline reached up to plant a Hagensen Pack over part of the support, staggered, and went down, a hole the size of a fist blown through his spine. Truett crawled over, picked up the dropped pack, and started tucking it into place. Men died. The work continued without letup.

The last primacord knot was tied, the last Hagensen Pack in place. Back in England, practice and experience had reduced the number of packs necessary from twenty to sixteen, but those charges would still make one hell of a blast when they went off. Richardson unrolled a length of fuse, then crouched to attach a pull-wire igniter.

But he couldn't fire it.

The first group of soldiers had moved on, but eight more members of the U.S. 1st Division, survivors from that LCVP he'd seen caught in the machine gun burst, had obviously decided that the huge Belgian gate made splendid cover. They crouched behind the ten-foot-square face of the obstacle, the water of the incoming tide swirling past their legs, a little higher up the beach with each incoming wave.

Richardson left the others with the fuse and stalked back down the beach. "C'mon, you guys!" he yelled. "You gotta move! We're gonna blow this thing!"

Some of the men blinked up at him with empty eyes.

Others refused to meet his eyes at all, and one sergeant reached out with a hand that trembled and extended his middle finger. An 88-mm shell detonated thirty yards away, an ear-tearing thud as it exploded in the wet sand and hurled a geyser of mud into the sky. Somewhere close by, a man was screaming with raw, unendurable agony.

Richardson looked at the huddled men again, searching for the highest rank present. As he'd feared, the sergeant was the only noncom there. The rest of them were privates. *Kids. . . .*

Crouched over, Richardson moved closer to the sergeant. "Sarge! Listen to me!" he shouted. "You've got to get your men in hand! You can't stay here, you understand?"

"Go fuck yerself," the man muttered at him. "These ain't my men!"

Richardson reached down with his left hand, grabbed the sergeant by his collar, and yanked him upright to his knees. With his right hand, he reached back, swung hard, and slapped the sergeant hard across the face.

"I don't give a fuck whose men they are," Richardson bellowed, his face inches from the sergeant's. "You're a soldier in the United States Army and you're fucking well going to assume the responsibility that you've got in those stripes you're wearing on your arm. You read me, mister?"

The sergeant stammered something and Richardson slapped him again, then gave him a furious shove that sent him sprawling back onto the sand, beyond the cover of the obstacle. Stooping quickly, Richardson picked up the man's M-1, snapped it to a crisp, military port arms, then threw it at him. The sergeant reached up just barely in time to catch it.

"You!" Richardson bellowed, pointing at the sergeant. "Move to that sea wall! That's an order!" He spun, pointing now at the other seven soldiers, who were watching the drama unfolding beside them. "The rest of you, all of you! Go with him! Now *MOVE!*"

The sergeant scrambled to his feet. For one horrifying moment, Richardson thought the sergeant might be tempted to shoot him. Certainly, the man was wavering between two choices. Then his face cleared, and he nodded jerkily. "Yes, sir! Come on, men! Follow me!"

He sprinted toward the sea wall, running wildly, falling in a spray of sand, getting up, and running again. First one . . . then three more of the soldiers followed him, hurling themselves up that deadly shelf of beach in a literal race for their lives. A machine gun on the hillside opened fire, its evil chatter clearly audible across the bark and bellow of exploding shells. One of the runners staggered, threw his arms high, and collapsed facedown in a motionless pile. The man behind him stopped to check on him, then he was hit as well, twisting away as blood splattered from his face in a broad crimson arc.

Three men remained behind the barricade. Richardson reached down and grabbed one of them, dragged him into the open, and dropped him. "Get the hell off my beach!"

The soldier rose, hesitated as though thinking over the matter of property rights, and then turned and ran after the sergeant. The next soldier needed no further urging. He bolted for the open as Richardson turned to confront him.

The last private continued to huddle facedown and motionless on the sand, and Richardson, with a horrible presentiment, reached out and grabbed the man's shoulder. When he pulled him over, he saw the bullet hole, staring like a red-rimmed eye from the kid's forehead, just beneath the rim of his helmet.

The Belgian gate was clear. Richardson took out one of his marker smoke grenades, pulled the pin, and tossed it into the area. As purple smoke boiled across the blast sight, he raced back across the sand, threw himself flat, checked to see that the rest of his team was clear, then grabbed the fuse igniter, already carefully packaged inside its watertight prophylactic.

"Fire in the hole!" he yelled, and yanked on the igniter wire. A moment later, white smoke sizzled off the burning fuze, cut for two minutes. Richardson sprinted to where the rest of the team was hiding, huddled about the base of another obstacle.

Seconds later, there was a roar, and the Belgian gate vanished in a twinkling of flashes and a swirling cloud of smoke. When the smoke cleared, nothing was left of the gate but the flattened tangle of twisted, severed steel girders.

GAT-1
Dog Green Beach

Wallace hooked the bare end of one wire over the battery terminal and clamped it down, then hooked the other end to the hellbox, the hand-held detonator.

"Hang on, Chief," Frazier warned him. "We got problems!"

"I see what you mean."

A dozen soldiers, crawling out of the water, had taken shelter behind the Belgian gate. He couldn't crank up the hellbox until they were clear.

"Hand me a couple of igniters," he told Kaminsky. He took them, checking to see that lengths of cut fuse extended from the tied-off prophylactics. "Be right back," he told the others.

Wet sand kicked and splattered about his feet as he ran, and once he felt something pluck at his shirt collar. The ground shook with the concussion of an exploding 88, and he nearly fell headlong.

Sliding to the ground behind the Belgian gate, he grinned at the startled soldiers. "Show time!" Wallace told them. He pulled out the two fuse-and-igniter assemblies, tucked them into empty slots in the face of the gate, and yanked on the igniter wires inside their prophylactics. "You guys better run 'cause this fucker's gonna blow! You got two minutes!"

The fuses started smoking and the soldiers started running. By the time the fuses burned out harmlessly, the area was safely clear. He tossed a purple smoke grenade and then ran back across the beach. Accepting the detonator from Bronson, he reattached a wire that had been pulled for safety and twisted the plunger.

With a shattering detonation, primacord and plastic explosives erupted in smoke and flame, thundering through a tightly contained pattern of obstacles. When the smoke cleared, the Belgian gate, two ramps, and a large number of mined stakes and hedgehogs had all been flattened or blasted to bits.

"Good job," Wallace said. "Let's get on to the next bunch."

GAT-5
Fox Green Beach

Tangretti was on the beach, but he had no equipment, no explosives, not even a .30-caliber carbine, no way to begin the daunting task of removing beach obstacles unless he was willing to start digging them up with his helmet.

Keeping low, he'd picked his way past the rows of mined obstacles until he reached the high-tide line. There, a weathered sea wall huddled against the sandy bluff overlooking the beach. He could hear the bark and rattle of gunfire from the heights overhead but couldn't see the enemy.

It was a strange reflection on modern warfare, he thought. Not once yet had he actually seen one of the enemy. He knew where they were, certainly, from the sounds of gunfire. If he stood up and looked, he was sure he would have been able to see their muzzle flashes, but only an idiot would so expose himself on that beach that morning for the sake of simple curiosity.

Obviously, the enemy had no trouble at all seeing the Americans. Those pathetic clumps of waterlogged men sheltering behind the beach obstacles made ideal targets. Better targets were the men still moving in the surf, or those who'd waded onto the beach and were trying to reach the sea wall. As he watched, man after man staggered and went down.

Other men had managed to brave the fire and reach the sea wall. Some had reacted with that age-old instinct of soldiers everywhere and started to dig, creating a trench in front of the sea wall. Several medics crouched nearby, giving first aid to wounded men.

Tangretti held no claim to being a military genius, but he could look at the wreckage and death cluttered across Omaha Beach and know that the invasion was in serious trouble. Most of the men were pinned down at the water's edge; the only reason they hadn't been swept back into the sea, ironically, was the cover provided by the beach obstacles intended to stop them there.

But they wouldn't be able to stay there for long. The tide was coming in, and very quickly, each foam-edged wave lapping farther up on the sand than the last. Already, men who'd been sheltering behind Belgian gates on dry sand were now crouched in water a foot deep. Inexorably, the incoming tide was driving the soldiers up the beach. Soon, the mass of humanity pressed against the sea wall, leaderless and disorganized, would become too vast and cumbersome, and far too demoralized, to do anything at all except surrender.

A dull but savage boom from the water's edge caught his attention. There, to his left as he faced the hills, some three hundred yards farther to the east, smoke boiled from the sand and surf in a pattern he knew only too well.

Demolitioneers were working there!

Tangretti was overcome with something akin to loneliness. He knew none of these hollow-eyed men huddling behind the sea wall beside him, though he felt a certain kinship based on the simple fact that all of them had made it from the boats to this desolate strip of sand and rock.

But down there, at the water's edge, someone was blowing gaps through the obstacles.

A GAT. It had to be.

Rising, his knees a little shaky, Tangretti started walking along the sea wall, heading east toward a point above the gap-clearing operation. Here, next to the wall, he actually felt fairly safe, for the Germans on the top of the ridge couldn't depress their weapons enough to hit the men behind the wall.

And he had to reach that clearing team. He might find only Army engineers but, hell, at least they would speak the same language he did.

He nudged his walk into a slow, sand-eating trot.

GAT-1
Fox Green Beach

Wallace's CDU had completed the task of blowing a gap through the obstacles all the way from the water's edge to the high-tide mark. They'd then begun the painstaking and dangerous task of moving up the cleared lane, tying green buoy markers on precisely measured lengths of line to the obstacles on either side. When the tide moved in, submerging the obstacles, those buoys would mark the safe path for incoming boats.

That task done, the Navy men moved up beyond the high-tide line and began assisting the Army engineering platoon in their task.

At the water's edge, a DD tank rumbled up out of the sea, water cascading in green and white torrents from the accordion folds of its canvas apron. The M1A3 Sherman rumbled twenty feet up out of the water, paused, and then its turret traversed a few degrees to the left. There was a bark, flame licking from the muzzle of the Sherman's 75-mm gun, and the whole tank rocked back on its treads. Wallace didn't see where the shell went, somewhere into the mist-shrouded hills above, he guessed. The tank rumbled forward once more, wet sand spilling in small avalanches from its whirling tracks.

Wallace lay in the sand, watching it move up the beach toward the GAT. Belching diesel fumes, it rumbled squarely through the gap his team had just blasted through the obstacles. There were a number of tanks on this half of the beach. Earlier, while talking to an Army colonel about which obstacles to take on next, he'd learned that on the east side of Omaha, off Easy Green, Easy Red, and Fox Green, the DD tanks had been a disaster.

There, the LCT skippers had released their tanks, as planned, a full three miles off shore. In those rough waves, and with the scything, devastating sweep of German fire, very few tanks had survived the long, deadly swim to shore. The situation on the western half of Omaha, Wallace had been told, was better. An alert LCT skipper had seen his first DD tank sink and drown the instant it rolled off the ramp, taking its entire crew to the bottom with it. He'd braved the fire from shore, then, taking the remaining DD tank ashore, and the other LCT skippers had followed suit. They took serious damage from mortar and artillery fire, but most of the DD tanks were safely landed in water shallow enough for them to run up to the shore in a conventional manner.

An explosion erupted among the steel tetrahedra forty yards away. A second blast followed, closer, and then a third, the last one close to the Army engineers working on the inner lane of obstacles. The 88s on this part of the beach, Wallace had already noted, tended to fire in quick groups of three.

Lieutenant Caldwell, the CO of the engineering platoon working with the GAT, threw himself down in the sand next to Wallace. "Those damned tin-can jockeys are drawing fire!" he yelled.

The tank was drawing closer now, the rumble of its engine drowning out the clatter of small arms fire from the hills at Wallace's back. More bullets spanged off the hull of the Sherman. Another 88 blast tore up the sand, and shrapnel rattled off three-inch steel. The next explosion landed among the engineers and the CDU, hurling Kaminsky like a broken doll twelve feet across the beach. Two engineers writhed on the sand, suddenly, shockingly, bloody.

"Aw, shit!" Caldwell snapped.

"Take care of your boys," Wallace told him. "I'll see what can be done about that tank!"

He lay in the sand until the third round howled overhead, exploding farther down the gap. Then he rose to his feet and sprinted down the open gap. The tank stopped, its turret traversing again, aiming at a point almost immediately behind and above Wallace's back. He threw himself flat as the gun howled again, and he felt the breath of the 75-mm shell slap his back as it passed. Rolling on his side and looking back, he saw the Sherman's target—a squat concrete pillbox located atop the ridge, perhaps two hundred yards away. Funny. That damned thing had been sitting up there all this time, and Wallace hadn't even noticed it.

The Sherman was in a duel with the pillbox, but it was obvious that the tank's 75-mm gun wasn't powerful enough to more than scratch the armored strongpoint's casement.

He got up and ran again.

Something struck him from behind, high up, behind his left shoulder. There was no pain, nothing more than a slight shock, as though someone had punched him. He kept running. Bullets sang and shrieked off the Sherman's armor, leaving small gray smudges to mark their passing.

Reaching the Sherman's side, he yelled for the commander to open up. There was no response, save another thunderous roar from the main gun. Looking around the beach, Wallace found an M-1 rifle lying in the sand. Picking

it up, he trotted back to the Sherman. His left arm felt a little numb after the blow he'd experienced, so he reached up
as high as he could with the right and slammed the butt of
the rifle against the base of the turret once . . . twice . . . and
again, the impacts ringing loud. After a moment, there was
a clank from inside, a hatch on the turret swung up, and the
Sherman's commander, his face black with grease and powder, peered down at him from above. "What the *fuck?*"

"Would you mind parking this thing somewhere else?"
Wallace yelled. "You're drawing fire and killing my men!"

"Just where the fuck do you suggest we go?"

Wallace pointed to a clear strip between two lines of obstacles to the east. "Through there! No mines, we checked!
And you can join up with a couple more tanks down there!"

Another 88-mm round thundered farther down the
beach . . . and another . . . and another. Sand and gravel
splattered across the tank's engine cover.

"Shit!" the tankman barked, and vanished. The hatch
came down with a clang. The engine raced, spewing fumes,
and Wallace had to jump out of the way as the drive reversed the left track and threw the right track forward. The
tank slewed left, then clattered toward the engineering platoon. He was starting to feel the strain, he thought. He was
tired, and his arm and side felt numb.

"Aw, shit, Bill," the lieutenant said. "What happened to
you?"

He looked down then and saw that the left side of his
shirt was soaked with blood. Until that moment, he'd not realized that he'd been hit.

"You'd better sit down."

"I'm okay, Lieutenant. Arm's just a bit numb." He tried
to work the fingers of his left hand, but they responded
sluggishly, as though they were asleep. It looked like the
round had passed clean through his upper shoulder, from
back to front. Strange. There was still no pain. He'd thought
being wounded would hurt more.

"Sit down! That's an order. Medic! Medic!"

An Army medic scrambled up, clutching his satchel of
first aid supplies. As he opened it, Wallace noticed that it
was almost empty.

"Just put a patch on it, Doc," he told the soldier. "I've got work to do."

Moments later, the engineers fired the last set of charges and the gap was clear all the way from the water to the foot of the bluffs. Wallace glanced at his watch and was astonished to learn that it was 0655 hours.

He's been ashore for just twenty-two minutes.

Chapter 31

Tuesday, 6 June 1944

Above Fox Green Beach

Frank Rand had been crouching in the shelter of the sea wall for half an hour, watching the incoming waves of infantry. He felt a strangely detached, floating sensation, as though this hell of noise and blood and fury were simply a rather fragmented dream.

All of his life, Rand had wanted to accomplish something great, something for which his Marine-hero father might have been proud. Looking down on the beach now, watching the shambles of blood and flame and smoke that the quiet beach had become, he knew that he had accomplished something.

But what?

Since swimming ashore from the wreck of the LCC, he'd seen nothing like an organized plan for getting off the beach. Men continued to straggle up out of the water, some sheltering behind obstacles, some making it all the way to the sea wall, some with their weapons and equipment, many without. Along his portion of the sea wall, Rand saw no officers and only a few noncoms. Without leaders, the men were more like survivors than soldiers, cold, wet, and numb from the steady bombardment and machine-gunning. From one end of the beach to the other, so far as Rand could see, the Omaha invasion had been stopped cold almost at the water's edge—exactly as Rommel was supposed to have planned it. He could see at least five tanks burning, DD tanks that had survived the heavy seas only to be blasted by the 88s mounted on top of the bluffs. A few tanks continued to move and fire, but they were clearly outclassed by the defensive emplacements and guns. They would continue to be picked off one by one until the draws penetrating the ridgeline at the back of the beach could be taken and cleared.

So . . . how to do that?

Carefully, with a slow deliberation learned at the Fort Pierce Scouts and Raiders School, he examined his Thompson submachine gun, checked each moving part, careful not to get any sand into its workings.

It would be nice, he thought, if he could actually fire the damned thing sometime this morning.

This hill at his back wouldn't be so difficult to climb. He could do it with his bare hands. The first twenty feet or so were pretty steep, but he knew he would find handholds in the rock. Then the face of the slope started angling back. He would find cover in the draws and saddles molded into the hill.

With a satisfying *snick* he slapped a thirty-round box magazine into the magazine well, then dragged back the charging lever, locking the bolt. The soldiers crouched behind the sea wall to either side watched him incuriously or else ignored him entirely.

Screw them. Rising, he swung a leg over the sea wall, dropped to the other side, then started moving up the slope. The soldiers, most of them, watched, but none stirred from their spots.

With his Thompson slung over his shoulder, he started climbing.

After the first few feet, he discovered a gully in the slope, an eroded channel in the soft rock that formed a kind of steep path cutting across the face of the hill toward the left. Following this, alert for trip wires and booby traps, he soon reached a place where the gully angled back to the left, a clear path zigzagging toward the crest of the ridge.

Thompson in hand, he followed it.

GAT-4
Fox Green Beach

Richardson lay flat in the sand. Purple smoke boiled across the blast area. "Hit the deck!" he yelled. "Fire in the hole!"

He yanked the igniter wire, then scrambled for cover. Moments later, a tremendous explosion tore through the dozens of ramps, dragon's teeth, and hedgehogs scattered above the high-tide mark.

A good job. Moments before, a DUKW, an amphibious six-wheeled vehicle, half boat and half truck, had driven up the beach . . . and right across a length of primacord linking two sets of charges. Richardson and Chief Williams had dashed forward to tie the severed cord together again. A burst of machine gun fire had slashed into Williams, wounding him. Richardson had completed tying off his length of primacord, crawled back to Williams and fixed his section, then carried the wounded man back down the beach.

But now the gap had been cleared. The way was open now all the way to the beach end of the Colleville draw.

That ravine was a final, seemingly insurmountable obstacle, sealed off by barbed wire and backed up by concrete emplacements and machine gun nests, both in the ravine itself and atop the bluffs on either side. Richardson, stooped over as gunfire sleeted past, trotted up the beach to the sea wall. There, sheltered from the fire above, Lieutenant Pinkowski was crouched in a shallow ditch with some of his surviving engineers.

Four of the eight Navy men were dead, as well as ten of the engineers. "Lederson!" Richardson shouted. "Truett! Get back down there and start marking the lane."

"Aye, aye, sir!" Truett snapped. "C'mon, Lederson!"

The two CDU men scrambled back down the exposed beach. Richardson turned to the lieutenant, jerking a thumb over his shoulder. "Looks to me like our next job is that ravine. Can we take it together?"

Pinkowski shook his head. "Unfortunately, Lieutenant," he said, "that was the last of our explosives. We didn't salvage much off the boat."

"Damn! Where can we get some more?"

"God, I don't know." His eyes looked wild, haunted by the incessant shelling. "It's all coming apart. What are we going to *do*? Half my men are dead—"

Richardson reached down, grabbed the lieutenant's shoulder, and shook him, hard. "Easy, sir! Easy! We'll pull it off! Can do, okay? *Can do!*"

Pinkowski was trembling, his eyes glassy. Shock, Richardson decided. The man had just been hit by too much, too fast.

Standing, Richardson looked around at the surviving engineers. Many of them didn't look like they were in much better shape than their commander. "Okay," Richardson shouted, addressing them all. "We need explosives. Bangalore torpedoes for the wire. Satchel charges for the wall. You!" He pointed at a sergeant. "And you!" He pointed at a corporal. "Round up as many men as you can and start scouring the area for stuff we can use!"

"Damn it, Lieutenant," one engineer said. "We *did* our bit—"

"Our *bit* isn't done until the Army's got tanks and men moving up that damned ravine inland! We're gonna blow that roadblock! We need explosives! Find them!"

" 'Scuse me," a voice called behind Richardson's back. "Will *these* do?"

Richardson spun, eyes wide. *"Gator!"*

Tangretti stood there, five feet away, with a silly, lopsided grin on his face. Heavy in his arms were two forty-pound bags of Hagensen Packs.

Richardson advanced on his friend. "God*damn* it, Gator!" He threw his arms around the startled Tangretti, hugged him so hard he dropped both satchels, then stepped back and clapped him on the shoulders. "Where the hell did *you* come from?"

"Oh, just down the beach. I sort of lost my unit, and I lost all my shit, too. I didn't want to show up empty-handed, so I kind of scrounged this stuff along the way."

"Where? And if you give me your shit about never telling on your sources, so help me I'll—"

Tangretti pointed. To the west and halfway down the beach, a DUKW rested in the sand at an odd angle, nose half buried, its left front wheel shot away. Richardson realized with a shock that it was the same vehicle that had run over his primacord line earlier.

"Any more down there?"

"Yeah. It's a Seabee vehicle. Looks like, oh, eight or ten more of these satchels, and a bunch of Bangalore sections."

"Sergeant!"

"I hear ya," the engineer said. "Okay! Wilson! Sutton! Crooke! With me!"

The engineers moved off down the beach, angling toward the disabled DUKW.

Omaha Beach

Everywhere on that blood-soaked shingle of sand and rock, heroism became commonplace. On each beach section, men of the Army-Navy Gap Assault Teams did what they could with the equipment available. On Beach Easy Green, one crew rode out four vicious barrages of German rockets fired from pits behind the hills, then went on to blast a gap fifty to one hundred yards wide through two lines of steel ramps and hedgehogs.

On the next beach east of Easy Green, code-named Easy Red, Carpenter's Mate William Raymor was wounded when a German shell exploded inside his LCM before it even reached the shore. In spite of his wound, Raymor teamed up with the engineering platoon, planting explosives on dozens of obstacles and blowing a fifty-yard gap clear through to the sea wall. This time, the GAT had no problems with U.S. soldiers getting in the way. There *were* no soldiers on that beach, except for the engineers and Demolitioneers, and they received the full attention of the German machine-gunners as they worked. Ensign Lawrence Karnowski and his men moved among half-submerged obstacles, working from their rubber raft on blowing a line of ramps in a race against the rising tide. They took down one set of ramps . . . then another. The Demolitioneers finally waded ashore after

blasting a fifty-yard gap through the obstructions, with
Karnowski carrying a wounded man who otherwise would
have drowned. To the far east of Easy Red, Chief Aviation
Ordnanceman Loran Barbour tied packs of explosives to
dozens of obstacles, running lines of primacord between
each charge. Barbour was just about to light off the warning
purple smoke when a German 88 struck one of the explosive packs, detonating it, the primacord, and every other
loaded obstacle in the area.

The blast tore through the GAT personnel who'd not yet
moved to cover. Five of the eight Navy men were killed
outright. Barbour and all but two of the GAT engineers were
wounded, while the engineering platoon suffered fifteen
killed and injured.

But the blast opened a gap through the obstacles. Barbour
remained on the beach, directing the evacuation of the
wounded and helping to mark the new channel for the incoming boats, until he finally collapsed and was carried
ashore. Other survivors of the GAT carried on as the tide
continued to rise, making certain the channel was marked
and directing new waves of landing craft safely through to
the beach.

The original plan called for sixteen separate gaps to be
blasted through the obstacles in time to start feeding the incoming troops and vehicles ashore. By shortly after 0700
hours, when the incoming tide had risen so far that most of
the demolition work had to stop, only five complete gaps
had been opened and marked. Those five were enough,
however, for at least some troops and heavy equipment to
struggle in to the beach and unload.

In the sheltered area along the bottom of the bluffs,
meanwhile, in hastily dug trenches and behind the sea wall
that ran along the top of the eastern half of the beach, soldiers of the 1st and 29th Infantry Divisions who'd made it
past the obstacles and the fire-swept shelf above the water's
edge were beginning to organize themselves. Platoon leaders and company commanders—sergeants and lieutenants—
took charge of squad-sized bands of men and began leading
them up the face of Omaha's bluffs. In the draws, fierce
firefights between infantry detachments and barricaded Ger-

man strongpoints raged as the American troops began seeking paths off the deadly beach and into the heights beyond.

Above Fox Green Beach

Rand hugged the sandy ground, hidden in a clump of dune grass clinging to the crumbling slope. The path, masked from German fire both by the slope and by drifting smoke, had debouched here, near the top of the bluff. Thirty feet ahead, along the crest of the ridge, a concrete casement had been erected atop the hill. There was movement inside, behind a three-high wall of sandbags. Raising his head to peer through the grass, he saw two . . . no, three German soldiers. Two were servicing an MG 42, firing at the beach below in short, aimed bursts. The third was an officer, holding binoculars to his eyes. Lowering the binoculars, he touched one of the soldiers on the shoulder and pointed, indicating a new target.

Raising his Thompson, Rand took quick aim and squeezed the trigger. Deliberately aiming low as the weapon bucked in his hands, he saw spurts of sand blasted from the sandbags, then walked the fire up and across the machine gun crew. One pitched back, screaming and clawing at his face, while the other slumped forward across the sandbag wall. The officer dove for cover just as the burst found him, slamming him against the far wall of the gun pit.

Bullets slapped into the sand close by Rand's position and whispered through the air just above his head. Other gun pits had been erected along the top of the bluff, connected by trenches and set up to provide mutual cover and interlocking fields of fire. Slithering forward on his belly, Rand crawled through the sand to the silenced gun position, molded himself to the casement wall, then rolled over the sandbag top. Inside, one soldier was still clutching his bloody face and moaning; the officer, an *oberleutnant*, was alive as well, blood drenching his shattered right shoulder.

The man held out his left hand. *"Bitte! Mein Gott, bitte—"*

Too close to use the Thompson, Rand slipped his black Sykes-Fairbairn commando blade from its boot sheath, moved closer to the *oberleutnant*, then lunged, slicing the officer's throat with a quick, sure thrust-and-slash. The man gurgled once and died, and Rand quickly dispatched the wounded soldier nearby. His right hand and sleeve were soaked with their blood.

A shouted order, in German, brought him back to his feet. A squad in coal scuttle helmets and *feldgrau* were clambering out of a trench and starting to move toward him. One stopped, yanked the ceramic ball and string from the handle of his potato masher grenade, and cocked his arm to throw.

Rand came to his feet, Thompson blazing. The burst chopped through two riflemen and the grenadier, who dropped back into his trench, taking the grenade with him. A second later there was a savage blast in the trench, followed instantly by a boiling pall of smoke, and screams.

Turning, Rand took a quick look at the beach below. He was high atop the rounded bluff just to the west of the Colleville draw. The view was spectacular—hundreds upon hundreds of vessels, ranging in size from a handful of cruisers and battleships on the horizon to uncountable swarms of landing craft drawn up on the beach or making their way through the surf to deliver the second wave. He could see a literal sea of beach obstacles, now more than half submerged by the rising tide, and he could see several of the broad lanes already blasted through them. As thickly planted as the obstacles were the men, moving up the beach through savage fire, huddled in the shelter offered by beach obstacles or sprawled motionless on the sand.

To his right, almost at his feet, the bluff dropped away in a sheer cliff, and he found he could look down into the German positions stretched across the floor of the Colleville ravine. He counted five large rifle or machine gun pits, dozens of trenches, layers of barbed wire, and several larger, roofed-over structures, pillboxes or emplacements for 88-mm cannon.

An explosion went off just outside his gun pit, showering him with sand. Rifle shots rang out, and one round clanged off the receiver of the German machine gun beside him.

There was not a hell of a lot more he could do here, not alone. What was needed up here was at least a company . . . and possibly some engineers to clear out some of these hardpoints.

And now he knew how to get them up here.

Swiftly, using a procedure learned months before at Fort Pierce, Rand stripped open the MG 42 and smashed the belt feed mechanism. Next, he took one of the two AN-M8 HC smoke grenades attached to his web belt, pulled the pin, and tossed it behind him into the pit. The smoke would cover him for the few moments he needed to get over the wall.

As heavy smoke gushed from the canister, blanketing him in a choking white cloud, he rolled over the sandbags at the front of the casement and started back down the gully worn into the face of the hill.

GAT-4
Fox Green Beach

Tangretti lay next to Richardson, threading in the next section of the Bangalore torpedo, then shoving the long tube farther up the draw. Machine gun fire crashed and echoed off the cliff sides, and bullets snapped into the dry sand in front of him, or shrieked as they ricocheted off bare rock.

Directly in front of the two men, dense coils of concertina wire lay across the mouth of the draw like huge, rusty springs. There were almost certainly mines up there, too, though he'd not seen any signs reading *"Achtung! Minen!"* Before the infantry could advance up the ravine and off the beach, that wire would have to be cleared.

Richardson handed him another section of pipe. He screwed it into place and shoved the now ponderously heavy Bangalore torpedo another three feet ahead.

He remembered Franklin's story about the training accident at Fowey. If he hit a mine now, the torpedo would detonate and he and Snake would be history. They were almost all the way through the wire now. Just a little farther. . . .

The torpedo wouldn't move. He shoved harder, but it was like pushing against a heavy rock.

"It's hung up on something." Cautiously, he lifted his head. The far end of the torpedo was buried in the sand.

"Pull it back," Richardson suggested, also staring up the draw. "Try again to the side."

"Right."

Gently, gently, he pulled the long pipe back a foot, levered to the side, then pushed ahead again. This time it slid past the obstruction easily. A machine gun hammered at them from the gun slit in a pillbox fifty yards farther up the ravine.

"Good," Richardson said. "You were hung up on a land mine, that's all."

"Aw, shit, Snake! Don't tell me these things!"

"Here. One more should do it."

That last section threaded into place, the Bangalore torpedo was shoved all the way past the last of the barbed wire. Richardson attached the end of an electrical wire to the final section, then began paying the wire out from the reel they'd brought with them.

"That does 'er," Tangretti said. "Let's get the hell out of here!"

"I'm with you!"

Flat on their bellies, they moved back down the draw. The spot they'd selected to start the Bangalore torpedo, just below the first tangle of barbed wire, had been sheltered somewhat by a low sand dune stretched across that part of the draw, providing them with a margin of cover while they worked. Farther out, however, they were exposed to heavy fire from farther up the draw. Machine guns chattered, flinging up puffs of dry sand. An 88 barked from its emplacement, and the thunder of its blast hammered at the two men.

As the dust and smoke avalanched around them, however, Tangretti yelled "Now!" Together, partly sheltered by the smoke, they rose to their feet and dashed the last fifty feet down the beach as bullets sniped and hissed around their feet. Outside the mouth of the draw and to the west, the other engineers and GAT personnel were sheltering behind the shell-broken end of the sea wall.

Throwing themselves flat, Richardson took the end of the wire and began connecting it to the hellbox. Explosions walked across the beach below them, as tall and as slender and as evenly spaced as poplar trees.

Richardson connected the last wire. "Ready!" he shouted. "All clear?"

Tangretti checked up the draw. Nobody in sight. "Clear! Blow it!"

Richardson turned the handle. Nothing. He checked his

connections, picked up the hellbox, and again twisted hard at the handle.

Nothing.

"Shit, Snake," Tangretti said. "That last explosion must've cut the wire."

"We won't be able to splice it," Richardson said, rising to peer over the wall. "We'll have to fire it with a fuse."

He started stripping off the heavy gasproof coverall he'd been wearing all morning.

"What the hell are you doing, Snake?"

"Setting that fuse. It's damned hard to run in this getup, and I haven't seen one Kraut gas attack yet, have you?"

"Sit down, Snake. I'm already stripped for action. Gimme an igniter, huh?"

"No, Gator," Richardson said. "I'll go."

"Uh-uh. No way. You got that sweet little wife to go back to, right?" He accepted a length of fuse from Truett, made certain the T-wire igniter was firmly attached and safely wrapped up in its rubber prophylactic. "We got any smoke left?"

Truett shook his head. "No, Gator. Used the last of it on the beach."

"Damn."

"Gator, you can't do this!"

"The hell I can't! Be right back." He scrambled past the end of the wall and raced back into the mouth of the draw.

Fox Green Beach

Rand found a colonel behind the sea wall. More and more officers were appearing there as successive waves of boats reached the beach and disgorged their cargoes of troops and equipment.

"Only two kinds of men are gonna stay on this beach!" the colonel yelled. He was pacing along the line of men huddled behind the sea wall, haranguing them, oblivious to the explosions thundering across the beach. "Those who are dead, and those who are gonna die! Now let's get the hell out of here!"

Rand hurried up to the colonel, saluting. "Begging your

pardon, Colonel! I thought you might like to know. I've found a path up that part of the cliff."

He pointed, and the colonel studied the slope. "All the way to the top?"

"Yessir. I was there."

"Could you lead a party of men back up there?"

"Yes, sir, I could."

"What's your name and rank, son?"

"Boatswain's Mate First Class Rand, Colonel."

The colonel looked him up and down. "Navy, huh?"

"Yes, sir."

"Well, we'll sort out the service bullshit later. As of right now, you're an Army second lieutenant!" He pointed. "Take charge of these men and get them moving up that hill."

"Aye, aye, sir!"

"We don't say 'aye, aye' in the infantry, son. Just get in there and get the job done!"

As the colonel walked back up the beach, still yelling at his men, Rand approached a sergeant who'd been close enough to overhear the exchange. "Who *is* that guy, Sarge?"

The sergeant grinned. "Colonel George A. Taylor, Lieutenant. Sixteenth Infantry Regiment!"

"Listen, then. If you can get your troops together, I'll take 'em up that hill. Have you seen any engineers around here?"

The sergeant pointed to the east. "There are some working at the mouth of the draw down there. Maybe fifty yards."

"Okay. Get your people organized. I'll be back in a minute with some satchel charges."

"Yes, *sir*!"

GAT-4
Fox Green Beach

Tangretti lay at the lower end of the Bangalore torpedo, attaching the fuse and rubber-wrapped igniter. He'd crawled most of the way up the mouth of the draw, seeking cover from each depression, each tumble of rock lying in the sand. He'd have to be faster coming back. The fuse had been cut for two minutes, enough time for him to make his way back to the sea wall, but only if he ran.

He hoped.

The Germans knew he was here, all right. Rifle and machine gun fire kept banging and yammering away, the bullets snapping just inches above his head or slamming into the dune in front of him, sending up blossoming spurts of sand.

That should do it. Bracing himself, he took a deep breath, then yanked on the wire through the condom, made certain the fuse was burning, then turned and dashed for the sea wall.

The machine gun burst caught Tangretti in the legs from behind, lifting him up, twisting him in midair, then slamming him again to the ground. At first, he didn't feel anything, only a numb and dizzying shock.

Then the pain began.

GAT-4
Fox Green Beach

"Gator!" Richardson lurched up from behind the sea wall when he saw Tangretti knocked down by the machine gun burst. Several hands tried to pull him down. *"Gator!"*

"Damn it, Snake," Truett yelled. "Get down! He's fired the fuse!"

"We've got to go get him!" Richardson broke free of Truett's grasp and raced up the mouth of the draw. He could see Tangretti's face now, paste-white and drawn, as he weakly tried to wave Richardson back.

Richardson kept going, counting to himself as he ran. He knew how long the fuse was cut for, and he knew when Tangretti had fired it. Fifteen ... fourteen ... thirteen ...

Something slamming into his side, hard, grating against a rib. He staggered and fell, and when he pulled his hand away from the wound it was slick with blood.

Nine ... eight ...

He scrambled ahead a few more steps, then threw himself flat, arms curled over his helmet, face buried in the sand.

Five ... four ... three ...

The explosion struck him through the ground, lifting him

clear of the sand and leaving him momentarily dazed. Lifting his head, he saw Tangretti, almost buried in sand, with only his head, shoulder, and one arm showing.

He wasn't moving.

Richardson crawled to his friend's side. "Gator! *Gator!* Are you okay?"

There was no answer. Pulling off his helmet, Richardson started digging away the sand.

GAT-4
Fox Green Beach

"You guys engineers?"

The Navy petty officer turned, looking at Rand, obviously not sure what to make of this stranger. "That's right."

"Where's your CO?"

For answer, the man pointed up the draw. Forty yards up the slope, one man was furiously digging at the loose sand, trying to uncover another. Through a haze of smoke, a machine gun stuttered.

Without thinking, Rand pulled his last HC smoke grenade from his belt, pulled the pin, but held the safety lever down. Vaulting the end of the sea wall, he ran forward, zigzagging to make himself a harder target. The machine gun stopped firing at the two Navy men and started trying to knock him down. When he'd run as far as he could, Rand ducked behind a boulder close to the side of the ravine's cliff, reached back, and hurled the smoke grenade as hard and as far as he could. It bounced on the sand close to where a broad gap had been blasted through layer upon layer of tightly coiled barbed wire.

As the smoke began spilling across the ravine floor, he was up and running once more.

The Colleville Draw
Fox Green Beach

Richardson was just dragging Gator free of the sand when the newcomer dropped to the ground next to him. Richardson thought he might be familiar but didn't recognize him.

"You're wounded," the man said. "Can you run?"

"Try me!"

Smoke filled the mouth of the ravine at their backs. Together, they hoisted Tangretti between them and started dragging him down the slope.

Richardson's side was starting to hurt. He didn't think it was bleeding too bad, but a rib had definitely been broken. He could feel the jagged ends grating together as he moved.

He felt a little short of breath. No problem. He was desperately worried about Tangretti, though. It looked like one of his legs had been shot clear through above the knee, and there was an awful lot of blood.

They reached the protection of the sea wall and slumped down on the sand. Richardson was having a lot of trouble breathing now; every breath hurt, and he felt the scary, almost panicky sensation of not being able to get enough air.

He felt very warm inside.

Tangretti stirred. "Damn you, Snake, you son of a bitch!" he said. "What the hell'd you go and do that for?"

"I was worried about you, buddy," Richardson replied. *Damn!* Why couldn't he ... get enough ... air? He had to fight for each shallow breath. "Couldn't ... let you ... go ... alone."

He was lying on his back, looking up into an overcast sky. He didn't remember lying down. Someone was shouting *"Medic! Medic!"* over and over, but the voice was a very long way off. Truett's anxious face bent over him, and he felt hands tearing at his clothing.

Getting dark. Must be almost night, though the last time he'd looked at his watch, it had still been morning.

Can't ... *breathe!*

He tried to capture Veronica's face and failed. Strange. He could summon Tangretti's face to mind easily.

"We're ... partners ..." he said. "Remember?"

GAT-4
Fox Green Beach

"He's gone, Gator." Truett shook his head. "Chest wound. I think his lungs collapsed."

"No ... *no!*" Rising on one elbow, gritting his teeth against the pain of his broken leg, Tangretti grabbed Rich-

ardson's shoulder, shaking him, trying to lift him from the
sand. Richardson's head lolled to the side, blood trickling
from nose and mouth, and his eyes had a vacant, faraway
look to them. "No, damn it, Snake! No! Don't die! *Don't
die!*"

"He's dead, Gator."

Tangretti let go of Richardson's shoulder, slumping back
next to him on the sand. Snake? Dead? It wasn't possible.
In a few minutes, a medic would arrive. He'd be able to
patch Snake up. He'd be able to bring him back. No problem. No problem. . . .

His face was wet with tears.

What a fucking damned waste!

Omaha Beach

Slowly, slowly, the infantrymen pinned on Omaha Beach
at last started to fight their way out. Single squads, assembled on the spot by officers or noncoms, slipped over the
sea wall and climbed the face of the bluffs beyond. Strongpoints were silenced one by one. Infantrymen used hand
grenades, satchel charges, and rifles to rush bunkers and
pillboxes, cleaning them out in sharp, vicious little firefights
fought at point-blank range.

Before long, it was recognized that the pushover defenders, the third-rate 726th Division, had at some point in the
past been replaced by the crack 352nd Division. In fact, the
352nd had been behind Omaha for the past two and a half
months, but for a variety of reasons that critical intelligence
had not been discovered in time.

That intelligence would have made little difference.
Omaha was absolutely vital to the Allied landing plan, the
single place where a landing was even possible between
Utah Beach to the west and the British and Canadian landings farther east. If the Americans failed to take Omaha, the
Germans would have a powerful, possibly a deadly, wedge
between the American and British beachheads allowing both
to be dealt with piecemeal.

The American soldiers fighting their way up those bluffs
cared little for whether they faced the 352nd or the 726th.

Germans were Germans, and too many of their comrades had died on the beaches below for them to be forgiving.

At first, they took very few prisoners.

Above Fox Green Beach

Crouched to one side of the slit in the bunker, Rand nodded at the young soldier across from him at the far side of the firing port. Together, they yanked the fuse igniters on the forty-pound satchels of explosives provided by the CDU men on the beach. They counted down the seconds, then together slung both packs up and neatly through the opening.

"Achtung!" sounded from inside. *"Zurückerhalten! Zurück—"*

The detonation of eighty pounds of C-2 inside the concrete enclosure of the bunker rang like the tolling of some enormous bell. Smoke blasted from the slit, followed by a spattering of concrete rubble as the ceiling inside collapsed. The muzzle of the 88, protruding from the slit, was twisted at an angle now, and pointed at the sky.

Rand signaled, and the rest of the soldiers with him cheered, rushing up the slope and past the knocked-out bunker. Two Germans in dust-whitened *feldgrau* appeared, stumbling out of a trench. *"Nicht scheissen!"* one called. An American corporal with the Big Red One emblem of 1st Division on his shoulder cut them both down with five rapidly triggered shots from his carbine and ran on past without even breaking stride.

There was, Frank Rand now knew, no glory in war.

Tiredly, he unslung his Thompson and sat on a broken stone wall. The soldiers who'd followed him up the hill, members of 1st Division's 16th Regiment, mostly, but with a few members of the 26th Regiment who'd just started arriving on shore, were spreading out across the top of the hill. Most of the pillboxes and trenches on the top of the bluff had been cleared out, though doubtless more Germans would be flushed from hiding as the day wore on. The Germans down in the Colleville draw, subjected to heavy fire from the top of the cliff, had already started pulling out.

Omaha Beach spread out below Rand, an impossibly jumbled panorama of ships and vehicles and men. The tide

was all the way in now, and the Navy was taking advantage
of the fact to put reinforcements ashore, as far up on the
beach as they could. Five lanes, marked by the Army and
Navy demolition teams, remained open, though the sinking
of a couple of LSTs in close to the beach had nearly
blocked one. The fire from the surrounding bluffs was still
intense, but for the first time that morning, Rand was certain
that the Omaha landings would succeed.

And he'd played a part in that success.

Not bad for a scrawny kid from Michigan.

Bucklew had been right. The only kind of heroism that
counted in a place like this was doing your job. Doing your
duty. And for the first time in his life Rand felt as though
he were a part of one powerful team.

He thought about the demolition men he'd seen by the
sea wall, wondering if any of them had been in the briefings
and lectures he'd given the CDUs back in England. Or his
students back at Fort Pierce. Possibly. He'd met so many of
them. Good men, all of them.

Damned good men.

GAT-1
Dog Green Beach

It was mid-afternoon, and the chaos on the beach had, if
anything, grown worse.

Still, Wallace thought, it was now *organized* chaos. Landing craft continued to come in and disgorge troops and
equipment. In the first wave, only six of an expected sixteen
bulldozers and tankdozers had made it ashore, and three of
those were knocked out in short order.

But the equipment kept on coming in. More bulldozers.
More tanks. More demolition gear and explosives. The
handfuls of soldiers who managed to push their way up
those sheer bluffs behind the beach could not exploit their
gains, or even hope to hang on against the inevitable German counterattacks, unless more ships got through the mo-
rass on the beach with artillery, with mortars, with
ammunition, with more and more and more men.

High tide peaked around noon, and the Navy demolition
men and their Army counterparts followed the ebbing wa-

terline down the beach, destroying more obstacles as they went. By evening, thirteen gaps had been blown through the beach obstacles and the lanes clearly marked.

Wallace, his arm in a sling, stayed on the beach, directing his men as they continued to set charges on German obstacles, and stopping several times to drag wounded men up the beach and out of the line of fire. It wasn't until dark when Lieutenant Commander Gilbert himself ordered him aboard an LST. "What are you trying to do, Wallace, grab all of the glory for yourself?"

"No, sir. But there's still some more obstacles—"

"Save it, son. There'll *always* be more obstacles. And men to take them out. You've done your part. Now let us do ours."

"Aye, aye, sir." He saluted. Turning away, he suddenly felt very tired, and taking even one step seemed more than he could manage on his own. Someone took him by his good arm and helped him down the beach.

He thought of Alice, back in England. It was going to be great to see her again. Wallace wondered if she still wanted to marry him.

He was ready, if she was.

Chapter 32

Monday, 12 June 1944

The Pentagon

Galloway read again the lurid headline on the front page of a newspaper tacked to the wall of his office. "INVASION!" the headline screamed. In only slightly less extravagant type, the subhead proclaimed "Allies Land in France, Smash Ahead; Fleet, Planes, Chutists Battling Nazis."

The dateline was 6 June, six days ago.

No mention of the infantry, unless you counted that "Allies Land" part. There rarely was. No mention of the heavy resistance as the Germans dug in their heels and fought back. That would be bad for morale.

Still, little by little, the story was coming out. Even so, it might be years before most people realized just how near a thing Omaha Beach had been. General Omar Bradley, aboard the command cruiser *Augusta,* had at one point actually talked to the British about funneling subsequent waves of troops bound for Omaha to the British beaches.

Omaha had come *that* close to complete disaster....

Things were looking better, however. Just that day, the long-sundered gap between Utah Beach in the west and Omaha had at last been closed up. The VII Corps was advancing up the Cotentin Peninsula toward Cherbourg, and Allied planes were now operating off captured airfields. Fresh troops were pouring ashore, and the beachheads were toughening up.

The Allies had returned to the Continent, and they were there to stay.

But Galloway had the grim, proud, inner assurance that the Omaha beachhead would not have been won and held without the efforts of the small band of Navy men comprising the Combat Demolition Units.

Returning to his desk, he picked up a sheet of typewritten paper. He'd just finished typing it up and was about to send it to Admiral King's office for final approval.

"For outstanding performance in combat during the invasion of Normandy, June 6, 1944. Determined and zealous in the fulfillment of an extremely hazardous mission, the Navy Combat Demolition Unit of Force O landed on 'Omaha Beach' with the first wave under devastating enemy artillery, machine gun and sniper fire. With practically all explosives lost and with their forces seriously depleted by heavy casualties, the remaining officers and men carried on gallantly, salvaging explosives as they were swept ashore and in some instances commandeering bulldozers to remove obstacles. In spite of these grave handicaps, the Demolition Crews succeeded initially in blasting five gaps through enemy obstacles for the assault forces to the Normandy shore and within two days had sapped over eighty-five percent of the 'Omaha Beach' area of German-placed traps. Valiant in the face of grave danger and persistently aggressive against fierce resistance, the Navy Combat Demolition Unit rendered daring and self-sacrificing service in the performance of a vital mission, thereby sustaining the high traditions of the United States Naval Service."

With King's approval, the paper would go across the river to the White House, where it would be signed by President Roosevelt, a Presidential Unit Citation awarded to every Navy CDU man who'd fought at Omaha.

Setting the Unit Citation aside, he picked up another sheet and read it. This one would also go to King's staff for approval.

"For extraordinary heroism as a member of Naval Combat Demolition Unit TWELVE, attached to the ELEVENTH Amphibious Force during the assault on the coast of France, June 6, 1944. Braving heavy German artillery and small arms fire, Lieutenant Junior Grade (then Chief Machinist's Mate) Wallace took command of his unit when his commanding officer was killed in the assault, going on to lead them in an attempt to blow a fifty-yard gap through the formidable beach obstacles. Though seven of the thirteen-man unit were killed or wounded by the terrific gunfire, he succeeded in accomplishing this perilous and vital mission. Heedless of his own safety, and despite serious wounds of his own, he repeatedly exposed himself to intense gunfire to recover wounded personnel and bring them to a place of comparative safety. By his inspiring leadership, aggressive fighting spirit, and unwavering devotion to duty, Lieutenant Junior Grade Wallace contributed directly to the success of his vital operations and upheld the highest traditions of the United States Naval service."

That citation would accompany the award of Wallace's second Navy Cross . . . and the confirmation of his field commissioning to Lieutenant j.g. Galloway thought about Chief Wallace—no, *Lieutenant* Wallace, now—and grinned. Like Galloway, he had been a part of the demolition teams from the very beginning—Sebou River, Fort Pierce, and now Normandy. Hell, if he knew Bill Wallace, he wouldn't care much for the promotion, but in this case the interests of the service definitely came first. The Navy needed experienced demolition men as never before . . . and they needed officers to lead them. Experienced officers, tested in combat.

Galloway thought about Richardson. Damn, he could still remember him and Tangretti standing here, in this very office. Richardson had been put in for a Navy Cross at Omaha, but the powers that be, for reasons mysterious, had downgraded it to a posthumous Silver Star.

The Silver Star.

That was ironic. Richardson had deserved the Navy Cross—hell, he'd deserved the Medal of Honor—every damned bit as much as Wallace, as much as any of those kids who'd bled and died on that bloody Omaha beachhead. In the end, though, a bit of metal and colored ribbon could not possibly tell the story of the *man* who'd won it. It would be stark comfort indeed, Galloway thought with a sharp, inner pang, to Richardson's young widow in England.

Carefully, Galloway slipped the two sheets of paper into a folder, then got up and took his coat down from the rack in the corner. It was time to take them up to King's office.

He still wished he could be one of the men of the UDTs, wished he could be going into action with them. Damn it, even Coffer—bad eyes and all—had received orders for the Pacific. The last Galloway had heard, Coffer had been at Maui, preparing to board ship' for yet another invasion—Saipan. The lucky bastard.

He wished him, and the men sailing with him, well.

Galloway had followed the exploits of the CDU and UDT men—of *his* men, as he thought of them now—closely, of course. He'd particularly immersed himself in accounts and after-action reports of their heroism in the hell of the Normandy invasion. Casualties during D-Day had been savage; fully forty percent of the Navy Demolition Unit men involved had been killed or wounded, and that was the percentage of *all* of the men involved. Of the 175 Navy CDU men at Omaha alone, 31 had been killed and 60 wounded, a casualty rate of fifty-two percent.

But they'd carried out their missions brilliantly. He was certain that Omaha would have failed without their efforts.

The Navy was already evaluating the lessons learned at

Normandy and putting them into play. The melding of Army and Navy units, for instance, had proven cumbersome, the lines of command prone to breakdown. In the future, the Navy UDTs, as they were calling them now in the Pacific, would work alone. They would also go into an enemy beach *ahead* of the invasion, not with the first wave, so that their job would not be complicated by infantrymen hiding behind the obstacles they were supposed to clear. They would also drop the heavy coveralls and gas masks. Those had proven to be more trouble than they were worth, and many of the CDU men at Normandy had discarded theirs the first chance they'd had.

As for Galloway, he'd learned a lesson or two himself. Battling the Pentagon's bureaucratic tendencies to do nothing while accumulating power had proved to be as challenging for him as tackling the ramps and hedgehogs and dragon's teeth of Normandy.

He chuckled over something David Coffer had said just before shipping out for the Pacific. *"They too serve who only shuffle papers."*

Besides, he had the vicarious thrill of following the exploits of the unit he had helped to create.

The CDU.

The Demolitioneers.

The *Teams* . . .

He thought of Virginia. After all this time, Galloway figured, he finally had all of his shit in one seabag. He decided he would stop by her office after seeing Admiral King and see if he couldn't arrange an evening with her tonight. They had some long-unfinished business to attend to.

Closing his office door behind him, the file tucked under his arm, Lieutenant Commander Galloway started off down the long Pentagon corridor, his shoes clicking briskly as he walked.

SEALS
THE WARRIOR BREED

by H. Jay Riker

The face of war is rapidly changing, calling
America's soldiers into hellish regions where
conventional warriors dare not go.
This is the world of the SEALs.

SILVER STAR
76967-0/$5.99 US/$7.99 Can

PURPLE HEART
76969-7/$5.99 US/$7.99 Can

BRONZE STAR
76970-0/$5.99 US/$6.99 Can

NAVY CROSS
78555-2/$5.99 US/$7.99 Can

MEDAL OF HONOR
78556-0/$5.99 US/$7.99 Can